"A science fiction-powered, epic reimagining of the Bible's Book of Revelation, the fourth installment in the pseudonymous Joseph's *This Generation* saga (after 2016's *Penance*) culminates in a jaw-dropping conclusion that is simultaneously apocalyptic fiction and visionary utopian fiction.

The highly appealing blend of Christian eschatology and apocalyptic thriller notwithstanding, the power of this series comes in Joseph's adept character development. Identifiable and endearing characters like Will Marron, who heroically attempted to assassinate Kurtoglu only to have the evil creature resurrect itself into a virtually unstoppable enemy, and Gloria Jolean, the disgraced wife of a morally bankrupt televangelist whose harrowing spiritual journey of self-discovery will touch all readers, give the grand-scale story an intimacy and emotional intensity. The breakneck pacing and nonstop action—coupled with Joseph's fluid and clear writing style—make for an undeniably page-turning read.

This is Christian science fiction at its very best—entertaining and edifying. Comparable to the *Left Behind* series by Tim LaHaye and Jerry B. Jenkins, this saga is, in a word, transformative."

—*BlueInk Review*

PAROUSIA

THIS GENERATION SERIES: BOOK 4

PAROUSIA

THIS GENERATION SERIES: BOOK 4

TC JOSEPH

ARCHWAY
PUBLISHING

Archway Publishing books may be ordered through booksellers or by contacting:

Archway Publishing
1663 Liberty Drive
Bloomington, IN 47403
www.archwaypublishing.com
1 (888) 242-5904

ISBN: 978-1-4808-6474-0 (sc)
ISBN: 978-1-4808-6472-6 (hc)
ISBN: 978-1-4808-6473-3 (e)

Library of Congress Control Number: 2018950347

Printed in the United States of America.

Archway Publishing rev. date: 1/15/2019

My books are always dedicated to my family. I would also like to dedicate this one to the friends who have become family over the years.

ACKNOWLEDGMENTS

I value my privacy and have joyously written under a pseudonym to preserve it. All in all I think it was a marvelous decision, but it is troubling when it comes to an acknowledgments page because it precludes me from thanking, by name, so many who have been instrumental in the production of this book. The failure to mention individuals is no reflection of the gratitude I feel. So I would like to offer special thanks for the encouragement of a veritable cadre of family and friends who started this series in draft form. Each word of encouragement is met with a grateful heart.

I also would like to thank the staff at Archway Publishing for taking time to make this the best book series it could be.

PREFACE: CATCHING UP

The This Generation series of books chronicles the lives of the characters over the course of several decades. As we arrive at *Parousia*, the fourth book in the series, I find it difficult to summarize the preceding three novels in sufficient detail to allow for the smiles of remembrance that play throughout this book. Nevertheless, *Parousia* is an exciting tale and a great read on its own. So, I offer the following brief overview of the story thus far:

Michael Martin was born to Kim Martin, who got pregnant to thwart genetic experiments performed on her by the Lady, an extraterrestrial with a psychic connection to Kim's nefarious brother, Father Benjamin Cross. The Lady subsequently gave Michael extraordinary intelligence. Later, Kim adopted Michael's best friend, Gabe, only to learn that he and Michael shared a father. Over time, Kim fell in love with Benny's assistant, Father Chris. Given his vows as a Catholic priest, they agreed to a platonic relationship in which Chris assisted in parenting the boys.

Father Chris's friends Tom and Fran Ellis were missionaries in Africa when Tom died. Their daughter, Gloria, grew to be a woman who eschewed the altruistic side of Christianity and fell in love with a greedy televangelist, Zack Jolean.

All the while, Kim's brother, Benny, rose through the ranks of the Catholic hierarchy by using bribery, subterfuge, and murder.

The families met on a cruise, during which Gloria fell instantly in love with Michael. Nothing came of their attraction as Gloria was married and Michael was approaching his ordination as a Catholic priest. With Benny's help, Zack killed his parents and tossed them overboard, rather than letting them close their lucrative ministry.

Zack also had an encounter with the Lady wherein he offered Gloria to carry an alien–human hybrid crafted from DNA sequences chosen from Michael, Gloria, and Zack to give it the appropriate genome to attach to a third strand from the Lady's leader. The aliens harvested the embryo, raised it to the age of ten, and then inserted the boy in the household of the Turkish prime minister in a religious act to convince imams of the child's divine origin. The child, Isa Kurtoglu, eventually became Benny's friend and coconspirator as they both rose in power.

Given Michael's intellect, gift for languages, and training in archeology, the Vatican tasked him with the translation of information from a previously unknown advanced ancient culture. The information was bound electronically to a golden disc in a very dense information pattern. As Michael unraveled the mysteries of the disc with the help of five programmers, he learned that it contained advanced scientific information from the Lady's civilization.

Overwhelmed by the knowledge contained on the disc, Michael took several actions to protect it. In an attempt to harmonize its discrepancies with Christian belief, he forged a revised Gospel of John and salted it into a Turkish archeological dig. While retrieving it, he was kidnapped and rescued by "the agent," a member of the Vatican's secret service. Michael also agreed to his subordinate's plan to safeguard the information on the disc by manipulating the minds of the programmers through the formation of alternate personalities.

Michael's actions appalled Gabe, who had become a minister and author of books about end-time events. Their relationship nearly ended when Michael shared his lack of faith in the Bible with Gabe's daughter, Michele. After a cooling-off period, wherein Michael seriously entertained Gabe's contention that the Lady was a demonic apparition, the two reconciled at an open-air pizzeria in Rome. As they hugged, the sky was rocked with lightning, and Gabe disintegrated in Michael's arms. Recognizing from his previous conversations with Gabe that the rapture had occurred, he ran headlong into a crowd in Saint Peter's Square as gunmen created pandemonium.

The agent pulled Michael from the panicked crowd and led him to the Roman catacombs. There he explained to Michael that they were experiencing the Dark Awakening, a time when millions of people with hidden multiple personalities were activated to create panic. In its wake, the Antichrist would arise to restore order. Michael gave his life to Jesus at that moment and vowed to help Christians during the tribulation reign of the Antichrist.

To his horror, Michael learned that his deranged uncle Benny had usurped the papal miter during the rapture. The new pope offered to keep Michael and Gabe's kids safe if Michael would agree to become the papal assistant. As the crowds of the Dark Awakening attacked the Vatican, Michael and Benny escaped in a harrowing trip back to the family estate in Georgia. During their journey, they masked their identities and used the pseudonyms Jake and Lucky. On their way to the family estate, a magician and crossbow performer saved Michael from two demented men with multiple personalities. The man offered his stage name, Will White. When he revealed his real last name, Michael realized the young man to be his brother Gabe's illegitimate son.

At a meeting of the UN, Isa and the Lady installed in Benny a demon named Nergal. Then they revealed Isa's hybrid nature and assured the world that he alone could protect Earth from the approach of the sun's stellar twin, Nemesis, and the aggressive populace of its largest planet, Nibiru. He also promoted the idea that the Dark Awakening was the direct result of magnetic interference from a solar discharge and detailed a plan to prevent future occurrences through an inoculation containing his own resistant DNA.

Michael and Will worked with Isa and Benny in the construction of the New Vatican on the Temple Mount in Jerusalem. There the three major religions united around Isa as symbolized by the construction of a new Solomon's Temple, new Dome of the Rock mosque, and new Saint Peter's Basilica. Although the time spent with Isa and Benny was demoralizing, Michael took comfort from visits with raptured family members and with two mysterious prophets who preached in front of the Wailing Wall the message that Isa was the Antichrist.

In a bizarre turn of events, each of the computer programmers in whom Michael had instilled alternate personalities disappeared.

In the United States, Michele took control of the family's massive corporate holdings. She and Gloria worked together to bring aid to displaced people in government detention camps, only to learn that the displaced were actually Christians who refused to accept Isa's new blended religion. With Michele's fiancé, Jimmy, they conspired to steal documentation from a government camp to build fake detention centers in orphanages previously run by Gabe. Zack took advantage of the situation to frame Gloria for the murder of a guard at the government camp. He used the falsified information to counter Gloria's threat to expose his murder of his parents, the incriminating evidence of which she had given to Michael for safekeeping.

On the day of Michele's wedding to Jimmy, the celebration was marred by the revelation that Jimmy's mother was Naomi DeRance, Michele's nemesis at the family business. Michael suspected a plot by Naomi to take over the company, but his thoughts were cut short when he was drugged and abducted. On Gloria's return from the wedding, she was arrested for the murder.

Will was desperate to find Michael, but Benny coerced him to stay in Jerusalem until the completion of the Temple Mount dedication ceremonies, which began with Isa's murder of the two prophets at the Wailing Wall. Distraught by their deaths, Michael's disappearance, and Gloria's arrest, Will killed Isa with his crossbow during the ceremony. Immediately, Gabe took the crossbow and handed it to an old monk, who ran into the crowd to be shot as the perpetrator of Isa's murder. Then Gabe put Will into a deep sleep, during which Will gave his life to Jesus.

And now the saga continues as Will awakens ...

Enjoy the read, my friends.

TC

HALF A TIME

ONE

Will Marron awoke with a start. His head reeled as he looked around. He was in a large bedroom. Ornately carved black furniture stood in stark contrast to the alabaster-white walls of the enormous room. He sat up on the oversized bed on which he had been lying. Where was he? How did he get here? His mind was foggy. He ran an inventory to pull himself back to the waking world. What was the last thing he remembered?

"Oh Lord!" he exclaimed to the empty room as images began to flood his mind. He had been a performer when the rapture occurred. Afterward he found his true family and went to work with his uncle Michael in the service of the pope. "Some pope," he muttered as he thought of all the treachery Benny had brought to the family. He had been working in a security detail at the opening of the New Vatican on the Temple Mount in Jerusalem.

He drew a sharp breath as the images focused. He had shot Isa Kurtoglu, the Antichrist himself! Then some old monk took his bow and ran into the crowd, taking the blame. After that, Gabe, his father, put him to sleep. As he fell into unconsciousness, he gave his life to Jesus.

"Thank You, Lord," he whispered, and a feeling of warmth enveloped him. He spoke a quick addendum: "Sorry it took such horrible circumstances to finally turn my heart to You."

He saw his phone on the nightstand. Numerous texts from his sister inquired about his safety. He texted a quick reply: "I'm okay. Will call as soon as I can."

Leaving the bedroom, he walked down a wide, long hallway. When

1

he passed an elevator bank, he recognized his surroundings. *This is Isa's apartment! I rode that elevator a couple of days ago to witness Isa's nuclear attack on the USA, Europe, and Russia.*

In a hurry to leave the lair of the beast, he sprinted down the hallway to the expanse of Kurtoglu's office. Looking neither to the left nor right, he headed straight for the door.

"Going somewhere, Will?"

The call startled him. He turned to find his great-uncle Benny, the pope, seated behind Isa's desk.

"Benny," Will said with great relief, "you startled me."

"You scared me as well. You've been out for hours. I had the guards put you in my bedroom so we could keep an eye on you."

"Your bedroom?" Will asked suspiciously.

"Alas, William, the old monk who took you down was much less kind to Isa. He killed the greatest man to ever live. I was there as Isa died. It was a nasty affair," Benny said with an unctuous lilt and an air of distaste.

Will tried to strike a look of terror. "I can't believe Isa is dead!"

"Now, now, Will. There's no need to panic. Everything is under control. There's a new sheriff in town, and you're looking at him."

"You are now the president of the world?" Will asked. This situation could well be worse than the previous one.

"President. Pope. They're such archaic words. I prefer the title potentate. It brings together the concepts of spiritual and physical control over all things, don't you think?" Benny asked with a proud grin.

Will questioned his great-uncle as he sat slowly in a chair in front of Isa's desk. "So ... the Lady made you potentate when Isa died?"

"Oh, heavens no," Benny replied with a chuckle. "She's gone too. Turned into a puddle of goo. If you ask my opinion, she was little more than a puddle of goo when she was with us." He made a *tsk* sound and screwed up his face, "A smelly puddle of goo at that!"

Will leaned back in his chair and crossed his arms. In the past, he had disliked Benny, seeing him as the pervy uncle one would be embarrassed to say was a relative. Now, renewed in his spirit by his relationship with Jesus, Will saw just how evil Benny was. The evil poured off of him in nauseating waves of dark power. *How did Uncle Michael manage to work so closely with this horror?*

The thought of his uncle Michael, to whom he often referred as Jake, drew to mind the search for the missing man. *What did Dad say just before I went unconscious?* He searched his mind while Benny continued to extol the Lady's lack of virtue. *Go to Petra.* He knew what he had to do.

"Well, it seems you have everything under control here, Lucky," Will said briskly.

Benny cringed at the moniker. "No thanks to you, I might add. Your services were decidedly lacking in the protection of our first president. I would be angry with you, but your ineptitude moved me to the top of the pile, so I'll be magnanimous. From now on, you have special permission to carry firearms to protect me."

"The only respectable thing for me would be to resign, given the magnitude of my error," Will offered in an attempt to bring to an end the nightmarish job of working for Benny.

"Will, I have a scant bit of time to consolidate my power, bring the world to heel, and prepare for an invasion from outer space. I need to be surrounded with people I trust. You may not be the best at what you do, but you're family, which means we have shared interests."

"Our major shared interest is Uncle Michael, and I won't rest until I find him," Will said.

A somber look overtook Benny at the mention of Michael. He rubbed his face with both hands. "I miss him too, Will. More now than ever. I could really use his skills to help me reign. Even though I am the most logical successor to Isa, there are bound to be pretenders to the throne—the leader of China, for example."

"Then let me go find him, Benny. For you and for me. And for Michele."

"We've been through this. The agent is more than qualified. He—"

Will interrupted. "He's taking too long, and his position hasn't changed in days. I sneaked a microscopic tracking device in with the evidence I gave him."

Benny beamed. "You may be brighter than I gave you credit for, William." His demeanor darkened as he asked, "Do you think the agent is purposefully slowing the investigation?"

Will weighed his answer. "In a word, yes, but I have no proof. What do you know about him?"

"He's inscrutable and has no background," Benny said with a furrowed brow.

The look of concern on Benny's face moved Will to push further. "Could it be he was taking orders from someone else? Isa, maybe?"

Benny shook his head. "I asked Isa myself if he had anything to do with Michael's disappearance. He assured me he didn't."

"Was Isa always truthful with you?" Will asked cautiously.

Benny looked worried. "I doubt Isa was really honest with anyone. Anyway, it would be hard to tell with that alien nature of his."

"Well, you said it yourself, Benny: there's a new sheriff in town. Give me the go-ahead, and I'll find Michael. I'll leave you to deal with the agent if we find he has been double-crossing us."

"I give you permission to find your uncle," Benny said.

Will jumped from the chair. It wasn't far to Petra. He could be there before nightfall.

Benny raised his voice, saying, "*But first*, you must stay here with me through my installation as the new potentate in two days."

Will glared at Benny. "I don't want to put this off another two days, Benny!"

"Be that as it may, I need you to have my back until this one public ceremony is over. And in those two days, you can train one of the monkeys on your staff to do your job while you're away."

Will hated the answer, but there was something niggling at him, telling him it was best to wait. Was it the Holy Spirit? He prayed silently while Benny stared him down. The peace of God immediately enveloped him, and he knew it was the Lord's will that he stay the next two days.

Will released the tension in his body, smiled slightly, and said, "You drive a hard bargain, Lucky. I'll stay until you are installed."

"What a welcome turn of events it is to see your cooperation. Twice in one day I've been impressed by you. If you keep this up, you'll be as invaluable to me as your uncle Michael."

"Great!" Will exclaimed, rolling his eyes.

"In the meantime, let's go to my old apartment. This bland bit of black and white is getting on my nerves, and the food options here are nearly nonexistent."

"I'm at your service, Lucky, but once I walk you back to your place, I want to go to my meager quarters to shower and change."

They walked silently to Benny's quarters. When they passed the closed door to the sanctuary, Benny opened it quickly and peered in at Isa's body, as if to make sure he was really dead.

The opening of the door brought with it an arctic chill that cut Will to the bone. He had never encountered such a pervasive feeling of evil. He stumbled for a second as the feeling overwhelmed him, closing his eyes and fighting an urge to vomit. As cold sweat broke out on his forehead, he said in a whispered whine, "Close the door, Benny. Just close it."

Benny threw the door shut with whimsical flair. "Not so happy to see the result of your failed security detail, are you, Will?"

Will said nothing, just stared.

"Well, that's okay. Uncle Benny's in charge now."

Will was up early the next morning. Tomorrow would be Benny's installation ceremony, to be held concurrent with the burning of Isa's body on a pyre in the center of Abraham's Courtyard, the section of the Temple Mount fronting the new Solomon's Temple, the new Dome of the Rock mosque, and the new Basilica of Saint Peter II. After that, Will would be free to look for Uncle Michael. He quickly checked his cell phone to see if the microscopic trackers placed with evidence forwarded to the agent had changed position. Nope. They were still showing Petra as their location. Will mused that the agent could have detected them and left them in Petra to throw him off the trail. Yet, he didn't believe this to be so because of his father's direction to go there.

"Dad, I sure wish you could visit another time to help me find Uncle Michael," he said aloud. Then he waited for a few seconds, hoping to hear his father's familiar voice. Silence. Disheartened, he remembered Michael saying raptured family members wouldn't be able to visit once the world entered God's wrath.

"So, we're going to experience the wrath of God," he whined. For so many years, it had just been an expression. Now he would find out what that phrase really meant. He sure wished he had Michael around to help him discern the times. Well, with any luck, he would soon be free to find him. If it were up to him, he and Uncle Michael would squirrel away in the family estate with Michele and Jimmy and just pray and praise God until the darkness passed.

"I have a funny feeling that's not what You have planned for me, Lord." He put on a fresh uniform, the clownish Swiss Guard attire, and checked his firearm, wishing for the familiarity of his crossbow.

Entering Abraham's Courtyard, he took stock of the added security measures Benny had ordered. There were new checkpoints erected at all Temple Mount entrances, brightly festooned tents at each. There, Jerusalem police would unceremoniously strip visitors of their clothing. Every item in their pockets, backpacks, and pocketbooks would be confiscated as "sacrifices" and laid on the funeral pyre with Isa's body.

"It would be just like Benny to usher in his reign with such a gruesome event," Will said to nobody in particular. He wiped his eyes. Still sleepy, he would need to grab a Starbucks as soon as he finished his tour of the Temple Mount.

Next he came upon the crew building the funeral pyre in the center of Abraham's Courtyard. He shook his head slowly at the monstrous pile of wood stacked there. It was easily eight feet high and thirty feet wide. In its midst were various fireworks that would sputter and spark for dramatic effect. Will chuckled to himself as he thought, *Benny sure is sending his predecessor out with a bang!* Surrounding the pyre in a circle were flowers of every sort, placed there in homage to world's dead emperor. Will had to wonder where Benny had gotten them. Since the rapture, growing flowers was a luxurious waste of land, water, and human capital for a world hell-bent on defending itself from a foreign invader. He shook his head in disgust. That was for the normal people. Benny and Isa had any luxury they desired.

Behind the pyre, between two large pillars near the entrance to the Jewish temple, a stage was erected. It stood about ten feet off the ground, and it was there that Benny would conduct Isa's funeral service. Will could only imagine the confabulation of religious traditions Benny would stitch together to honor the late Isa Kurtoglu. One thing was for sure: Benny would be the star of this show, not Isa. Will wondered if his shooting of Isa had brought about a much worse ruler. Was Benny the Antichrist all along? Will shivered at the thought. Isa was horrible, to be sure—cold, harsh, and ultimately inhuman. But Benny was filled with anger at the entire world. His intentional meanness played worse than Isa's callous disregard in Will's book. "You should have let the Hashashin take care of the Benny problem when we had the chance, Jake. And I'll happily tell you to your face, once I hug you and welcome you home!"

Making his way from Starbucks, Will silently thanked God that coffee crops had done surprisingly well and that the government allowed coffee shops to operate around the globe. Latte in hand, he strode through the early morning streets of Jerusalem, remembering the times he would look for Michael only to find him at the Wailing Wall delivering coffee to the two witnesses, Moses and Enoch.

It was still early in his day, so he decided to take a detour to the Wailing Wall, if only to feel closer to his uncle for a few seconds. As he approached, he saw the yellow police tape strung around the bodies of the dead witnesses. In all the commotion over Isa Kurtoglu's death and the recent nuclear exchange, nobody had taken steps to remove the bodies. Gingerly, he approached the corpses, his mind filling with memories of the bloated, stinking bodies with which he'd had to contend during the Dark Awakening.

The memories assaulted him, but he steeled his resolve. He would make sure these two great men of God were respectfully moved to the tombs beneath the old city to join their fellow patriarchs. As he got closer, he noticed the beautiful smell of roses in bloom, certainly not the odor he had anticipated. Looking over the tape, he saw the bodies were not bloated, even after days in the hot sun. They looked like they were in a deep, peaceful sleep. There were no traces of blood or bullet wounds from the shots Isa had fired to bring them down.

"Thank You, Lord, for preserving Your saints!" he exclaimed in a hushed tone of awe. He examined the area across the police tape. The camera placed there to record Isa's historic encounter with the witnesses was still trained on them. He would have to move the camera before he could remove the bodies. After that he would have a very small amount of time before the crew monitoring the video feed would come to see what was going on. Transporting the bodies would require a Jeep from the motor pool, but he would have to hurry if he wanted to get one. As Jerusalem awoke for another day, the possibility of witnesses to his crime would grow exponentially.

He hurried to the motor pool and signed out a Jeep, noting on the sign-out form that he had taken it for use in the preparation of the upcoming ceremonies. It wasn't exactly a lie. He guessed the new potentate wouldn't want the bodies lying around on the day of his ascension to the throne.

He saluted the soldier in charge of the motor pool and drove the Jeep to the Wailing Wall. Checking his watch, he wondered if it was already too late in the day for such a daring plan. He parked the Jeep in front of the police tape and exited, carefully surveying the surroundings to ensure that he was alone. Only one ragged person passed by in the distance. The man looked neither to the left nor the right, totally oblivious of Will's gaze. Like many of the inhabitants of Jerusalem these days, he kept his head down. No one wanted to run the risk of offending Isa, Benny, or one of their men.

Once the man left, Will moved quickly to the other side of the police tape behind the camera. He grabbed the tripod on which it sat when he felt a strange rumbling beneath his feet. An earthquake?

"William, do not move the camera," a voice called to him. He looked around to see who had spoken. He saw nobody, but whoever had called out to him knew his name. His cover was blown. He crossed back to the other side of the police tape, preparing to get in the Jeep and drive away.

He turned to see the bodies one last time before he left. To his amazement, they began to glow, just a little at first, but then with brilliant intensity. The one Michael called Moses sat up first. While seated, he looked intently at Will. In his mind, Will heard the prophet speak: *I was the one who called to you, William. Your intentions were honorable, but as you can see, we do not need to be buried.*

The intense light subsided as Enoch sat up next. He looked at Will as well. "We require your services to record in detail what is about to happen."

Will was ecstatic with joy at their awakening, but at the same time he was fearful of the incredible power emanating from the two. He moved behind the camera as he'd been told, but his knees were weak.

The witnesses stood. Looking into the camera, Moses said, "Woe to the inhabitants of Earth, for Satan has come down to you."

Enoch added, "He is filled with wrath because he knows his time is short."

Moses continued the thought, saying, "Now is the time to accept Jesus as Lord and Savior. Only in Him can you find the strength to stand against the evil to come. Only in Him is there eternal life."

Will's spirit quickened to their message and the hope it contained. Just yesterday he had made that commitment and found the peace only Jesus could give.

The witnesses stood next to one another in silence. Their message had been delivered. Will thought he could see a quick nod from them as their bodies began to glow again. The ground rumbled beneath him again, and a huge flash of lightning parted the sky. The thunder that followed was deafening, but it carried the full message "Come up here!" It echoed in successive languages until it died down to a slight rumble.

The witnesses levitated for a second. Will moved the camera to follow them. Then they began to rise—slowly at first, as if they were saying goodbye to their beloved Jerusalem. Then their speed increased as their bodies shone brighter. Will managed to follow their light with the camera until they were high in the sky. Then a cloud covered the view.

Will broke into praise of the Lord, but he did so softly so as not to be heard by the camera. "Lord, I can't believe You allowed me to witness this amazing event. Thank You, Lord. Thank You!"

His jubilant feelings lasted only seconds as his attention was drawn to further rumbling. Unlike the earlier tremor, this one did not dissipate. It grew progressively stronger until Will could no longer stand. Crawling away on heaving paving stones beneath him, he looked in vain for a safe place, frantically trying to get away from the undulating boulders in the Wailing Wall behind him. Endless thunderous booms assaulted him as buildings throughout Jerusalem gave way to the quake. Each crash sent him scrambling with fear that the wall had collapsed.

The quake lasted more than a minute, which seemed to Will like an eternity. And then it was over. Alarms and sirens from all points in the city pierced the sudden stillness. Will looked back to the Temple Mount to see if it had survived intact. None of the stones of the Wailing Wall had broken loose. He sat on the pavement for a few seconds, taking it all in. The roller-coaster ride of emotion had left him temporarily dumbfounded. As his wits returned, he stood. He knew he needed to get to the Vatican to assess the damage, but there was something more important to be done first.

He ascended the stairs to the Temple Mount as the first of many aftershocks rocked the land. Although not as intense or long as the first quake, this one was plenty fierce. Will struggled to keep his balance on the stairs as they weaved back and forth beneath him. More crashes and more sirens split the air. This time the noise was punctuated with wails of pain and fear throughout Jerusalem. Panic set in for a second, but Will swallowed hard and forced himself to act calmly, climbing one step and then another. If it was his last act on earth, he had to get to the control room beneath Saint Peter's Basilica to make sure the video feed of the witnesses's resurrection was not deleted from the record. The world had to see their message!

Blackness surrounded Michael. He was aware of the drugs in his system and fought to retain consciousness. Nothing could be worse than the drug-induced visions: Satan in all his hideous glory—bluish complexion and massive wings—calling to him, laughing at him, and then laughing at Gabe's dead body. He didn't know how much more he could take.

"Think, Michael!" he said aloud to himself. "Focus!" In his mind's eye he conjured up the image of a photo he had found years before in his mother's safe. The photo showed much younger versions of the important people in Michael's life … and a mystery. They had all posed together for the photo years before they had met one another. How could it be?

To keep his mind active, Michael recalled details of the photo for the thousandth time. Chris was wearing shorts and a striped shirt. Sneakers? He concentrated on his memory of the photo. No, not sneakers. Hiking boots …

TWO

Gloria lay in her bunk at a Houston detention center, formerly a Walmart. She knew she wouldn't get to sleep that night. The events of the past days whirled in her head, and she felt the near suffocation of panic, the feeling of a trapped animal.

When the police arrested her at George Bush International Airport, she assumed she would be taken to a precinct house and booked on the charge of murder. Zack had murdered the prison guard and framed her. She had an attorney poised to come to her aid in the event Zack dared to follow through with his threat. She was hurt by his betrayal and annoyed at the inconvenience but felt sure she would be out on bail within twenty-four hours.

She couldn't have been more wrong. The police delivered her immediately to the FEMA camp. As they pulled up to the facility, she demanded to see her attorney. They laughed at her.

"There are no attorneys and no trials for the Christian militia," one cop said smugly.

The other joined in with the government line. "We only have a short period of time to unite the planet. Civil rights no longer apply to people who refuse to leave their noninclusive religions."

"It's a fact, ma'am," the first cop added. "Nobody wishes you harm, but subversives must be detained and deprogrammed. It's for the safety of us all."

"But I committed no crime!" she protested. "I was set up by my husband so he could make off with his secretary!" she shrieked as tears filled her eyes.

"Just following orders, ma'am."

They pulled her from the back of the police car and removed her handcuffs. She used her newly freed hand to wipe frantically at the tears on her cheek, looking briefly at her hand to see the smudge of mascara and makeup there.

The police handed her off to the booking officer with her documentation. The man barely looked at her as he scanned the credentials and led her into the converted store. She looked around the cinder block facility, now devoid of merchandise and cash registers. Instead, she saw rows of steel metal bunks, three high, each fitted with a thin mattress and an even thinner pillow. From the ceiling at either end of each row of beds hung a huge television screen. Near where the bakery had once been were rows of steel tables. At the opposite end of the store was a row of open showers and toilets. Not even a hint of privacy here.

The booking officer took her to what had obviously been the Walmart hair salon. A stern-looking woman greeted them.

The booking officer said emotionlessly, "Strip."

"I beg your pardon!" Gloria snapped. "This is still America, and I still have rights!"

The booking officer struck her with an open-handed slap to the face. She was flabbergasted and reflexively reached to her cheek. He then grabbed her hands and forced them into cuffs behind her back. Pulling upward on the bound wrists until they hurt, he held her there. The woman moved in with a sharp pair of shears and cut the dress off her. Next came her bra, panty hose, and underwear. In minutes she was standing naked and crying before her captors.

The booking officer unlocked one of the cuffs and led her to a barber chair. He cuffed her to the chair, and the woman went at her with a pair of clippers. Inside another minute, Gloria bore a crew cut. She sat in awe, looking at her shorn locks lying in a heap on the floor.

Next the woman doused her head with an acrid-smelling powder. The woman barked at the booking officer, who was checking his cell phone. "Hair is cut and deloused, Frank. Move on!"

Frank led Gloria to another cubicle. The back wall was filled with hooks that at one time held eyeglass frames in the Walmart vision center. There he made her lie down, cuffing her to what looked like a doctor's examining table.

"Just a bit of disinfection," Frank said with a leering grin. "We run a clean shop here."

She heard him running a pail of water and smelled the pungent smell of Lysol. First he removed her jewelry, missing her wedding band, and then he began to wash her—no cloth, just his meaty hands. He went after her makeup first. Her eyes stung from the Lysol, and its odor made her cringe. She didn't know how she would be able to survive the indignity about to occur. She got a good look at Frank as his hands moved to her neck. He was heavy, really heavy. Greasy black hair hung over his pimple-ridden face. It was hard to guess his age, but she figured he was maybe in his late thirties. As he leaned into her, she got a whiff of him. Suddenly she was thankful for the smell of Lysol.

She gritted her teeth, closed her eyes, and prayed hard as Frank's cleansing routine lingered around her breasts and crotch. The Lysol stung, but it paled in comparison to the sting of Frank's violation.

"Do you like what Uncle Frank can do for you?" he asked. She said nothing and forced herself to be still. Minutes passed like hours, but finally he was done. He unbound her and led her to the open showers.

"Rinse off!" he barked. *Oh, Uncle Frank sounds rejected,* she thought sarcastically. She could feel hatred toward him rising in her heart. She took the little bit of shower time to confess the hatred and ask Jesus to show her His love for the man. She left the shower, in no way wanting to be friends with good old Frank, but at least she had a better attitude than before. He handed her a thin robe, much like a hospital gown that had been sewn in the back.

"Underwear?" she asked softly. He laughed.

Next he took her to a more kind-looking old woman in the Walmart shoe department.

"What size do you wear?" she asked with a soft tone. Gloria felt a tinge of hope when she heard the underlying kindness in the woman's voice. She looked into the woman's weathered, wrinkled face for a sign of compassion.

"Size," the woman said blandly. Gloria told her and received a pair of work boots in the male equivalent to her size.

"Thanks," Gloria said. The woman offered no response other than shoving a pair of socks toward her.

Frank walked Gloria down a row of bunk beds and stopped near the middle. The metal bunks were three high with a ladder at the end of each. "You'll be in the middle bunk."

She looked at her new home. Not much to see. A mattress, a pillow, and a thin blanket. As she placed one foot on the ladder, Frank grabbed her wrist.

"We tell you when it's time to hit your bed. There's about an hour before the rest come in from the factory for dinner. While you wait for them, you are on toilet cleaning detail." He marched her to the row of toilets, where he handed her some cleanser and a brush.

She set to work, thinking she would prefer the company of dirty toilets to Frank any day. As the hour passed, she thought about how Zack had betrayed her—not just now, but throughout their married life. She prayed for God's grace to forgive him, knowing this wouldn't be a one-and-done prayer. It would take awhile to forgive and look past a lifetime of heartless actions on his part. She needed to be shed of him, done with him. She removed her wedding ring, the one piece of jewelry Frank hadn't taken, and the one piece of jewelry she didn't want. She threw it into the toilet and flushed it with the cleanser-filled water. It should have felt bad, but it didn't. It felt liberating. There was a chance her heart would be freer in a FEMA camp than it had been at Riverside. With this in mind, she looked forward to meeting the other detainees. It would feel good to be surrounded by real Christians. Their shared beliefs and torment promised an opportunity to forge a church more intimate and powerful than any in which she had ever participated.

Her optimism proved to be unrealistic. As the others marched into the facility, each stood behind a chair at one of the tables. Frank marched Gloria to an open chair. She would later learn they were seated in the order of their bed assignments. To her left and right were the women with whom she would share a bunk. To her left was a young girl; Gloria estimated her age at seventeen or eighteen. The woman to her right was four decades older. She might have been pretty at one time, but her hair had grown in as a shaggy gray mop after the initial buzz cut, and puffy dark circles surrounded her eyes. Her pallor suggested that she hadn't seen the sun in a while.

They were ordered to sit. Gloria spoke to the woman at her right, "Hello. My name is Gloria."

"I would know you anywhere," the woman said flatly. "I used to send money to Riverside. You may not be the sole reason I am here, but you're a big part of it."

Gloria was crushed. "I'm so sorry for those years. Only after the rapture did I realized how wrong we had been. Please try to forgive me." She touched the woman's hand. The woman pulled away.

Gloria turned to the young girl on her left. "Hi. My name is Gloria."

"Yeah, I heard," the girl said. She stared down at the table, not bothering to face Gloria.

"What's your name?"

"Kimmy."

"Well, Kimmy, I'm pleased to meet you. If you ever need anything …"

"I need you to be quiet," Kimmy said in a low voice. "They don't like us talking."

It was only then that it dawned on Gloria. The room was silent except for the filing of detainees, one table at a time, to the food line. She kept her head down like the others, not wanting to stand out. When it came time for their table to eat, she followed along to receive a scoop of mashed turnips, a slice of stale bread, and a paper cup of warm water. Michele's food donations had definitely not made it to this camp.

Once all had been served, the lights were dimmed in favor of the television monitors hanging from the ceiling. They blared speeches given by Isa Kurtoglu. He talked endlessly about the need to band together to fight against the coming Anu invasion. He prattled on about the dangers of noninclusive religions. The cumulative effect for Gloria was a headache. She couldn't believe this beast with the hypnotic voice had once shared her body. She shoveled the turnips into her mouth and rubbed at her forehead.

She was thankful for the end of dinner as she joined the ranks for the cleanup ritual. Going by table, each woman took her tray and silverware to an open spigot. They were allowed a few seconds to let the water wash off what it could, and then they were directed to leave the items in a pile. Gloria assumed they would then be put through a dishwasher, but she later found that she was wrong. They were merely stacked in place to be ready for the breakfast service.

And still, Isa droned on. The detainees returned to their tables and sat like stones for another couple of hours of his video badgering. The women all kept their heads down.

At last the order was given for them to return to their bunks. The lights were turned off, but the mugging face of Isa Kurtoglu was frozen on the television screens as a sort of subtle reminder that he would be watching. The inmates around Gloria fell quickly to sleep, but her mind raced.

The rhythmic breathing and snoring around her was interrupted by a different sound. Dim light from the televisions showed a security guard sneaking slowly among the bunks. What need would their captors have to creep around like that?

As the guard neared, Gloria lowered her head and tried to breathe softly and rhythmically, pretending to sleep. He stopped at her bunk. She could smell his breath. Then she heard subtle movement in the lower bunk: Kimmy's bunk.

"Please don't do this again," Gloria heard Kimmy plead softly.

The man chuckled. "I love it when you resist."

Gloria heard Kimmy whimper. The bunk moved as he planted himself on Kimmy's bed. Gloria panicked. She didn't know what she would do, but she wasn't about to let a teenager be assaulted by some brute with all the power.

"Let her alone," she said softly.

"What?" the guard snarled from below.

Gloria raised her head. "She's just a girl. Let her alone," Gloria said with a flat monotone in what she hoped was an authoritative voice. She felt the bunk move as he got off of Kimmy's bed.

He stood. His head was even with Gloria's. Leaning in toward the bunk to put his face mere inches from hers, he said, "You're the new one ... the televangelist, right?"

"Yes. I don't want any trouble. Please don't hurt that poor girl," Gloria said in a more conciliatory tone.

"Is that what you really want?" he asked with a creepy leer. "Because I'm thinking you don't want her to have all the fun. I'm thinking that pretty-boy husband of yours wasn't man enough for you." The warmth of his garlic breath brushed at her face as he spoke.

"Think what you want, just let the girl alone, okay?"

"And if I do?"

Gloria didn't respond. He reached out fiercely and cupped her breast. "I'll make you scream 'Oh God' for real, darling, not that fake stuff you did on your church show."

She removed his hand in a sharp motion. As she touched him, she had a strange feeling from the Holy Spirit that the man was not totally in control of himself. Maybe he was possessed by some demon?

She prayed silently for a second and then announced strongly, "In the name of Jesus, I command you to stop!"

He jolted as if he'd just received an electric shock. "Wh-what?" he stuttered.

"Stop hurting this girl. And leave me alone while you're at it!" she said more forcefully.

He said nothing, looking confused, and continued on with his rounds.

"My name's Iris," said the woman on the top bunk. "I thought you were a fraud, but you walk the walk."

"I was a fraud until the rapture, then I gave my life to Jesus."

"Same here," Iris said.

Gloria climbed out of her bunk to check on Kimmy. She found the girl curled in a ball on her bed. She sat next to Kimmy and stroked her hair. "It's okay now. He's gone."

"For now," Kimmy sobbed as she sat up. "But he'll be back, and the next time it will be worse. He told me he'd kill me if anyone found out." She leaned into Gloria's shoulder and cried. Gloria held her as she heaved with sobs. Soon the sobs quieted, and Gloria spoke in a motherly tone to her, "I had a friend named Kim. She was one of the bravest people I knew. Do you know what made her so brave? She knew she could do anything, put up with anything, as long as she had Jesus's love. She was right. And I'll tell you something else, you resemble her more than just in your name. You're brave too. I can tell ..."

When the girl had fallen asleep, Gloria returned to her own bed and closed her eyes. Her emotions were a wreck. She dreaded what she would see and endure in this godforsaken camp, but she was happy to know the Lord could use her to bring His peace even to this insanity.

It wasn't long before Isa's image on the television was replaced with another of his loud, droning speeches—apparently serving as reveille for the camp. The women rose from their beds, folded their blankets, and silently stood next to their bunks, eyes downcast. Gloria followed their lead. One by one the rows were called to form a breakfast line.

Breakfast was a watery oatmeal concoction. There was no sugar or milk and no coffee, just another small paper cup with warm water. Gloria was beginning to understand the robotic, trancelike demeanor of the ladies. They were malnourished. The thought of eating like this day after day until the Lord's return was dismal. For a second, Gloria's mind drifted toward memories of the fabulous breakfasts Rosalita made for her and Zack, the luscious French toast, pancakes, burritos, creamy oatmeal, and fried potatoes. *Stop it!* She pushed the images out of her mind. They were from a totally different reality. This was her reality now, and she knew that to pine for the past would be the equivalent of mental and spiritual suicide. Instead, she forced herself to focus on the future, when Jesus would return to set things right. Then there would be no more hunger, no more abuse. The world would be characterized by praise for its Redeemer and people's displays of respect for each other. It seemed like an impossible dream, but it was a scant three and a half years away. She told herself she could do anything for three and a half years with Jesus by her side.

Although she didn't feel gratitude yet, Gloria willed herself to thank Him for the privilege of being counted worthy to suffer on His behalf. The simple admission brought her a powerful feeling of peace and warmth.

In short order, the guards excused the tables one by one. The women went like trained animals to the open toilets, each robotically doing her business before the start of the workday. Gloria followed suit and smiled softly to herself when she was assigned the toilet into which she had flushed her wedding ring. The lack of privacy nearly prevented her from releasing her bladder. Yet another thing she would have to get used to.

They lined up to be marched to the weapons factory. Gloria wondered what she would be doing but guessed it would be some sort of mindless assembly line job. Put one part into another and push the contraption down the line to the next woman. There was no time to build automation if the weapons were to be ready when the Anu arrived—at least that's what the government said. In all probability it was the best way to keep the world's citizens engaged in the fight.

18

To the extent there was a spiritual component to the weapons, it certainly didn't hurt that they were infused with the negative energy of Christian suffering. She had read once that demonic entities actually fed on the misery and despair of humanity. Well, there was plenty for them to feast on in this hellhole.

As the guard ordered the women forward, Gloria's old friend Frank pulled her harshly out of line. "Not you, TV star. We have something special for you." Those around her stared more intently at the floor. Gloria stared into Frank's eyes, hunting for a shred of compassion or human dignity. He struck her across the face. "Eyes down!" She immediately obeyed as the welt grew on her cheek.

He motioned for her to follow him to the loading dock of the original store. Once there, he shackled her wrists to cuffs bolted onto the wall. Panic ran throughout her body, and she choked back a sob of fear.

A man entered the loading dock, carrying a folding chair. "Man" might have been a stretch. Gloria guessed he was at most twenty years old. Slicked-back blond hair sat over the scowl on his narrow, angular face. Sitting on the chair, he stared at her for a long time. She kept her head down, not wanting to make the mistake of meeting his gaze.

Finally he spoke. "My name, oddly enough, is Christian. I'm the head counselor at this camp. In other words, I run it."

Gloria spoke softly, "Nice to meet you, Christian."

He chuckled in a threatening manner. "You were very naughty your first night here."

Gloria said nothing.

He continued, "Our records indicate you interfered with a guard's duties."

She erupted, saying, "He was trying to have his way with a young girl!"

He raised an eyebrow and smirked. "When you have been here long enough, you may realize that physical affection is more coveted than feared."

His notion was ridiculous. She didn't respond.

"To make matters worse, it looks like you prayed and comforted one of our guests in the name of a noninclusive religion. I assume you know that is unacceptable."

"So I've heard," she said softly.

He smiled slightly. "Well, it's your first infraction. We'll go easy on you ... this time. Frank!" Frank answered his master's call, carrying a fire hose.

Christian said to Frank, "I'll leave you to it, then." He sauntered off the loading dock.

Frank grinned and braced himself as he pulled the nozzle on the hose. A torrent of water smashed Gloria's face, taking her breath away. She turned her head first to the left and then to the right. No matter what she did, there was no air to breathe. She tried to hold her breath, but the water kept coming. Her burning chest could stand it no more, and she involuntarily inhaled, taking water into her lungs. She began to cough. The water stopped.

She coughed up water and breathlessly gulped at the air. As she panted, Frank spoke, "We're going easy on you today, so I'll only do this a few more times. You really want to learn to fit in here. It's very unhealthy to go against the grain."

Far away in a foreign land, another water cannon fired at a naked man whose eyes, ears, and mouth were covered and bound in thick tape. His bound hands hung from a meat hook. The cannon fired at him once, twice, and a third time.

"I will not crack. I will not give into this," Michael chanted resolutely in his mind.

"I will not crack!" the Lady mocked before morphing into the blue-winged Satan.

"Jesus, help!" Michael screamed into the tape over his mouth. The images went away.

As he calmed, reason returned. Whatever drugs had been administered were starting to wear off. He had no idea how long he had been drugged and in sensory deprivation, but he recognized the protocol used to fracture the personalities of Vatican programmers in his employ years before. He knew he must be toward the end of the process. So far Jesus had kept him sane ... so far.

THREE

I t had been a tough day for Michele Sheradon, but then again, they were all tough days. She was a bundle of nerves. Still no news about Uncle Michael, and texts from Will were short and to the point. Information gathered from news reports detailed a mad monk who incapacitated Will and shot Kurtoglu with one of Will's arrows. It seemed odd to Michele that Will could be so easily taken down by an old fellow. And it seemed even stranger that the old guy would just happen to be a crack shot with a crossbow. Even in a day and age when the unthinkable had become routine, this scenario smelled of a contrived news story.

She asked herself if Will could actually bring himself to commit murder. Sure, he had killed to survive in the Dark Awakening, but could he cold-bloodedly plan and execute the assassination of a world leader—*the* world leader? Then again, the Antichrist was destined to feign a return from death. Surely Uncle Michael had told Will an attempt on Isa's life would be playing into his hand.

She was tempted to wipe her hands over her face in frustration, but she stopped at the last minute so as not to smudge her makeup. She had no time to reapply it. The driver was at the door to take her to company headquarters. She was about to go through yet another all-hands meeting to scope out where their businesses stood after a disaster. It was like the Dark Awakening all over again, except this latest disaster was nuclear. With half-lives lasting into the thousands of years, the new reality for the United States was grim.

She smiled and waved to the car's driver. Swiss Guard. She would rather drive herself, but Will insisted his men perform the task. He worried for the security of the family and felt personally responsible for the lapse in security resulting in Uncle Michael's abduction.

Uncle Michael's abduction. Whatever Will was up to. Gloria's arrest. It felt like the world was closing in on Michele. And now she had to go spar with Naomi, her supposed mother-in-law. She made a mental note to have a private investigator drill into the woman's suspicious claim of maternity. For Jimmy's peace of mind and for the sake of her marriage, she had to learn the truth about Naomi. In the meantime, there were two imposing priorities—to find Gloria and plan a rescue and to see if the remains of the family business could be used to serve the Christian community. Jimmy was searching databases for Gloria's whereabouts.

The family business undoubtedly fared better than those with headquarters and manufacturing plants in the blast zones. None of the family's facilities had been bombed out of existence. Michele took a long, deep breath to push back the need to cry. The news reports were so dire that they strained her ability to believe them. Aerial and satellite photographs of New York, DC, Chicago, and Los Angeles bore no relation to the cities they had once been. In their stead, cratered landscapes and twisted metal bore silent testimony to the power that had leveled them. Ash from the explosions covered the surrounding areas, leaving a moonscape, colorless and hostile to life.

Radiation at the sites was too high to conduct search and rescue operations. If by a miracle some had survived the original onslaught, they would be dead in a matter of days from nuclear fallout. Because of prevailing winds, most of the East Coast fallout moved into the Atlantic Ocean and came ashore in Europe. Greenland, Iceland, France, Spain, and England caught a lot of the United States' fallout—their own fallout hitting their Eastern European neighbors. But the ash clouds were immense and driven high into the atmosphere. Scientists estimated they would circle the Northern Hemisphere and precipitate out in rain and snow for the next several years. Radioactive water would kill off animals and crops. The implications were horrifying.

Areas closest to the blast zones were in pandemonium. People who had survived the blasts and were now affected by the fallout were clamoring to leave and seek medical help. There was no help for them. Soldiers in radiation suits fired at will on anyone attempting to leave the designated hazard zones. The people who survived there awaited lonely, bitter deaths from radiation poisoning.

As the car pulled up to the office, Michele thought, *Well, at least Isa made good on one promise.* His program for hardening the electric grid had paid off. There was little electromagnetic pulse impact from the nukes, just temporary outages as power was rerouted along the grid, but nothing too terrible.

For the first time in her life, Michele didn't like the cheery décor her grandmother had chosen for the office building. Life had gotten too tough. There was too much despair and too many deaths for her to be calmed by the subtle tones. Given the way Michele felt, she would prefer the space to be decorated in some macabre black and bloodred color scheme.

Entering the conference room with a sigh, she could tell by their faces that her staff felt demoralized as well.

"Are you okay?" Naomi asked. Her concern startled Michele for a second.

Michele shook her head. "I'm so sad. I never knew a time when nuclear war wasn't a possibility. I grew up with the idea, but somehow I never thought I would see it."

"I know you think I'm ancient," Naomi said with a wry smile, "but it was a possibility for my entire lifetime too. When I was in grade school, we had to practice drills of what to do in the event of a nuclear exchange. It was real to me when I was little, but so was Santa Claus. When I got older, I assumed no government would actually be so insane as to start a nuclear war." Her voice trailed off as if she were searching for some lost innocence.

John Santos joined the conversation. "Even with all the prophecies about the end times, I never imagined New York, DC, Chicago, and Los Angeles obliterated in a nuclear exchange."

Tanya, the head of human resources, said, "*Exchange* is the keyword. It looks like our bombs took out their share of the Russian populace too."

"Good," said Pak, head of risk management. "I wasn't born in America. I came here with my parents when I was ten. I adopted this country as my home, and I'm happy for every bit of damage we did to the people who started this."

"But the people didn't start it," Tanya protested, "just a couple of lunatics in government."

Michele called the meeting to order. "I assume our factories fared pretty well. We obviously lost distribution in the affected areas, but there is nobody left to ship product to anyway," she said with a scowl. She hated the clinical tone she used, but she would break down completely if she allowed any emotion.

Naomi answered, "Basically, you're right. We lost assets we no longer need given the casualties. We have records of our bank deposits in those cities, but they were very small since we sweep cash into our Atlanta banks at the end of each day. Production delays from the power outages were manageable. And there's a possible upside."

"What could that be?" Michele asked.

"Well, for one thing, there are no longer Department of Justice records of an investigation into our charitable giving. And there are no longer rating agencies to rake us over the coals for being under investigation."

Michele nodded. "I'll be honest with you, I'd rather be under investigation with a thriving country."

"I agree," Naomi said, "but we shouldn't look this gift horse in the mouth. It will be years before the DC agencies are up and running again. I'll be shocked if we ever hear anything about those investigations."

"Well, we sound like we are in a pretty good position to provide disaster relief," Michele said, eliciting groans from the other end of the table.

"With all due respect," Pak said forcefully, "it's not our responsibility to tend to society. We're a business. Our job is to make money. I thought you would be more sensible with your uncle out of the way."

Michele grew irate at the idea that there was any benefit to Uncle Michael's disappearance. She couldn't contain an eruption of the pent-up emotions that had been brewing since the time of his abduction. "More to the point, Pak, you think you can bully me now that my uncle isn't here. Well, guess what, you can't. Pack your things. We really don't need you."

There was a huge inhalation of breath from all those around the table. For some ridiculous reason, Pak stood his ground. He stared fiercely at Michele.

She glared back. "I'm giving you ten minutes to get out of the building, or I'll have security remove you."

Pak's expression changed from impudence to subservience in seconds. "Can't we talk about this?" he pleaded.

"I won't have another person speak ill of my uncle in my presence. Does everyone here understand?" she barked.

There were murmurs of affirmation from around the table.

"Good," Michele said sternly. "Pak, you now have nine minutes and thirty seconds."

Pak left the room in dismay.

Naomi looked upset with Michele, and Michele couldn't care less. Naomi spoke in a soothing voice to those who remained. "You have to understand, this is a family business. We in the family stick together ..."

Michele cut her off abruptly, saying, "No, Naomi. This business belongs to Uncle Michael, Will, and me. Not to Uncle Benny, not to Jimmy, and most certainly not to you. In fact, in order to prove my point, I am reassigning you. From now on, you will perform Pak's role."

Turning to John Santos, she said decisively, "John, you are someone I trust, someone I have always trusted. From now on, you are going to be my right-hand man around here."

John squirmed in his seat, not liking the shake-up any more than Naomi did, but Michele had to continue down this path. If she vacillated now, she would appear weak. "Naomi, go sit where Pak was seated. John, take Naomi's seat. Tanya, when the meeting is over, get the HR documents together to effect this management change. Naomi will earn Pak's old salary. John will earn Naomi's old salary."

Naomi huffed to Pak's chair. She was livid. Under her breath she cursed her new daughter-in-law. Michele heard it. "What was that, Naomi?"

For the first time since Michele had known her, Naomi looked frightened. She put her head down and said, "Nothing."

"I thought as much," Michele said indignantly. "Now, if nobody else has issues with who controls this business, let's proceed."

They all nodded their agreement, happy to be past the tirade.

Michele continued, "I know it varies for each ingredient depending upon sourcing and our ability to keep things fresh, but can we get to all of our food businesses and ask them to stock up on commodities? There is no telling what nuclear fallout will do to the crops."

25

"Fair point," John said. "The last report from the provisional government states they aren't sure if there was enough ash blown into the atmosphere to bring about a nuclear winter. That's great news. We may still have growing seasons for the next few years."

Naomi wiped her face in despair. "That's if we can trust the government's assessment."

"Everything is a total mess to be sure," Tanya added. "As you know, most insurance policies exclude acts of God and acts of war. I'm hearing rumors of our health insurance carriers trying to exclude radiation effects from our medical coverage."

"That's ridiculous!" Michele exclaimed.

"But not unheard of," Tanya said sadly.

"Okay," Michele said, taking it all in. "John, are we still sitting on a pile of cash?"

"Yes, but buying up commodities and continuing aid efforts will eat into it."

"I see," Michele said gravely. "But we have an obligation to our employees. Tanya, can you work your sources to get a feel for the cost of service they are trying to walk away from? We'll need to engage our actuaries to see how those numbers play out vis-à-vis the location of our facilities and the known path of the radioactive cloud."

"I see where you're going," John said with a grin. "The actuaries could then give us a statistical estimate of the cost to cover our employees."

"Right." Michele grinned. "Given the long-term effects of radiation exposure, the projected amount will be heavily discounted. We'll then invest that amount to fully fund our obligation."

"The employees will sure be happy to hear it," Tanya said.

"Of course, we'd only need about three and a half years of payments," John said with a smile.

"Oh, please," Naomi said with disdain. She didn't look up from her phone when the others turned in her direction. Instead, she turned ashen and stared intently at it.

Michele ignored the comment. "But we'll fund the full amount. It will be important to our employees to hear that their care will be completely covered by the company."

"Point well taken," John said.

Michele moved the meeting forward. "We also need an analysis of our survival food business. I know it's small compared to our other food businesses, but we have to run it in three shifts. Find out if there are any quick capacity changes we could make to ramp up production even further. If there is a nuclear winter, we'll need every pound of freeze-dried food we can produce."

"Currently that business makes the products it freeze-dries," John said. "When we bought it, we did an analysis of which of our existing food products would work with their preservation systems. There are quite a few. We may be able to divert products in bulk from our other factories to be freeze-dried."

Michele picked up the thought, "And if our survival food business focuses only on preserving the food and our regular businesses source the raw materials and perform the manufacturing, we should be able to increase production a lot. We'll need to study this quickly."

John concurred. "Like I said, the biggest part of the analysis was done during the acquisition to target synergies, but we didn't pursue them vigorously."

"Let's set up a meeting with the business heads. Make it a daylong affair. I want us all to brainstorm—no silos, nobody protecting their fiefdoms," Michele ordered.

"I'll get you the meeting," John said, shaking his head as he wrote a reminder to do so on his notepad, "but you're going to have to force cooperation."

"I'll do it," Michele said sternly. Looking around the table, she asked, "Does anybody have any other business to discuss?"

Most of the group did not. Michele looked to Naomi, who was still captivated by her phone. "Naomi," Michele said briskly to break her from her trance.

"What?" Naomi asked, looking up. Michele was baffled by the look of terror on Naomi's face.

"Is there any other business you want to bring to the table?" Michele asked with concern.

"N-no," Naomi stuttered, "but I really need to have a word with you after we adjourn."

The meeting ended quickly. The staff made beelines out of the room, clearly anxious to be away from the drama they thought would unfold. When they were gone, Michele closed the conference room door. "Naomi, I'm sorry I acted so abruptly, but …"

"I don't care about the job," Naomi said in a tense whisper. "I just need you to know I'm on your side. I need your protection."

"My what?" Michele asked, confused.

Naomi handed Michele her phone, which displayed an email from Benny. The pontiff was none too pleased with Naomi's attempt to take control of the company. The text was scathing and hinted at horrifying punishments if she should ever step out of line again.

Michele gulped at the tone of the document. She had never seen Uncle Benny's wrath, but she had heard plenty about it. "Naomi, I don't know what to say …"

"Say you'll talk to him. Tell him you were rash when you told him about my relationship to Jimmy. Tell him I made it up."

"Did you make it up?" Michele asked.

Naomi burst into tears, shaking her head. She tried to speak, but no words came. Finally she said, "No. It was a rape. I'm not the motherly type, so I gave the baby up for adoption."

Michele moved closer to the woman, her mother-in-law, whom she'd just demoted! She patted Naomi's shoulder. "That must have been so painful. I had no idea."

"It was a long time ago. When I realized who Jimmy was, I tried to capitalize on it because I disagreed with the way you and Michael ran the business. Then I got an email from the Vatican telling me to assist the government in their search of the estate. The next thing I know, I'm being questioned as if I had something to do with Michael's disappearance. I didn't, Michele. You have to believe me. I disagreed with just about every decision he made regarding the company, but I would never, ever hurt him." She broke into long, heaving sobs.

Michele tried to put the pieces together, "Naomi, I don't share any information with Uncle Benny. I didn't tell him you were Jimmy's mother. Maybe Will mentioned it. I don't know."

"Well, now he thinks I'm dangerous. The most powerful man in the world thinks I'm dangerous! What am I going to do, Michele?"

Michele read the email again. It was ruthless. She offered a suggestion. "How about this? I'll write him an email explaining you really are Jimmy's mother, but the circumstances surrounding that fact are very painful. That's why you were secretive about it. I'll also explain that you have been demoted as punishment for any appearance of deceit that may have upset him."

"Oh, Michele, would you? Would you please do that for me?" she pleaded.

"Yes, Naomi. We haven't often agreed, but I have heard enough about Uncle Benny's temper to know I don't want you in his crosshairs."

"I've known your grandmother for a long time, and I've seen what Benny can do. And now that he has all this power—well, people can just disappear."

"I know," Michele said sympathetically. "Like I said, I'll send him the email, but you better pray that Will finds Uncle Michael. When it's all said and done, he's the only one in the family who can keep Uncle Benny at bay."

Just then Michele's phone rang. Looking at the home screen, she saw it was Jimmy and decided to take the call.

"What's up, honey?" she asked.

"I found where they're keeping Gloria."

FOUR

I t was a bright, beautiful day in Jerusalem. There wasn't a cloud in the deep blue sky, but the city was still—more quiet than Will had ever heard it. The earthquake had been devastating. Most of the twentieth-century architecture had toppled to the shaking earth. The old city construction, close to the ground and largely made of stone, handled the quake much better.

"It's like You restored the city to its ancient form," Will said to the Lord as he walked the perimeter of the Temple Mount. Today was Benny's big day. He would declare himself potentate of the world. The very thought was nauseating to Will, but at least he would be free to search for his uncle Michael after the audacious ceremony Benny had planned.

The stage was set, and Isa's burial pyre was ready to burst into flame. Will double-checked the security. His reputation was on the line. He laughed at the very thought! As far as he was concerned, the world would be better off if Benny fell into the flames with his beloved leader.

"Who am I kidding?" he spoke to the wind. "We all know the Lord has a plan. Benny will survive. So I have to play my part and run security."

He watched for a couple minutes as the men in charge of pyrotechnics pored over Isa's pyre, making sure things would go off as planned. Next, he went to the studio under the basilica to check the camera angles and the flight paths of the drones. He also double-checked his wireless access to those feeds through his phone.

His rifle felt odd on his shoulder. Benny had ordered his crew to carry them, but Will wasn't nearly as sure of his abilities with a rifle as he was of his expertise with a crossbow. When push came to shove, Will knew he could aim and shoot, but it was a brute weapon in his hands. It had none of the finesse and subtleties of the bow. He looked at his watch and at the doors to the basilica. They opened at 9:00 a.m. on the dot to reveal Benny ready to lead a parade of interfaith leaders to the stage. Behind them, the remaining leaders of the world's governing regions held Isa Kurtoglu's body aloft on a wooden slab.

Will marched to Benny and saluted.

"Is everything in place, William?"

"Yes, sir," Will said briskly.

"We had this same conversation a couple of days ago, and you know what happened," Benny said, making a terse reference to Isa's death. "Have you done a better job this time?"

Will bristled at the comment but let it pass as part of the show. "Yes, sir," he snapped.

"Good! Well done. Let's get this show on the road!"

Will stepped back into the ranks of a row of Swiss Guardsmen behind Benny, and the parade to the stage began. The air was still. All in attendance were silent as a lone snare drum pounded out a morbid beat. Will scanned the crowd and periodically checked image feeds on his phone. There weren't likely to be any problems. The place was locked down tight.

As they neared the podium, the world leaders deposited Isa's body onto the arms of a forklift, painted black to reflect the solemnity of the occasion. As the world leaders took their places on the stage, the forklift raised the body. Inching forward, the machine moved toward the pyre. Will looked uncomfortably at the way the body jostled with the movement of the lift. If Kurtoglu were to fall off the wooden slab, it certainly would sour the festivities. For a second, Will allowed himself to think of the dark comedy that would ensue, and then he quickly wiped away a smirk forming on his face.

After what seemed to be an eternity, the forklift placed Kurtoglu's jiggling body on its final resting place atop the massive pile of kindling and fireworks awaiting Benny's first act as potentate—to incinerate his predecessor.

Benny began his remarks. "Fellow citizens, I come to you with the saddest task. Today we bid farewell to the most unique man ever to grace earth. Isa Kurtoglu stood head and shoulders above us all. His alien DNA combined with ours forged a truly remarkable being. We were his brothers and sisters, but only in part. He was also a member of a great galactic federation of civilizations.

"As you know, from the time Isa became our leader, he pursued a marvelous plan to use alien technology in our defense. In so doing, it was his greatest desire that we come together as a people and thereby prove to the federation the value of our inclusion in its ranks.

"Sadly, our esteemed leader and my beloved friend has been taken from us—nevermore to lead us in revolt against the noninclusiveness that has plagued us from time immemorial.

"As if the news of his barbarous murder were not enough, I have more bad news. Two days ago, I witnessed the ultimate in self-sacrifice as the Lady literally poured herself into Isa's healing. While I don't understand entirely the process, she drained the last bit of her spirit to bolster Isa and bring him back from the verge of death. Alas, dear friends, her efforts failed."

Benny paused to hold up an ornately decorated wooden box containing the goo left behind by the Lady in the holy of holies. "This is all that remains of her. I commend her spirit to join Isa's."

Will watched, aghast, as Benny unceremoniously chucked the box onto the pyre and dusted off his hands. Will had a hard time stifling a giggle.

Benny continued, "The times are dark, and the hour of humanity's greatest challenge rushes toward us, but we are not without hope. The plans set forth by Isa and the Lady are as valid today as they were three days ago. I can assure you, I remain the sole confidant of our alien benefactors. I alone know the extent and timing of actions to fulfill their plans.

"In short, we have not been left destitute. I am extremely confident that I can carry out the remainder of their plans and save us from the impending peril.

"For this reason, and this reason alone—the welfare of every man, woman, and child on earth—I am taking the reins of the Kurtoglu administration. With you under my guidance as both political and spiritual leader of the world, we will find the resolve to unite as never before to eradicate once and for all this Anu threat.

"The great prize is still in sight. By a show of hands from the assembled world leaders, I ask them to pledge their loyalty to me so that we can proceed without further delay."

The world leaders seemed shocked by this request. Will wondered if they hadn't been clued into this part of the program. He watched expectantly as Benny turned from the microphone to face the seven remaining world kings. All media coverage was on Benny and the world leaders. Cameras failed to cover an armed drone behind the would-be potentate of Earth. There didn't need to be much more convincing. These leaders were the weakest of the original ten. One by one, the men raised their hands to pledge their support to the new world leader.

Benny turned again toward the microphone to the soft applause of the small group gathered at the Temple Mount. He spoke with a humility Will found to be decidedly convincing. If he hadn't known Benny personally, he would have believed in the man's sincerity. "It is with honor and a bit of trepidation that I accept the task you have given me. In this harshest of hours, I believe it would be unsettling to our goals if I were to abandon my papal post to assume the presidency. For the benefit of all, I will work tirelessly to fulfill both roles. I have opted for the title of my combined posts to be the simple word *potentate*. Therefore, I stand before you today as Potentate Peter."

Like clockwork, the musicians broke out into a musical amalgamation of "Hail to the Chief," "God Save the Queen," and "Ave Maria." The schizophrenic mélange of instrumentals left Will's head spinning. Like Benny himself, the musical concoction was outlandish, over the top, and on the cusp of insanity. As the band played, Benny held his arms aloft in a victory pose that turned into an awkward papal blessing as a squadron of jets flew over, tipping their wings to the new leader.

When the fanfare finally subsided, Benny took on a solemn posture. "My unfortunate first task as potentate is to commend the spirits of Isa Kurtoglu and the Lady to the great beyond. They were my mentors and my dearest friends. I cannot begin to tell you all the tales of their kindness and generosity."

That's because there are none, Will thought.

Benny continued the eulogy. "Instead, I will focus on what they meant to all of us. They were beacons of light pointing toward a future where men and women of goodwill would work together for the good of the planet. They showed us a future where violence, distrust, and fear could melt away in the forging of global unity. We may have lost their presence, but we have not lost their vision. We have not lost their hope for a brighter tomorrow. And we have not lost their faith in the human spirit!"

Applause filled the air. Benny paused to smile at those gathered, and then he looked into the camera broadcasting his message to the entire world. "With the support you have shown me, and with the lessons I have learned from these two most marvelous beings, I will not let their legacy be forgotten. I will not let their deaths be in vain. And I will not stop until we have achieved the bright, bounteous future they envisioned!"

Applause again. This time Benny smiled into the camera, but it was a wistful smile, a smile of hope tainted by the pain of loss. "And now it is time to bid farewell to the two beings who have done more than any others to benefit humanity. Gentlemen, please light the solemn pyre."

The pyrotechnical team advanced on the pyre from all sides, each member carrying a lighted torch and moving dramatically to a military cadence. The precision steps, the billowing torches, and the rigid sound of the snare drum worked together to create an atmosphere of great expectancy. Will and his men moved to form an outer circle around the pyre. He then commanded his men to aim and fire in a twenty-one-gun salute, followed by the desperate wail of "Taps" played on a solitary trumpet.

Despite his disdain for both the Lady and Kurtoglu, Will couldn't help but be moved by the ceremony. He imagined all the people on earth feeling the same. Will and his men lowered their arms and performed white-gloved salutes. This was the signal for the pyrotechnical team to place their torches on the pyre.

The fire started slowly, allowing the pyrotechnical team to retreat to a safe position. The smell of wood tinged with accelerant filled the air. Will wondered how long it would take to incinerate the dynamic duo and if Benny would dismiss the crowd or make them stand there until nothing was left but a pile of smoldering ash. *Well, this is Benny we're talking about. I doubt he'll want to stand that long.*

It wasn't boring for long. The pyrotechnics sputtered to life with a row of sparklers around the outer perimeter of the pyre, making it seem as if it rested on a bed of light. Their brilliance continued as a second row of fireworks caught, sending glistening Roman candles into the air above the Temple Mount. Next, a row of fireworks surrounding the body erupted in large shooting flames. The bright white flames obliterated any view of the body. Will kept blinking, resisting an urge to break his attention and shield his eyes from the hot glow.

Soon all the wood was ablaze. The heat of the flames could be felt as far as the stage, where Benny patted his forehead with a linen handkerchief. Will felt sweat run down his face. Then he saw something. He blinked his eyes to make sure it wasn't some sort of illusion. It wasn't. His knees went weak. Kurtoglu's body was moving!

Will stared hard at Benny, trying to muster the older man's attention. Eventually, Benny looked in his direction. Will rapidly moved his eyes toward the body. Benny's gaze followed. He looked intently into the flames and then had to grasp the podium to keep from falling. *So Benny sees it from his perspective as well.*

Will's mind raced. *Maybe the muscles somehow twitch when being consumed by fire.* That had to be it. Kurtoglu was certainly dead.

Will looked again toward Benny when he heard a collective gasp from the assembled crowd. Looking back at the pyre, he saw Kurtoglu's body in a seated position. Nobody moved. There was no sound other than the roaring flames. It seemed every person there was trying to make sense of the scene.

The head of the flaming body turned in Will's direction. Will felt immediate nausea. In his mind he heard Kurtoglu's voice. *Thank you, William. Without you, I might not have made this marvelous transformation.* Will heaved and swallowed hard.

The body stood, looking like the Human Torch in a *Fantastic Four* cartoon. The creature raised his hands to the heavens. His thunderous voice echoed around the Temple Mount, saying, "Citizens of Earth! *I am* the phoenix. *I am* Kurtoglu. *I am* God, come to rescue you!"

The stunned audience cheered the man of flame, and all of the drone cameras zoomed close to catch his likeness. Kurtoglu spread his hands out over the flames and said in a softer voice, "Be still." The flames died instantly, leaving Kurtoglu standing on the pyre in perfect health. He looked immaculate—the perfect human being—even as smoke drifted off his once-flaming suit.

Kurtoglu turned to Benny and said, "I am well pleased with your intent to carry on in my absence, Potentate, but as you can see, I am more than able to perform my duties."

Will drew his breath. Impressive as Kurtoglu was, Benny wasn't the type to relinquish control—of anything. The being inside Benny cried out worshipfully, "With the power vested in me as potentate of the world, I make my final act to restore to you all power and titles of my office." He then kneeled with a slight stumble. Lowering his head and extending his arms in worship, he finished his proclamation with the words, "My Lord and my God!"

Those attending the service did the same. Will saw the knees of his men starting to buckle. "Attention!" he called, to let them know they would not join in the adoration. Kurtoglu looked at Will with a slight smile. All of Will's men fell to their knees. Will could feel the pressure of an unseen force moving him toward the ground. He prayed and felt slight relief. He prayed harder, sweat pouring down his face. Kurtoglu stared at him, and the pressure increased. Then some force hit his knees from behind, and he fell.

Isa stepped on unseen stairs down from the pyre. With amazing vigor and rapid movement, he ascended the stage to stand next to Benny. He motioned to the adoring crowd to stand, and Will felt an instant release of the pressure that had held him down.

"I have been to the other side," Isa said with a grin. "I have conquered death. The conjoined nature of my alien and human DNA has resulted in even more remarkable abilities than anybody could have imagined! Through my death and resurrection, I have become one with the universe in a way even I couldn't have dreamed a few short days ago.

"I have returned, my people, from the cosmic void. I have taken up my life again with one purpose, one dream, and one mandate: the salvation of humanity. With my newfound insight, we will easily defeat the Anu. I will usher in a golden age for humanity that will far exceed the confines of the galactic federation so highly valued by the Lady.

"Rest assured, there will still be a time of hardship until we defeat the Anu, but following their demise, I will lead humanity to its brightest future."

The audience cheered as Isa first blessed the crowd and then those present on the stage. With a final wave, he descended the stairs with Benny in tow. Will ordered his men to rush to the stairs. There they surrounded the two most powerful men on the planet and escorted them in the walk to their quarters in the basilica. Isa smiled, waved, and offered brief comments to reporters as they strolled across Abraham's Courtyard.

Will got a good look at Isa as they proceeded. There was still a scar on his head from the arrow that had killed him. His face and demeanor were the same, but something had definitely changed in the man. Around him, Will could nearly see a dark energy, like a barely visible mist. Then he recalled books written by his father years before about the Antichrist. At some point, Satan himself would inhabit the Antichrist. *Satan!* Will gulped. The change in Isa made sense now. His body was little more than a skin to cover Satan's spirit.

Will escorted the president and pontiff back to Isa's apartment and stood guard outside. He winced at the sounds of fury he heard from within:

"So you thought you would be the new leader of the world, did you, Benny?" Isa screamed in a deep growl.

"I … I thought you were dead, Isa," Benny said, groveling. "I meant no disrespect."

Will heard a scream, a thud, and a moan. He guessed Isa had thrown Benny against a wall.

"You were there when I inhabited this body! You knew I wasn't dead!" Isa bellowed.

"Isa, please, please," Benny muttered over and over.

"This is the last time I'll speak to you, you pathetic pretender to my throne. From this time forward, only Nergal will grace my presence. Do you understand?" Isa screamed.

There was another crash from within, followed by a howl of pain. Then there was silence. After a minute, the door opened softly.

"William, could you help me to my apartment?" Benny asked in a whisper.

Will turned to see the older man's face bruised and misshapen. He grasped Benny's left hand and slid his body under Benny's arm. They moved in silence, punctuated by an occasional moan from Benny. Will felt a terrible, claustrophobic fear. Satan had literally come to Earth, and there was nowhere to run, nowhere to hide, and no place of escape.

He helped Benny to his bed. "There you go, Benny. You look horrible. Do you want me to call a doctor?"

"No!" Benny shouted in a panic. "Nobody can know what just happened! Let me rest and I'll be fine."

"Okay," Will said uneasily. It sure didn't look like Benny would be fine.

"William," Benny said in a harsh whisper as he grabbed Will's sleeve.

"Yeah?"

"I've made a terrible mistake. Isa isn't who I thought him to be. You have to find Michael. He may know what to do. Go find Michael."

Michael was somewhere between consciousness and deep sleep—not a dream state, but a muddled fog. He felt a pinch on the underside of his forearm. A needle?

"The beast has awakened, Father. And so you must as well."

FIVE

t took awhile to get permission to fly to Houston. Air traffic in North America was very tightly controlled after the nuclear attack, a necessary precaution because of radioactive dust in the upper atmosphere. When prevailing winds brought radiation with them, the government halted air traffic. In times of precipitation, public service announcements warned people to stay indoors. Government agents with hazmat suits and Geiger counters patrolled the streets to monitor the environment.

Michele hated postnuclear life. The invisible threat of radiation poisoning was never long out of mind. There was no way to live a normal life when any rainstorm could turn an area radioactively hot for days. And that wasn't even the half of it. While she and Jimmy waited to board the company jet, the airport's television monitors covered Isa Kurtoglu's remarkable recovery from death.

She took Jimmy's hand as they stared in disbelief at the screens. "Even though I knew about this, it's still shocking to witness."

Jimmy squeezed her hand. "*Shocking* isn't even the word for it, babe. Even from here, I can feel a spiritual darkness resonating from him."

"Well, the Bible says he and his angels will be cast down to earth. We've been invaded. I don't know if the world will feel safe again before Jesus comes," she said sadly.

"Probably not. But there's nothing for us to do but keep busy. We have to save as many as possible. Getting Gloria will be a good test of whether our phony credentials can pass muster."

They settled into club chairs in the waiting room, sipping coffee and listening to the newscaster's astonished recounting of Isa's resurrection. Michele's ringing cell phone startled her. Looking at the screen, she said, "Will," before taking the call.

"Will! Where are you?"

"I'm in a Jeep, heading into Jordan."

"We've been watching the coverage from Jerusalem. How horrible is it?" Michele asked.

"We have a lot to catch up on. The earthquake damaged most of the modern buildings around the Temple Mount," he said.

"I saw the reports. They said the bodies of the two witnesses are buried under the rubble."

"Not so!" Will screamed. "I watched them ascend to heaven. I have a video of it. At some point, I have to figure out how to pirate it onto a worldwide telecast."

"What about Isa?" Jimmy asked. Michele relayed the question. "Jimmy wants to know about Isa."

"He was scary before, but he's terrifying now. There is such palpable evil surrounding him. Even Benny is afraid of him."

She relayed his comments to Jimmy and then asked, "How is Uncle Benny?"

"Well, the new Isa beat him up pretty bad for presuming to become the world leader. I don't think Benny is likely to make that kind of mistake again."

"You mean physically beat him up?" she asked, aghast.

"Yeah. I helped him to his bed. He said he made a terrible mistake and that I need to find Jake. He said that Jake might know what to do."

"To help Uncle Benny? He's too far gone," Michele said with a scowl. "Do you have any leads on where to find Uncle Michael?"

"It has only been a few days since we last spoke, but a lot has gone down. The crazy monk who attacked Kurtoglu was a ruse Dad cooked up. He took the blame for something I did."

"They were pretty good shots. I was wondering how the old fellow managed to disable you and pull off such a precise execution," Michele said.

"Well, you're the only one who has questioned it so far, but Isa knows I did it."

Michele gasped. Her heart pounded in her throat at the thought of the potential danger to him. "Will, how do you know?"

"He got into my head at his resurrection. In fact, he thanked me for enabling his transformation."

"Oh," Michele said softly, realizing Will's self-recrimination for being an unwitting vehicle for such evil. "Will, you have to give your life to Jesus. He can protect you."

"I already did that," he said cheerily. "The best decision of my life. When Dad put me out to make it look like the old monk incapacitated me, everything hit home. The old guy's sacrifice for me bowled me over. The next thing I knew, I was in front of the cross, and I understood Jesus's sacrifice in an experiential way. So, I gave my life to Him."

"Will! I'm so happy to hear that!" she screamed into the phone. "You have no idea how worried I've been about you!" Jimmy tugged at her arm with a questioning expression. "Will gave his life to Jesus," she said with a grin.

"Tell him congratulations," Jimmy offered.

"Jimmy says congratulations, Will. We're both very happy and greatly relieved."

"Same here," Will said. "I just hope to be able to share the news with Jake soon."

"Do you have any leads?"

"Just before I passed out at Isa's assassination, Dad told me to go to Petra. That's where I'm headed now."

"Just Petra?" she asked. "Couldn't he have been more specific?"

He chuckled. "I have a location of sorts. Do you remember me telling you I put trackers on the evidence I handed over to the agent?"

"Vaguely ..."

"Well, those trackers haven't moved for a while, and guess where they are?"

"Petra?"

"Yep. But the fact that they haven't moved makes me nervous. I could be walking into a trap, so I'll have to do some reconnaissance. This is no time for me to be a bull in a china shop."

"Agreed. I'm worried about you ... and Uncle Michael ... and Gloria. I sure would like it if we could have a few safe moments to catch our breath."

"Well, hopefully I'll be smart enough to find Jake and bring him home. Then we can concentrate on Gloria," he offered.

"Actually," she said cautiously, "Jimmy and I are at the airport right now. He found out where they're holding Gloria. We're going to get her."

"What? No!" Will screamed. Michele held the phone away from her ear.

Returning the phone to her ear, she said, "This is the perfect opportunity to find out if our credentials will do the trick."

"But Michele, you'll be on your own. Neither Uncle Michael nor I will be at the Vatican to run cover for you if they decide to check up on you. I wish you would wait to rescue Gloria until he and I can lend some assistance."

"We've cleared our flight plan, Will. We're going through with this. God only knows how much trouble Gloria is in. We have to do something while we can."

Will let out a long, theatrical sigh. She grinned at the drama. Finally he said, "Okay, but promise me you'll be careful."

"We will be. We'll be dressed in FEMA coveralls, and we have Vatican papers demanding her transfer to a Vatican detention facility. Do you really think anyone is going to try to call Jerusalem to check on us when the whole world is buzzing about Isa's resurrection?"

"Probably not," Will admitted.

"So, you agree this is the perfect time for Jimmy and me to execute our plan."

"I didn't say that. I just asked you to be careful."

"Do me a favor," she said. "You be careful too. And call me as soon as you find Uncle Michael. I can't wait until he is safe."

He hemmed and hawed. "Listen, about that. We haven't heard from him in weeks. There's no knowing what kind of condition I'll find him in. He may even be—"

"I know," she said, cutting him off before he could say the word. "But I think if he were gone, I would feel it somehow."

"I hear you. I just want you to understand it may not be good news."

Jimmy pulled on her sleeve. She looked in his direction to see it was time to board the plane.

"I've got to go. Our plane is boarding."

"Again, be careful. Don't take any unnecessary chances," he ordered.

"Same to you, Will. I love you."

———————————

Jimmy pulled the rental van up to the gate of the former Walmart where Gloria was being held. A man in a small guard building opened a window. Jimmy rolled his window down.

Jimmy's baseball cap was pulled down low over his eyes. He said nonchalantly to the guard, "Detainee transfer to the Vatican system. Here are my orders." He handed the man his electronic clipboard. It looked authentic enough, and the programming had been lifted from a real clipboard he had stolen from another FEMA camp.

The man at the guard station barely examined it. He glanced at the clipboard and saw the transfer authorization sheet on the screen. "Too bad you're only here for one. This camp is getting pretty crowded," he said with a sardonic grin as he handed the clipboard back to Jimmy.

Michele leaned across Jimmy to get into the conversation. "We still have room to accommodate more detainees. The Vatican takes the ones most entrenched in the old Christian dogma. Our reeducation methods have proven to be the best in the world."

The guard said blandly, "I'll call ahead. I'm sure they could round up a few Holy Rollers to send your way."

Michele bristled at the comment but smiled as if it were one of the cutest things she had ever heard. "Thanks. We appreciate it."

He opened the gate. They drove through as Jimmy put up his window. He looked straight ahead but spoke sternly. "Just remember our mission is to liberate Gloria. She is our priority."

"Yes, but if we can get more …"

"We don't want to look too eager. Try to be as bland and lazy-looking as the guy we just left." He was right. She had to be careful not to blow their cover.

Jimmy drove the van up to the former store's entrance, where another guard greeted them.

"How are you doing today?" the man asked with a broad smile. There was a certain softness to his voice and kindness in his smile that put Michele at ease.

"We're doing fine," Jimmy answered dully. "And you?"

"I'm over the moon!" The man beamed. "Have you seen the television reports? He's back! President Kurtoglu isn't dead!"

"We heard some reports," Michele said, pointing to the van's radio, "but we've been traveling most of the day."

"Well, come inside then," the guard invited happily. As they exited their van, he held out his hand. "I'm Lucas. Nice to meet you."

Jimmy shook hands first. "Hi. My name is Barney." He pointed to the clipboard showing his name as Barney Collins. Michele had rolled her eyes when he came up with their names, exhibiting his love for the old horror soap opera *Dark Shadows*.

"My name is Angelique Bouchard," Michele said. She wanted to laugh at how ridiculous she felt giving that name. In the end, it came out as an authentic smile.

Lucas returned the smile and ushered them past the security station at the entrance to the facility and into the main area. He pointed to rows of large television screens hanging from the ceiling, each displaying the endless coverage of Isa's miraculous reappearance.

"We've been watching this all day. I can't get enough of it!" He waved his hands with excitement. "This is the best I have felt about our chances since I first heard of the Anu. If ever a man could save humanity, it is Isa Kurtoglu."

"It's amazing," Michele said, feigning being impressed by the news as she looked around the open facility. Rows of bunk beds, open showers, open toilets. Rows of propaganda-spouting monitors. It was so depressing. She couldn't wait to get Gloria out of here, but already her heart broke for the women whom they would have to leave behind. The idea of converting her parents' old orphanages into mock detention centers had thrilled her while she and Jimmy planned it, but now she could see their efforts would make a comparatively small impact, just a drop of rescue in an ocean of terror.

"I could watch this all day too," Jimmy said with a motion toward the monitors, "but we have to get on the road with our detainee. How long will it take to process her into our custody?"

"Not long at all. When you showed your orders at the front gate, the guard entered the transfer into our computer. It automatically sent an order to bring your detainee back from the munitions factory."

"That's good to hear," Jimmy said. "We have a long drive, and I wouldn't mind having dinner with my wife tonight for a change."

"I hear you, but I've got to tell you," he said in a soft conspiratorial tone as he leaned in close to Jimmy, "the best desserts are here, if you get my drift."

Michele heard it all and scowled.

"Hey, it's a different world now," Lucas said defensively. "We're not doing anything wrong. We relieve some sexual tension—theirs and ours. And we aid in the reprogramming by breaking down their old Christian morality."

Neither Jimmy nor Michele responded. Michele's mind raced. The horrors of FEMA camp life just became more real and more disgusting to her.

Lucas shifted uncomfortably. "Maybe I can rush things along," he said as he beat a hasty departure.

Michele could barely contain her anger. She looked at Jimmy and was about to erupt in a torrent of angry words about what she had just heard.

"Not here," he said softly. He pointed to one of the monitors to make it look as if he were calling her attention to the Kurtoglu coverage.

She followed his lead, staring blankly at the screen. "It's so much worse than I imagined."

"This is probably a *good* location. Your upbringing left you unable to imagine some of the harshness in the world." He was right. He had lived in institutional settings from a young age. She wanted to hug him nearly as badly as she wanted to get out of the detention center.

In short order, Lucas returned with a heavyset guard and a detainee in a threadbare hospital gown. For a second, Michele didn't recognize the detainee as Gloria. Her once luxurious blonde hair had been shorn to a crew cut, leaving nothing but dark and graying roots. Her eyes looked dark and puffy as if she hadn't slept in days. Without makeup, her eyes looked small and pale, not the brilliant, shining eyes for which she was famous.

"Is this the prisoner?" Michele asked. She thought the sound of her voice would bring Gloria's attention, but it did not. Gloria looked only to the floor. What had they done to her?

"This is the one, and she's more trouble than she's worth," said the guard.

"This is Frank." Lucas introduced the taciturn guard. Frank nodded.

Jimmy and Michele nodded in return.

"How has she caused trouble?" Michele asked.

Frank answered with a snarl, "She's really entrenched in the noninclusive religions. She even interrupted a night guard's conjugal session with her bunkmate."

Jimmy caught Michele's eye at the misuse of the phrase "conjugal session." His stern look told her to stay calm.

Jimmy said, "So the bunkmate is a troublemaker as well, I assume. We've got empty beds at our facility. We can take her off your hands, too, if you'd like."

"You could take them all for all I care," Frank said briskly.

"I have room for three or four in the van," Jimmy offered.

"Might as well take the woman on the top bunk too," Frank offered. "This one's been getting chummy with her as well." Michele caught him looking cautiously toward Lucas to see if he had overstepped his bounds. If he had, Lucas showed no indication of it.

"If you give me their names, I'll process the orders," Jimmy said, calling up a screen on his clipboard.

"In the meantime," Michele said sternly, "let's begin to process this one out of here. Do you have the things she came in with?"

Lucas offered a sick grin. "We're not in the habit of giving those things back. They usually end up in the custody of the staff."

Michele was livid. She spoke sharply, "Well, she's a Vatican prisoner now, and her things belong to us. I want every piece of jewelry and her clothes. I have uses for them."

Lucas looked to Frank, who hemmed, saying, "I could check to see if any of it is still here," before he huffed away.

"Make sure you have the personal effects of the other two as well," Michele called after him.

Frank turned and stared at Lucas, who then explained, "Those two aren't high-profile detainees. They didn't come in here with much."

"Find what you can," Michele said sharply. To Lucas she said, "You go help him. I'll take the detainee and wait by the entrance."

Lucas and Frank left, and Michele grabbed Gloria's arm to lead her to the front of the facility. Gloria looked up, and Michele finally saw recognition in her eyes. Gloria produced a barely perceptible wink, and Michele squeezed her arm. For the first time since she and Jimmy had entered the facility, Michele began to relax.

Within half an hour, Jimmy had processed the transfer documents and the other prisoners had been delivered to the front exit. Michele's heart broke upon meeting Gloria's bunkmates. They had clearly been in the system longer than Gloria and stared only at the floor as if they had no concern about where they were being taken.

Jimmy put handcuffs on each of the women before moving them to the back of the van. Michele sat in the front passenger seat. Jimmy took the driver's seat and drove through the gate that the guard opened for them, giving a wave.

When they were finally on the open road, Michele gave way to the relief she felt and the euphoria of a completed mission. "Aaagh!" she screamed. Jimmy broke into uproarious laughter.

Gloria broke her silence as well. "Praise God! How did you guys find me?"

Michele petted Jimmy's bicep. "Jimmy has become really good at getting around the FEMA computer systems." Michele took the handcuff keys from her pocket and passed them back to Gloria. "Here, get out of those cuffs. I can't hug you if your hands are bound."

Michele put down her sun visor to use the mirror. She wanted to see the expression of Gloria's bunkmates. They were still silent.

Gloria undid her own cuffs and then those of the two women. Their moods slowly lifted as she explained they were rescued. Then it really hit them. First one and then the other burst into tears.

Kimmy spoke excitedly about returning home. Michele grew silent.

"You can't go home," Gloria said softly. "None of us can."

SIX

W
hen Will commandeered a Jeep from the motor pool, he thought he could make the three-hundred-mile trip to Petra in six hours, eight at the most. He hadn't considered the tremendous damage done by the Jerusalem quake. Leaving the city was a nightmare. All work by the rescue crews to clear the roads had stopped at the news of Kurtoglu's resurrection. People excitedly cheered in the streets with tearstained faces, jubilant that their leader had returned to protect them from the unknown terror of the approaching Anu.

"Anu!" Will said to himself as he found yet another street too blocked for the Jeep to navigate. In all the speeches Kurtoglu had given, he had painted them as a warrior race bent on the destruction of humanity. Yet he never offered any proof. They were as mythical as the monsters under a toddler's bed, but the world couldn't see it.

Entire sections of the King David Highway had buckled from the stress of the quake, reminding Will of the Dark Awakening. He would travel for a little while, only to find a section of the highway impassible. Then he would have to turn around to exit the highway and find an alternate route. It took him hours to get out of the city and onto Route 90. The road would take him due south to Eilat, where he would enter Jordan and then travel due north to Petra. It was a circuitous route, but he didn't trust himself to take the Jeep off-road to find a more direct passage.

As Route 90 wound around the Dead Sea, Will was excited to see the deep blue of the lifeless waters against the bleached desert rocks. The setting sun, nearly hidden behind the horizon, cast a pink hue upon the entire area. It was certainly beautiful. He pondered that the scene he viewed probably had not changed much since Jesus stood there looking over the tranquil sea.

"And in another three years and change, I could be looking at it with You, Jesus," he prayed. The awesomeness of the statement took his breath away. Jesus would be back soon to set things right. The very idea made his heart soar.

Will's trip from Jerusalem to Eilat took nearly ten hours. There he filled the Jeep's gas tank. By this time it was well into the middle of the night. He weighed his options. He could continue on and be in Petra by early morning, or he could check into a hotel to get a few hours' sleep. Not knowing what to expect in Petra and wanting to be in top form when he got there, he decided on the latter.

The motel lobby sported a long-empty vending machine. Will looked at it furtively. Junk food had gone the route of extinction in the new world. Farm areas had to concentrate on staples for the workers of the world's munitions factories. Will stared at the machine. What he wouldn't do for a bag of chips and a Coke!

The room was small and nondescript, but it had an air conditioner and a television. He lay down on the bed and turned on the tube. There he saw Benny, looking far more fit than he had when Will left him less than a day before. As Benny spoke, Will recognized Nergal was in control.

"We are proud to announce the very heart of our plan to defeat the Anu. Our scientists have completed the production of a nanochip DNA-enhancement vaccine that will render every citizen on earth immune to the effects of radiation and the increasing Schumann resonance frequency. For more than three years, we have lived in fear of the radiation that brought about the Dark Awakening. And thanks to our glorious risen leader, we have finally found the cure. Through some very advanced nanotechnology, our vaccine will reprogram the DNA of every world citizen to provide everyone with the aggressive immune system of President Kurtoglu. This enhancement not only will protect us from the onslaught of future radiation but also will be an immunization like no other. In less than two months following this inoculation, words like *cancer, flu, cold, multiple sclerosis,* and *muscular dystrophy* will be confined to the past.

"It will be a great day for the world, and the sooner we all are inoculated, the sooner that great day will arrive. To that end, we have turned every hospital, urgent care facility, and doctor's office into an inoculation clinic. We will serve the people of Earth twenty-four hours a day, seven days a week, until every man, woman, and child has been set free from disease. In the six weeks following inoculation, the DNA of each person will have changed sufficiently to ensure continued good health. The newly liberated medical staff will be trained over the next three years in the newest medical technologies in the event we suffer casualties at the hands of the Anu."

Will turned off the television. The mark of the beast had arrived. He knew from the Bible that acceptance of the mark would render an individual incapable of salvation. Will wiped his tired eyes and after a while found fitful sleep.

After only a few hours, he awoke to a sunny day. The temperature was moderate, but the sun shone brightly as he approached the border with Jordan. The border was really only a technicality in this day and age since Jordan was a part of Isa's caliphate, so Will was shocked to see a mile-long line of cars waiting to cross. He stayed in the line for a few minutes. Every so often, a car at the front of the line would turn around and head back to Israel.

"This could take all day," he said tersely as he hit the steering wheel. He weighed his options. He could wait hours in this line, or he could pull Vatican rank. The next time the line inched forward, he used the freed space to put the Jeep into the other lane. Driving slowly to look for oncoming traffic, he studied the people in the cars beside him. Almost all were families, their cars weighed down with possessions. For all the world they looked like refugees.

After a short while, he reached the Jordanian border, where a particularly annoyed-looking soldier stopped him, speaking Arabic. Will had no hopes of understanding the man. He raised his hands to show he was unarmed and then gingerly retrieved his passport from the console between the front seats.

The soldier took the passport, instantly recognizing the Vatican insignia. "You are from the Vatican?" he asked in halting English.

"Yes," Will answered, "I work security for Pope Peter. What's going on?"

The soldier returned Will's passport and then wiped at his brow. "People fleeing the Jerusalem quake. And what brings you to Jordan?"

"The pope has sent me to develop security plans for a celebration he would like to hold in Petra at the completion of the inoculations." Will hoped his excuse didn't sound as ridiculous as it felt. He added a bit to tighten the lie. "I guess it's all about symbolism. Petra is a stone fortress signifying strength, and once we are all inoculated, we will be strengthened against the Anu."

The soldier smiled and nodded. "I get it."

"So, you think all these people are refugees from the Jerusalem quake?" Will asked in disbelief. It didn't make any sense for the displaced Israelis to go to the desert when provisions for them had been made available throughout Israel.

"An ancient tale has frightened them. Something said by Prophet Jesus. 'When you see the abomination of desolation, flee.' If you ask me, they all need to be reprogrammed."

"I hear you," Will said. He waved as the guard allowed him to pass through to Jordan.

The ride to Petra was uneventful. The sun was brilliant in the sky, and he was on the infamous Desert Highway. It was aptly named. The landscape to his left consisted solely of bare rocky mountains in varying soft shades, from a salmon color near the road to a gray color at the peaks. To his right was sand, miles and miles of sand. He pounded his fingers nervously on the steering wheel. He needed a plan, but he had too little information to develop one.

"This may be a fool's errand, Will," he said to himself. He wished his father had given him a little more to go on. All he could do was follow the tracker signals, but for all Will knew, the agent had chucked the trackers out the window somewhere. There was no guarantee he would find them with the agent, and even less of a chance they would lead to Uncle Michael.

He pounded the Jeep's steering wheel in exasperation. When he was on the Temple Mount, he only wanted to get away from Benny and Isa and find Uncle Michael. It all seemed so plausible to him then, but the realities of a vast desert and the uncertainty that lay ahead drove him to despair. He pulled the Jeep to the side of the road, grabbed his phone, and dialed quickly.

"Hey, Michele," he said, trying to sound nonchalant. "How did it go with Gloria?"

"It went really well, Will. We rescued not only Gloria, but also her bunkmates. They're here at the house with us now, getting a little R & R, but Gloria is adamant she wants to manage one of our facilities. We're just waiting for a friendly face in the Vatican to help us get her a new name and a Vatican passport."

"I should be able to help with that. If I can't do it, Jake surely can," he said softly.

"Do you have any more leads as to his whereabouts?" she asked hopefully.

Will drew a long, hard sigh. "No," he whined as he pushed the hair back from his face.

"Will," Michele said with great compassion, "I know this is hard."

"It's not that it's hard, Michele. It's that I don't know what to do next. Even if I track the signal, it doesn't mean Uncle Michael is at the other end of it. If I don't find at least a clue to where he could be, I'm out of luck. I have nothing else to go on."

"You sound really stressed right now, Will, and—"

"Damn right I'm stressed!" he exclaimed. His voice cracked.

"And," she interrupted, "that's not a wise way to go into this."

"Maybe I just don't trust myself. I'm not trained for any of this," Will complained.

"Maybe you shouldn't trust yourself," she argued. "Maybe you should trust the Lord. What were Dad's last instructions to you?"

"Go to Petra."

"Right. And that's what you're doing," she said with deliberate calm.

"But I don't know what the next step is ..."

"The next step is an act of faith, Will. You're new at Christianity, so listen to your sister. Faith isn't about knowing all the answers; it's about knowing the One who knows the answers."

Will bristled for a moment. From anyone else, he would have taken the remark as a useless platitude, but this was different somehow. He could tell Michele was speaking from the heart. "I hear you, but out here on the Desert Highway I wish I could see something a little more tangible."

She chuckled a bit, and he felt his tension wane. "That's why it's called faith, Will. We're called to walk by faith, not by sight."

"Okay, but say I walk by faith and fail. Could you forgive me if I don't return with Jake?"

"No," she said bluntly.

His heart sank.

She continued, "Because there would be nothing to forgive. Will, you are doing everything humanly possible to bring Uncle Michael home. I would never think less of you if you don't succeed."

He sounded morose. "I took the Vatican job to be close to him and protect him, but I failed, and now—"

"You didn't fail! Will, haven't you noticed we are in extraordinary times? We are all just trying to get through them, to get to Jesus's return. I have never felt anything but proud of you."

Will gulped back a sob. He heard Gloria say, "Let me talk to him."

"Will. This is Gloria," she said in a motherly tone.

"Hi, Gloria. I'm glad to hear your voice," Will said, trying to hide his despair.

"I praise God I can talk to you as well, sweetie. Listen, Will, I know you didn't have much in the way of parents, and I never was one. But I want you to listen to me as I try my best to give you some motherly advice."

Tears coursed down his face. Never had anyone offered him motherly comfort. "Okay," he said quietly.

"You are greatly loved, not only by Jesus and the Father, but also by us. That love isn't based on performance. If you find Michael, and I think you're going to, it will be wonderful. But if you don't, you haven't let any of us down."

"Thanks, Gloria," he croaked.

"I mean it, Will. It's time you put this in God's hands. If we are meant to find Michael, we will. If not, then we'll see him in a few years."

Will could feel the words having their effect. He moved the conversation away from his own doubts. "They will be long years, Gloria. I got a look at Kurtoglu close up. There's no doubt in my mind he's Satan incarnate."

"I know. They'll be long years with or without Michael. Are you feeling any better about what you have to do?"

"A bit. I just wish I had more direction."

"We're Christians, honey. We don't wish. We pray. Bow your head, and let me pray for guidance for you."

Will did as he was told. "Okay."

"Father, we know these are perilous times. Nothing is sure in this day and age other than the fact that You love us. We commit our lives to You, Lord, knowing our imperfections and limitations, but also knowing the strength and wisdom You promise to give those with willing hearts and willing hands. We ask You now to send Your Spirit on Will. Protect him as he proceeds on his mission. Guide his steps and quicken his path. Bless him with the knowledge that Your strength and Your guidance are all he needs to succeed. And finally, Lord, we ask You to heal the brokenness in his heart. Let him know with absolute certainty that You love him beyond all telling and that we love him very much. We ask this in the name of Jesus, the ruler of this world, who is to come. Thank You, Lord. Amen."

"Amen," Will croaked. Warmth permeated his body. His head swam with the intoxicating feeling of God's love. If someone had told him two weeks ago that he could ever feel this way, he would have scoffed. He opened his eyes to see that he was surrounded by a golden glow.

"Did that help, Will?" Gloria asked. "I can really feel the Lord's presence on this side of the conversation."

"I feel it here, too, Gloria. I don't think I've ever felt such peace. It's like my whole perspective has changed," Will said with astonishment.

"You're looking at things from God's perspective now. All things are possible in Him."

"Gloria, I can't thank you enough. Is Michele still there?" he asked.

"Yes."

"Can you put the phone on speaker?"

Gloria complied. Will said softly, "Listen, I never say it enough, but I love you guys. And I want to tell you how happy I am that you have come into my life."

"Back at you, Will," Michele said. "I can't imagine my life without my big brother. If it weren't for you, I would never have known how silly men looked in the Middle Ages."

"Yeah, yeah, yeah." Will laughed. "Thanks again, though."

"Thank you for all you have brought to our lives too. Now are you going to sit there being sensitive, or are you going to find Uncle Michael?" Michele asked with forced lightheartedness.

"I'm going to find Uncle Michael." Will grinned. "He won't know what to make of the new Christian me. I can't wait to show him."

"That's the Will I know. Go get him, buddy. I love you," Michele said encouragingly.

"Love you too," Will said just before he hung up.

The change in him was dramatic. He felt like he could fly the rest of the way to Petra. As he continued down the road, the once drab beige desert looked bright and inviting. He sang to himself, "Jesus loves me, this I know, for the Bible tells me so." It was the only hymn he knew.

"Note to self," he said aloud. "Get some worship music."

He entered the town of Petra and initiated the tracking app on his phone. It appeared his tracking devices weren't in the town proper but somewhere to the north and east. He remained on King's Highway, traveling northeast, until he came to the trackers' location at a fenced government building standing alone in the stark rock hills.

Made of corrugated metal, the building was about the size of a large garage. Once white, the metal had begun to rust. Its windowless shell gave the appearance of desolation, like the building had been abandoned for years. Will parked the Jeep and looked through the fence. It was dilapidated as well. The only new thing in the area was the sign on the fence designating the property as belonging to Kurtoglu's world government. Will touched the fence gingerly. It wasn't electrified. It wasn't very tall either. Whatever this government facility was, it wasn't very secure. He checked his phone again; the trackers were definitely here.

Easily climbing the fence, he drew his rifle and proceeded slowly around the building, looking for an entrance. On the back, he saw a single door. He tried it. Not locked. He backed away for a second. Could this be a trap? It seemed too easy. Releasing the safety on his rifle, he entered. The darkness of the shed threw him after the brightness of the sun. As his eyes adjusted, he heard a footstep. Before he could turn in the direction of the sound, he was hit from behind. The blow knocked him forward just as bright overhead lights came on.

Will looked up to see the agent pointing a revolver at his head.

"Even with tracking devices, it took you an inordinate amount of time to find us, William."

"Well, I was busy," Will said tersely.

"Oh yes. That nasty business shooting the Antichrist and all," the agent said smugly.

"Exactly," Will said sharply. "Why did you have to hit me?"

"You were carrying a weapon. What did you expect?"

"I'm not really sure," Will said as the agent held out his hand for Will's rifle.

Once Will handed it to him, the agent put away his revolver.

"Well, you might as well join us," the agent said with a hint of whimsy. "Your uncle is just awaking from a long sleep."

SEVEN

They descended in an elevator to a cave beneath the metal warehouse. The bare cave walls gave way to a large steel door. Facial recognition software gained the agent admittance.

"Where are we?" Will asked.

"It's a rather ingenious facility set up by your uncle a few years ago. It appears the Holy Father at the time threatened to remove him from his work decoding a disc of information from a prehistoric advanced civilization." The steel door swung open, revealing the hallway of a modern facility. Bright overhead lights cast a harsh glow on white walls.

The agent continued, "Your uncle didn't appreciate the threat very much, so he created this facility as a back door to anonymously access the disc."

At the end of the hallway, they turned to the right. The agent again stood in front of a camera to gain access to a large room filled with computer equipment. They walked through it to an office, where Michael lay on a cot. He looked pale and emaciated.

"Where did you find him?" Will asked. "Shouldn't we get him to a hospital?"

"He's fine. Although you are a little slow on the uptake. I didn't find him. I took him."

Immediate rage overwhelmed Will. "You took him? What kind of sick game is this?" he screamed.

The agent grimaced. "I assure you, it's no game. He should awaken any time now. It might be helpful if he sees a friendly face. So please try not to scream."

Will took a deep breath to calm himself—it would do no good to overreact. He went to Michael and looked closely at him. He appeared to be sleeping. In measured tones, Will asked, "Why did you take him?"

"He'll have the same questions, and I'd rather not answer them twice. Talk to him."

"Jake, it's Will. It's time to wake up now." He held Michael's hand. It felt clammy.

The agent readied a syringe. Brushing Will aside, he unloaded its contents into a vein in Michael's arm. "This should wake him."

Almost immediately Will saw color come to Michael's cheeks. He again took the older man's hand and spoke to him. This time Michael squeezed Will's hand in return.

"He's squeezing my hand," Will said with a smile.

"He'll wake up feeling fine, but he'll be a bit disoriented," the agent said clinically.

"He'll be more than disoriented," Michael murmured.

"What?" Will asked. "Jake, it's me, Will. What did you say?"

He spoke more deliberately. "I said, I'll be more than disoriented. I'll be royally pissed off."

"There, there, Father," the agent said casually as he approached with a glass of orange juice. "You'll understand it all very shortly. You should be thirsty. Try to sit up."

Michael struggled. Will reached under his back and cradled him into a sitting position.

More alert now, Michael smiled wanly and said, "Will, you are a sight for sore eyes."

"Back at you, Jake," Will said as he wiped away a tear.

Michael took the glass. At first he drank gingerly, but soon he gulped the liquid. When the glass was empty, the agent poured him another.

"Your strength should soon return, Father," the agent said. "When you are ready, I will explain to you and your nephew what has transpired over the past few weeks."

"I have more memory than you imagine," Michael said. "I was drugged and held in an isolation tank, the same procedure used on my programmers years ago. How did you rescue me?"

"Oh, but I didn't, Father," the agent said with a touch of a grin. "I was the one who performed those procedures on you."

"You!" Michael spat.

Will's mind spun with rage, and he lost control of himself. "I could kill you," he screeched as he pounced on the agent. In a flash, the agent pinned Will to the floor.

"Given our relative levels of training, I highly doubt it," the agent said dismissively to Will. Looking toward Michael, he said, "Please let me explain."

"Okay," Michael agreed. "Let him up." Michael said to Will, "Come on, Will. Sit next to me. Let's hear him out."

"Do you know where you are, Father?" the agent asked with a grin.

Michael answered, "If I'm not mistaken, we're in my secret facility outside Petra."

"Correct."

"But that facility is useless without the programmers. ... The programmers! You kidnapped them!" Michael exclaimed.

"Correct again." The agent smiled with pride.

"What have you done with them?" Michael demanded. Will watched carefully. He wasn't sure what to make of the conversation.

"Well, to begin with, I had to undo your programming and reintegrate their fractured personalities. Not an easy task, I might add."

"You healed them?" Michael asked. Will heard hope and relief in Michael's voice.

"Well, I freed them of their programming, but I was left with five young men who were very angry at you. I explained to them that true healing could only come from accepting Jesus as their Savior. Given your parochial status, they weren't open to the suggestion."

Michael wiped his forehead. "I understand. So, you ended up with a security problem. These men have access to the secrets of the universe, and there's no way to contain that knowledge."

"Exactly. I abducted these men to keep them from Kurtoglu, but in the process I turned them into loose cannons. With full consciousness and the ability to access the disc, they could subvert any of the false information you planted to delay the implementation of the inoculations."

"So where do I come in?" Michael asked.

The agent winced. "As a bit of a wager, I'm afraid. I refused to let them go, but I was remiss at finding myself more their captor than you."

Will shook his head. "I'm confused," he said to Michael. "Catch me up."

"One of the worst decisions of my life was allowing my assistant to establish alternate personalities in five computer programmers. We did it to keep safe the secrets on a disc from what I thought was an advanced prehistoric civilization. Now I think it contained fallen angel technology. In order to keep that technology out of Isa's hands, the agent abducted the programmers. He tried to give them their freedom by reintegrating their personalities, but he created a new problem for himself. With their personalities intact, they could no longer be trusted to access the fallen angel technology."

"Which is moot anyway," Will said gravely. "The chief fallen angel now lives in Kurtoglu."

Michael shook his head. "Someone tried to assassinate him? How long have I been out?"

"About three weeks," the agent said.

"And that someone was me," Will said with embarrassed softness. "I killed Isa with an arrow to the head."

"I don't know what to say," Michael said with a look of horror.

"Before you do, let me just add that it was meant to be. Dad was there. He and a priest had this old hermit take my crossbow and run into the crowd on the Temple Mount. He took the blame for me, and they killed him."

"Father Vinnie and Father Ignatius," Michael said knowingly.

Will continued. "When I saw his sacrifice, I realized the weight of Jesus's sacrifice for me. I gave my life to Him."

Michael's worn face drew into a broad grin. "I've been praying a long time for this. I'm so happy, Will!" Michael leaned over to hug him. Will returned the hug, noting how thin Michael felt.

Turning to the agent, Will said tersely, "None of what you said explains why you did this to him."

"It lays the groundwork. I told the programmers a life with Jesus would have made them immune to the personality-splitting program years ago and that any life they could have outside this facility would be greatly enhanced if they turned their hearts to Him. That argument didn't totally convince them, so I offered to prove it."

"By demonstrating my personality wouldn't break," Michael said somberly.

"That's sick!" Will exclaimed.

Michael shrugged. "It's my penance. I stole years from those men."

"More importantly, Father, what was at first motivated by revenge in their hearts has turned to stunning curiosity and compliance. Over the course of the past three weeks, each has agreed to give his life to Jesus if you come out of the process unshaken in your faith."

"I'm totally unshaken in my faith," Michael said resolutely. Then he paused, shook his head, and grimaced. "I guess it would have been too easy for you just to ask me to witness to them?" he asked with annoyance.

"They were very angry, Father. Their anger needed to be satiated."

"And ..." Michael led.

"And for years you weren't on the side of good. I saw your allegiance to Christ in the Roman catacombs, but as time passed I wondered if you had relapsed to your old ways."

"If I had, I might tell Benny or Isa you had taken the programmers," Michael said with a nod.

"They and I would have been killed. I would have gone to heaven, but not these young men."

"It makes sense to me," Michael said with a shrug.

Will took it all in disbelief. "Jake, you can't seriously tell me you think he's right! Think of what he put you through! Think of what he put all of us through!"

"I'm sorry for the pain of the family, Will, but what he did makes sense to me. And from a spiritual perspective, if I can help these men find redemption in Christ, it is all worth it."

"I thought you would understand, Father," the agent said. "And for what it is worth, I am sorry for your treatment. I could think of no other way to accomplish my objectives."

"Fully forgiven from my standpoint," Michael said.

"I'm not there yet," Will said sternly.

Michael stared at him for a moment. "Will, his plan was ingenious! I've wanted to find a way to get to this facility without Benny and Isa knowing about it. But even if I got here, I'd be hopeless without the help of the programmers. The agent found a way to bring us all together."

"But to what end?" Will asked. "They've already started inoculations with the chip."

"That means they have transferred the contents of the disc to quantum computers," Michael said. "Only a quantum system could keep track of every chip in real time. The disc was like the consciousness of the Lady. In a quantum system, it will be very autonomous, almost lifelike."

The agent added, "I haven't allowed the programmers to upload any information to the device, but we checked your connection to ensure we could still get access. The programmers believe the disc now sits at the periphery of the quantum system, directing its processing."

"As a real-world interface," Michael said softly, thinking aloud as he pulled it all together. "Effectively, quantum computers process information in alternate dimensions."

"What?" Will asked. His head was spinning.

"Normal computers look at information linearly. If you give a computer a maze, it will run each path until it finds the right one. A quantum computer will run all the paths simultaneously and then choose the right one. To do that, it relies on the idea that a subatomic particle exists in all of its states simultaneously until the wave function collapses. In our example, it would collapse at the proper solution to the maze."

"Yeah," Will deadpanned, "that's not helping. I'll have to take your word for it."

Michael shook his head. "The disc will utilize the computational capabilities of the quantum computer but remain separate from it. It makes a lot of sense now that I think about it," he said.

"And the fact that we can hack into it means we may be able to throw a few cogs in the wheels of progress," the agent said.

"In small ways," Michael replied. "We won't be able to defeat the system, but we should be able to find ways to help Christians and maybe get a handle on Isa's plans. If I'm right, he is so demented, he actually thinks he can defeat Jesus when He returns."

"Demented I can agree with," Will said. "He is unlike anything I've ever seen. You thought Benny's demon was bad; wait until you see this thing. It even has Benny scared. The last thing he said to me was 'Find Michael. He may know what to do.'"

Michael rolled his eyes. "Benny is way beyond anyone's ability to help him, but if he's afraid of the new Isa, he'll want us around. We may be able to keep our positions at the Vatican."

"There's nothing I'd like less," Will said dismally, "but from the Vatican we can help others by running interference."

Michael stood shakily as he said to the agent, "What's next on the agenda?"

"We meet with the programmers."

"Let's get to it then," Michael said. He stumbled a bit as he tried to walk. Will caught him and held him up.

"I still have my sea legs," Michael said with a grin.

Will stayed close to offer a steadying hand if needed as they walked out of the office and into the bright hallway. Michael squinted and used his hand to shield his eyes.

"The sensory deprivation has made you very sensitive to bright lights, loud sounds, et cetera, but the effect should go away in a few days," the agent said. He led them through another door to a dimly lit lounge, where the programmers were waiting.

Will drew his breath. He wasn't sure he wanted to meet this group of geeks who'd let their savage mentality drive the experiment done on Michael. He surely wasn't expecting the reception they received. When they walked into the room, the five men smiled and applauded. A string of Italian ensued. Michael provided Will with brief summations of their conversations.

"They're happy I made it through okay. At first they wanted revenge, but then they began to root for me," Michael explained as first one and then all of them came to shake his hand.

Michael made quick introductions as he spoke with them. Not trusting them, Will made careful note of each. "Will, this is Savario Scharpacci." Savario was of medium build with hazel eyes behind thick glasses. Long, thick brown hair swept from his face and barely touched his shoulders.

"*I suoi cappelli sono belli,*" Savario said to Will as they shook hands.

Michael leaned in toward Will. "He thinks your hair is nice."

"Yours too." Will grinned nervously.

So it went with the others. Giacomo Stuarti, who was a little over five feet tall, was the second to shake Will's hand. Will noted that old Giacomo was not only short of stature but also short on deodorant. Michael grinned at Will to show he knew what the younger man was thinking. Will was pleased to see the old Michael's wit.

Eduardo Benno, a very tall man with hawkish features, spoke to Will in halting English. "You are *nipote* of Father Michael?" he asked with a grin.

Not sure what to answer, Will said, "I am very *nipote* of Father Michael."

"Yes," Eduardo said with a confused look. The agent laughed loudly.

Michael said, "Will, *nipote* means nephew. Eduardo asked if you are my nephew."

"And I said I'm very much your nephew," Will covered, blushing and giving a chuckle. At this Michael and Eduardo began to laugh as well.

As the afternoon proceeded, Michael talked at length with the group about his sorrow for what he had done to them. He explained the need for salvation and then laid out the road map of Bible prophecy concerning the end times. Will understood very little of the Italian, but he enjoyed watching the interaction. It reminded him of C-3PO telling tales to the Ewoks.

After hours of conversation, Michael slapped Will's leg. "Come on, buddy. You can join in. The guys are ready to commit their lives to Jesus."

Will shook his head in disbelief as the gravity of the situation settled on him. Michael could have been angry with these men—should have been, in Will's estimation. Instead, he forgave them and led them to a life of eternal joy when Jesus returns. This is what Christianity was all about, the changing of lives. Will didn't think he had ever been more proud of anyone in his life as he and the agent joined Michael to pray for each of the programmers in turn. They accepted Jesus with earnest tears of joy, and soon all were filled with the Holy Spirit. The spiritual energy in the room was like nothing Will had ever experienced, and he wished it could go on forever.

"After a few more short years of torment, it *will* go on forever," he muttered to himself.

"What?" Michael asked.

"Just talking to myself. Soon we'll be able to live in this kind of joy forever."

Michael put his arm around Will. "I'm so happy to see you in the Lord, Will. I've been praying hard about this for a long time now."

Will returned the gesture, putting his arm around his uncle. "Thanks for all the prayer. I don't know what took me so long to come to the right conclusion."

"Genetics," Michael said somberly. "You are like your old uncle in the most unfortunate of ways. You're a hardhead, *capo tosto*, as these guys would say."

"*Sì, io sono capo tosto*," said Luigi Canzotti with a smile.

"*Anch'io*," the others said as they clapped Will on the back.

"So we're just a bunch of hardheads," Will said with a chuckle.

They ended the day with a long dinner. No longer prisoners of the agent, the programmers agreed to stay on in Petra to follow Michael's instructions for hacking into the system. The agent contacted Benny to say he and Will had found Michael and eliminated his abductors. He convinced the pope of Michael's need for rest at home in the United States. Will arranged a Vatican plane to fly them to Atlanta from Amman, Jordan, the next day.

Finally, they fell exhausted onto beds in the Petra facility. Will had his first sound night of sleep since Michael's abduction.

EIGHT

Michael was horrified and overwhelmed by the destruction that had occurred since his abduction. The ride from the Atlanta airport was morose. The once freely traveled roads were now burdened with checkpoints. Not that it mattered. Few people were on the roads. Their driver explained that every morning's weather forecast came with a measurement of radioactivity on a color-coded scale. Today was a yellow day. If it had been a red day, one in which prevailing winds brought radiation from the west into the area, all outdoor activity would have been curtailed.

"That seems to be very little by way of protection," Michael said to the driver. "Radioactivity can get into houses too."

"I hear you," said the driver. "The government recommends each homeowner use a Geiger counter to assess his property." He pointed to one on the front seat beside him. "I check the car every day. Sometimes I have to wash it three times a day to keep the radioactive dust off it."

"There is nothing left of New York, DC, Los Angeles, or Chicago," Will said with a sigh.

"Damn Russians!" cursed the driver.

Will shook his head slightly and stared in Michael's direction. "I have a lot to tell you."

Michael nodded. "I probably don't want to hear it, but I need to."

"I wanted you to have some rest and good food before laying everything on you, but some of it I should tell you now. Zack framed Gloria for the murder of a guard at the FEMA camp she and Michele visited, and she was arrested."

Michael seethed. No doubt Zack had figured out that he held

Gloria's insurance package of information against him. He sighed. "It doesn't surprise me. Gloria had proof of Zack's complicity in the death of his parents. She left the information with me as insurance. When I disappeared, so did the threat she held over him."

"Well, that's the bad news," Will said. "The good news is that Michele and Jimmy arranged a transfer from her FEMA camp to ours. Gloria is staying at the estate for the time being, but she wants to run one of our camps once we get her a new identity and Vatican citizenship."

"We'll do it the instant we get back to Jerusalem," Michael said.

"Aagh," Will groaned. "Don't even say the name of that city for the next couple of days. Benny has given us only five days to make you better. Trust me, you need to be at the top of your game in the new Jerusalem!"

The limousine stopped at the gates of the estate, where Will saluted the guards. As the car wound its way up the long driveway, Michael looked out over the wintering orchards. He wondered if their fruit would be edible anytime soon given the radiation. He sighed. At least it was good to be home.

Standing on the porch were Michele, Gloria, and Jimmy. They had done up the porch pillars in yellow ribbons to welcome him home. He wiped at a tear. So much had transpired at this old house. His mind flooded with memories as he exited the car.

The women swooped down on him, giving him hugs and kisses. Michael was astounded at Gloria's appearance. The FEMA camp had shorn her once beautiful locks, leaving nearly nothing.

"You had us scared to death, Uncle Michael," Michele yelped through tears.

"I honestly didn't think I'd ever see you again in this life," he cried as he held her tight.

As he hugged Gloria, Michael said, "Will has been protecting me by not telling me all the news. He did clue me in on your capture and subsequent rescue, though."

"Well, I'm a little worse for the wear." She swiped nervously at her head. "But Michele and Jimmy did a brilliant job rescuing me and my bunkmates."

"Right now her bunkmates are staying in Joseph's old house, but they're registered in our soon-to-open detention facility," Jimmy offered, referring to the home of the butler who managed the estate during Michael's childhood. Michael mused that he was the only one there who remembered the dear old man.

Michael extended his hand to the younger gentleman. "Hi, Jimmy. Great job with the rescue." Jimmy held onto his hand for a brief moment. Michael didn't share the sentiment. His last memory of Jimmy was the disastrous disclosure that Naomi was his mother.

Will dismissed the driver and joined the group, but all the attention stayed focused on Michael. "Is *anyone* here happy to see me?" he asked with a grin.

"Come here, you," Gloria said as she gave him a huge hug.

"Gloria and Michele shored me up when I had doubts about my ability to rescue you," Will said to Michael over Gloria's shoulder.

Michele then hugged Will and said, "Speaking of which, you have been pretty quiet about how the rescue went down."

Michael chuckled. "Imagine that! From what I understand, the rescue lasted about thirty seconds before Will found himself at gunpoint."

"You exaggerate," Will said with a grin. "I bet I lasted forty-five, maybe even sixty, seconds."

"You can tell us all about it over dinner," Michele said, leading them into the house. "But the news reports from the Vatican are saying Will and an undercover agent found you and eliminated the terrorists who abducted you."

"Well, Benny and the truth are rarely in the same room," Will said, shaking his head.

The soft scent of polished wood bathed Michael in the comfort of home. For a second, he saw himself playing hide-and-seek with Gabe in the formal rooms and looking for some imaginary unknown treasure in the estate's expansive basement.

"I can't tell you how good it feels to be home," he mused as they went to the kitchen. Michele had the table set, and food was on warming plates.

"I wish I had your favorites, Uncle Michael, but given the radiation levels, we've moved mostly to packaged foods. However, thanks to Grandma's aquaponics, we have some really nice trout almondine and fresh salad."

"It all smells heavenly," Michael declared. "Let's say grace and dig in."

The meal filled them to the full, and Gloria had even managed a cake from sugar and flour held in the estate's basement storerooms.

"Kudos to Gloria on the cake," Michele said. "I wouldn't know where to begin to turn raw ingredients into an actual cake!"

They all echoed her praises for the delicious dessert and started to tell each other what had transpired after Michele's wedding.

"As it turns out, Naomi is really Jimmy's mom," Michele said. "It was a pretty sad situation. She was raped."

"It still smacks of an attempted takeover of our company, if you ask me," Michael said.

"Not just you," Michele agreed. "Uncle Benny has been threatening her. She asked me to put in a good word for her at the Vatican, but Uncle Benny hasn't answered my emails."

"Well, if nothing else, maybe he scared her into our camp," Michael said. "I'll give her a call tomorrow. So, after your wedding you guys found me missing. The feds tossed the house, but Will managed to assert Vatican domain. Do I have it right so far?"

"Yes," Will said. "I was crazy without you. Isa and Benny said I could go to look for you once the Temple Mount opening ceremonies were completed."

Michael wiped his forehead. "I had forgotten all about those ceremonies. How did they go?"

"Well, you're rushing me a bit. Before the ceremonies even began, Isa and Benny mowed down the two witnesses for all the world to see."

"And let them lie in the streets over the Christmas holidays, until they were resurrected three and a half days later," Michael continued the tale.

"Who told you?" Will asked.

"The Bible. It's all in the book of Revelation."

"Well, did the Bible tell you I was there when they woke up?" Will asked with a grin.

"No way!" Michael screamed.

"Better than that, I have it all recorded on a flash drive. Some programmers we know might be able to ship it off to every television and computer on earth, don't you think?"

"Do you have the drive with you?" Jimmy asked.

"In my pocket. We'll have to look at it before we hit the hay tonight."

"When the witnesses ascended to heaven, a huge earthquake tore Jerusalem apart," Michele added, "but the world barely noticed because of all the turmoil from Russia's nuclear attack."

"That's not what really happened," Will said. "Russia had planned a march on Isa's kingdom. Vladimir had teamed up with Isa's brothers to take him down. As fate would have it, the Russian and Turkish armies were wiped out by a meteor storm. They never knew what hit them.

"Benny and I watched it with Isa from his bunker. Then Isa called Vladimir on his computer to say goodbye. Apparently the US and Russia had not been forthcoming about the destruction of all their nukes. Somehow Isa got the launch codes for the ones they held back and set off the nuclear exchange. It was disgusting. He and Benny laughed like mad hatters.

"I got enraged, and somehow Isa got in my head to shut me down. I woke up thirty hours later in my apartment. I saw the devastation on television and learned of Gloria's arrest on a news crawl. It was all I could take. I knew I had to do something. So, I hid beside the temple while the Jewish opening ceremonies commenced. There was no camera coverage close to the temple because Isa and Benny didn't want to televise the animal sacrifices. I know, the two butchers who nuked half the world were suddenly sensitive to the slaying of a few animals. They're nuts."

"Certifiably," Michael agreed. "So, when did you shoot Isa?"

"The moment he got to the stage. But as soon as I fired, I heard Dad calling me. He was with a priest and a hermit. Dad took the bow from me and gave it to the hermit. He ran into the crowd waving the bow and calling out Kurtoglu as the Antichrist until the Swiss Guard mowed him down."

"Did Isa die immediately?" Michael asked.

Michele picked up the tale. "From the television coverage I saw, Uncle Benny and the Lady took him into the temple in case there were more potential assassins. Only Uncle Benny came out alive. Isa was dead, and the Lady was never seen again. Do you think Uncle Benny finished the deed? He did try to assume control once Isa was declared dead."

"I don't think it lines up with prophecy, but I wouldn't put anything past Benny," Michael said. "That having been said, Isa bleeding all over the holy of holies would certainly constitute the abomination of desolation spoken of by the prophet Daniel."

"I don't think Benny did it," Will said. "He seemed genuinely distraught about Kurtoglu's death. Of course, he seemed even more distraught about Isa's reanimation, and I can't blame him. It's Isa's body, but the personality is different. Jake, do you remember that demon fog we saw when we were on the hajj? It's like that. Something palpably evil surrounds him now."

Michael nodded. He remembered the day very well.

"It's funny you say that," Michele said, "because all the news coverage talks about the aura of power and light he displays since his resurrection."

"Resurrection, my foot!" Gloria exclaimed. "Satanic possession of a dying body, maybe. Resurrection? Not a chance."

"Well, we all know who he is now," Michael said. Then in a whine he added, "I really don't want to go back to work for him and Benny. No lie, in some ways an isolation chamber and mind-bending drugs were like a vacation from those two."

"Ouch!" Will exclaimed. "But I might have to agree with you. It's bad, Jake. Real bad."

The conversation fell into a lull. Michael could sense the deflating feeling of knowing they still had over three years until the Lord's return. He changed the subject. "On the positive side, I'm here with you all, and I'm very thankful. I'm also so glad you got out of the camp, Gloria."

Gloria smiled and nodded. "Not unlike you, I would have to say it was bad but, in some ways, more liberating than my former circumstances. Lies, subterfuge, and a constant battle of one-upmanship with Zack wore me down. I can honestly say I am more at peace now than I have ever been. For years I had Zack and no real relationship with Jesus. Now I have Jesus and no Zack. This is infinitely better."

"Amen to that," Michele chimed in.

Gloria continued, "And praise God, we were able to walk out of there with two more souls. They're good women, Michael, but they're disoriented and confused. One is pretty young. She was used as a sex toy by a really unsavory guard."

"You know the facility and his name, right?" Will asked.

"Yes. Why?" Gloria countered.

Will raised an eyebrow. "Maybe a few keystrokes from Benny's office could get him transferred to a road crew, where all he can lay is pavement."

"Crudity aside," Michele said, "I think it's a great idea."

"I agree," Jimmy said. "And for the record, I didn't think the comment was all that crude."

Michele rolled her eyes.

"These women don't trust strangers much. That's one of the reasons they opted to stay in Joseph's house when they learned you two were coming. I was hoping I could take you guys to visit with them tomorrow. Maybe you could talk to them about the Bible and the love of Christ. I think it may really help in their healing."

"Sure," Michael said.

"*Healing* is the operative word," Gloria said somberly. "When Jimmy and Michele came up with the idea of fake detention camps, I thought the idea was brilliant. I saw the camps as incredible places where the saints would pray, encourage one another, and anxiously await the Lord.

"I was naïve. Maybe the camps can grow into that scenario, but it won't happen right away. These people have been stripped of their dignity and abused in the foulest manner. They need healing before they can fully function as the body of Christ."

Michele placed her hand on Gloria's. "I was naïve as well. In my mind, I thought these liberated people would only need the creature comforts we could give them, but now I see their mental health is poor. They are so demoralized."

Gloria continued, "Even though I was only in a camp for a short time, I have a much better idea of what will be needed in our fake detention centers. That's why I want to run one for women."

"I think it's a wonderful idea, Gloria," Michael said. "My understanding is that you need a new identity. I can work on that when I get back to Jerusalem. But that does raise another issue, namely, another gender."

"I hear you," Michele concurred. "I have an idea for the person to head up a men's camp. I want to run it by you."

"Who?" Michael asked.

"John Santos." Michele grinned.

"Interesting choice," Michael said. He thought John was up for the job and trusted him implicitly. "Do you think he'll go for it?"

"To be honest," Michele said, looking first to Jimmy with a shrug and then at Michael, "I think John is tired of the Naomi drama. She keeps people on their toes, but she does it by continually stirring the pot. It often puts John in a bad position."

Jimmy jumped in. "To be clear, I entertain no fantasy about Naomi. I know she is difficult. My dealings with her have been far less like family and more like extortion."

Michele explained, "She told Jimmy she would make it look like the two of them were in cahoots to steal the company if he didn't convince me to stay home after we were married."

"Cahoots?" Will aped. Michael chuckled. For years Michele had teased *Will* about using theatrical language.

"Yes, cahoots." Michele smiled. "I guess you're rubbing off on me."

"Here's my concern," Michael said. "Who will be at the company to keep a lid on Naomi?"

"I will," Michele said. "Besides, running afoul of Uncle Benny has really humbled Naomi. I think she would rather stay loyal to the sane side of the family."

"For as long as she can, at least," Will said.

"What do you mean by that?" Michael asked.

"Well, while you were away, Benny and Isa announced a plan to rapidly 'inoculate' the entire population of the planet in a month. In their announcement to the world, Benny explained how people who take the mark will actually get the part of Isa's DNA that gives him a superior immune system. Disease will be wiped off the face of the earth. Having seen Isa close up and personal, I can't imagine this insane world sharing his DNA."

"So that's how they'll accomplish it," Michael said with an astonished look. "The Bible says that people who take the mark cannot be saved. That statement always seemed weird to me, given Jesus's loving nature. But if the mark changes DNA, they'll be like the Nephilim, something other than human. As a consequence, Jesus's sacrifice wouldn't be effective for them."

"That's some heavy stuff," Will intoned. "Do you think we'll see a difference in them?"

"It could be bad. Some extrabiblical literature indicates that these half fallen angel, half human beings were exceedingly violent and had little to no respect for life." Michael wiped his forehead. He couldn't think any further about it tonight. "How about we watch your video of the witnesses's ascension and then hit the hay. It's been a long day."

The estate was quiet when Michael awoke in the middle of the night. He checked his watch; the time was a little after 2:00 a.m. He went to the office in the suite of rooms he referred to as his bedroom. He turned on the desk lamp and opened his safe to retrieve the flash drive containing Gloria's evidence of Zack's crimes.

"Lord, I'm not really sure if I should do this. In some ways it feels like revenge, but in another way, it seems like a good thing to nullify his message of 'Christian' compromise to Isa's world system." Isa! The thought of Isa alone made him want to take Zack down. His betrayal of Gloria to the Lady was beyond treacherous.

Plugging the flash drive into the computer, he looked through the evidence. He would have to scrub it so it didn't incriminate Benny. Benny would only take action if his own reputation were at stake. Michael knew he could easily send the documentation to global authorities with a Vatican cover letter. But was it the right thing to do?

He decided to take a break from the information, resolving to clear his head before making a final decision. Pulling from the safe the now familiar envelope left by his mother, he took out the large black-and-white photo of a picnic long ago. Staring back at him were the faces of his mother, Chris, Father Vinnie, Father Morton, Gloria's parents, Zack's parents, Benny, and Naomi. Despite the fact that they had only met one another much later in life, there they all were in the same photo. He looked to the back of it to see his mother's handwriting identifying the people she knew, along with a note questioning how they all could have been together and yet none of them remembered the event.

He mused about the photo. Benny was the oldest child in the group, probably in his mid- to late teens. Maybe he would have a memory of it. But even if Benny remembered it, was there a chance he would actually tell Michael the truth? No way. He wouldn't ask Benny about it.

"Well, that's settled," he said as he placed the photo and note back into the envelope. "For now, I'll have to be thankful that this photo got me through my time in the isolation tank. Maybe someday I'll figure it out.

"Now what about you, Zack?" He thought for only a few moments more. Zack's parents were in that photo, and he had mercilessly killed them. Zack had worked with the Lady to bring about Isa's conception. Something evil had happened to all those people in the photograph. Their lives had been ruthlessly manipulated in the same manner Zack manipulated those around him. The decision was made. Michael pushed the button to send the incriminating evidence.

NINE

Riverside Church was filled to capacity. All of the attendees loved Zack. No more did he have to share an audience with Gloria. The news of her treachery had galvanized the congregation, leading them to rally around their bereaved pastor. His word was gold. Literally. Despite the hard times, his coffers kept growing. His plea for relief funds following the Russian attacks had brought in millions of dollars. Whereas a small portion would actually find its way to people who had been displaced, the lion's share of the profits would go to the ministry. By "the ministry," Zack meant the underground palatial estate he had begun to construct on the grounds of the parsonage. If his sheep wanted to stand and face the Anu, well, more power to them. Zack intended to spend the whole ordeal cuddling with his secretary and a safe full of gold. Once the danger had passed, he would proclaim divine providence kept him through the worst of it. The world would sorely need his message as it rebuilt.

Rebuilt. The very word implied there would be something worth rebuilding. By comparison to the state of the world today, the new world would be light-years ahead. New technologies, a smaller population, and a united world would bring in a golden age dreamed of by philosophers through the ages. And Zack planned to be at the forefront of that new civilization. He would link himself inextricably to Kurtoglu tonight by accepting the inoculation in front of his parish in a sort of New World communion ceremony.

Zack had believed most of his life that Jesus rose from the dead, but he hadn't seen it. In contrast, Isa, his very own son, had risen from the dead for the entire world to see. How could Zack have been so fortunate to share genes with the greatest man ever to live? Isa was the new god for the new age.

Smiling broadly his signature smile, he said, "Sisters and brothers, you know I have gone through a rough patch since learning of my former wife's horrible deeds. I thought maybe there was nothing to live for. I wasn't sure I had a purpose anymore.

"My grief was compounded when some reprobate Christian fanatic decided to end Isa Kurtoglu's life. Isa Kurtoglu! The last hope for a world about to be besieged by alien forces and catastrophic natural disasters.

"I was like to give up when I saw them haul his bloody body out of the holy temple in Jerusalem." He paused to wipe a tear from his eye. This was no manufactured tear; the very image of Isa lying dead had shaken him to his core. "I didn't know if I wanted to go on.

"And then, just when it seemed the world was without hope, the most miraculous event of our age transpired. The once dead leader of the world miraculously sat up on his funeral pyre!" His voice turned to a taut whisper to elicit a sense of awe. "Think of it. Go on! Close your eyes and remember every detail of that moment. You actually got to see a man rise from the dead!

"I was overjoyed in that moment. At that exact second in time, I suddenly had hope and a reason to go on. Jesus rose from the dead. I believe it with all my heart. He died to take away our sins. But God has sent another son, and this one died to save us from the certain catastrophe of the Nemesis passing. Just like Jesus, this one was killed for his efforts. And just like Jesus, he took his life back up again.

"One man died and came back to life to give us a sinless existence, and one man died and came back to life to lead us into a great age. As time goes on and our theology is rewritten, we will come to recognize that the sacrifice of one is of no value without the sacrifice of the other.

"In the very same way Jesus is a son of God, Isa Kurtoglu is as well. You know, when Jesus was on earth, He confused people when He said 'eat My body and drink My blood.' Think of the horrible cannibalistic overtones of that statement. People thought he was crazy.

"But follow my line of reasoning here. For His day and age, this was His way of telling people to incorporate His very essence into their own. And our second savior has made the same offer, but this offer has teeth to it.

"In Jesus's day, there was no way to actually transfer His essence, His DNA, into the lives of His followers. They had to rely on spiritual transformation. That was a pale foreshadowing of a day when another messiah would offer his *actual* essence to his followers. That day has arrived. We have the opportunity to partake in the DNA of divinity."

He paused for a moment, folded his hands, and closed his eyes. "Can you sense the gravity of such a statement? Sure, we all have heard of the health benefits. Those alone would make the inoculation worthwhile. But it goes so much deeper to transformation of our very natures. We will become as he is, and for the first time, we'll be able to live the sinless life modeled by Jesus.

"Can you see the stunning partnership of these sons of God? Can you possibly question whether Isa Kurtoglu is as much divine as Jesus? Can you see the beautiful synergies of their respective sacrifices? Can I get an 'amen'?"

The crowd erupted in shouts of amen. They got to their feet, applauding their newfound hope. Zack smiled at them and blessed them in the name of Isa until the applause diminished.

He motioned for them to take their seats and said, "I hope you will share with me this most special of communion Sundays. For today, we have members of the government's inoculation team to administer the savior's DNA directly to us. To participate in the DNA of the divine, all you have to do is come forward. The government has advocated the two most receptive sites for the inoculation to be the right hand and the forehead. You can choose either. As for me, I want it right on my forehead, where our friends from the Eastern religions locate the third eye. Oh, Lord Isa, open my third eye that I may be as you are!"

He went to the edge of the altar and closed his eyes. A large photo of Isa Kurtoglu's face filled the screen behind him as the choir sang. "Keep your eyes upon Isa. Look full in his wonderful face, and the things of earth will look strangely dim in the light of his glory and grace."

The crowd sang along, swaying from side to side, arms raised in worship. A government worker wiped Zack's forehead with an alcohol swab. The inoculation itself felt like a slight pinprick, but the weight of the moment nearly knocked him off his feet. He could swear he could feel the effects of the holy unction the second it penetrated his skin. His head became hot, and his breath grew shallow. Then the heat in his head slowly dripped down his arms, and he felt strength he had never known before. By the time it reached his legs, he felt as if he were a superman.

"Praise you, Isa. Praise you," he said over and over as he swayed to the music and soaked in the holy energy. He knew it would be great, but he had no idea of the euphoria it would bring. It was as if he could feel his body changing, growing into something more than a man.

The night ended late. They had 100 percent participation in the ritual. All over the sanctuary, men, women, and toddlers swayed to the music with joyous expressions. Zack had never been in such a powerful, meaningful worship service. Finally at midnight, the high of the night began to lose altitude, and Zack returned to a more normal state of mind. He dismissed the crowd and left the church with his secretary.

But the night was far from over. The rejuvenation he had felt on the altar translated to his bed. He didn't think he was ever so sexually aggressive, even in his youth, and his secretary was with him every step of the way. He fell to satisfied sleep thinking, *This must be how the gods make love.*

———

He awoke three hours later, fully refreshed.

"It looks like enhanced DNA doesn't need as much sleep," he said to himself as he went downstairs for a cup of coffee. The sun was just rising. He took his coffee to the backyard. There was a bit of a chill in the air, but it felt invigorating. Everything felt invigorating. The colors of the sunrise seemed more vivid than he had ever remembered.

The government workers said it would take six weeks for the inoculation to take full effect. Zack couldn't imagine how great he would feel in six weeks. He took a long drink of coffee and contemplated the wonderful gift he had given the world in the form of Isa Kurtoglu. Of course, Gloria had participated as well. His mouth moved to an involuntary sneer at the thought of her. She had been a sort of mother of a god, and yet she threw it all away to chase after the memory of Jesus. How foolish!

And yet, he had loved her as much as he had ever loved anyone. His thoughts ran to his secretary asleep in his bed. Some physical companionship and a look of adoration—that's all she was to him. In contrast, for a while he had thought he and Gloria were soul mates, bound inextricably in spirit. Well, he was relieved of that delusion years ago on that cruise. She had never looked at him the way she looked at Michael Martin.

Damn him! Life would be pretty good right about now if only Michael hadn't been found. The news release from the Vatican announcing his safe return was the only thing spoiling Zack's mood. There was perhaps an upside. Zack may have paled in comparison to Michael in the past, but Michael was tied to the old religion. He would never take the inoculation. The government said the populace would undergo an expansion of IQ from Isa's DNA. Maybe Michael would be a comparative dullard in as little as six weeks. Or better still, maybe Isa would finally brand him a heretic. How wonderful it would be to have his god remove his nemesis!

"O let it be, Lord Isa. Remove my nemesis as willfully as you plan to remove the Nemesis entering the inner solar system."

Looking out toward the horizon, he saw light reflecting from an approaching car. He gulped down his coffee and rushed up the stairs. It wouldn't be good for visitors to see the pastor in his skivvies. Running into his bedroom, he grabbed a pair of pants and a T-shirt. To his stirring mistress, he held one finger over his mouth to indicate he needed her silence.

"Someone is coming. It's too early to announce our relationship. Do not make a sound until I tell you the coast is clear," he warned.

She mumbled her acknowledgment in a sleep-filled daze.

Returning downstairs, he fixed his hair in the foyer mirror. He looked good—in fact, too good for a man coming to terms with his wife's treachery. He tousled his hair, making it a bit more unkempt, and sucked in a little at his cheeks to give a gaunt appearance. Finally he practiced yet again at turning the corners of his mouth slightly down. It was hard for him. He had practiced his trademark smile for so many years that the muscles at the bottom of his mouth had atrophied.

The doorbell rang. He ignored it as he completed his look.

The bell rang again. "Coming," he yelled as he slowly approached the door. Whoever was paying a visit this early in the morning certainly didn't merit much in the way of social graces.

As the bell rang the third time, he opened the door to see two of Houston's finest. They didn't look happy.

"Officers! What can I do for you this fine mornin'?" he drawled.

The older of the two announced officiously, "Reverend Jolean, we have a warrant to search your home and to retrieve your computers." He held out an official-looking piece of paper. Zack snatched it from his hand and read it briefly. It certainly said they had the right to take his computers.

As they entered his house, Zack said in an appeasing tone, "Now, now ... j-just hold on here a second, officers. There must be some kind of mistake. I can't think of any reason the government would be interested in my computers."

"Sir, would you please lead us to your computers. We'll take them and be about our business."

"No, sir, I won't!" Zack snapped. "Am I under arrest?"

"At this time you are not, sir."

"Well, then, you can just take your warrant and shove it. I know my rights!"

The younger, burlier officer floored him in seconds. One moment Zack was in their faces, and the next moment, Zack's face was plastered against the tile floor.

The older cop explained, "You may mistakenly be remembering your rights as an American citizen. Those rights apply in local matters, but global laws take precedence in global affairs."

As the younger cop cuffed him and lifted him to his feet, Zack said in a demanding tone, "This is ludicrous! Do you know who I am?"

"Yes, sir. You're a man under arrest for attempting to prevent us from doing our duty. It's a federal offense. You have the right to remain silent ..."

Zack didn't even listen. He had heard the Miranda rights read on television shows since his youth. Instead, his panicked mind raced. What might his computers show? Bank records could prove he commingled the money from the nuclear cleanup fund with his own, but a good lawyer could easily plead that he still planned to use the funds for their intended purpose. At worst, he could be accused of a clerical error.

Considering that, he complained loudly, "I'm telling you two for the last time, you are making a big mistake. I have done nothing illegal. I'm a minister, for crying out loud!"

Paying him no attention, they walked him to their squad car and placed him in the back seat. Another car of officers arrived to perform the search. "Where are you taking me?"

"Downtown to a holding cell," the driver said. "Tomorrow you'll be arraigned for interfering with a police investigation. The judge will set bail, and you'll be back home by noon."

"You mean I'll have to spend the night in jail? This is outrageous!" Zack exclaimed.

He complained throughout the booking process. Not once did the officers acknowledge his complaints. They spoke over him as if he weren't there. This enraged Zack. All his life people had waited—waited!—to hear what he had to say.

Of course Zack called his lawyer at the first opportunity. And, of course, he was not at home. Zack left a voice mail.

His cell was six feet by eight feet. A mattress lay on a concrete slab extending from a cinder block wall. A toilet and a sink stood in the open next to the "bed." The entire area disgusted him.

Sleep never came. He thought repeatedly about what they could be after. If it was the relief money, he would pay it back with interest. One sermon about how he was falsely charged would bring in millions. He thought briefly about the evidence Gloria had found on him, but those files were erased shortly after she lowered the boom. They wouldn't find those files.

Breakfast was watery oatmeal and even waterier coffee. If it were possible to enjoy, he would have had scant time to do so. After Zack had taken a few bites, a guard took him to see his lawyer.

In a dimly lit interrogation room, his lawyer, Jerry, sat on one side of a table. An empty chair sat on the other side. The room's walls were two-toned, forest green on the bottom with a slightly lighter shade of forest green on the top. Steam whistled from an ancient radiator. The room was ghastly. Zack's scowl wasn't hard to come by this morning.

"Zack," Jerry said glumly. He stood to shake Zack's hand.

"Why so somber, Jerry?" Zack asked. "Whatever bail they levy, we'll pay it and take this up in court on another day when I have showered and shaved."

"Things have changed since last night," Jerry said. "The police have dropped the interference charges."

Zack grinned broadly. "Well, praise God! This might not be such a bad day after all!"

"Not so fast, Zack. They dropped their complaint in favor of international charges," Jerry said gruffly.

"International charges! What the hell is that supposed to mean?" Zack asked impatiently.

"It means the world government is charging you." Jerry pulled from his briefcase a copy of the complaint. "They are charging you with the murder of your parents, the murder of your former church secretary and her husband, and many incidents of fraud. The alleged murder of your parents occurred in international waters, and the alleged fraud is worldwide given the demographics of your donors. So, the crimes fall under international jurisdiction."

"This is ridiculous!" Zack screamed. "They have no proof, because none of this ever happened!"

"Apparently there were incriminating files on your computer ..."

"Jerry, this is bull crap. I cleaned all old files from my computer years ago. Those files don't exist." Zack fumed.

"Forensic detectives retrieved them from your hard drive." Jerry sighed.

"Well, there must be a misunderstanding then. We'll fight this all the way, Jerry. I don't care how much it costs. For now let's just concentrate on getting me out of here."

Jerry shook his head. "I can't represent you."

"What?" Zack screamed.

Jerry spoke in a low tone. "Nobody can. There are no personal rights. International law in the Kurtoglu regime is totally one-sided. The accusation and conviction are nearly synonymous."

"So, you're saying I'm presumed guilty?" Zack asked in disbelief.

"No. I'm saying you have been declared guilty. As we speak, the government is seizing all your assets."

Zack couldn't sit still. He jumped up from his chair and paced the room. He ran his hands through his hair, sending loose curls down over his face. "Jerry, you have to let them know there's been some mistake."

Jerry shrugged. "I tried to do just that by calling the guy who filed the complaint, a Father Michael Martin. He hasn't returned my call."

"Michael Martin?" Zack spat. "I can tell you right now, this is a setup. Gloria set me up!"

"Well, she did a pretty good job of it, Zack," Jerry said with disgust, "because from a legal point of view, our hands are tied."

"Not quite," Zack said with a menacing grin. "I don't care how you do it, but get me a call with the pope today. I have several numbers for him on my cell phone if you can get it out of evidence. Regardless ... I don't care how you do it. Get to the pope and tell him everything is about to come out in the open. He'll know what to do."

"I can't just dial up the pope!" Jerry protested.

"Do it! I want to talk to the pope today!"

TEN

Five days had passed far too quickly. Michael certainly felt better than he had at the end of his captivity, but he wasn't sure he was strong enough to return to Jerusalem. The return flight should have been routine, but he noticed an awful reality taking shape in his interactions with the cabin steward. The man had clearly taken the mark. He wore it proudly as a red dot in the middle of his forehead, smaller than a Hindu marking, but clearly present. He was standard issue in Benny's air force: tall, muscular, dark hair, and blue eyes. It always gave Michael the nauseating feeling Benny patterned them after Chris.

"Welcome aboard. My name is Ryan, and I'll be taking care of you during this flight. We have a nice vegetable lasagna for you today," the man said.

"Thanks, Ryan," Michael said. He did a double take as he looked at the young man. There was something different about him. To Michael it looked like his skin had a slight green pallor. He wiped his eyes as the man left the cabin.

"You saw it too. Didn't you?" Will asked.

"I'd say yes, but I'm not sure what I saw."

"To me, it's like he doesn't look entirely human. To tell you the truth, something about him looks reptilian to me."

"That's interesting," Michael said, lost in thought.

"How so?"

"The Hebrew word we translate as 'serpent' in the Garden of Eden narrative is *nachesh*. But it can also be translated as 'seraph.'"

"Like an angel?"

"Yes," Michael said. "I always wondered if the fallen angels would look reptilian to us. When you read the book of Enoch, you see God saying there is no redemption for the offspring of the fallen angels and humans."

"Book of Enoch?" Will asked.

"It's not in the Bible, but Jesus and His disciples were very familiar with it. Jude referenced it in his epistle."

"So tell me about it," Will said.

"Enoch said two hundred fallen angels came to Earth and impregnated women. The offspring were described as twelve-fingered giants who had total disregard for humanity. God declared there was not even the potential of salvation for them because their DNA had been corrupted with the angelic DNA."

"Why does that matter?" Will asked.

"Jesus was fully human and fully God. His sacrifice enables the redemption of humanity. For some reason only known to the Father, the fallen angels aren't entitled to redemption. The mixed DNA renders the hybrids unfit for salvation as well," Michael said with a slight shrug.

"It sounds kind of sci-fi, don't you think?" Will asked.

"More than any of the other stuff we've seen?" Michael asked with a raised brow.

"Well, when you put it that way ..."

Michael continued his explanation. "When we move forward to the book of Revelation, we're told that salvation is unattainable for those who have taken the mark of the beast. Now I think I know why. They have been contaminated with fallen angel DNA."

"And because of the word *na, nach* ..."

"*Nachesh*," Michael corrected.

"Yeah. Nachesh. I might have gotten it eventually," Will said with a grin. "Because of that word, you think we may see reptilian tendencies in people who took the mark?"

Michael nodded. "Intriguing, right? At least we'll be able to quickly identify them."

Will commented, "The question I have is, how do they see themselves?"

"What do you mean?"

Will explained, "When they look in the mirror, do they think they look different?"

"I doubt it. They probably think they haven't changed, believing instead that we've become pale or something."

"If so, then they'll be able to instantly identify us as well," Will warned.

"You're probably right," Michael said glumly as the steward entered with their dinners.

"Here you are, sir," he said to Michael. "A hot meal should help to bring some color back to your cheeks." Michael raised an eyebrow toward Will.

"And one for you as well," he said to Will. "I'll be right back with some wine, and you two will be set to go."

He poured the wine as the two men sat in silence. Michael's mind moved to what awaited him in Jerusalem.

After a while, Will asked, "One thing that confuses me is the 666 in Revelation. What's that all about?"

Michael sighed. "The only part of Revelation that *everybody* knows! There are lots of ideas. In Hebrew numerology, seven is the number of completion or perfection. The number three is associated with the Godhead. Six is one less than seven, representing imperfection. Some people say 666 represents the perfect imperfection or the imperfect god."

"I thought it had to do with his name," Will said.

Michael answered, "Hebrew letters also have number values. I could build a case that a certain Hebrew spelling of Isa's name adds to 666, but it's hardly an exclusive club. Some people say that 6-6-6 in Hebrew spells out *vav-vav-vav*, or *www* in English. They say that's because Isa couldn't rule without the World Wide Web.

"Still others say that the Greek letters that spell 666 closely resemble Arabic markings worn by the Muslims as head wraps when they declared Isa to be the Mahdi.

"Others say that three sixes add up to eighteen, which just happens to be the number of characters in Isa's citizen ID number.

"There's also the thought that 666 is a reference to Solomon because the Bible says he received 666 talents of gold each year. It's the only other time that number is mentioned in the Bible. Because of this they say the person who rebuilds Solomon's Temple is the Antichrist."

"So which is it?" Will asked.

Michael answered glumly, "Any or all. Take your pick. They all point to Kurtoglu."

Their plane landed in Jerusalem and taxied to the papal hangar. Michael had not seen much sleep on the flight. Each time he nodded off, the winged creature from his dreams greeted him.

He was anxious about going back to Jerusalem. He had fairly hated it before, but at least he could rely on the comfort of occasional visits with Moses, Enoch, and raptured family members. Those comforts seemed long gone, and in their place loomed Satan himself. He didn't know how he was going to deal with it. He prayed for the Lord's protection.

When they arrived in the hangar, Michael was shocked to see Benny waiting for them. He had a black eye and some heavy bruising on his face. He tried to cover it with makeup, but it didn't match his new pallor. Clearly he had taken the mark.

Without his usual ceremony, he ran to Michael and hugged him fiercely. Overwhelmed by the sentiment, Michael returned the hug.

"I'm okay, Benny," Michael said softly.

The man shook in his arms. Through tears, he whined, "Michael, I'm so happy to have you back, but I've done a terrible thing. I've backed the wrong side all these years, and now there's nothing I can do about it."

Michael spoke in his ear. "I know, Benny. I guess I've always known, even before I met Jesus." Michael felt an involuntary cringe shake Benny's body at the mention of Jesus's name.

Benny pulled away. He reached into his pocket for a handkerchief and dotted his tears. Noticing the makeup stains on his handkerchief, he said, "Well, you can see where he beat me. That's not the half of it, Michael. We were in the holy of holies after that madman shot Isa, and then the Lady ... oh God, Michael!" He started to cry again, and his words were unintelligible.

Michael looked intently toward Will as he led Benny to a chair. "Will, can you get Benny a bottle of water?" To Benny, he said, "Try to be calm, Benny. I can't understand a word you're saying."

Benny took several deep breaths. Will arrived with the water. Benny took a long drink. "Thank you, William."

"You're welcome," Will said kindly, all the while staring at Michael.

Michael prodded. "Tell me what happened in the holy of holies, Benny."

"The Lady turned into Lucifer. She wasn't an alien, Michael; she was Lucifer. And not the light-bringer I had expected Lucifer to be, but a monstrous being with blue skin and ugly, bat-like wings. I still can't stand to think of how he looked at me. I had never known such unadulterated contempt. He dug his talons into Isa's face. Isa screamed. I screamed, and the next thing I knew, I woke up to Isa's dead body."

Benny's description rocked Michael. It was too close to his dreams to be a coincidence. He felt his hands shake but willed them to stop. There would be plenty of time to ponder their similarities, but there would be little time with Benny before Nergal came forward.

Michael spoke cautiously. "The book of Revelation says the Antichrist will die of a head wound, only to be inhabited by Satan in a mockery of Jesus's resurrection."

"Well, that certainly would explain his personality!" Benny spat before opening to a new wave of tears.

"Why are you telling us all of this, Benny?" Michael asked.

"Ohhh," Benny whined. "Since taking the inoculation, I've had a very difficult time being myself. The ascended master Isa installed in me is taking over. I don't know if I'll be able to resist the merging of our personalities any longer."

"You've got to fight it, Lucky," Will said with encouragement.

"It's a lost cause, Will. I made many bad choices over the years. They've led me to this point—the merging of my consciousness with one of a higher order. It is something I wanted from the time I was young. Now that it's staring me in the face, I haven't got the courage."

"Aw, Benny," Michael said somberly, "if you hadn't taken the mark, I would tell you how you could change it all by accepting Jesus."

"I wouldn't anyway. He's the only person who scares me more than Isa," Benny said glumly.

"So, what do you want from me?" Michael asked suspiciously.

"Nothing *from* you, Michael. I want to warn you. Isa has changed, and very soon I will change as well. Consider it a final act of love—at least as much as I'm capable of love."

Something broke in Michael, an uncharacteristic compassion for the man. He put his arm around Benny and gently hugged him. "Coming from you that means a lot, Benny. Probably more than I can convey."

"Thanks, Michael. I knew you would understand." He rose from his chair and turned to Will. "Will, take good care of your uncle. He's the only one you have."

"I will, Lucky. I promise," Will said. Michael saw a tear in Will's eye.

Then Benny trudged toward the door of the terminal. Before exiting, he turned to them and said, "Oh, by the way, Isa has requested a meeting with the two of you in an hour. I'll be there, but probably only in body." He sadly left them to gather their bags.

Michael and Will were walking across Abraham's Courtyard toward Saint Peter's Basilica.

"I sure would have liked a day or two to see my apartment and go through my mail before our little tête-à-tête with Satan," Michael said glumly.

"If it weren't true, it would be one of the most ridiculous things I've ever heard you say," Will replied with a hint of irony.

Michael sighed. "Your description of him was bad enough, but seeing Benny in that condition just now ... well, it scares the crap out of me."

"Maybe we'll be lucky. Maybe he'll fire us," Will said hopefully.

"I think termination for Isa means death. And don't get me wrong; I'd be more than happy to be with the Lord right now, but what about Michele? What about all the people we could help? Death seems to be the wrong answer from the standpoint of the kingdom of God."

Will put a hand on Michael's shoulder. "Well, then, let's go in there as soldiers of the kingdom of God."

"You mean put on the armor of Christ?" Michael asked, bemused by the change in Will.

Will shrugged. "I guess. We'll pray before we go into the room.

When you're speaking, I'll be praying. When I'm speaking, you'll be praying. When Isa and Benny are speaking, we'll both be praying."

"Sounds like a plan," Michael said. "It may aggravate them if they catch on, but Jesus is Lord even over the likes of Kurtoglu. I'm with you."

"I have a theory, Jake. I think the Lord is the best undercover operator in the universe. He can protect us and not give us away. It won't aggravate Isa; it will mollify him."

They stopped in the silent splendor of the basilica's sanctuary and prayed together on the way to Isa's apartment. Once there, they notified his guard, who led them to Isa's office, which was white on white on white with an enormous black desk. Michael always had found it sterile and cold.

Isa joined them from the opposite hallway. "Father Michael, what a pleasure to see you returned to us!" To Michael's surprise, Isa seemed charming.

"Thank you, President Kurtoglu. It's good to be home." Michael smiled.

Isa continued, "Hello to you, Will. The agent's report said you were very helpful in the tracking and elimination of the good father's abductors. I commend you."

Will spoke with downcast eyes, "Thank you, Excellency. It's an honor to serve."

"Of course it is!" Isa said with a near shout. "Come, gentlemen, take a seat." He pointed them to three black chairs at the front of his big black desk. "Your uncle will be joining us shortly."

They took their seats. "I'm sure you are wondering why I called this meeting," Isa said jovially. "Well, I thought it might be good to get a few things on the table. First of all, I should tell you I'm not overly fond of the human race. It's nothing they've done; I just don't like them." He shrugged and threw his hands in the air.

Michael had no response other than "Uh-huh." Will remained silent.

Isa continued, "You two are different. Michael, your enhanced intellect has always intrigued me. It makes you closer to my equal than anyone on earth. Add to that the genetic qualities you contributed to this perfect body of mine, and it's a no-brainer. You're one of my favorites."

Michael willed himself to halt an involuntary cringe. His mind raced with the thought that he would rather be executed than be Isa's favorite pet. Again he said, "Uh-huh."

"And as for you, Will, what can I say? Your arrow enabled me to become all I am today. Your hatred of me, along with your bravery, brought all this about. I think you are a man after my own heart."

It was Will's turn to say "Uh-huh."

"So there you have it. One of you touches my brain; the other, my heart."

Michael felt a quickening in his spirit. Throughout the conversation, Isa had been attempting to get into their heads but was unable to. The prayer cover was working. He also thought Satan seemed entirely mad, unhinged in a way psychologists could only imagine.

Isa grinned smugly. "So, now I have a dilemma. Two of my favorite humans have done the unimaginable. They have embraced the old religion. Imagine my sense of betrayal."

Neither Michael nor Will said a thing.

"So, you don't deny it?" he demanded.

This was a biblically significant moment. Jesus warned in the Gospels not to deny Him. "I don't deny it," Michael said with studied calm.

Will followed his lead. "Neither do I."

Isa continued, "So, I am faced with the decision to terminate your services or to keep you around. I have decided on the latter. Because I find you two amusing, I will give to you the rare chance to live and work in my regime as Christians."

"That's very magnanimous, Excellency," Michael said.

Apparently at a loss for words, Will said suspiciously, "Ditto ... Excellency."

Isa folded his hands and placed them near his mouth as he stared at the two. "You see, I've made a sort of wager with myself. I bet I can convince you to serve me." He waved his hands in a grandiose manner. "I know, you don't think there's so much as a remote possibility, but I'll let you in on a little secret."

He abruptly stood and walked to their side of the desk. Leaning against the desk, he continued, his face mere inches from theirs. "The secret is that Jesus isn't dead. He's very much alive ... for now. He, my friends, will lead the Anu invasion. And I will gloriously shoot Him from the sky."

Michael could feel Isa's breath on his face. The intensity of the meeting was wearing him out. "So, you acknowledge Jesus is more than an ancient fiction," Michael said sternly, catching an "Are you crazy?" look from Will.

"I think I just did. Do try to keep up with me, Father. I don't like it when people don't pay me the proper attention," Isa said with a deprecating whine.

"I'm just trying to understand your premise," Michael answered.

"My premise is that I will destroy Him when he comes. And because I like the two of you, I will give you time through His death to worship me. In fact, Father, you claim to love this Jesus so much, I'll let you lick His blood from my boots in an act of worship to me."

"To be honest, I can't envision that as my future," Michael said, crossing his arms in front of him. Again speechless, Will followed Michael's lead and crossed his arms as well.

Isa grinned too broadly, insanely. "Thus the very nature of my little wager. Will the dynamic duo fall down to me or not? It's my own little reality show."

At that moment, Benny entered the room. His eyes were vacant, and his face had the contemptuous look Michael had learned to associate with Nergal. He announced, "Excellency, the package you requested is waiting."

"Wonderful, Holiness! As you can see, I have been entertaining our guests."

Benny moved to a position beside Isa. In this huge room, the four of them were in a tiny, confined space. "Yes. Father Michael, it is good to have you back. You too, Will."

"Thanks, Benny," Michael said. Will grinned and nodded.

"Henceforth, I think it would be better for you to refer to me as Holiness," Benny said. "I have become so much more than the uncle who used to rock you to sleep."

"Yes, Holiness," Michael said softly.

"Don't be dismayed. Your old uncle is still here, safe and sound, and I will still honor his commitment to your family. But I'm head honcho in this body."

"I see," Michael said. This encounter made the time with Benny in the airport all the more poignant.

"Well, down to business," Isa said. "As much as I like the two of you and want to keep you around, it wouldn't be prudent for me to put blind faith in your loyalty."

"And to be fair, you've already been naughty, Michael," Benny added.

"I'm not sure what you mean," Michael responded.

Benny accused, "Setting up Vatican subsidiaries without consulting me. Why, I learned more from Naomi in one conversation than in all the time I spent with you."

Michael shrugged casually, feigning nonchalance. "Admittedly, I used Vatican pull to help our company. I didn't think you would want to be involved in the petty matters of my life."

"Petty matters," Benny mocked. "Modesty is just as much an ill-fitting suit on you as it is on me."

"This is family business, Benny. Do we really need to hash it out in front of His Excellency?" Michael asked harshly.

Benny rolled his eyes. "No, we don't. I merely raised the issue to support His Excellency's point that your agenda is not always synonymous with ours."

Isa intervened. "See there? No recrimination, just a look into the pecking order of your loyalties. As we've already discussed, I want to keep you around to see the demise of your God, but your loyalty to Him gives me pause.

"Not to worry, though. I do believe I have found the solution to our problem. My new assistant will have the primary responsibility to ensure the inoculation of the world's entire population. Another of his duties will be to monitor your performance."

"Holiness, would you like to make the introductions?" Isa asked with a devilish grin.

Benny left the room. Michael looked in Will's direction and quickly raised his eyebrow. Whatever this was, it wasn't good. The last thing they needed was someone to look over their shoulders. Michael thought the most useful person in that position would be the agent. Had the agent duped them all along? If so, the Petra secrets had been exposed already.

Benny entered, trailed by Zack, sporting his trademark grin.

TIME

ELEVEN

The conference room was the same, but the attendees certainly were different. Things had changed in the eight months since Benny mandated the inoculations. Michele missed John Santos. His work at the men's shelter was much more important, of course, but she wished there could be another Christian around the conference room table. Long ago, the authorities had taken Tanya from human resources for failure to receive the mark. Her rescue was as easy as Gloria's. In fact, all the rescues had become easier. With Uncle Michael's access to government supercomputers, Jimmy had actually managed to arrange transfers whereby the real FEMA camps delivered detainees to their fake detention centers.

Those were the victories she lived for. Days in the office with the marked masses were another story. It boggled her imagination that they couldn't see the changes in themselves. The slightly green tint of their skin and their hollow eyes were haunting. True to Uncle Benny's word, they were smarter and more efficient workers. Eradication of disease led to no sick days, but frivolity was gone. Spontaneity was history. In their wake were high-performance slaves with little capacity for love and immense hatred for those who opposed their resurrected leader.

Reinstated to her former position, Naomi began the meeting. "As you can see, our businesses are doing quite nicely. Although we thought the food businesses would suffer shortages with the loss of our major crops, the inoculations have made human metabolisms so much more efficient. The world's population simply doesn't need as much food."

That's why you all look like concentration camp victims. Isa is killing these people, and they're thanking him!

Michele gave up her inner commentary to catch the remainder of Naomi's summary. "Thankfully we were able to off-source our redundant workers to the government's munitions factories—and with a handsome tax break at that."

Michele noted, "I can see from the income statement. Margins in the food business have never looked so good. Even though volume is down, the higher prices of our products and the reduction in labor costs have resulted in a net increase to the bottom line."

"Not to mention the tax benefits. Tell me the truth, Michele, don't you feel a bit silly about the way you and your uncle were suspicious of the new government? As it turns out, things are going pretty well. And I might add, it is no coincidence that the benefits to society occurred simultaneously with the loosening of the stranglehold of old, exclusive religions."

"Well, I certainly can see the changes in all of you since the inoculations," she said, trying her best to sound sincere without overdoing it. They so strongly believed in their new messiah, there was little chance they would see her remark as sarcastic.

"I'm very sorry the inoculation won't work for you," proclaimed Ellis Baker, the new head of risk management. "I honestly don't remember ever feeling better in my life." Michele had previously told them that a rare genetic mutation in their bloodline prevented the inoculation from working for her and Uncle Michael, and therefore the pope had exempted them. To the people around this table, they were pitiable for not being able to share in the herd immunity afforded by the shot.

"I'm with you," sang Patricia O'Brian, the new head of human resources. "The very act of inoculation has greatly streamlined my job. I'm the head of an HR department that hasn't seen any sick days, unmotivated employees, or complaints in over six months. It's unheard of in my profession—and my counterparts in other companies are seeing the same thing."

"Sounds like there will be redundancies in HR," Michele said in an attempt at humor.

Patricia missed the joke. "Already ahead of you. We have managed to cut our staff in half by asking for volunteers to serve in the munitions factories. We actually had too many volunteers. In the end, we had to raffle off the spots." Michele was in awe of the lady's satisfaction—just so happy to make previously unheard-of advanced weapons for the cause.

"Well, we're less than three years away from the anticipated arrival date of the Anu," Michele said. "I'll rest easier when that is past." She meant it. She couldn't wait for Jesus to return and rid Earth of Isa and his evil regime.

Naomi said, "The Anu event is on the horizon in our three-year planning process. Frankly, I think we should run three plans: best-case, worst-case, and most-probable scenarios."

"Do you mean annihilation by the Anu as the worst case?" Michele asked. "Because if you do, it's a pretty easy plan. Everything is destroyed. Nothing matters."

"Well, maybe not the absolute worst case. And to be honest, I have faith our risen lord will save us, but good business practices would demand we look at a darker scenario."

"Which is?" Michele asked with exasperation.

"I hesitate to bring this up, but I've been doing some research. From what I have learned, the Anu consume humans. It would take just a little bit of tweaking of the machinery in our processed meat plants to give them what they want."

Michele gasped. "You're planning a scenario where we kill and process human beings?"

Naomi shrugged. "Not at first, at least. There will be a lot of casualties of war if the Anu win. We would just be offering our services ..."

"For heaven's sake, Naomi! Do you really want a buck that badly?" Michele screeched.

"I said it was a worst-case scenario. I don't think it will happen, but I want to be prepared in any event," Naomi said defensively, raising her voice.

Michele tried to remain calm. Everyone else in the room was calm, despite the absolute horror of Naomi's suggestion. "And you have done the preliminary analysis?" she asked with resignation and a sigh.

"Yes," Naomi said with a satisfied grin. "Along with the cost to poison the bastards with our products. You have to figure the only way they'll win is if they kill Kurtoglu. He beat death before; he can beat it again. The people lost in the war will already be dead, so we might as well use them to buy time for him to resurrect."

"I see," Michele muttered, stifling a cringe. Turning the topic of conversation, she said, "But enough with the worst case. I assume the best-case scenario is that we win decisively and that the Nemesis crossing won't produce too many catastrophic natural events."

Naomi nodded. "Yes, although I think that scenario will be as unlikely as the worst case. I think the most likely case is the third scenario. This plan anticipates significant damage to crops and infrastructure from natural disasters and the war. Under that plan, we would plow every spare dollar into our expanding freeze-dried food operations."

"That is a plan I can buy into," Michele said. "If the natural disasters occur, they'll happen in advance of the Anu attack. I say the sooner we increase capacity in freeze-dried foods, the better for us and for the world."

"I agree," said Enrique Jones, the new CFO. "There is no way of knowing the casualties to come from the natural disasters or the war, but given the shelf life of our freeze-dried products, there is virtually no chance we can have too much inventory."

"Do you have an inkling of the reduction in margin this plan will entail?" Michele asked.

He thought for a second before answering. "If we go full tilt, moving all available production, we'll be breakeven in the food business. In terms of your total holdings, though, you'll be fine. The aircraft and armament business is working three shifts to keep up with orders for His Excellency's high-tech weapons, and our oil and gas wells are running at full capacity."

"I just asked as a courtesy, and to let you know I'm on top of things," Michele said. "Of course we'll do whatever it takes to ensure the availability of food to the global population."

The rest of the meeting was much more mundane—no talk of canned human treats for alien conquerors. Michele breathed a deep sigh of relief when it ended. She made hasty goodbyes, packed her briefcase, and hit the open road, which truly was open. Gone was the Atlanta of the past with its traffic-tangled roadways. In the new world, there were no pleasure trips, no trips to parks, and no time at the mall, just routine travel to and from work. If you missed rush hour, the roads were nearly empty.

While the empty highways held a definite apocalyptic feel, she was happy for them today. She easily made up for lost time and arrived at the orphanage-turned-detention center a bit early. After showing her ID at the gate, she parked her car in front of what had been an old high school building her parents converted into an orphanage. It was a sizable brick edifice with granite windowsills and doorframes. The building reminded her of the 1950s visited by Marty McFly in *Back to the Future*. She grinned at the reference. Could life ever have been so innocent and carefree?

Gloria stood on the front stoop of the old building and waved as Michele approached.

"I thought I would be late," Michele said with a grin, "but I think I drive like my dad."

"I've heard stories." Gloria chuckled. She held out her arms to hug the younger woman.

"About my dad's driving or mine?" Michele asked as they embraced.

"Both," Gloria answered with a chuckle.

Michele pulled back from the hug to admire Gloria's hair, which had grown in significantly since the buzz cut she'd received at the real detention center. Her hair was still luxurious, but she wore it shoulder length and no longer colored it. Dark brown with gray highlights completed a more studied look now that she wore glasses instead of contact lenses. "I really like the look!"

"It feels good, too. So much more honest than when I had to play Barbie to Zack's Ken."

"Well, he's Uncle Michael's problem now—and Will's."

"I can't believe Benny rescued him. It's a shame." Gloria shook her head sadly.

Michele looked at the cloud passing over Gloria's face. It wasn't a look of sadness for the loss of a man she once loved. It was the heavy weight of regret for years gone wrong. She offered a bit of solace: "Well, at least Riverside was shut down."

"Too bad it wasn't shut down before Zack's inoculation communion service."

Michele agreed as she put an arm around Gloria's shoulder and led her into the facility. "So what time do we start?"

"In about fifteen minutes, John will arrive with the men's group.

Then the prayer meeting will begin," Gloria said. "It was tough going here at first, but once I earned the trust of a few women, things started to snowball. We have a pretty regimented system, but it's all done at the will of our guests. Early rise, earnest prayer, long Bible studies, and meal preparation. That's pretty much the sum total of our days, but we feel really strong spiritually and take seriously our work to provide prayer cover for Christians living in the world system."

Michele grinned, looking at the place as they headed to the auditorium. The women's side housed about two hundred guests. On the men's side, John had nearly one hundred fifty more. John patterned their days after the women's. The groups usually ate dinner together and then gathered for evening prayer.

"Mostly, people are happy here," Gloria said, "but there are a few married couples who don't appreciate the gender segregation. I was hoping to introduce you to a younger couple tonight. John and I can vouch for their maturity in Christ."

"All I need is a recommendation from you two. As soon as they can be ready to run a family camp, I have a refurbished apartment complex where we can house up to fifty families. It's in a rougher part of town, but the fencing is strong and electrified. I think our people will be safe there."

"As safe as anyone can be in this crazy world," Gloria said with a sigh.

"Thank God that every day you don't have to deal with the inoculated," Michele said sternly. "I just came from a meeting at headquarters. These people become less human every day."

"Truly, I don't know how you do it," Gloria said.

"How you do what?" John grinned as he approached for a hug. Michele was taken by the change in him. Following the rapture he was a broken man, constantly nagged by the fact that he'd found Jesus too late to join his wife and kids. For a while, he threw himself into work to get over it—just putting his shoulder to the grindstone and counting off the days until Christ's return. Running the men's camp had given him a purpose. She saw confidence in his step, and his bright eyes glowed with hope as he smiled at her.

"Interact with your former colleagues." Michele rolled her eyes in an exaggerated gesture of annoyance.

"I can't say I miss it," John commiserated.

"Yeah, well, they've gotten even wackier since the inoculation."

"It's hard to imagine Naomi getting any worse."

"Well, she's kind of green now to begin with. And today she set out scenarios for the three-year plan, one of which included canning humans and feeding them to the Anu."

John's eyes grew as wide as saucers in an expression of disbelief. "Wow, I guess things did get worse!"

"No shop talk, Michele," Gloria chimed. "And that's no way to talk about your mother-in-law!" she teased.

"Yeah, don't remind me."

"How is Jimmy handling her?" John asked.

Michele said, "Better than I am. But then again, Uncle Michael has him setting up Vatican detention centers in other English-speaking nations. He's been in Canada and the UK for weeks at a time. Soon he'll be headed to Australia."

"Leaving you to handle Mommy Dearest," John cracked.

"Exactly."

Gloria motioned to the auditorium door. "We'll be starting soon. We should get in there." Gloria took the stage, followed by John and Michele. Gloria walked up to the microphone. "We're going to do our regular praise and worship tonight, but I wanted to take a few moments to acknowledge Michele Sheradon. Some of you have met her; many of you have not. Michele and her husband, Jimmy, are the designers, creators, and owners of this camp and several more like it."

The room burst into applause. These men and women had been rescued from concentration camp conditions. Now they lived Christian lives in a world where Christianity was banned. They knew full well they were among the very most fortunate people on earth—all due to the foresight, commitment, and courage of Michele and Jimmy.

Michele walked to the microphone. "I appreciate the applause—I really do—but I don't deserve it. Jesus left me with the means to do this, led me to the idea, and gave me the grace to see it through. Won't you join me in extending that warm applause to our Redeemer Jesus—the One who will come to reign in less than three years' time!" The building erupted as the audience stood, applauded, and stamped their feet.

Gloria asked them to return to their seats and then ushered in a time of peaceful prayer and worship. To Michele, it felt like she was already in heaven. The worship, prayer, and singing of hymns lasted about an hour. Then an image grew on the screen at the front of the auditorium. Bright light in the background obscured the surroundings of a man who sat only in shadow. This man only went by the moniker "the preacher." Somehow, he managed to break into the global news channels to preach brief words of encouragement. World authorities were livid. Uncle Michael had told Michele that Isa was frantic to find the man and kill him.

"Ladies and gentlemen," the preacher began. His voice was heavily modulated electronically so as not to give any hint of his identity. "Today's message will be short. Do you remember the story of Shadrach, Meshach, and Abednego? A proclamation throughout Babylon demanded everyone to worship the king. Daniel's friends Shadrach, Meshach, and Abednego refused.

"I believe this account has a lot to do with our situation. Where do you suppose Daniel was? This is his book, but there is no reference to where he was when his friends went through the flames. There are a lot of mundane reasons for his absence, for instance, he may have been away in a remote part of the kingdom on royal business. But we can look past those mundane reasons to see a pattern, one that may be prophetic. Daniel wasn't part of the persecution. He was removed from the situation. In this instance, he is a symbol of the rapture. He was snatched away like our believing loved ones. In the wake of his departure, the king grew strong in his opposition to the Lord. The same thing is happening now.

"When Shadrach, Meshach, and Abednego were given one more chance to fall in worship of the king, their response was the King James equivalent of 'Up yours, O King.'" The audience laughed aloud. "The important thing isn't their impertinence but their faith. They would rather be thrown to the flames than deny the Lord. But guess what, the flames didn't harm them. In fact, the Bible says they didn't even smell like smoke when they came out of the hot furnace.

"When the king looked into the furnace, he said he saw 'one like a son of god' with the three young men. I submit to you, ladies and gentlemen, that he didn't see 'one like a son of god.' He saw *the* Son of God!" The audience cheered.

"We are living in the worst time of human history. We have only one job—to hold fast to the faith. Whatever the threat from the current regime, do not bow to it. And trust me on this: just as Jesus was with Shadrach, Meshach, and Abednego, He will be there with you and me as we walk through the flames of this horrific time.

"Be strong, my brothers and sisters. Be courageous. This world in its current form has nothing to offer us. If we are called to die in Christ, bring it on. If we are called to live through this in Christ, bring it on!" His voice grew louder. "If we are called either way, bring it on, because in Christ either is victory!" The crowd rose up and cheered.

He resumed in a soft tone. "Alive or dead, I am Christ's. The same applies to you. We have less than three years left before our glorious Savior cracks the sky to bring justice and peace. To live or to die, either is gain in Christ.

"I pray the holy peace of God upon you tonight. May the Holy Spirit rest upon you, dwell in you, and energize you for the days to come. In Jesus's name, amen."

Michele felt the glow of the Spirit's warmth as it coursed through her body. She didn't want to move. She only wanted to luxuriate in the power of His love. They sat in silent worship for half an hour, being refreshed by God.

Michael was wakened by his ringing telephone. He flung himself out of bed to answer. "Hello," he said sleepily.

"It happened again!" Zack screamed into the phone.

"What happened?" Michael asked, as if he didn't know.

"The preacher!" Zack screamed. "He got onto all of our stations again!"

"Did you trace the signal?" Michael asked.

"We tried. It came from no identifiable source."

"So, why are you calling me?" Michael asked.

"Isa's going to kill me when he finds out we can't track the signal!" Zack exclaimed.

"Good," Michael said as he slammed down the phone. They would never trace the signal. The good thing about a quantum system is its interdimensionality. In the quantum world, the signal exists and doesn't exist at the same time. For a brief moment, the signal flipped its potentiality and existed in the worldwide network, and then it simply ceased to exist.

"Really, Mom," Michael said to his dark apartment, "I can't wait to thank you for buying up those shares in our quantum computer company."

He returned to sleep, praying not to have another dream of the blue Satan murdering Gabe upon Jesus's return.

TWELVE

The agent's flight landed in Almaty, Kazakhstan. Once the capital of the nation, the old city had been abandoned by the political elite in favor of Astana, a newly created city in the north. At first, the change doomed Almaty to a slow-motion economic decline, but the fall of communism and the subsequent drilling of the nation's vast natural gas deposits brought the city back to life. The resultant cityscape of Almaty was a striking contradiction in terms as Western architecture and neon lights stood in stark contrast to the nondescript concrete buildings of the Soviet era.

Customs was a challenge. A large metal case carried the agent's rifle. In his suitcase were two pistols: one he carried with a shoulder holster, and a smaller one he wore around his ankle. The government had outlawed firearms for everyone but police and the armed services. He showed them his Vatican clearance, but his Russian wasn't good and the customs officials weren't conversant in English, Italian, or German, all of which he spoke fluently.

With enough haggling and a phone call to the officer's supervisor, who had a cursory knowledge of English, his admittance to the country finally was cleared, albeit grudgingly. People didn't trust a world government operative entering their nation with weapons.

The agent rented a Niva, a Russian jeep, and drove south toward the Muyunkum desert, a barren land resembling Monument Valley in the United States, but with a much colder climate. His informant had told him to go toward Tortkuduk, a town built around uranium mining. In the local bar there, he would meet a man named Dmitry— no last name.

The drive was very scenic. For a few hours he pondered the state of the world. The inoculated masses were zombie facsimiles of the people they had once been. He held no disdain for those who had taken the mark. He pitied them. They had been duped into following their leader to hell. First a hell on earth that barely fazed them in their delusion of preparing for an existential battle with the Anu. After that they would suffer an eternal hell, where their faculties would be restored to them only to face endless regret that they hadn't chosen Jesus.

The desert vista gave way to the Karatau Mountains in the distance. He drove toward them, knowing he would find Tortkuduk at their base. Soon enough he arrived at a ramshackle collection of buildings almost too small to be called a town, just a large factory in the scrubby desert surrounded by very meager homes. Life didn't look any too easy in Tortkuduk.

He found the bar, a dilapidated establishment in a run-down wooden building that looked as if it hadn't seen a coat of paint since the Soviet days. He pushed on a crookedly hung door to find that the interior of the building was as depressing as its exterior. Dark walls faded to black in the shadow of a bright fluorescent light hung in the center of the ceiling. There was a bar to his right and a few tables with steel legs and worn linoleum tops to his left. It was the middle of the day. The place was empty except for the tired-looking bartender and a heavy woman who was sleeping off a hangover at one of the tables. He strode up to the bar and ordered a beer, *"Pivo, pozhaluysta."*

He pointed to a bar tap with Cyrillic writing. From what he could tell, he ordered a Kazakh beer with a name that translated to Red Wolf. He tasted the brew—obviously watered down—and smiled. *"Spasibo,"* he said. "Thank you."

"Gde Dmitry?" the agent asked. (Where is Dmitry?)

"Dmitry?"

"Da."

"Odna minuta," the bartender answered, indicating that the agent should wait a minute. Then he left to find Dmitry while the agent nursed his beer. He looked at the television. In the old days it might have shown a soccer match. Today it was yet another Kurtoglu speech to encourage tireless work.

True to his word, the bartender reappeared in only a minute with

Dmitry in tow. Dmitry was a short, squat man with beady eyes and a bushy beard that did a lot to hide the green pallor of his inoculation.

The agent stood. "Dmitry?" he asked.

The man nodded. He spoke English, as their mutual contact had instructed. "And you are?"

The agent smiled. He never gave his name. "The one sent to meet with you," he answered.

"What I should call you?" Dmitry asked.

"Don't call me anything," the agent said briskly.

Not all people who took the mark changed in attitude. Some, like Dmitry, had been old horse traders before the mark, and inoculation just made them more efficient and ruthless in their pursuit of gain. "Let's get down to business," the agent said.

"Yes, business. I want a thousand credits to my account."

"Done," the agent said. With the programmers accessing the global system, he could easily transfer the funds to Dmitry's account.

"When will I receive money?" Dmitry grunted.

"When you have given me your information. It is a simple deal."

"Fine," Dmitry said. "My sister is married to a renegade. He refuses inoculation. Says Lord Kurtoglu is Antichrist, and inoculation will take his family to hell."

"Imagine that," the agent said with a deceitful grin of disbelief.

"I know!" Dmitry exclaimed. "People like him will ruin life for the rest of us. The Anu will take advantage of our lack of unity. Chain only as strong as weakest link." The agent recognized those words from a public service announcement issued by Kurtoglu and the pope.

"How many are we talking about in total?" the agent asked.

"With my brother-in-law's family and some friends, probably *shto* ... how to say in English ... hundred."

"Do you know where they meet?"

"Barn. Up in mountains."

The agent pulled a small notebook and pen from his breast pocket. He clicked the pen, handed it to Dmitry, and said, "Draw me a map. Write your sister's and brother-in-law's names."

Dmitry drew the map. Mostly the route consisted of following a dirt road out of town until it turned into a path up the mountain. He doubted he would have any trouble finding it. Dmitry wrote the names in a Cyrillic hand. It took a few moments for the agent to decipher them. "Your sister is Adrina Slatpova?"

"Da."

"How often does the church meet?"

Dmitry shrugged. "Don't know for sure. I think every day, six o'clock."

The agent looked at the map and then at his watch. There was a strong chance he could complete his task today. He pulled out his cell phone and pressed a button. "Savario, transfer half of the funds to Dmitry."

"Half?" Dmitry asked.

"A down payment. If your information checks out, we will deposit the remainder."

Dmitry tilted his head toward the floor, raised his eyebrows, and opened his eyes wide, a typical Russian cussing stance. "*Mu'dak*," he said.

The agent knew enough Russian to understand the word would loosely be translated as "asshole." He grabbed Dmitry by the lapel, saying harshly, "*Idi syuda!*" (Come here!)

Dmitry blanched at the agent's iron grip. Seeing the fear in his eyes, the agent yanked Dmitry's face to within a centimeter of his own, pulling Dmitry up on his toes.

In slow, clipped English, the agent warned," You must always be polite with me, Dmitry. Bad things happen to people who aren't polite with me."

"D-da," Dmitry stammered with a dry mouth. He licked his lips.

The agent slowly lowered him and brushed away any wrinkles he may have left on Dmitry's jacket. Then he turned and left the bar.

On the ride out of town, the agent castigated himself. In the old days, he wouldn't have thought twice about putting a bit of fear into Dmitry. But since his commitment to Jesus, the actions felt forced and unnatural.

"Ah, Lord," he said aloud. "I don't know the right answer. If I have offended You, I apologize. On the other hand, if a little fear in Dmitry will help to keep a hundred of Your children safe, I gratefully accept the task."

He felt sudden serenity, taking it to mean his actions served a much greater purpose. "Desperate times call for desperate measures, right, Lord?"

He took the road until it ended at the base of the mountain and parked the Niva on a level spot near a grouping of trees. After exiting the vehicle and taking his rifle from its case, he took another look at Dmitry's map, estimating an uphill trek of a kilometer along a path winding to a steppe farmed by Slatpov's community. He moved slowly, trying to make no sound and staying close to trees for cover. Slatpov most likely had people watching. The last thing the agent wanted was for the community to go into hiding before he arrived.

The rustling of a brook! He relaxed with the sound cover, taking a quicker pace.

Then it happened. A teenaged boy with a fishing pole and some fish crossed onto the path ahead of him. He darted behind a tree, but it was too late. The boy had seen him and run off. The agent couldn't let him warn the others. He took off in a mad dash after the boy.

The kid was fast, and the agent was feeling his age. Ignoring pain in his right hamstring, he pushed harder, eventually overtaking and tackling the boy. Before the kid could scream, the agent covered his mouth as he pinned him to the path. The boy's eyes were wide with terror. The agent guessed he was around fifteen.

In Russian, the agent said quietly, "I mean no harm. I'm here to help. Do you understand?"

The boy nodded. The agent removed his hand.

"How can you help?" the boy asked in English.

"How did you know I speak English?" the agent asked.

"Your accent is horrible," the young man said with just a hint of a grin.

A smart aleck! The agent laughed. As he helped the boy to stand, the agent noticed he wore a cross—a risky act of defiance in the new world.

"What's your name?"

"Maks," the boy answered.

"Well, Maks, do you love Jesus?"

The question took him off guard. The agent could see the terror in the young man's face. He watched as Maks considered his options. Finally deciding he couldn't deny Jesus, he squared his shoulders, stuck out his chin, and said, "I do, and I always will. Even if you kill me."

The agent smiled and patted Maks on the shoulder. "I have no plans to hurt you, Maks, only to help you."

Maks sighed and motioned with a quick upturn of his chin. "You going to help me with that rifle?" he asked.

"In a way," the agent answered. "I have a plan to help your group, but I really could use a translator. Will you help me?"

"If I don't like plan, I don't help," Maks said decisively, looking squarely at the agent.

The agent didn't know if it was just teenaged hubris or if Maks had some serious courage. Either way, he found himself really liking the kid.

Maks led him to the barn where the congregation was gathering. They watched from the shadows of heavily leaved trees along the perimeter. The agent liked Maks and trusted him to a degree, but years of training left him untrusting of any coopted collaboration. He kept one eye on the growing group in the barn and one eye on Maks.

One woman hesitated to go in. She kept looking toward the path down the mountain. "My mother," Maks said quietly.

The agent said carefully. "Go to her with your fish and your pole. Tell her you are late and you will take the fish home and meet them in church."

Maks frowned. "She will tell me to wash. Disrespectful to come before God with fish smell."

"Agree with her," the agent said. "Just get her to go into the meeting."

Maks did as he was told. She berated him for his lateness and held her nose at the smell of the fish. Then she huffed into the barn. It went down just as Maks had said. He returned to the shadows with a broad grin and shrugged his shoulders. The agent chuckled.

They waited just a few moments until the service began. The agent heard the lilting sound of a hymn sung softly so as not to alert anyone to their presence. He left the shadows and motioned for Maks to follow him. "Do you remember our plan?"

Maks tapped his index finger on his temple. "Got it."

"Okay, let's go."

At the door to the barn, the agent swung his rifle from his shoulder, pointed it straight ahead of him, and disengaged the safety. He motioned to Maks to open the door.

The singing came to an abrupt halt when the pastor, Slatpov, yelled to the crowd to take cover. They all fell to the floor.

The agent said through Maks, "All prepared to die for Jesus, stand in front of me. Those who are not, you may leave."

The people rose from the floor. Slatpov, who bore the resemblance of a Russian Ichabod Crane, defiantly placed himself inches away from the rifle. His wife, Adrina, stood beside him, linking her arm in his. Like her brother, Dmitry, she was short and a bit overweight.

The congregation lined up behind them, each with a look of defiance and resignation. But the agent reasoned there had to be at least one mole in the group. The agent screamed his ultimatum another time. Maks dutifully translated, mimicking his intonation.

From the back of the crowd, a young man strode to the front. He was very gaunt, and his eyes looked vacant. He denied Jesus. Maks interpreted.

"Anyone else?" the agent screamed, followed immediately by Maks.

There was nobody. The agent trained his gun on the traitor and spoke to Maks in English. "Maks, do you have a handkerchief to wipe this man's face? If not, use your shirt sleeve."

Maks did as he was told. One wipe of the man's face revealed the pallor of inoculation. This could be a serious matter going forward. Until now, the agent had never heard of someone with the mark being aware of his own changes.

"Do you speak English?" he asked the man.

"Yes."

"You have done a fine job. I will handle it from here."

"A fee was offered," the man said gruffly.

"Fine," the agent said curtly. "How much?"

"Five hundred credits."

"Treachery comes cheap these days," the agent said in disgust. "Show me your hand."

The agent waved his phone over the man's hand to read his transaction data on the embedded chip. He forwarded the information to the programmers, who moved the credits.

"Done," the agent said. He pointed the gun at the traitor and said menacingly, "Now leave this mountain and never come back. I'll know if you do, and I will kill you."

The man burst through the barn doors onto the path down the mountain. The agent engaged the safety on his rifle and put it back over his shoulder while Maks explained that the plan had been to flush out the traitor. The agent asked if he could worship with them.

The group was still nervous, but they resumed their places. Slatpov started with the hymn again. The agent and Maks took places at the rear. The agent's Russian was rusty, but he got the meaning of Slatpov's sermon. Without a doubt the man had been anointed by God to minister to people in the end times.

As the service drew to a close, the agent asked if he could speak to the group. Through Maks he said, "As Christians you understand the inoculation is the mark of the beast about which we were warned in the book of Revelation. You have wisely decided not to take the mark and its embedded transaction chip in favor of living in a self-sufficient manner on this lovely mountain. You are to be commended. However, the government plans to hunt down and kill all resisters.

"My friends and I have developed a method to make it look as if you have received the mark in the government's computer system. We can hack the system and assign a fake nanochip transponder to your name. A separate program will feed the government system with false transactions, thereby creating a virtual you to take away your resister status."

The group applauded, but not too loudly, ever mindful of the secretive nature of their meeting. The agent continued, "I wish we could offer the same to every Christian, but it can only work for those who have formed remnant communities separate and distinct from the populace. We save who we can. We ask you to keep those others in your prayers.

"To process your information, I need you to tell my compatriot your name, birth date, and citizen identification number. He will use this information to establish your virtual presence."

The agent dialed the quantum-encrypted phone he'd received from Michael. When the programmer, Eduardo Benno, answered, the group formed a line to provide their information. During this time, the agent met individually with and prayed with most of the parishioners.

Then he took a bit of time with Maks, who had been an invaluable help. Pulling the notebook from his jacket pocket, he wrote down a phone number, ripped out the sheet, and handed it to the boy. "Maks, this is the phone number to a secure line. If you ever need my help, leave a message identifying yourself only as Maks. I'll do my best to get to you."

"Thanks," Maks said with a grin. "You are pretty nice for a foreigner with a gun."

"You're pretty nice, too," the agent said. Then he mused that he must be getting soft in his old age. The truth was that the Spirit of God was rounding out the sharp edges of his personality.

When they had all given their information, the agent took the phone. Benno reported, "Good job, boss. We got one hundred nine names. That brings our total close to five thousand."

"These are good people, Benno, and I'm happy to help them. Sometimes, though, I'm saddened by the millions we can't help."

THIRTEEN

Michael and Will had taken an early breakfast together before heading out to the desert. They were scheduled to attend a review of Isa's new weapons technology.

Will said as their Jeep left Jerusalem, "Jake, I have to warn you, Isa is rabid to find out who the preacher is."

Michael shrugged off the warning. "The messages are recorded on a quantum computer. Literally, Will, they disappear as if they never existed once the broadcast is complete. There is no historical signal for them to trace. There is no access point where the information feeds into their system. It simply is, and then it isn't."

"That makes no sense to me," Will said.

"You're in good company. Einstein called these phenomena spooky action at a distance. I'm an archeologist and linguist by trade, but I've had to learn a lot about quantum mechanics at the hands of the Lady's disc. It's fascinating stuff."

"Well, fascinating or not, I still feel a strong obligation to protect you. All I'm asking is that you make sure to keep *your* spooky action at a distance. Don't save your remarks. Destroy all outlines or notes. These guys are dead serious about finding the preacher and removing him."

"I know, and I'm about as locked down as I can be right now. But I can envision a time when I move into the base at Petra or the safe space under the chapel to continue the work."

"Just let me know before you bug out. I have no interest in staying in Jerusalem. If you go, I'm going with you."

"Will do. You're the only person in Jerusalem I can stand to be around," Michael said with a half grin.

"Wow! Thanks for the ringing endorsement. You mean I'm more fun than Zack?"

Michael acknowledged Will's quip with a grin and a shake of his head. "I can tolerate Isa and Benny better than Zack! They were prophesied in the Bible. They're destined to be here. But Zack is more than I want to bear."

"I hear you. You know, I always thought Zack looked a little reptilian, but since the inoculation, he's looking really bad. I mean, everyone else looks a little green and zombie-ish, but he looks like the Creature from the Black Lagoon."

Michael chuckled. "He doesn't look much worse than the others. It's just that we know him for the snake he is. It colors our perception of him."

"Listen, I didn't like him for who he was, and I hated what he did to Gloria, but that was nothing compared to who he has become. Did Ben-Nergal tell you Isa tasked Zack with lining up crematoriums around the world to deal with the Christian problem?" Will asked.

"Yes. How did you know about that?" Michael asked.

"I work hand in hand with Isa's security team. Those guys may be turning green, but they're good at their jobs. Nothing they observe is outside the realm of our staff meetings. I've harped on them repeatedly that even the smallest detail can tip us off to a potential security leak."

"I suppose that's true. Can you trust them?" Michael asked.

"The inoculation gave them a work ethic better than they ever had, and they're passionate about protecting our imperious leader. I trust their commitment to the job and to Isa—and I milk those tendencies for information," Will explained.

"Well done," Michael complimented.

Will continued, "Every day at four in the afternoon, Zack meets with Isa to tell him the number of Christians murdered in the crematoriums. It's Isa's happiest time of the day. My guys see Zack coming out of his office every afternoon with a big grin. Apparently the Reverend Jolean isn't above slaughtering the flock once he has fleeced it."

"I don't think Zack ever was a Christian. He's always been about as evil as Benny," Michael concluded.

"Speaking of which, what are your days like with old Nergal? You look miserable every time I see you with him," Will commented.

Michael winced. "It's a matter of the lesser of two evils. If I had to be around one or the other, I would choose Nergal over Satan." He wiped at his forehead. "Did you hear what I just said? I can't believe we work in close proximity to the Lord of Darkness."

"I hate it myself," Will said. Then with a mischievous grin he added, "But I console myself with the knowledge that at least he isn't smitten with me like he is with you."

Michael nodded in an exaggerated fashion. "Yeah, thanks for looking at the bright side."

"You have to joke about it, Jake. The fact that we're where we are is absurd, and it couldn't have come about without the hand of God. That very absurdity is what tells me on a daily basis that, despite all the hell coming to earth, God has everything under control."

"Wow, you sure have come a long way in your Christian faith. You're maturing quickly—and quite nicely, I might add." Michael was proud of the man Will had become.

"Well, time is short, and I have an uncle who is a pretty darn good role model."

Michael smiled and shook his head. "So what's happening today, Mr. Security Know-It-All?"

"We're going to get a firsthand look at a prototype of Isa's dark matter weapons."

Michael slumped in his seat. "You know, dark matter was just a theory until your role model teased information about it from the Lady's disc. Naturally, I sent my findings to CERN."

"Naturally," Will mocked with a grin.

"And it's probably a misnomer to call it a dark matter weapon. Dark matter doesn't react with regular matter. The information on the Lady's disc indicated that dark matter is in balance with superpositioned antimatter, sort of the uncollapsed waveforms of existence. When observation leads to the collapse of a waveform, the dark matter is freed from its entanglement to form regular matter. It's a stunning theory because it answers two of the overriding conundrums in physics: What is dark matter? And what happened to the antimatter formed at the big bang? Isa's weapon is likely made by untangling the dark matter to capture the superpositioned antimatter."

Will made an "I'm stupid" face, shook his head, and waved a hand over his head. "Really simple terms, please."

Michael spoke deliberately in a mocking tone. "Isa separate other-dimension antimatter from this-dimension matter. Make big boom."

"Now I understand!" Will exclaimed.

"Here is my concern," Michael said. "Because the antimatter is really just a superposition, it doesn't exactly exist in this dimension."

"But big boom here, not there," Will said with a caveman-like grunt. "Right?"

"Only partly. I think Isa is trying to take out players in higher dimensions."

"Like ..."

"Like Jesus when He returns."

"Okay. I know I'm the stupid one here, but who cares?" Will questioned.

"What?" Michael asked indignantly.

Will removed his right hand from the steering wheel, waving it to make his point. "Either you believe scripture or you don't. We know who wins. What do I care if Isa sticks pins into a voodoo Jesus doll? No matter what he does, he can't win."

"You're probably right," Michael said. "But the more I know about this and the more I see, the more I worry about Isa's potential to do damage in the spiritual dimension."

Will grimaced. "I'm sure you'll figure it out and come to my conclusion anyway. I just did it without all the math. Remember, I was an illusionist in my former life. Illusion is all about making the lie convincing and distracting the audience from the underlying truth. Isa is the father of lies. He can build all kinds of big, bad weapons, but they are just to distract us from the truth that in a little over two years, he's going down."

"You're right. I worry too much," Michael said, and yet his concerns weren't abated.

Will said, "Before we get to the test site, there's something I want to talk to you about—a potential project for the programmers."

"Okay, shoot."

"In the early part of the century, the US Navy developed insect-sized drones. Eventually they developed the technology to key those drones to specific DNA characteristics."

"How do you know this?" Michael asked as Will surprised him yet again.

"I told you, my guys hear a lot of stuff," Will said casually. "These drones sniff out DNA signatures. So, if you can identify a DNA signature specific to your enemy, you can send the drones to infect or kill them. The project name for the drones was Project Locust."

Michael asked incredulously, "So you think these are the locusts in the book of Revelation?"

"Yeah, I do. Isa and the boys are mass-producing them. Any human without Isa's DNA signature will be the target. Here's the thing, though: The individual locusts can't think. They are controlled by Isa's supercomputer," Will said with a broad grin and raised eyebrows.

"Which we can hack. We can change the programming to infect people *with* Isa's DNA," Michael said, continuing the thought.

"Thereby contributing to the fulfillment of prophecy," Will said with a huge smile. "And do you know what that means?"

"Tell me what you think it means," Michael said skeptically.

"It means we're in the book of Revelation. Not by name, but the results of our actions were predicted two thousand years ago. How does that make you feel about God being in control of everything?"

Michael smiled as well. "Pretty darn good, I have to tell you. You might have to cover for me for a day while I head out to Petra to confer with the programmers on how to do this."

"That shouldn't be too hard. We can tell little Ben-Nergal you have the flu. He'll feel all smug and superior that he has an enhanced immune system and you don't."

Michael and Will arrived at the test site before Isa and Benny. An army general graciously escorted them to a makeshift viewing area consisting of ten rows of chairs on a wooden platform. The general led them to the first row of five seats. As he was taking his seat, Michael scanned the attendees in the chairs behind them. Most were military bigwigs. One in particular looked familiar. Finally he recalled the man as the head of his family's aircraft and armament business, the family's original business established by his grandfather Stanford Martin. He went briefly to say hello.

"Graham! I didn't expect to see you here," Michael said cheerily.

"Hi, boss. I didn't expect to see you here either."

Michael shrugged. "I'm not sure why I'm here aside from politics. How about you?"

"These guys go through jets like nobody's business. I got the opportunity to come here to see what they're doing with them."

"Well, it's nice to see you," Michael said. "While I have you here, I thought maybe I could ask you if we are doing anything on Project Locust."

Graham grimaced. "The US Navy's Low-Cost UAV Swarming Technology on steroids! The goal is to produce bug-sized drones that can be used to deliver lethal poisons based on the DNA of the target. The plan is to keep them in reserve in case the Anu form a beachhead on Earth."

"But we don't have Anu DNA to use in programming the drones, do we?" Michael asked.

"None that I know of. We're using the inoculation DNA in tests. If the target identifies as humanoid but doesn't carry the inoculation gene, the drones swarm and strike."

"Wow!" Michael exclaimed in pretend awe to cover a sickening feeling that the tests were conducted using uninoculated human subjects. "Is our company responsible for programming the drones?"

Graham shook his head and explained, "The drones are programmed to assess targets according to a protocol based on criteria uploaded from the government's supercomputer."

Michael grinned. "Interesting technology." He shook his head. "I was such a sci-fi geek when I was a kid. I never thought I'd actually get the chance to live it."

"I hear you," Graham said. "If it weren't for the upcoming Anu threat, life would be about perfect for me."

With the possible exception you're on your way to hell. Michael saw the arrival of Isa's limousine and brought the conversation to an abrupt close. Taking his seat next to Will, he said under his breath, "Here come Larry, Curly, and Moe."

Will sniggered as a speaker blasted "Hail to the Chief" to announce Isa's arrival. The group applauded until Isa and Benny took their places, leaving the seat beside Michael open for Zack. Michael nodded hello. Zack grunted, and the show began.

An armored tractor trailer pulled onto the barren desert in front of the viewing stand. Doors in its roof retracted, and equipment resembling a large spotlight rose from inside. The driver of the truck stepped out in a uniform encrusted with medals, looking like the world's most distinguished war hero. He stood at attention, awaiting a signal to begin.

Isa waved his arm to commence the demonstration. The war hero spoke into a microphone feeding speakers alongside the viewing stand. "Excellency, Holiness, and our guests, you are about to see the culmination of years of scientific advances in particle beam technology combined with the most recent discoveries from CERN. I could take you through the details, but frankly a display of power is much more convincing than anything I could say."

The sound of fighter jets roared over the horizon. In seconds, they were over the viewing area. They turned around overhead and flew away while the beam weapon powered up. The spotlight glowed brilliantly and began to emit a loud, high-pitched hum.

Three jets flew over the horizon. Michael would have guessed they were going full throttle. The hum of the weapon grew louder until it vibrated the viewing stand on which they sat. Then a brilliant strobe of light cracked the air. For a second it looked like the planes stood still, and then they vanished into puffs of smoke.

The spectators in the viewing stand erupted with cheers and applause. The hero continued, "As you can see, Excellency, this technology should make it very hard for the Anu to enter our airspace. If they dare, they will be reduced to their constituent atoms as easily as these planes and their pilots were."

"Pilots?" Michael questioned aloud. "They weren't drone jets?"

Zack looked at him with disdain, whispering, "Think about it, Michael. Time is limited. We need to test these weapons in real-life combat simulations."

"So the pilots were vaporized." Michael snorted.

Zack answered with a smug grin, "Well, they weren't indispensable.

You would be amazed how many members of the armed services refused to be inoculated based on the old-school thought that we're in the end times—the kind of stuff your brother believed."

Michael blanched at the mention of Gabe. "They flew Christians to their deaths," he said briskly.

"They would have ended up there anyway. At least with this type of sacrifice, their lives have been a benefit to society." Zack smiled his trademark toothy grin. Michael had always found it insincere and haunting. Now with Zack's light green pallor, the smile had all the charm of a cobra. Michael shivered.

Will whispered into his ear, "I know it's hard to accept that good men were killed, but don't lose it. You have to play the game." Will was right. Michael suppressed a look of disgust.

They performed another test during which jets were tasked with shooting missiles at the weapon. Same result. The missiles and aircraft paused in midair for a second and then vanished into puffs of smoke. More deaths. More applause and cheers.

When the demonstration ended, Isa stood to speak to the observers. "Gentlemen, I trust you share my hopefulness about our efforts to thwart the Anu. We will soon finish our work on the next generation of these devices. I promise you, we will be ready, willing, and able to blow the marauders out of the sky."

For most of the ride home Michael was quiet, mulling the technology at Isa's disposal. "Cat got your tongue?" Will finally asked.

"No. Just the same fears I expressed on the way here. Isa has built weapons that may well work in the spiritual plane. It concerns me."

"God has everything under control," Will assured him.

———

Michael slept poorly that night. In his fitful sleep he had a very realistic dream. He and Gabe were standing in a crowd around the throne of God. God was no color and every color at the same time, like a diamond reflecting light from its many-prismed surface.

Next to the Father stood Jesus, but He also looked like a lamb. Nudging Gabe, Michael said, "Dude, I think we're in the book of Revelation."

"I think you're right," Gabe said, grinning from ear to ear.

"How did that happen?" Michael asked.

"Don't talk now, Michael. Pay attention. Jesus is about to break the seventh seal."

There was silence. The crowd of witnesses, of which Michael was now a part, stood in reverent awe as Jesus picked up a large scroll. He broke the seal, and the heralds of millions of trumpets rang out. Then seven angels marched to His side, each with a large golden trumpet.

The first angel blew his trumpet, followed quickly by the second and third. Michael looked at Gabe for an explanation. Gabe pointed over Michael's shoulder. Michael turned to see a swarm of meteors and a large asteroid bearing down on Earth.

"The Nemesis system is surrounded by debris accumulated from previous crossings into the solar system," Gabe explained.

"And the debris is heading to Earth now?" Michael asked.

Gabe nodded slowly, somberly.

Michael awakened with a start and went to his bedroom window. In the moonless night, the sky twinkled peacefully with stars. Yet, one star out there was on a path to bring incredible destruction.

FOURTEEN

Zack sat at his desk in the anteroom to Isa's apartment. Like the apartment, his office was a study in boredom: white on white with a black desk and black leather chairs. It certainly was a step down from his office at Riverside.

Jerusalem wasn't all Zack had hoped it would be. To be sure, the esteem of being Isa's assistant was a dream come true, but it came with a price. He hadn't fully appreciated Isa's demanding nature and violent disapproval. Until being conscripted to this task, Zack had imagined the temperate, supportive, caring personage portrayed to the cameras.

The reality of the situation was very different. Isa was mercurial. Zack never knew when he would erupt over any small thing. He was also tireless. If the man slept, Zack never saw it. That basically meant Zack lived on call 24/7.

He didn't mind the larger tasks. Setting up the worldwide network of crematoriums felt like real work. Yes, he understood the very nature of it was gruesome, but desperate times called for desperate measures. Everyone on earth had an opportunity to be part of the resistance. Those who refused became de facto parts of the problem. The stakes were exceedingly high, and Zack took his task seriously. His daily recounting of crematorium statistics found Isa at his most pleasant. Isa claimed he could actually feel the enhanced unity with the elimination of those who refused to share his DNA. In a small way, Zack thought he could feel it too.

That aspect of his job was fine. It made him feel like he was contributing to the cause. But Isa expected him to be equally enthused about the most mundane things. Isa was a terrible eater. Nothing pleased him. Constantly he would call Zack to berate his food, and Zack would work with the kitchen staff to develop different recipes. Sometimes the new food worked for a day or a week, but at some point, Isa would throw another fit, and Zack would be on the hook.

Still, Isa was better than the pope. Zack would never forget or forgive his sexual humiliation at that man's hands. Benny's newfound baritone voice annoyed him to tears. His fawning attention to Isa wore on him. But more than anything, he hated Benny's assistant.

"Michael!" The very name rolled off Zack's lips like a cussword. Because of him, Zack had lost Riverside, where he was treated like a god. Nobody in Houston *ever* got in his face about anything. Now he was stuck hoping against hope Isa would like the brussels sprouts in tonight's dinner.

There had to be a way to be rid of Michael. Zack would have thought the man's refusal to be inoculated would be enough reason for Excellency and Holiness to be done with him. God knows people all over the world shared far worse recompense for such a decision. But Michael was still Isa's favorite. There had to be a way to get Isa to like Zack better than Michael. A time would come. Zack would stay vigilant to recognize it.

He glanced at his watch. Jumping from his desk, he ran down the hallway so as not to be late for a security meeting. He hated the security team, but Isa recently mandated his presence at their weekly staff meetings, which were little more than rehashing of programs in place to keep Isa and Benny safe.

He understood the reason for the meetings but not the reason for having Will as head of Benny's security. As if Michael weren't bad enough, he had to look at Gabe Redux once a week. He entered the conference room just as the meeting began, quietly taking the remaining seat. Just his luck! He was seated across the table from Will.

There were only a handful of people in the meeting. Most grunted hello. Will did as well. He looked exceptionally pale to Zack this morning. The first speaker, the head of Isa's personal security team, Sharif Kawan, droned on about the group's progress against its annual goals—the first section of the weekly binder. Sharif's swarthy complexion, full beard, and intense stare bore testimony to his former life as a Hamas insurgent. Zack found him to be uncouth. Rather than pay attention to a man he disdained, Zack leafed through the information. The meetings followed the same agenda. He didn't know why they didn't just send out the binder each week instead of having these interminable sessions.

As he perused the binder, he went through the typical pages of computer printouts summarizing access to government facilities and unusual data requests by Temple Mount employees—all things that jazzed the imaginations of security analysts but bored Zack to tears.

Then his eyes fell on a curious notation in the middle of a page. Michael had requested astronomical images. How bizarre! Since Isa's assumption of power, he had made all such data highly classified. There was about to be a war with an extraterrestrial society, mandating the highest security clearance for all astronomical data.

Could Michael be using secure information about Earth's enemies to undermine Isa's plans? It certainly wouldn't be inconsistent with the Christian fascist belief that Isa was the Antichrist. Could this be the smoking gun Zack needed to get rid of Michael once and for all? There was only one way to know. Zack would request the same data once the meeting ended. He turned down the corner of the page. Looking up, he realized he had caught Will's attention and quickly changed his place in the binder.

Soon, it was Zack's turn to speak about the inoculation process. He cleared his throat as he began. "As detailed in my section of the binder, in the first month of inoculations, 75 percent of the planet's population was given Excellency's DNA enhancement. In the following three months, we picked up stragglers—people who weren't heavily invested in the new global order but succumbed to the economic pressure of not being able to transact any business without the chip included in the inoculation. That brought us to nearly 87 percent.

"The remainder has a different demographic. They cling to old religious symbols, stating they would rather die than be inoculated. It has been our policy of late to grant their desire." There was a chuckle from those seated around the table. Zack grinned with them and noted Will had not laughed.

"Even though the percentage of citizens not inoculated is relatively small, it still translates to sixty-five million to seventy million people. Relieving so many people of the burden of noncompliance is a daunting task.

"A few of the outlying communities eventually accept our system. Just this week, I learned of a group of one hundred or so who were inoculated in Kazakhstan. In the same period, crematoriums in our network removed another five thousand. But these numbers are a drop in the bucket."

There were grumblings around the table. Sharif said dismally, "Sixty-five million people could do a lot of damage if we see a repeat of the magnetic anomaly that brought about the Dark Awakening. To my mind, so many potential time bombs constitute an imminent threat. We can't be fighting them and the Anu at the same time." Most around the table agreed. Again, Zack noted that Will did not.

"You've been quiet, Will. Do you disagree?" Zack asked, putting the man on the spot.

"Just taking it all in," Will said with an oblique smile.

"But, do you disagree that these people are a danger?" asked Sharif.

"I think the main dangers are the Anu and the Nemesis crossing. Taking the focus off those threats is dangerous as well."

Sharif grumbled but accepted Will's answer.

Zack continued, "I'll be convening a teleconference of military commanders in the world's ten regions. So far, the existing crematoriums in our network won't be enough to meet our needs. We'll require the army corps of engineers to build large-scale facilities."

"But doesn't that divert the military's attention from the larger Anu threat?" Will asked.

Zack cut him off, saying with a sneer, "I don't think so. Even if it did, it wouldn't take long to build the requisite facilities."

Zack wrapped up his part of the meeting with a vow to eliminate those who refused the inoculation. He stared a hole through Will as he said deliberately, "Come hell or high water, I *will* have 100 percent compliance before the Anu arrive."

It was next Will's turn to talk about security around Benny's upcoming meeting of world religious leaders. "The purpose of the gathering is to provide hope and encouragement to the world as we near the arrival of the Anu. There's a possibility the pope's message might induce more people to accept inoculation, thereby helping Zack in his quest."

Zack chuckled. He noted how Will refused to meet his eyes as he said it. In Zack's mind there was not even a chance Will and Michael were working for the world order.

Will continued, "Jerusalem again will be on lockdown during the three-day meeting. You will be inconvenienced by scanners and other security measures every time you leave and reenter the Temple Mount. Basically, anything you can't take on a plane, you can't bring to the Temple Mount." There were dissatisfied groans from around the table.

Sharif sided with Will. "I don't care how much you dislike it, we must protect Excellency and Holiness at any cost."

Will thanked him and continued until he had finished his portion of the meeting. As Will always did, he asked, "Any questions?"

Zack jumped at the chance. "Excellency has been most annoyed by the preacher's broadcasts, particularly the manner in which his messages are delivered. Someone has found a way to hack into our worldwide communication network. The security implications are staggering. What are you doing about it?"

Will sighed and moved forward in his chair. "As you know, we've tried to trace the signal, but it doesn't have any identifiable source."

Sharif added in exasperation, "It is literally as if the message pops into existence as a burst of information and then ceases to exist."

Another member of the group in charge of information technology security added, "We're not exaggerating about it never existing. Even though we have seen the messages, they cannot be recorded."

Will continued, "You can't track a signal with no origin, no destination, and no evidence of existence after the fact."

"Yeah, well, I'll let you tell that to Excellency, because he blows a gasket every time he sees another transmission," Zack said in a raised voice. All around the table cringed.

Sharif spoke. "His aggravation doesn't help the situation. It would be easier for us all if he weren't riled up every time the preacher speaks."

"What are you implying?" Zack asked. "You don't want me to tell him when there's a breach?" He didn't like where this conversation was going. Soon they would be asking him to run interference with Isa on their behalf.

Will answered, "He can't have his fingers in everything. A large part of our job is to filter information and only bring to his attention the most important things."

"And you don't think it's important when our security has been breached?"

"There are varying levels of potential danger in a security breach," Will said. "If someone hacks into our weapons systems, it's a whole lot more dangerous than if someone preaches old world Gospel. Nobody is telling you to lie to Excellency, but maybe you could do a better job of filtering the information so that only the highest-priority stuff gets his attention."

Zack fumed. Suddenly this meeting was about him not doing his job! He glared at Will.

Will turned to the head of Isa's security staff. "Sharif, help me out here."

Sharif responded, "Excellency has a task nobody would want. He has to keep this world running and protect it from an unprecedented invasion. We have always tried to ensure he stays on task by limiting the issues we bring to his attention."

"By 'we,' you mean you fellows—before I came along," Zack snapped.

Will responded calmly, "We all know you want to impress him, Zack, but you'll soon learn he doesn't want gossip and palace intrigue. By virtue of the fact that you bring a situation to him, he thinks you can't handle it and need his help."

"Exactly," Sharif intoned.

Zack slammed himself back in his chair as if slapped.

Sharif remarked sternly, "You can act like an offended teenager, or you can listen to some advice. We've been dealing with him for a much longer time than you have. If you continue to take every little problem to him, he'll soon find you to be a useless drain on his time and energy."

Zack was still angry, but he listened. He didn't think for a moment Will had his best interests at heart, but Sharif? "What do you suggest? That I lie to him?" he asked.

"No," Sharif said sternly. "He will know in an instant if you do. Let me ask you this: How many preacher broadcasts has he seen?"

"All of them."

"How did he see them?" Will asked.

"I turned them on for him—called his attention to them," Zack admitted sullenly.

Sharif said, "Exactly. In your mind you were alerting him to some- one who showed him disrespect. Am I right?"

Zack didn't answer. Rather, he stared at Sharif with disdain.

Sharif asked again, harshly, "Am I right?"

Zack said sullenly, "Well, yes. I thought he would want to know of any dissent."

Will said with a roll of his eyes, "I think you were trying to display your loyalty by pointing out another's betrayal."

"How dare you!" Zack fumed. What was it about this family? Why were they destined to plague him wherever he was?

"It's not an illogical assumption," Sharif said coldly.

Zack pursed his lips rather than respond as he wished. He hated the mirror they held up to him, but in the back of his mind he began to wonder if they were right. He couldn't prove it, but he thought Michael was the preacher. Would he throw his own career under the bus for the opportunity to plant doubt about Michael in Isa's mind? He had to admit that the facts didn't look good. Softly, he asked, "What do you suggest?"

Will spoke in a conciliatory tone. "We've found it best to deal with him as silent servants. Speak when spoken to. He assumes you can handle your job without his help."

Sharif continued, "Every time you interrupt his day with an un- solved problem, you distract him from the very important tasks that consume him—namely, the safety of the entire planet. Why focus his attention on some pathetic unknown man with a message that died years ago?"

The IT security analyst chimed in. "When you bring an unsolved problem to his attention, it creates in him the perception you can't handle it."

"So, put yourself in Isa's shoes," Will said. "At some point, he's going to wonder about your value if you only bring to him problems and not solutions."

"I see," Zack said. "Let's say I think this preacher's breach of our systems is a problem. How do you suggest I handle it?"

"Well, first, assess the problem," Will answered sharply. "And that may mean you have to ask us about it. As discussed earlier, the threat level of this particular breach is pretty small."

"Agreed," said the IT analyst. "There have been absolutely no attempts to hack our weapons or critical infrastructure. None! From a
hacking perspective, the world has never been more safe."

"I didn't realize," Zack said softly.

"Because you ran to Isa before even asking anybody in security
about the threat," Will accused.

Sharif added, "You don't like the preacher's message. None of us
do. It's a slap in the face to a virtual god who has come back from the
dead to save us. If I found this guy, I'd kill him myself. But our job is
not to run to Excellency with things we don't like. It's first to assess
the threat, then prioritize it, and then neutralize it."

"These are things you guys are supposed to do!" Zack countered.

"These are things we've done," Sharif said. "We have looked into
this. We assign it a low threat level and, therefore, a low priority given
the much more horrific issues on our horizon."

"Fine," Zack growled. "I overreacted. It won't happen again."
Inwardly he seethed.

Later in his office, Zack used Isa's security clearance to access the information Michael had requested. It was a Hubble shot of the intruder
in all its smoldering glory. The legend said the photo was taken in the
infrared spectrum—light in a bandwidth below the eye's level to per-
ceive. The big red orb was punctuated with black striations and was
difficult to see through a reddish haze.

How could this matter to Michael? There was no denying the man
was a genius. Did he see something others hadn't? Then again, after
today's meeting, Zack was pretty sure nobody, including Michael,
would present any finding to Isa without vetting it.

"I don't know what you're up to, Michael Martin," Zack said with
a sour grin, "but I promise I'll find out."

FIFTEEN

Michael's workdays were different since he'd returned. He didn't like Nergal very much, and Nergal wasn't very fond of him. But unlike Benny, Nergal wasn't needy. So, their interactions weren't as time-consuming as Michael's constant care for Benny, allowing Michael a lot of time to work on the preacher's messages and to confer with the programmers in Petra.

He also studied the gathering of Jewish Christians in the ancient remains of Petra. The desecration of the holy of holies with Isa's blood, the ascension of the witnesses, and Isa's resurrection combined to sway the hearts of thousands of Jews. Following the great Jerusalem quake, they streamed out of Israel to Petra. At first, they were denied passage into Jordan, but eventually their numbers grew too strong. Going through the desert like their ancient ancestors, they found their place of refuge. For a while it looked like Isa would stop their exodus, but when a flash flood in the mountains separated his men from the fleeing Jews, he called a retreat.

"Just like You said in Revelation," Michael said in amazement to the Lord.

"Talking to yourself again?" Nergal asked with annoyance. Unlike Benny, who would never think to bring work to Michael, Nergal made the occasional appearance in Michael's space. Usually he was aggressive when he did so.

"Just a bit," Michael said with a sardonic grin. "What can I do for you?"

"I was bored and thought you might amuse me," Nergal said condescendingly.

"I'm afraid you made a wasted trip," Michael announced sternly.

"Maybe you could me tell how much our family's company is worth these days?" Nergal asked with a malicious chuckle.

"Well, let's be clear, it is not your family business—not yours, not Benny's."

Nergal laughed long and hard. Michael knew he had no interest in the business. It was just Nergal's way of passing the time by making him uncomfortable.

"Maybe I should consider visiting Atlanta to sort of take an inventory," Nergal offered.

This type of conversation had occurred several times in the past few days. Prior to that, it was only once a week or so. So far Michael had refused to be baited. But he could feel himself growing angry today, even though he knew anger was just what Nergal wanted.

"So, tell me," Nergal said with a thin smile, "what do you think of this preacher who has everyone so hot and bothered?"

"I haven't thought much about it," Michael said. He stood from his desk with a pile of papers. His back was to Nergal as he filed them. It felt good not to look at him.

Nergal changed tactics. "You don't like Zack much. Is it because you saw him with Benny in the family chapel? Because I have to say, that chapel has never seen such fun," Nergal teased.

Michael's back stiffened at the remark. He knew he wouldn't get through this meeting without losing it. An idea came to him. If it worked, it would be great. If it didn't, it would get him in some hot water with old Nergal.

Nergal came up behind him. Michael could feel his breath as he spoke. "But it's not Zack's affection for *me* that made you jealous. You couldn't stand the fact that Zack got Gloria."

Michael spun around, praying. For a second, Nergal looked confused. Michael said, "In the name of Jesus, retreat. I won't deal with you today. I want to talk to Benny."

Nergal stumbled backward and caught himself after a few steps. He bent over and put his hands on his knees as he breathed hard. He panted for about thirty seconds as Michael prayed. Finally, he stood upright and spoke in Benny's voice. "I don't know what you have done, Michael, but I feel so free."

"Well, I doubt he's gone for good, Benny," Michael cautioned.

"Definitely not, and I should warn you, he's angry with you … and a little scared." Michael wasn't looking forward to Nergal's wrath, but he liked the idea that the demon was frightened.

At that moment, Will walked in. "Jake, are you ready to call it a day?"

"I'll be ready in a minute," Michael said distractedly over his shoulder. Then to Benny he said, "We're going to grab some dinner. Do you want to join us?" Michael ignored Will's coughing sound, looking intently to Benny for his answer.

"No, you two go on without me," Benny said. "I'm tired, and you-know-who is fighting hard to regain control. I think I'll just take a nap."

"You-know-who?" Will asked. Coming alongside Michael, he took a hard look at Benny. "Lucky, is that you?"

"Yes, Will. It's nice to see you," Benny said, sounding uncharacteristically kind.

"It's … surprisingly nice to see you, too," Will offered in a confused tone.

Benny smiled sadly and said, "Well, I won't be here much longer. Nergal is pressing hard to take over, and I feel exhausted. I have to sleep now."

"Okay, Benny," Michael said. "Can I get you anything?"

"No. I'm just going to lie down," Benny said softly as he lumbered out of the room.

"What was that all about?" Will asked.

"Nergal really got to me. I commanded him to recede in Jesus's name."

"Whoa!" Will exclaimed. "You should do that more often."

They went to Michael's apartment and cooked dinner, packaged macaroni and cheese. Michael added some artificial bacon to flavor it. While Michael cooked, Will ran a check for bugs. Michael was sure there were none. Early in the process of building the Temple Mount, Michael had eschewed the idea of an apartment in the basilica, choosing instead an ancient apartment in the old city. It held a lot of charm for an old archeologist. Rough-timbered doorways and woodwork offset old plastered walls with just enough cracks, pits, and scars to add character to their off-white surfaces. Plumbing and electrical work, added centuries after the edifice was built, ran along the outside of the walls. High ceilings completed the look. Only one significant change was made to the architecture when the building was restored: a bank of windows filled the wall on one side of the apartment. The wall of windows facing the Temple Mount extended to every room.

More important to Michael was the security. With the electrical infrastructure on the outside of the walls, it was hard to imagine much by way of hardwired listening devices. Of course, external eavesdropping could be accomplished by tuning sensitive microphones to vibrations on the windows. Michael easily mooted that possibility with small devices that vibrated the glass with slight current, creating steady white noise that microphones couldn't penetrate.

"No bugs," Will said as Michael brought the mac and cheese to the table.

"It's a pretty secure building once you eliminate listening through the windows."

"True, but the external plumbing wigs me out a bit." Will grimaced.

"When you live with it, you barely notice it, and when you do notice it, you think it adds character."

"Yeah. Whatever," Will said with a sarcastic grin. "So tell me how you sent old Nergal on the run today."

Michael's face wrinkled with concern. "I ordered him to recede in Jesus's name. The New Testament is filled with instances where demons are brought to submission in His name."

"That's really cool," Will said. "Do you think it will work on Satan Kurtoglu?"

"No, and that's my source of concern about what happened today. The Bible is very clear that in the tribulation Satan will be given the power to overcome the saints. I think the Lord was gracious to me today, but for the end-time scenario to play out, Christians won't have the power or the opportunity to drive out evil spirits everywhere."

Will scowled. "That's a pretty grim assessment."

Michael nodded. "But I think it's an accurate one. I feel like I put God on the spot back there. He was gracious to me, but I have to be more cognizant of the times going forward."

Michael took a bite of his food. Technically, it was junk food, but it was comfort food for him. It reminded him of Friday nights in front of the television when he and Gabe were kids. The thought of Gabe jogged his memory. "Oh, by the way, I had the most realistic dream the other night that I was in the throne room of God, standing beside your dad."

Will chuckled. "You don't hear that every day! Did Dad have anything to say?"

Michael continued, "I was there with him, but the focus wasn't a visit. We watched while the seventh seal was broken. It was indescribable. The Lord was like this multifaceted diamond, just radiating everywhere. Jesus looked like a man and like a lamb at the same time. Then your dad and I heard the first three angels blow their trumpets."

"That's incredible, Jake!" Will yelled and gave Michael a high five across the table.

"As dreams go, it certainly was," Michael agreed. "But I think it means the trumpet and bowl judgments will start soon. Worldwide devastation is upon us."

Will frowned. "Do you have any idea about the timing?" he asked.

"Things like this can be confusing because of all the moving parts. The Nemesis system is traveling one way, and we're traveling another. I don't know enough about celestial mechanics to figure out exact timing. Anyway, I wanted a closer look, so I accessed recent Hubble images."

He stood from the table to get the images from his briefcase. Returning to the table, he said, "They're amazing. You almost can't see Nemesis and its planets because of the debris field. It doesn't follow Nemesis like the tail of a comet; it surrounds Nemesis like our Oort cloud."

"I'm not familiar with the—what was it ... Oort cloud?" Will asked.

"It's sort of a globe of debris surrounding our sun, way past the orbit of Pluto."

Will grinned as if to say, *Do I need to know all this?*

"Okay," Michael said with a shrug. "I think the debris field for this thing constitutes the first three trumpet judgments. Do you remember them?"

"You'd think I would, considering we live in the book of Revelation, but they're kind of jumbled in my mind."

"Understandable because the judgments mirror one another. The first trumpet is hail and fire mixed with blood. I think this is talking about a horrific meteor storm. The vast majority of the Nemesis debris is iron oxide, so it's red."

"So it's not really blood, but it looked like blood to John because it was red," Will concluded.

"Correct," Michael responded. "The second trumpet talks of a huge mountain thrown into the sea, turning a third of the sea blood red."

"A big meteor," Will offered.

"I think it's an asteroid, but you're basically right. Revelation describes the third trumpet as a great star like a burning torch falling on a third of the water, turning it bitter." Michael paused for a moment.

"I've got nothing," Will said. "What could cause that?"

"Thujone," Michael said with a grin, waiting for Will's reaction.

"Thu wha?" Will drawled.

"Thujone. It's a naturally occurring ketone, commonly known as absinthe or wormwood."

"Ah. Wormwood I recognize," Will said with a scowl.

"It has a bitter taste," Michael added. "There is some debate if this is the compound that gives absinthe its slightly psychedelic effects."

"So this stuff is going to get into the rivers how?"

Michael proposed, "Not all meteors strike the ground. In fact, most vaporize in the atmosphere. I think the one John saw was one of many that will disintegrate into a fine powder that will quickly rain out to pollute the rivers and eventually the seas."

"Why would it 'quickly rain out,' Professor?" Will asked with a mouthful of mac and cheese.

"Nice manners," Michael said, causing Will to laugh, some of the mac and cheese escaping before he could catch it with his napkin. "You've heard of cloud seeding, right?"

Will nodded, still wiping his mouth.

Michael continued, "In a similar way, thujone, which is a heavy compound, would gather water molecules and rain out very quickly to find its way to rivers, lakes, and oceans."

"So to pull it all together, the first three trumpets represent Earth passing through the Nemesis debris field," Will said.

"Yes, and I don't think it is too far away. Maybe three months."

"Around the time of Resurrection Day," Will mused.

Michael cringed at Will's use of the term the world had given to the anniversary of Satan's reanimation of Isa's body. "Don't use that term with me," Michael said. "Call it what it is, the anniversary of Satan's entrance to Earth."

"Yeah, that," Will said with a shrug.

"I have to get the church prepared. I'll call in sick for two days starting tomorrow. You'll have to cover for me. I want to get the programmers moving on the Locust Project and stop by to see the Jewish community. They can help get the word out about the trumpet judgments."

Will removed a folded paper from his pocket, unfolded it, and laid it on the table. It looked like some kind of computer printout.

"What's this?" Michael asked with a puzzled look.

Will pursed his lips. "It's a security screwup. When you used Benny's security clearance to access the Hubble data from your computer, you triggered an exception report on a security log. From now on, use the programmers to access a secure database."

Michael's head reeled with self-condemnation. He should have been more careful.

"What's worse," Will said gravely, "Zack turned down the corner of that page during our weekly security briefing. He knows you were there."

Michael rubbed his forehead. "So if the preacher talks about this information, Zack will know his identity."

"Worse. Isa will know his identity. I know he gets some perverse pleasure keeping us alive, but this could be the straw to break the camel's back."

"You're right," Michael said remorsefully. "I was so stupid to have accessed the system from here. I was just so psyched about the dream. I got careless."

"Don't beat yourself up," Will offered. "I have a plan. Take this page to the programmers. Don't release the preacher's report until they've removed all evidence of your data request. In the meantime, I'll steal that page from Zack's binder. He may suspect you're the preacher, but he won't be able to prove it."

"How are you going to steal it?" Michael asked cautiously.

"Sleight of hand," Will said with a shrug. "Old magician stuff. Redirect and move quickly."

Michael rubbed his forehead with his thumb and index finger. "I hate that I put you in such a position, and it still won't stop Zack from feeding his suspicions to Isa."

"There was an interesting exchange in our meeting today," Will said. "Sharif came down on Zack for running to Isa with everything. He explained how Zack was making himself look increasingly incompetent to Kurtoglu."

Michael leaned back in his chair and crossed his arms. "So Zack will start to fear the loss of his own position from oversharing. Good move on Sharif's part."

"I don't think he was insincere. He really was trying to give Zack some sound advice, and I think Zack heard him."

"Yeah, but if Zack thinks I'm the preacher, he'll take it to Isa. He wants to burn me badly."

Will grinned. "But he won't have any proof once the programmers cover your tracks. Zack will look like a hysteric with a grudge if he can't prove what he says."

"So I live to fight another day ..." Michael said.

"Or live to have another security breach," Will said sternly. "You have to be more careful, Jake. The stakes are too high, and not just personally. If we flip their locust program like Revelation says, we'll be doing a lot to protect the saints."

Michael chuckled. "Revelation has already been written, Will. We'll do it."

Will answered sternly, "It's good to have faith, but don't get reckless."

"It sounds like we've switched roles, Pop," Michael said with a raised eyebrow.

They grew quiet for a while, and then Will said, "Here's something that has always bothered me. Isa plays up the Anu threat, but he downplays the natural disasters Nemesis is bound to cause. Why do you think that is?"

"Satan has no interest in saving lives. In fact, he glories in the destruction," Michael said.

Will whistled through his teeth. "I remember how Isa and Benny laughed like madmen when the Russian alliance was destroyed. It's like they fed off it."

"So, for Isa the destruction will be a happy day," Michael said. "I know Nergal will enjoy it. And even before Nergal, Benny and the elite were looking forward to the reduction of the world's population to a more sustainable figure."

"Wow," Will said. "Isa and Nergal are evil beings not from Earth, so it's easier to comprehend their response. But the elite getting happy over such destruction seems worse to me—traitorous to humanity."

"And yet they think they're doing humanity a favor," Michael said.

"Then the preacher's warning isn't just for the church. It's for the entire world."

"I wonder if it matters," Michael said gloomily. "Anyone who has taken the mark is doomed anyway. It's all just so sad."

Will walked home from Michael's apartment. Crossing Abraham's Courtyard, he thought about the best way to get rid of the evidence against Michael. There were only five people at the meeting. He had already given his copy of the incriminating page to Michael. That left four more, but the really important one was Zack's.

The basilica looked beautiful in the golden spotlights that set it ablaze each night. The temple and the Dome of the Rock were beautiful as well, but the wattage was definitely turned up on the building inhabited by Isa. Will walked up the megalithic stone stairs and entered. In front of him were the doors to the sanctuary: to the left, a hallway to Isa's side, and to the right, a hallway to Benny's. Will instinctively turned toward Benny's side to get to his basement apartment, and then he stopped.

"Might as well check to see if Zack's office is open," he said to himself. It was nearly ten o'clock, and the interior of the building was dimly lit. He walked past the sanctuary, inhaling deeply the smell of incense. Ahead he saw light from Zack's office. Was Zack still working?

He walked slowly, quietly. He pressed himself against the wall and turned his head to get a peek into the room. Zack had his back turned, diligently going through some list of data on his computer. On the desk was his binder from the meeting earlier in the day. Will had an idea. Leaving quietly, he exited the building and ran to the Starbucks near the Wailing Wall.

He raced back to the basilica with a latte in each hand and was nearly out of breath when he entered. He walked slowly down the hallway, waiting for his breaths to become regular.

At the door to Zack's office, he asked, "Burning the midnight oil?"

Zack startled and jumped in his chair. When he turned to see Will speaking, he frowned.

"Here, I picked up a latte for you," Will said, placing the coffee on Zack's desk.

"I don't want to seem ungrateful," Zack drawled, "but why the sudden act of kindness?"

"Call it an act of conscience," Will offered with a sheepish grin. "I think it was a tough meeting for you today. It probably felt like everyone was coming down on you."

"It didn't feel like that. It *happened* like that," Zack snapped.

Will sighed as he took a seat in front of Zack's desk. "I was afraid you would feel that way. It was hard for me to fit in at first, too. We're Americans. We tend to hear comments like those at today's meeting in a way that's not intended."

Zack shrugged. "True enough. I feel very American over here."

"Well, if you don't mind my saying so, you are in good company. I had never left the States before I took this gig."

"And you think I'm taking their comments the wrong way?" Zack asked with less of an edge.

"You're taking them like any red-blooded American, but we're more rebellious than most. As an American who's been here longer, I don't think you took the comments as intended."

Zack put a finger to his lips in a thinking pose Will had seen him use in his televised sermons. He was a crafty one. Will would never know if Zack really believed him. "So, in their minds, they were trying to be helpful?" he asked.

"Absolutely!" Will exclaimed. "Although, it wasn't totally altruistic. They gave you good advice on how to handle Isa, but they were also trying to make their jobs easier."

"So, not altruistic, but still in my best interests," Zack said as he thought about it.

Will sighed. "Zack, Isa may be the resurrected savior of the world, but he's a pain in the butt as a boss. We've learned to band together

142

to keep things running smoothly around here. As to their appraisal of how Isa might view you if you run to him too frequently with issues—they're judging by the long string of assistants before you. They didn't last long, and they weren't sent to the unemployment office, if you get my drift."

Zack blanched. "I get your drift."

Will picked up his coffee in the gesture of a toast. "Here's to a long tenure with another American." Taking a big swig of the coffee, he quickly set it down on the edge of the desk as he began to cough. "Went down the wrong pipe," he choked out.

"Are you okay?" Zack asked.

"Not sure," Will croaked. He bent over in a cough and knocked his coffee off the desk. The lid, which he had loosened, burst open, leaving a pool of latte on the white tile floor.

Zack jumped from the desk. "Isa *hates* a mess!"

"Get some towels," Will said as he fell into another series of coughs. As Zack ran to the men's room to get some paper towels, Will quickly stole the incriminating evidence. By the time Zack returned, his cough had subsided, and he was on his knees by the spill.

As Zack handed him towels, Will apologized in a gravelly voice. "I'm so sorry about this."

Will wiped furiously at the floor with the towels. When the mess was clean and the towels disposed of, he took his leave. On the way to his quarters, he took the page out of his pocket and entered the sanctuary. Using the flame from an altar candle, he burned the evidence.

Following Will's interruption, Zack returned to the hunt. He wanted to know if he was a widower yet. None of the crematorium reports from the Houston area had mentioned Gloria. Earlier in the evening he had sent a request to the Houston FEMA center to determine her disposition.

While he and Will spoke, his inbox registered a reply. "Sent to a Vatican facility." Zack wasn't aware of any Vatican detention facilities.

SIXTEEN

Gloria couldn't remember when she had ever felt so fulfilled. True enough, the world was in dire straits, but for the first time in her life, she was truly helping others. She found the experience to be thrilling.

The women under her care were thriving, as were the men under John's care. The facility ran like clockwork. People who had been slaves to the system had become liberated prayer warriors. Of their own volition, the groups moved to three shifts so there was constant prayer. Although they found it a great idea, Gloria and John had to work hard administratively to make it happen. Kitchens had to stay open 24/7, work rosters had to be reconfigured, and quarters had to be adapted to allow for daytime sleeping. But it was worth it. The entire facility buzzed with the presence of the Holy Spirit. His presence was powerful every second of every day. The guests, as the inmates were called, had no doubt their constant vigil empowered and protected the saints living in hiding.

Gloria had just finished this week's chore roster when she got a call from the guard station out front. "What's up, Ethan?"

"I need you to come to the guard tower," Ethan replied. "We have a situation."

Could you be more vague? Gloria said to herself as she hung up the phone. She grabbed an umbrella and headed across the parking lot to the guard tower. Ethan met her at the door.

"What's the problem?" she asked as she shook raindrops from her umbrella.

He motioned over his shoulder to a woman with an infant. "I think she wants us to kill her baby."

"What?" Gloria cringed.

Ethan answered, "She doesn't want to inoculate him, and she thinks this is a Christian extermination camp. She would rather him die here and go to heaven than stay with her and take the mark."

"Oh my!" Gloria whispered before turning to the woman in tattered clothes. "Can I help you?" she asked.

Crying, the woman looked up. "I'm Maria Rosa." Gloria could see the gaunt pallor of someone who had taken the mark. "This is my baby, Manuel."

He couldn't have been more than three months old, and Gloria thought baby Manuel was the most handsome thing she had ever seen. His tawny complexion offset a perfect little nose, long black eyelashes, and a head of dark hair that fell in loose curls around his face. He sucked his thumb as he slept.

Maria Rosa looked carefully at Gloria and pronounced in a confused tone, "You are a Christian."

Gloria nodded tearfully, offering no explanation as to how a Christian could be running the detention center.

Maria Rosa continued. "I couldn't take it. I was afraid my baby would starve, so I took the mark. I was a Christian, but now I can feel the Lord has left me."

"Oh dear," Gloria said as she put an arm around the woman.

Maria Rosa continued through tears, "I did it to save my Manuel, but the men at the clinic said he would have to be inoculated too. I ran away. I can't let my baby go to hell!"

Gloria burst into tears as well. This woman's decision was gut-wrenching.

"But I'm changing now," Maria Rosa continued. "I can feel my love for him is fading. More and more I want to please Kurtoglu. If I keep Manuel any longer, I'm afraid I will take him for the shot. Then all will be lost." Maria Rosa broke into heavy sobs, waking Manuel. Gloria saw his pale green eyes and fell instantly in love.

Maria Rosa calmed herself as she cooed the baby back to sleep. "My Manuel is beautiful, isn't he?"

"The most beautiful baby I've ever seen," Gloria said through tears.

"Take him," Maria Rosa said. "You must let him die here to save him."

"I ... I don't know if I can," Gloria stammered.

"You have to!" Maria Rosa exclaimed in a fierce, tense whisper to avoid frightening the baby. "Better he die here with Christians than marked and beside me."

Gloria's head spun. She wanted to help. *Oh Lord,* she prayed, *what can I do to help her?*

The answer was jolting. She felt Him say in her spirit, *Take your baby.* There was no hope for Maria Rosa. Despite her best intentions, she had taken the mark. Her DNA was in the process of changing into something not quite human and therefore not covered by the sacrifice at the cross. Gloria took the child in her arms with huge sobs and a river of tears.

Maria Rosa placed her hand on Gloria's shoulder, and the two women cried. And then, Maria Rosa straightened herself, squared her shoulders, and walked away. Gloria held the baby for a long while and rocked him to a deep sleep. She asked Ethan to call John to the guard tower.

"What's up?" John asked as he entered.

"A young woman left me her baby," she said in a soft voice so as not to wake Manuel. "She took the mark, but when it came time to inoculate the baby, she couldn't do it. She brought him here to die with other Christians."

"Aw, he's beautiful," John said softly as he gently touched the child. "I remember mine when they were infants. There's nothing better than holding a sleeping baby."

Gloria's brow furrowed. "I don't have any baby things. I'm not even sure what I need. Can you coordinate with Michele? I'm hoping she can help."

John answered, "People at the office have taken the mark. They can buy supplies for her, and she can transfer the credits to their account through the expense reimbursement system."

"But she won't know what to get. We'll have to rely on your expertise," Gloria said.

John smiled and said with a shrug, "It's been awhile, but I think I can pull together a pretty good list. In the meantime, it's not like we're without resources. There's a couple living in the apartments with a six-month-old. I can score some diapers and a bottle from them until Michele can get things here. The diapers will be a little big, but they'll work."

"Oh, John, could you do that now? I'm pretty sure he'll be hungry when he wakes up."

He smiled. "It's a short drive. I should be back in fifteen minutes."

"Thank you, thank you, thank you," she sang, already relieved to have some help. She had always dreamed of having a baby, but her lack of knowledge about caring for one was daunting. If the mother gene counted for anything, she would be okay. Already she loved this little bundle and knew she would do anything to keep him safe.

When Gloria returned to the camp, the women all gathered around to see Manuel and offered to help with his care. He would be a toddler when Jesus returned; they just had to keep him safe and loved until then. Gloria handed him to Iris, her former bunkmate, when Iris asked to hold him. Gloria's arms felt empty without him. In no time at all she had bonded with him.

John returned with a couple of bottles, a box of diapers, and a container of formula. That would hold the baby until Michele could get there.

"John, in all the excitement, I forgot to call Michele!" Gloria exclaimed.

"These ladies have everything under control. Let's go to your office and call her together."

The phone rang. Michele answered, "Hello."

"Michele, it's Gloria and John," Gloria said.

John said, "Hi."

"What's the matter?" Michele asked cautiously. "You two never call me together."

Gloria explained what had happened, and Michele screamed into the phone, "What a wonderful gift from God! I can't wait to see him. I have a meeting to go to, but, oh, who cares. I'm the owner and the boss. I can play hooky if I want!"

"Not so fast," John said. "We need baby supplies, but without the mark, we can't buy them."

"Fair point," Michele said. "I do all our shopping online with Vatican accounts."

"We can't wait for items to be shipped to us," John said. "Little Manny has to eat and poo. It's what babies do."

"Now you're a poet, John," Michele teased at his unintentional rhyme.

John broke into a broad smile. "We were thinking someone there could buy them for you."

"Perfect answer, John. I'm sure my secretary will do it for me." She laughed heartily. "The whole office will be buzzing with the rumor that I'm pregnant!"

"Hey, it could happen," Gloria said enthusiastically.

"It would have to be by long-distance fertilization, the way Jimmy travels to set up new detention centers," Michele said. "Thankfully he'll fly home tomorrow if it's a low radiation day, and he'll stay for a while."

Gloria answered, "That's good to hear. You shouldn't be padding around that big house all alone. Maybe you will hear the pitter-patter of little feet one day."

"Only if they're Manny's when he comes to visit. There's no way I could responsibly bring a baby into the world. I don't think it's in the cards—at least not until the millennium."

Gloria knew the ache to have a child and the heartbreak of being unable. "You're right, of course, sweetie, but it's not long now until Jesus comes. Manny can be an older cousin to little baby Sheradon in a world where the lion and lamb lie down together."

Michele said, "It feels like a thousand years since the rapture. I almost can't remember life before, and I'm having a hard time imagining what it will be like after Jesus returns."

"That's because you spend too much time with green people," Gloria chided. "You should come here more. The constant prayer has created an incredible spiritual buzz around here."

"It sounds great to me," Michele said. "I'll be there shortly with baby supplies, as soon as you give me a list."

"Check your email," John said with a smirk.

"Ever efficient. I can't tell you how much I miss you around the office, John."

"No offense, but I can't say I miss being there. How's Jimmy's mommy?" He chuckled.

"She's been good since Uncle Benny scared her into line. Jimmy pleaded with her not to take the mark, but she wouldn't listen. In her mind, she would be the only person fit to run the business if Uncle Michael and I couldn't buy or sell."

"She sold her soul for your family business," John said with disgust.

"Yeah," Michele said. "First she was green with envy. Now she's just green."

Gloria and John laughed loudly.

"I can't believe I just said that," Michele said, her embarrassment clear in her voice.

"Got to laugh at something," Gloria said, "and we don't get many opportunities these days."

"Listen," John said, "I don't want to break up this party, but the sooner you get baby supplies, the sooner you can get here."

The remainder of the day flew by. Manny ate happily for Gloria. He was a very content baby, rarely crying. She wondered if it was the pervasive presence of the Holy Spirit making him feel secure and loved. Of course, a couple hundred aunts and uncles loving on him didn't hurt either.

Michele arrived with what seemed like a truckload of stuff—a rocking baby carrier, a crib, an industrial-size box of formula, a huge stack of diapers, soft baby food, blankets, clothes, and toys. Much of the stuff had to be assembled, but John and his guys got right on it.

"My secretary had a hard time finding these things. Green people aren't having many babies these days. We have enough items to start. I can get anything else we need online," Michele said.

Just then, one of the women brought Manuel to Gloria. His green eyes flashed, and he smiled when she called his name. "Oh, praise the Lord!" Michele screamed. "He's beautiful!"

Gloria squealed, "I honestly think he's the most beautiful baby I've ever seen."

"Oh, Gloria, I can't believe how excited I am to see this baby. For the first time since the rapture, I have hope for the future."

"I know." Gloria beamed. "He'll get to grow up in a wonderful world. All we have to do is keep him safe for a couple more years."

They grew silent. Gloria focused on the gravity of that statement. She looked at Michele, who had a sudden forlorn look.

Gloria said resolutely, "We'll do it, Michele. We'll do it because we have to."

Michele's phone rang. "Jimmy," she said. "I'll put him on video." She put the call on video and pointed the camera at the baby.

"I know I've been gone a long time." Jimmy chuckled. "But not that long. Is there something you want to tell me?"

"Meet your nephew Manny."

"Will's baby?" Jimmy asked suspiciously.

"No!" Michele laughed. She and Gloria excitedly told him the story as the baby reached for the phone.

"What fantastic news!" Jimmy yelled.

"It kind of gets me thinking about our kids," Michele said.

"Don't go all biological clock on me," Jimmy teased. "There's no good way to bring a child into the world as it stands. In a couple of years, it will be a completely different story."

"I hear you," Michele said. "In the meantime, though, we have Manny to hone our skills. I'll teach you to change his diaper when you come home."

In the midst of such long-needed happiness, Gloria's office phone rang. It was the front gate again, with a prisoner drop-off.

Gloria asked, "Jimmy, have you sent another person to us?"

"No. I've been too busy here in England to arrange any new transfers."

Gloria shook her head. "That's weird, because the front gate just called to say we're getting another guest—a young woman."

John smiled. "It would be kind of wonderful if the feds continue to feed us their worst Christian reprobates."

"It sure would," Gloria said excitedly. "This day just gets better and better." Turning to Manny in Michele's arms, she said, "Doesn't it, my handsome little man?" She looked up at Michele. "Can you handle our little bundle of joy while I admit another to our prayer group?"

"I sure can," Michele said. "I'll introduce him to his uncle Will and his uncle Michael while you're gone, if I can get either of them on the phone."

Gloria heard Michele signing off with Jimmy as she left her office. On the way through the group, she called to her former bunkmate. "Kimmy, can you help me get a new girl set up?"

"Sure," Kimmy said. "Do you need her on any particular shift?"

They walked together to the front of the facility. "Let's start her on days. It's what she would be used to from her old camp," Gloria said.

"There will be the normal period of distrust, but after she adjusts, say, next week, we'll put her in the rotation."

In the front of the building, a man in a dark suit from a dark limousine stood with a young woman. She was slightly built with spiked black hair. Gloria would have guessed her age to be eighteen.

"We don't usually get transfers by limousine," Gloria said cautiously as she asked to see the young woman's transfer information.

The limo driver smiled. "You don't understand. I work for her father. He has asked me to turn her over to the government for reeducation because she refuses the inoculation. He thought bringing her directly to you would eliminate the need for police and publicity."

Gloria forced a smile. Her father had decided to get rid of her quietly so he wouldn't be embarrassed. Nice fellow. Turning to the young woman, she asked, "What's your name, dear?"

"Chastity," she snarled. "My parents are big Sonny and Cher fans." There was something very abrasive about this young woman.

"You don't hear that very often," Kimmy said softly with a grin.

The driver unloaded Chastity's suitcase and beat it out of the camp as Gloria continued the introduction. "I'm Gloria, the director of the women's camp. This is Kimmy. She's going to get you settled in."

As they walked back to the camp, Chastity folded her arms in front of her and only answered "yes" or "no" to Kimmy's questions.

Gloria studied her. Chastity carried a look of disdain. Most of their inmates were happy to be in this camp because they had spent time in the real camps. This one would be different. Not only did she have to deal with the fact that her father turned her in, but also this was a step down, from the life of a spoiled young woman to communal living.

"Wow, an infant and an angry teen all in one day, Lord!" she said, returning to her office.

As she entered, Will was talking to the baby, "Gitchy, gitchy, gitchy goo."

Michele demanded drolly, "Did you just say 'gitchy, gitchy, gitchy goo'? Watch *The Flintstones* much?"

They all laughed. Gloria hadn't laughed in such a long time. It felt good. "Where's Michael?" she asked.

"On a secret mission," Will said with a grin. "He's going to take a couple of mental health days to spend some time in the desert."

SEVENTEEN

Michael relished the time away from the Temple Mount. The Jordanian desert was barren. Its austere mountains carried soft indigo and brown hues, in contrast to the various gradations of taupe and beige of the sand along the road he was driving. The azure sky was dotted with tiny wisps of white cloud. The landscape and sky felt expansive, as if they went on forever. Just that small hint of eternity sent Michael into worship and praise throughout his drive. By the time he reached the Petra base, he felt recharged by the Spirit and ready to work.

The meeting with the programmers was incredibly productive. They had become quite proficient at hacking into systems worldwide. Of course it helped that they had a back door to Isa's megalithic supercomputers.

"So, here's the deal," Michael said as they sat around their programming stations in the underground base. "Years ago, the US Navy developed an automated intelligence drone designed to look like an insect."

"The Locust Project," the agent said. "I know of it."

"*Anch'io*," said Savario and Eduardo. (Me too.)

"Well, good!" Michael exclaimed. "I had never heard of it until Will mentioned it. I understand they work by targeting specific DNA signatures."

The agent added, "Technically, these types of devices were outlawed by international treaty because of their eugenic capabilities. But nobody in the intelligence community really believed the US stopped working on them."

"Well, that much I can confirm," Michael said. "Our family aircraft business has been churning them out by the millions. My contact there tells me they aren't hardwired to a certain DNA signature. Their target data is uploaded to them from a controlling computer."

"Like Kurtoglu's supercomputer," Giacomo concluded.

"That's my guess," Michael said. "The filter profile will be Isa's genes from the inoculations. The locusts will attack anyone without his genes."

Savario added thoughtfully, "If they are broadcasting a simple signal like that, they're probably using IFTTT coding."

"Very easy to crack," Marco said.

"IFTTT?" Michael asked.

"Programming based on 'if this, then that' statements—simply a parameter and a result."

Michael looked at them gravely. "So, my question is this: Can the programming be turned around so that people *with* the DNA get stung?"

"Very quickly, if we can find the files," Luigi said. "We'll send a command to the drones telling them to do the reverse of the government's program."

Michael questioned them. "No offense to anyone in this room, but Isa is using the world's best. What's the likelihood they won't find your command?"

Savario drew a deep breath and exhaled slowly as he thought. "In regular programming, they would eventually hit on it," he said, "but if we use their quantum computer, the command will only exist while broadcasting."

"Like the preacher's messages," Luigi said with a grin. He and Savario high-fived.

"So it sounds doable to you guys?" Michael asked. They all responded with "yes" or "*sí.*"

"And we know it is." The agent beamed. "Otherwise it wouldn't have been written in the book of Revelation."

"True enough," Michael said. "Now to the next order of business." He pulled Will's purloined page from his briefcase and explained his security breach.

Marco took the page from Michael and looked at it closely. He spoke to Michael in Italian. "This is a system to which we already have access. We can expunge your record by the time you get to Jerusalem."

"*Grazie*," Michael said. "Have you had any luck developing targeted encrypted video?"

"Sí," Eduardo said. "It is like the technology we use to broadcast the preacher, but we just send it to a pinpointed location. And it is helpful that the location you chose is across town."

"Good," Michael said. "So, I could send a message to the Petra community, and—"

"It will appear on all of their cell phones and computers simultaneously," the agent said with a grin. "At least you will have their attention. What you do with it will determine if you also get their cooperation."

"I have the encrypted message on this flash drive. Let's give it a try," Michael said.

The energy in the room exploded as the programmers got to work. This was innovative technology for them. Their animated faces displayed their pleasure. Within moments, the message was uploaded to the system.

"Whenever you're ready, Father, we'll play the message," the agent said. "In quantum communication, everything is 'now'; therefore, we won't be sending an encoded message so much as playing your message here and simultaneously on their equipment."

"There's no time like the present," Michael said, making what he thought was a very witty allusion to the perpetual now spoken of by the agent. Nobody laughed. Michael was happy Will wasn't present to see him be too nerdy even for this bunch.

"Here goes," the agent said, directing their attention to the preacher's dark silhouette on an overhead screen.

"Hello to God's elect, the one hundred forty-four thousand Jews called by the Lord. This is the preacher speaking to you. You have no doubt seen my global broadcasts and know I am your brother in Yeshua.

"I know you are a well-fortified group living in exile from the world community. I also have seen God's supernatural protection over you. Because of your might, I am sending this directed message to your computer systems. In short, I wish to meet with your leader. I believe he could use my technology for global broadcasts to influence the estimated fifty million to one hundred million citizens who have not yet taken the inoculation.

"I will arrive at your border in one hour in a white Jeep with a Vatican insignia. I ask your guards to escort me to a meeting with your leader to discuss the details."

The message concluded. Michael thought it sounded more convincing when he recorded it. In playback, he thought he sounded a bit desperate. But then again, he was. That group had a Masada mind-set. They were militarized and willing to go down with the ship, taking out all enemies with them. There was no way Michael could just stroll up to their perimeter and offer a deal, especially if they recognized him as Benny's assistant and the fraudster who had perpetrated the Antakya Codex scam on the world.

The agent said somberly, "Well, they're just ten miles away. You have time to get a cup of coffee and go to the bathroom first."

"Time to throw up," Michael said fearfully. "If I don't make it back, be sure to go through with the Locust plan."

"You'll be fine," the agent said. "After all, you'll be with a man who is a trained killer."

"You're going with me?" Michael asked hopefully.

The agent smiled. "It seems I have a history of protecting you from yourself."

———

They rode in silence to Petra. Michael drove while the agent examined his concealed weapons. As their Jeep approached the ancient Petra dwellings, they were stopped by two men with machine guns in *thawbs*, the long white tunics worn in the Middle East, their heads covered with white knit hats to shield them from the desert sun.

"*Ani poh laheepogesh im ha manhig shelach,*" Michael said, making use of his Hebrew. (I'm here to meet with your leader.)

"*Ani yodeah,*" answered the one with a swarthy complexion. (I know.) Michael guessed he was in his early twenties. He and his compatriot motioned for Michael and the agent to exit the Jeep. Each was searched, and they took the agent's shoulder gun and each of the pistols strapped to his ankles. Michael raised an eyebrow at the agent.

The agent winked quickly in response to tell Michael he wasn't out of weapons.

The swarthy guard placed the barrel of his gun between Michael's shoulder blades and pushed slightly. "I guess he wants me to walk," Michael said to the agent, who was experiencing the same thing.

"*Ken. Lach!*" the guard said, confirming that he should begin walking.

"*Atah meveen angleet?*" Michael said over his shoulder, asking the man if he was able to understand English.

"I speak it too," the guard behind him said without accent. His voice was light as if the revelation of his ability was fun.

Michael asked, smiling over his shoulder at the young man, "Are you taking us to your leader?"

"Yes, Yitzhak is expecting you. You would call him Isaac in English."

"Which does he go by?" Michael asked.

"Either. His friends call him Isaac, but he uses the Hebrew when he acts as our leader to reinforce the connection to our roots."

They walked for about ten minutes, ending up at a tight mountain passage with sheer stone walls on either side. Michael knew where they were headed—the iconic Khazneh, the building carved into the sheer stone cliffs of Petra. As they exited the passage, the light stone of the Khazneh glistened in the strong desert sun. Michael had always loved this site. In the bright sunlight, the open main entrance looked like a foreboding black square. A tall figure with broad shoulders came to the door wearing a thawb.

"Is that Yitzhak?" Michael asked over his shoulder.

"Yes."

They walked up the couple of steps onto the portico in front of the door where Yitzhak stood. The guards made them stop. They waited for a moment as dim light shone off Yitzhak's face. He was clearly checking his phone. *Definitely a Millennial,* Michael thought.

Suddenly Michael heard loud laughter. "I don't believe it!" Yitzhak exclaimed with a slight accent as he strode through the doorway. He had caramel skin that complemented golden-brown eyes. His teeth shone brightly as he smiled. "Father Michael Martin! The pope's assistant is the infamous preacher!" he exclaimed.

"You recognize me?" Michael asked.

"I thought I did," Yitzhak said, holding out his phone, "but I had to look you up to be sure. I remember seeing your interviews about the Antakya Codex."

"Don't remind me," Michael said dismally. "I've changed since then. I've given my life and my heart to Jesus."

"I don't think ill of you. I myself was not saved at the time, but I remember you because of your passion for archeology. You're one of the reasons I studied it at Hebrew University." He made a motion toward the guards, who then pointed their weapons to the ground.

"Thanks," Michael said. "Your men were very nice, but I'm not a fan of a machine gun pointed in my back."

"A necessary precaution," Yitzhak said with a wave of his hand.

"Yitzhak," Michael began.

Yitzhak interrupted, "Call me Isaac. My American friends do. Before we begin, shouldn't you introduce your friend here?"

Michael chuckled. "I wish I could. He's a brother in Christ who has done amazing exploits for our cause, but he works undercover. In all the years I've known him, I've just called him 'the agent.'"

"Alvin," the agent said, extending his hand. Isaac shook it warmly.

"A-aaalvin?" Michael asked with a gaping grin and a reference to the Chipmunks.

The agent held up a fist with the little finger extended. "I can kill you with just this," he said, returning the grin.

Michael rolled his eyes and shook his head. Isaac laughed. Three men brought chairs and drinks, leaving them to talk on the ancient porch.

"To what do I owe the pleasure of your visit?" Isaac asked.

"You've seen the preacher's transmissions, I take it."

"I have," Isaac affirmed. "I'm still a little amazed he's you."

"The Antichrist and the false prophet would be too, but I'm not likely to be caught because of the technology we use. The preacher's videos are quantum communications created with entangled photons. The messages are real while they're transmitted, but when the transmission ends, they cease to exist—no trail of them streaming and no metadata."

"Totally untraceable," the agent added.

Isaac let out an airy whistle. "Amazing! I didn't even know the world had such abilities."

"Well, technically, only Kurtoglu does," the agent said.

"You're using his computer!" Isaac exclaimed. "That's brilliant!"

Michael smiled. "On the off chance they could find a way to trace the signal, its origin would be the same computer monitoring the inoculation chips."

"Hah!" Isaac shrieked, shaking his head as if he couldn't believe it. Then his look grew quizzical as he asked, "You have the powerful toys and access. ... What do you want from me?"

"Seeing how you have galvanized this group, I believe the Holy Spirit has given you evangelization skills I could never dream of," Michael said. "I want to use my encrypted system to send your messages to the entire world. Well, to be more precise, I think the Lord wants me to offer it to you. Many who haven't taken the mark aren't Christians. Your community's defiance of the global government will open the door. Your preaching will open their hearts."

Michael looked closely at Isaac. He could see the wheels turning in the younger man's head. Michael added, "There's another reason. The preacher's anonymity only goes so far before it looks conspiratorial and elusive. The church needs a shepherd it can see and relate to."

"Those are all really good points," Isaac said, "but my main work is here. I belong in Petra."

"Well, there's a bit of a surprise in that regard," the agent said. "My team and I are just across town. We can come here, record your messages, and transmit them."

"Or I could just drive to you," Isaac offered.

The agent frowned. "Here's the deal. Our facility is top secret and a massive security threat to the Kurtoglu regime. I'm not too keen on anyone knowing its location."

Michael added, "A-aaalvin has a long history with secret service activity. He doesn't share much information." The agent again raised his little finger at Michael's mispronunciation of his name. Michael laughed.

"It's an opportunity I can't turn down," Isaac said. "We may be able to save millions of people from hell and edify the Christian community."

"So you're in?" Michael asked.

"I'm in!" Isaac exclaimed.

In the next couple of hours, they laid out strategies, also determining what the messages would look like and their frequency. Finally they all prayed together. They left as friends, with Isaac walking them to their Jeep. Isaac moved with the lithe, easy stride of an athlete.

There was one last question nagging at Michael. As they walked, he said, "There is one favor I'd like to ask, although I hope it never comes to it …"

"Sounds ominous." Isaac smiled.

"If the government would ever find our base, could my people take shelter here? I know your community is for Jewish Christians, but in a pinch, would it be okay?"

"You're right. We are a Jewish community, but we are also responsive to the needs of our brothers and sisters in Christ. Your people would be welcome."

"Thanks," Michael said with a sigh. And then another thought hit him. "Same thing if my family and I have to escape from Isa and Pope Peter?"

"I would never turn away the man who stared down the barrel of a gun to bring me this opportunity from the Lord," Isaac said as he bent to hug Michael goodbye.

"My family, too, right?" Michael asked again in the embrace.

"Yes. Of course," Isaac said. *"Baruch haba vmishpacha shelcha."* (You are welcome—and your family.)

Michael held him tight and patted his back. Isaac's men returned with the agent's personal arsenal. When he had returned his weapons to their places, he took the driver's seat and motioned for Michael to get in.

"Home, A-aaalvin!" Michael yelled as they pulled out to Isaac's laughter.

The agent shook his head. "You don't really think that's my name, do you?"

"You mean it's not?" Michael asked.

"I didn't think the negotiation would go very far if I couldn't show Isaac I trusted him with my name. Alvin is the first thing that came to mind."

"Because it also happens to be on your birth certificate?" Michael asked with a grin.

"Don't be silly," the agent said with a scowl. "My birth certificate and all other records were expunged years ago. I'm like your quantum thingamajig. I only exist when I want to."

"Good enough, Agent Q," Michael said, shaking his head. As they left the mountains, his phone buzzed. Pulling it from its holster, he saw Will had tried to call him on his encrypted line. He returned the call. "Will, I've got great news. Everything we wanted to accomplish can be done," he said without saying hello.

"Great!" Will exclaimed. "You haven't left Petra, have you? I stumbled on something here that may be of value if our guys can check it out."

"No. I'm in the Jeep with the agent. We just left ancient Petra and are on our way to the base. What's up?"

"I stole that computer page from Zack's binder, so he has nothing on you."

"Good man," Michael said.

"Now, don't get mad. I may have been a bit reckless."

Michael said carefully, "Will, just tell me what you did." The agent turned his head to stare at Michael, who then put the phone on speaker.

"I couldn't sleep, which is another story. Anyway, I sneaked back into Zack's office to snoop around. I figured it would be good if I could get some dirt on him—something we may be able to use as leverage someday."

"Okay," Michael said slowly.

"Long story short: I accessed Zack's password from security logs. It appears that Reverend Jolean spent too much of his life with the ladies and a fortune. I found one of Isa's accounts with a ridiculous number of charges for porn and prostitutes. Either Satan has discovered Isa's penis, or Zack is living it up on the boss's dime."

"I'm sure he is, but how do you know Isa isn't enabling it?" the agent asked. "Satan has used sex for ages to control people."

"Well, here's what I want you to check out: There's also movement of large-dollar credits from Isa's government accounts to a string of accounts, all of which immediately transfer the exact same amount to a receiving account. I bet the receiving account belongs to Zack. I'm hoping your guys can track it."

"Good work, Will," the agent said. "That is the textbook pattern of malfeasance. If you text me the account numbers, I'll pass them off to the programmers to hack."

"I'll sure like having some leverage in my back pocket if Zack gets too treacherous," Will said.

"I agree, but no more midnight raids to Isa's side of the basilica. Do you hear me?" Michael said sternly.

"Yes," Will responded. "Hey! Don't you want to know why I couldn't sleep?"

"Not particularly," Michael teased.

"I got a call from Michele and Gloria ..." Will began.

"Uh-oh. What happened now?" Michael asked with dread.

"A lady who took the mark dropped off her baby boy with Gloria. His name is Manuel, and he's absolutely beautiful."

"Finally some good news on the home front!" Michael cheered.

"Well, there's more. Your demented uncle had me fill in for you while you were 'sick.' He's going to soak in some hot spring over Winterfest, so I nagged him about our request to go to Georgia for Christmas. It's not a lot, but we'll have Christmas Eve and Christmas Day at home to play with little Manny."

"I can't say I've had a better call from you, Will!" Michael exclaimed. "The agent and I will brief the programmers on our meeting. I should be home tomorrow."

"Okay. See you tomorrow," Will said. Then he hung up.

Michael said, "Put the pedal to the metal, A-aaalvin!"

EIGHTEEN

A fter my dream," the preacher said somberly in his transmission, "I came upon these images of the Nemesis system." The screen moved to the Hubble images. "As you can see, the system is surrounded by a large cloud of debris. This cloud will affect Earth's orbit shortly, resulting in the disasters depicted by the first three trumpet judgments of the book of Revelation."

Zack grinned. He grabbed the security binder and trotted to Isa's office. He knocked lightly on the door and drew a deep breath. Isa didn't take kindly to interruptions.

"What is it, Zack?" Isa asked. Zack couldn't tell if his boss was annoyed at the interruption.

"Um ... the preacher is online, and I think I may have a clue as to his identity."

"Come in," Isa said slowly. It felt like something Vincent Price would say. Zack had loved Isa from a distance for years, but up close and personal, he could be a little creepy. Zack pondered it only for a second before Isa lost his temper.

"I'm a very busy man, Zack. What do you have?" Isa barked.

Zack held out his phone so Isa could hear the preacher droning on and on.

Isa listened intently. Speaking in nearly a whisper so as not to eclipse the preacher, he said, "It sounds like he is trying to pin a scientific backing to John's fiction in Revelation. He's wrong, of course."

"Notice the images of Nemesis," Zack said. He couldn't stifle a grin at the thought of channeling Isa's ire toward Michael.

Isa snatched Zack's phone to look closely. "These are fairly recent images. I've seen them."

"Downloaded from Hubble," Zack said. "It stands to reason we could trace the preacher to the image download."

"I'm listening." Isa grinned.

Zack grabbed his security binder and turned to the appropriate section. He rifled through the pages to find the one with the turned corner. He couldn't find it. He rifled through the pages again. *He couldn't find it!*

Isa crossed his arms and stared woefully at Zack.

Zack met his eyes and stammered. "B-but I have evidence, Excellency. I must have misplaced it." He turned the pages violently. *Where's the page showing Michael's access to the information?* "Excellency, let me describe the evidence. Our security records show that Father Michael accessed these exact Hubble images in the last week."

"It should be easy enough to check, Zack," Isa said, glaring. Zack feared Isa was about to blow his top. He rifled through the pages yet again.

Isa hit a button on his speakerphone to connect with the scientists in his bunker.

"Yes, Excellency?" a voice rang through the phone, that of the most recent head scientist.

"Call up records for access to Hubble in the past week," Isa demanded. "I'm looking for unusual access."

The scientist typed on his keyboard. "Just the scientists in the control room, Excellency."

Zack frowned.

"Oops. Looks like we have one unusual entry, Excellency."

Zack's grin returned. He couldn't wait to see Isa explode and then tear into Michael.

The scientist said, "Your assistant went into those records using your security clearance—I assume on your behalf."

Zack felt the color drain from his face. His breaths became rapid and shallow. He spoke rapidly, wincing at the terror in his own voice. "Excellency, I went to those files to see what Father Michael accessed."

Isa grimaced. Into the phone, he said, "Specifically search for access by Father Michael."

More typing. "Um … nothing, Excellency. I don't see anything about Father Michael."

"Thank you," Isa said calmly before pouncing on the disconnect button. He threw Zack's phone. It landed on the floor behind Zack, who scampered to retrieve it and backed away.

"No you don't!" Isa screamed as he stood from his desk. "Don't you back away from me! You've been courting my attention for years under your delusional premise that you're my father. Well, now you've got it!" He strode to within an inch of Zack.

Isa's hot breath pummeled Zack's face, his eyes drilled into him. "Excellency …" Zack began, not really knowing what he would say after. His mouth felt too dry to speak.

Isa stared until Zack's knees felt weak. Pain echoed through his head. Black swirled around the edges of Zack's vision as the pressure of Isa's presence in his brain became too much to bear. He passed out, only to awaken on the couch in his apartment. He hated this apartment, a windowless basement abode of seven hundred square feet. He missed his mansion on the Caribbean. What he wouldn't do to be on the veranda of his home, smelling the salt air!

Well, that would never happen again, thanks to Michael. Michael! His mind filled with vague images of his recent encounter with Isa, but he drew a blank trying to recall the time following their conversation with the head scientist. Try as he could, he found no memory of the meeting's end or how he'd gotten back to his apartment. Could it have been a dream?

He saw the security binder lying on the coffee table in front of him and scanned it again, looking for the turned corner. It wasn't there. So it wasn't a dream. Then he looked carefully at the page numbers. Page 35 was missing. That must have been the page with the turned corner! But how did it go missing?

His mind zeroed in on the only time Will had come to visit him in his office. "Damn!" Zack screamed to the empty room. "Will must have taken the page when he spilled his coffee!"

Zack was sick at how gullible he had been. "Did I want to talk to another American so badly that I fell for his stupid act? Damn Michael, and damn his rotten nephew!" he screamed to the empty apartment.

It was clear to Zack that Will and Michael were out to sabotage him. Was the entire thing a setup? Will had seen him turn down the corner of that page; Zack was sure of it. He paced the room, feeling like a caged animal. Not only were the walls closing in, but his enemies were too. Well, they would pay. Zack wasn't sure how, but he would find a way to make it happen.

He went to his computer to find the only balm for his pain. With a few clicks he ordered a redhead and a brunette to assuage his ego.

"Charge it to my son!" he exclaimed with a mad laugh. "In fact, I think I deserve a little bit extra for my services today." He moved another hundred thousand credits from Isa's account to his own.

He had a pang of conscience—more like some hidden fear—as he held his finger above the return button to verify the transfer. He tapped his foot anxiously as he considered his action. Finally, he smiled as a Bible verse came to mind. "The Lord owns the cattle on a thousand hills," he said with a grin. "And Lord Isa owns even more. Surely he wouldn't deny his old pop some comfort."

And with that, he pushed the button.

"You wanted to see me?" Benny asked in Nergal's rich baritone voice as he entered Isa's office.

"Yes, it's about Zack. His time may be cut short."

"Do whatever you wish, Excellency," Benny replied. "I only asked you to bring him here to keep Michael off-balance. As luck would have it, with the exception of one unfortunate incident, Michael has been manageable."

"Zack thinks Michael is the preacher," Isa said slyly.

Benny felt sure Isa was gauging his reaction. "Preposterous! He spends nearly every waking moment near me. I think I would know if he were sitting in his office preaching Christ to the masses." Nergal realized it could be true, but the Benny side of their awkwardly conjoined personality wasn't about to throw Michael under the bus.

"Messages can be recorded," Isa said.

Nergal won out for the moment. "True enough, but you're the one who wants to keep Michael around. Why not dispose of him instead of Zack?"

Isa laughed heartily. "That is the response I want to hear from you. Your allegiance to me must be stronger than allegiances to your family."

"I'm totally devoted to you, Excellency. You've risen from the grave. I worship nobody else."

Isa smiled at the acknowledgment of his godhood. "To answer your question, I like having Father Michael around. He is one of the few humans I found palatable before my resurrection, and I hope to save him. One day he will bow to me, and I will reward him."

"Yes, Excellency," Benny said. The Benny side of his personality was at once relieved that Michael would live another day and envious that Michael would reap some kind of reward after operating in opposition to Isa.

"Now, now, no need to be jealous, Holiness. I see you as a companion, a compatriot. My feelings for Father Michael are more like a human would have for a pet. His blistering intellect amuses me, and his conscience confounds me. I find him interesting. No more. No less. But I want him alive to see the destruction of his Lord."

"As for Zack," Benny said in Nergal's rich baritone. "In his defense, he has taken very well to his crematorium duties. Not many humans are so pliable."

Isa waved his hand. "Your memory is short. I had an entire country performing those duties for me less than a hundred years ago. Benny would have remembered it."

Nergal frowned. "This human you gave to me is very obstinate. He resists me at every turn. I thought our personalities would have merged completely by now."

Isa chuckled. "Well, Benny always was a man after my own heart. Maybe I was wrong to try to keep you in control. Maybe a full merger will only come if both of you are free to express yourselves. Right, Benny?"

Nergal receded, and Benny came to the surface, gasping for breath. "Oh, Lord Isa, I don't know how to thank you for setting me free."

"Relax, Benny, Nergal is still around, but I think I might have been rash in demanding to deal only with his personality."

Benny tittered. "He is just a tiny bit boring, isn't he?"

"Compared to you, yes," Isa said. Benny could feel Nergal's rage beneath the surface.

"If I'm not mistaken, Excellency, we were speaking of Zack. Unlike Michael, he's too imaginative to be plagued by concepts like trust and loyalty. Those aspects of Michael's character make him eminently more controllable than Zack," Benny said, although his interests lay elsewhere. He hadn't been in full control of this body for a long while, and he had some serious eating and drinking to do before he let Nergal overtake him again. And if he played his cards right, maybe more.

Isa smiled as if acknowledging Benny's thoughts, before saying contemplatively, "To be honest, Zack annoys me, but his continual attempts to sabotage Michael amuse me. We'll let it go this time. He knows he has seriously crossed me by coming to me with an unsupported accusation. I don't believe for a moment the evidence didn't exist. I rather surmise he was bested by Michael or, maybe, Will. To the extent that is the case, he has sharpened them like steel to a blade. It's fun to watch. At least for a while. When I tire of Zack, I'll let you know. In the meantime, I'm sure he will be punished sufficiently."

Benny smiled broadly and let out a mischievous chuckle.

The prostitutes had behaved in a way that was a credit to their profession. Zack slept happily in his bed until his doorbell rang. Throwing on a robe, he sprinted to the door. He opened it to find Benny in full papal regalia—old school, not the sleeker attire designed by Isa. Benny entered ceremoniously, ducking slightly to avoid hitting the papal miter on the doorjamb.

"To what do I owe the pleasure of this visit, Holiness?" he asked suspiciously.

Benny threw off his robes to reveal leather underwear and little else. "I just came from Isa. You've been naughty. I'm here to deliver your punishment," he said as he struck Zack with the papal shepherd's crook.

NINETEEN

The ride from the airport was colorful, if nothing else. Isa's zombies had worked overtime to decorate homes and streets in colored lights for Winterfest. Even Isa's misappropriation of Christmas couldn't get Michael down today. He and Will only had a few days to spend with the family. He wanted it to be a wonderful Christmas. Only God knew where they would be next year, once the wrath of God started in earnest.

"Is it just me, or does having a baby around make Christmas new again?" Will asked.

Michael chuckled. "I remember how Christmas suddenly felt warmer and more magical when Gabe had his kids. It's quite a gift to watch kids experience things for the first time."

"I've never been around a baby, and I don't know if I'll ever have kids," Will mused.

"Don't say that!" Michael exclaimed. "You're a young man, and the millennium is less than two years away. I can picture you meeting a lovely Christian girl and settling down in a world run by Jesus."

"I can't imagine it," Will said somberly. "So much destruction has to occur before then."

"True enough," Michael agreed, "but when Jesus comes, we'll work with Him to set the world right. You'll work for a purpose you can get behind. You'll come home at night to a lovely wife. And you'll have a slew of kids—each uglier than the last," Michael teased.

"Nice," Will said with a grin.

"All kidding aside, Will, you'll be able to raise kids in a world where sin is a thing of the past. There'll be plenty for everyone, and Jesus will reign supreme. It will be wonderful."

"If we can make it through the next couple of years. Do you really think we can last that long on the Temple Mount?" Will asked.

Michael shook his head. "I've had my fill, and I know you have too. At some point God may give us permission to leave. Isaac said we can join the Petra community if we need to."

"I was ready to leave Benny's service the moment you were abducted. And while we're on the subject of your abduction, I still don't like the agent after what he did. And yet, without him we wouldn't have the programmers on our side or access to the technology to turn the Locust event around. It's all a part of prophecy I guess."

"I believe it is," Michael said with a smile, "and ultimately I'm just happy to be part of the winning team."

"The team that beams Isaac's teachings to the world," Will said with a satisfied smile. "His messages are so inspired. They're incredible!"

"He does a great job," Michael concurred. "He's on fire for God, and it comes across in his sermons. He blows the preacher away by a mile! And I couldn't be happier. It takes some of the heat off me."

"I'm thankful the preacher has moved to only occasional messages. I about wet myself when I saw your name on the security access report," Will confessed.

"You know, I never thanked you for covering my butt on that one. I don't know how I could have been so careless," Michael said as they pulled up to the gate guarding Castello Pietro. Michael felt an involuntary wince. He just hated that name.

"You're welcome." Will grinned as he saluted the Swiss Guard at the gate. Then he turned sober for a moment. "Everyone is careless at some point. To be honest, I'm surprised we lasted this long with the Kurtoglu regime."

"We wouldn't have if Isa didn't have a strange fascination with me," Michael complained.

"That's because you're his dada," Will mocked.

Michael shook his head. "Just park the car, smarty-pants. Let's get this holiday going."

Notified by the front gate, Michele and Jimmy came to the front porch to greet them. Michele hugged Michael fiercely. "It's been way too long!" she exclaimed.

Michael quipped, "Well, we literally have Satan for a boss, so ..."

When Michele hugged Will, Michael hugged Jimmy. "I can't thank you enough for your work with the international detainee centers. Over two thousand Christians have a home now because of your fine work."

"Thanks, Uncle Michael," Jimmy said with a smile. Then his demeanor darkened. "I appreciate the compliment, but there are so many in need of our help. Sometimes it feels like we're trying to drain the ocean with a paper cup."

As they headed indoors, Michael answered. "It's the worst time in history, Jimmy. We'll never be able to help everyone, but we have to keep trying."

The house looked festive. Michele had done a good job of winding broad red ribbon through four stories of stair rails. Nestled in the stairwell was a six-foot pine tree decorated in red bulbs and cranberry garland. "The place looks great, Michele," Michael said.

"Thanks," she replied. "It's a shadow of what the professional designers did for Mimi. Obviously there's no twenty-foot tree. This is what Jimmy and I could get."

"Well, it looks great," Michael complimented.

Will sounded disappointed. "Aren't we missing something? I thought there was going to be a baby for me to play with."

"They'll be here in about an hour," Michele said with a laugh. "Gloria has a few things to wrap up at the center. But I have to warn you: Manny is a bright kid. You'll have to do better than 'gitchy, gitchy goo.'"

Michael cackled. "You *actually* said that?"

"What is this, pick on Will day?" Will asked with a feigned hurt expression as Jimmy led him to the family space in the back of the house. Michael and Michele lagged behind.

"I was talking to Will about how great it will be in the millennium. Maybe he'll find a nice girl and have oodles of kids in a world with no sin. Same goes for you and Jimmy."

"I can't wait," Michele said dreamily. "Being around Manny gives me optimism for the future. I know we're only a couple of years away from Jesus's return, but these last five have seemed like a millennium. And we haven't even started the worst of the judgments."

"They're around the corner," Michael said somberly. "But we have to get through them to get to the other side, and I'm anxious to be done with the tribulation. I've seen enough of Isa and Benny to last a lifetime."

"I'm sure you have," Michele answered.

"Not that it's been easy on you. The company can take its toll even in the best of times."

"I spend less and less time there, Uncle Michael. Nicely put, everyone is green, and their pallor is the least of it. They are increasingly inhuman, just little automated pieces of flesh. I actually miss the times I fought with Naomi. At least there was honest emotion then."

"How is Naomi?"

Michele rolled her eyes. "Green and living every day to honor her risen savior. She takes it easy on me because she feels bad for a genetic anomaly preventing you and me from taking the inoculation."

"They bought that lame excuse?" Michael asked with astonishment.

"Like the dutiful lizards they've become."

"What does she think about Jimmy not taking the mark?" he asked.

"She was tough on him at first. He said he wouldn't take it out of love for me, kind of like when a person shaves his head for a wife undergoing chemo. After a while, she thought it was romantic. And by now she has stopped caring. She almost never calls him anymore."

"Is he okay with that?" Michael asked, thinking how much he missed his own mother.

She shrugged. "I think he's relieved, to tell you the truth."

Before long the front gate notified Michele of Gloria's arrival. They all went to welcome her. Michele threw open the front door and rushed to take Manny.

Michael hugged Gloria. "I like your hair," he complimented.

"Thanks," she said a little nervously. "I don't have to be Riverside's Barbie doll anymore, so I went with my natural color."

"Good for you. I think it's very flattering." He smiled.

"As do I." Will smiled as he moved in for a hug.

"And who do we have here?" Michael asked as he lightly touched Manny's foot. The very sight of his tiny shoes brought a smile to Michael's face. Manny grinned.

"This is the best boy in the world!" Gloria exclaimed. "Aren't you? Aren't you Mama's best boy?" Manny grinned, gurgled, and salivated.

Will moved in to get a good look at him. It was a little too close for Manny's comfort. His face puckered into a soft cry.

"That's okay," Gloria cooed. "Will's a nice boy. Look," she said as she hugged Will.

Michele laughed. "I felt the same way about him at first, but I grew to love him."

Will shook his head. "Gloria, they've been picking on me all day."

Michael scowled. "We've only been here an hour."

Gloria took the baby from Michele. "You have to move more slowly, Will. Just touch his shoe like your Uncle Michael did. And speak softly to him."

"Hi, buddy," Will whispered in a high voice. Safe in his mother's arms, the baby smiled.

They enjoyed a dinner of freeze-dried stroganoff. Michele apologized for the army-type rations, explaining that she had saved the only fresh food for their Christmas Eve dinner.

The next day was Christmas Eve. They spent the day making some Christmas cookies with flour, sugar, and shortening Michele had managed to find. Michael became acutely aware of the absence of chocolate—most of his mother's recipes called for it.

Taking a bite of a chip-less chocolate chip cookie, he said, "I guess we were chocoholics. Almost all of Mom's recipes used chocolate." He waved the cookie as he spoke about it.

Will swooped in to take a bite of Michael's cookie as he waved it. With cookie still in his mouth, he said, "Still, beggars can't be choosers. We're lucky to have these, and to tell the truth, they're pretty tasty."

"They'll have to do," Michele said, "because I have to close up the cookie factory to get our Christmas Eve dinner ready."

Dinner came together quickly with everyone helping. They had broiled fish, mashed potatoes, and carrots from the hydroponic garden.

The baby had his first taste of mashed potatoes. He swirled the first bite around in his mouth and then pushed it out through pursed lips. The next bite went better. Finally, he came to love them.

"Can I feed him?" Will asked.

"Sure, just a little bit on the edge of the spoon," Gloria cautioned.

The baby waved his arms anxiously, awaiting each bite. He punctuated each with a loud "Mmm" that drew squeals of delight from the adults. Michael laughed at the thought that the adults enjoyed Manny's mashed potatoes more than he did.

"You'll be a great dad someday, Will," Gloria said to the grinning younger man.

"I think she's right," Michael added. "I can't wait for the millennium, when you guys will get busy making some playmates for young Manny here."

"Guess there's nothing left to do but practice in the meantime," Jimmy said with a leer.

"Down, boy!" Michele chuckled.

Following dinner, they each gave gifts to Manny. He gloried in the attention but played with the boxes. Will fell to the floor to demonstrate how to play with each new toy, bringing laughter and looks of awe from the baby. Michael joyfully watched the group, silently praying they would all survive the coming disasters.

After about an hour with the baby's toys, they went to the chapel, where Michael celebrated Christmas Eve Mass. His message was somber. "First, I want to say merry Christmas to each of you. This is the fifth Christmas since the rapture. In those early days, I couldn't imagine how any of us could survive this long. But we have, and although it has been exceptionally hard, we have all grown in Christ. When you think about it and remember who we were before, you'll discover we are each a miracle of God's grace and Jesus's redemptive power.

"I suspect that, like me, you have days when it's hard to remember the time before the rapture." He paused to acknowledge the smiles and nods. "It seems as if I've lived a lifetime since then—a lifetime filled with anxiety, fear, and uncertainty. And yet, underlying all those negative feelings has been a deep, abiding knowledge of Jesus's love.

"We're going to have to dig deep to hold on to that feeling of love as we enter the final days of the tribulation. The trumpet and bowl judgments are around the corner. We are about to see horrible destruction, pain, and confusion as Earth is plunged into a two-year dance with the Nemesis system." He wished he could preach a more uplifting message, but he had to prepare them for the imminent destruction.

"By next year at this time, the Lord will have broken the bedrock of everything we know and love about Earth. Throughout all the up-coming turmoil, we'll have to remind ourselves that a new civilization will be built when Jesus returns. We will finally live in a world of peace. Satan and sin will be bound for a thousand years as we work with Jesus and our raptured family members to rebuild a veritable Garden of Eden.

"This is why Jesus says, 'When you see these things, look up, for your redemption is nigh.' Although we have to live through the trials to come, we are told to joyfully expect His return. But how do we accomplish this?

"The truth is, we have to forgo our attachment to this world and adopt an eternal perspective. Although much of the world's population will be decimated in the coming two years, Jesus sees anyone who took the mark as already dead. He has already grieved for their decision. They are lost to Him, and they are lost to us. That doesn't make the coming events any less frightening, but it makes them less tragic, because already we have witnessed the greater tragedy. What remains is merely fallout.

"Live or die, we will soon be with Jesus, reshaping this world for His reign. I'm especially excited for that opportunity tonight because I can imagine the future more completely when I look into Manny's eyes. He will be too young to remember any of this hardship. He will grow up in a world of sunshine, joy, and peace and with physical knowledge of the Lord! He is the future of Earth, and he is what we're fighting for—his future and the future of the ones to come after him. The Bible says of the millennium that a person who dies at the age of one hundred will be considered a youth. That means we get to watch not only Manny grow up but also his children, grandchildren, and great-grandchildren.

"Do you know what this tells me? The Lord is a creator, not a de-stroyer. He's the author of life, not the end of it. For in the very moment when the people of Earth have chosen to side with hell, there are seeds like Manny who will grow up in Eden and repopulate a wonderful earth without pain and suffering.

"And so, this is the challenge we face: to let go of the current world in order to embrace the seeds Jesus has already planted for a much better world to come."

Everyone was complimentary of his remarks. But then again, they were about as disposed to like him as any group of people. The real test would come the next day when he held services for the men and women in the detainee camp.

As time went by, they all left to get some sleep, but Michael wasn't tired. Although he knew the truth of his message, he couldn't shake a foreboding feeling. He had found it difficult to concentrate since his time in the isolation tank, and his continuing nightmares robbed him of peace. To calm himself, he read the Bible in the estate's library until he grew tired.

Wincing at the creaky boards on the old stairs, he wound his way to his third-floor bedroom, trying to be silent, taking a step and waiting a few seconds before taking another. When he was on the landing to the third floor, he heard a soft chuckle. No, not a chuckle exactly. What was it? He smiled when he realized it was the baby talking to himself in his crib. He sneaked quietly into the room that Michele had turned into a nursery for Manny.

"What are you doing up, little man?" he whispered to Manny. The baby smiled in the glow of his little lamb night-light. Then he gurgled again. Michael was sure Manny was trying to talk to him. He reached into the crib and gently raised the baby to his arms.

"How about some rockabys to help you sleep?" he asked. The baby snuggled against him. Michael noticed a full bottle on the table next to the rocking chair.

"So that's what you want," Michael said softly. "Are you a hungry boy?"

The baby gasped at the sight of the bottle, moving his mouth in a sucking motion as if the nipple had already hit his lips.

"Yeah, you're just using Uncle Michael to get some num-num, aren't you?" He sat in the chair and inserted the nipple. Manny drank happily. "I speak fifteen languages fluently, and you've reduced me to saying 'num-num.' What are we going to do with you, Manny?"

Gloria appeared in the doorway. "You know about baby monitors, right?" she asked with a smile, to indicate she had heard him all along.

"I do now." Michael grinned. "I hope you don't mind. I heard him in his crib and decided to check on him."

Gloria sat on the floor next to the rocking chair. "You know, he's going to need a father as well as a mother in the millennium."

"Oh, uh," Michael stammered. "Are you offering me the job?"

"I can't think of anyone I'd trust more."

"Listen, Gloria, I have no idea if I will be released from my vows in the millennium. You may meet a man you can actually marry."

"If I can't marry you, I'll be happy to have a coparenting relationship like the one your mom shared with Chris," Gloria offered.

This was totally unexpected. Michael took a deep breath to savor the moment. "I'm overwhelmed. You know, I've wondered about us and prayed about it, but I just don't know what the priesthood will be like in a couple of years. In any event, coparenting with you would be like a dream come true."

"You and Manny and I can be a family," she said with a smile as she laid her head on his knee. He reached out to stroke her hair and then pulled back. He didn't know what the future would hold, but he knew in the present he was a priest. He needed to stay in his lane.

"It's a deal," Michael said. "And when Jesus arrives, we can ask Him if marriage is a possibility. I meant what I said in my sermon tonight. There is such a bright future on the horizon, but the old cliché still holds: it's always darkest before the dawn."

He was interrupted by Manny's squirming. The bottle was empty. Michael flipped the baby over his shoulder and patted his back. One large burp later, he asked with a suspicious scowl, "Why do you suppose my shoulder is wet?"

Gloria giggled, pointing to a small towel on the arm of the rocking chair. "He threw up a little bit. You should have placed the towel over your shoulder. Welcome to parenthood. If you're lucky, I'll let you change a diaper."

───────

Christmas Day was a blur. After breakfast, they went to the detainee camp. John Santos had gathered the men and women in the space that had once been the orphanage gymnasium.

As they entered, John greeted Michael warmly with a hug.

"John, you look better than the last time I saw you," Michael complimented with a smile.

"Getting out of the corporate environment and actually doing something to help people has done wonders for me." He smiled. "Don't get me wrong, I still long for the day I'll be with my wife and kids again, but this will keep me busy until Jesus returns with them."

"Good man," Michael said.

John introduced him to the group, and Michael preached his Christmas sermon. The men and women at the camp seemed to be moved, except for one young woman in the back who yawned as if she were bored to tears.

He next led a Bible teaching, followed by prayer and worship. The day was beautiful, a little taste of heaven. The Holy Spirit was present, leaving not a dry eye in the house.

"Well, actually there were two," Michael said to himself. That young woman in the back seemed angry. There was something about her he didn't trust. He doubted she could be a Christian given her display of disregard for the service.

Afterward, while everyone sat down to Christmas dinner, Michael motioned his eyes toward the young woman and asked Gloria, "What's her story?"

"A new detainee. Her name is Chastity."

"As in Bono?" Michael asked with a grin.

"Yes. Her parents were Sonny and Cher fans."

Michael raised an eyebrow. "Really? What were they, ninety when they gave birth to her?"

Gloria chuckled. "Why do you ask?"

"Her reaction to the service today. I'm not sure she's a Christian," Michael said quietly.

"She says she is, but I don't see it either," Gloria said in a whisper. "But she doesn't have the mark and doesn't want it. We might find ourselves in the position that we catch a stray person who is against Kurtoglu for reasons other than Christianity. We can't turn them away. We just have to hope they'll come to love Jesus from their time with us."

"I never really anticipated non-Christians at these locations," Michael pondered. He didn't say anything else. An unsaved person in this environment seemed unsafe and problematic to him, but the very nature of Christianity was evangelism. Despite his unsettled feelings, he said nothing more, choosing instead to enjoy the day.

TWENTY

Michele was just about to get out of bed on December 27 when she heard her phone signal a text message. Reaching to her nightstand, she opened the text from Gloria. It read, "Zack is here with local police. Bad situation."

She jumped from bed and roused Jimmy. "Jimmy, get up! We have a problem. Zack is at the facility with the local police."

"What?" he asked from a dead sleep as she slipped into jeans and a T-shirt.

"Get the car. I'll meet you out front!" she called as she left the bedroom.

She ran as fast as her legs would carry her to the chapel. There she pounded the specific three stones to gain entrance to the underground bunker. "Come on. Come on!" she screamed as the floor opened to reveal the stairs.

"Oh God, I hope I'm doing the right thing," she screamed as she went to the armory her grandmother had left. Quickly grabbing two automatic rifles and lots of ammunition, she ran up the stairs and rapidly pressed the stones in reverse to hide the underground facility.

Again she ran as fast as she could to the back door and through the house to the front, where Jimmy was pulling up in the Hummer that had brought Uncle Michael and Will home during the Dark Awakening.

Jimmy threw open the passenger door. She quickly handed him the weapons and jumped in. As they sped down the driveway, she called Will.

"What's up?" he asked casually.

"Zack is at our camp with the local authorities. Can you get rid of the cops?"

"On it right now," he said crisply. She heard him pounding his computer keys.

"Keep me on the phone," he commanded. "I've sent an urgent communiqué to the mayor, the governor, and the president telling them to get their men off Vatican property this instant."

"Good," Michele barked. She held tight as Jimmy made a speedy right-hand turn.

"Will," Jimmy said, "we'll be there in ten minutes, and we're armed. Will the police be out of the way by then? I'm not looking for a confrontation with the authorities."

"I don't know, Jimmy!" Will shrieked, "In no event will you produce your weapons to the police! Do you hear me?"

"I'm with you on that one," Jimmy said.

"I'm sending the Swiss Guard from the house to assist," Will said as his keyboard rattled.

They heard a ping. "Okay," Will said. "The governor has just ordered the local police to vacate the premises immediately."

"Good!" Michele exclaimed as she loaded ammunition into their rifles.

"Uh-oh," Will said glumly. "The governor apologized for any casualties and damage done to the facility. Looks like it was a raid."

The Hummer careened through the security gate as Michele shrieked. Jimmy joined her.

"What? What is it?" Will cried.

"It's ... it's on fire," Michele screamed. "Oh God! Will, I can see nothing but flames."

"I'll tell the mayor to send firefighters. Do you see the police?" Will asked.

"No. Wait. There's a limo coming toward the gate. Jimmy, block him!" Michele screamed. Jimmy moved the Hummer directly in the limo's path. Michele holstered her phone and jumped out with a rifle. She released the safety and pointed the barrel at the limo's back seat. Jimmy jumped from the Hummer with his rifle pointed at the driver.

As Michele watched, Zack slowly exited the limo holding Manny. Chastity followed.

"Give me the baby!" Michele shrieked. She wanted to kill Zack. Her mind raced with the prospect of taking out the man who was trying to rob them of the little happiness they had found.

Zack didn't move but held the child in front of him as a shield. Michele pulled the trigger in a rage, shooting into the limo. Manny wailed in fear.

"Give me the baby!" she screamed at the top of her lungs. Her trigger finger itched to finish the deal, but Manny's cries moved her to reason. She wanted to comfort him more than she wanted revenge.

Zack stood there, frightened and confused. Jimmy moved toward him silently, his gun barrel pointed at Zack's head. "Do it!" he yelled, startling Zack, who had not taken his eyes off Michele. Cautiously, he held Manny out to her.

Michele engaged the safety on her rifle and handed the weapon to Jimmy. Her tears and sobs echoed Manny's as she took him from Zack and held him close to comfort him. Only after her heartbeat slowed did she realize Will had been screaming to her through the phone. Holding the baby close with one arm, she pulled the phone out of its holster.

"Are you okay?" Will demanded. "I heard gunfire."

"We're okay. Jimmy has a gun on Zack and Chastity." Turning toward the young woman, she screamed, "Chastity! We were never anything but nice to you! Why would you do this?"

Chastity remained defiantly silent. Zack spoke for her. "Money. Of course," he said smugly.

Michele accused, "Gloria would never have handed Manny to you unless ..."

"You're right. She's dead," Zack said with no emotion.

"Why, Zack?" Jimmy asked. "She wasn't hurting you."

Zack shrugged. "I couldn't let Michael be the hero yet again. The man ruined my marriage. I wasn't about to let him ruin my chance to be a widower."

Zack haughtily flashed his trademark smile. "And I'll tell you something else: when Isa finds out what you guys have been doing behind his back, your whole damned family will wish they had died as quickly as Gloria."

Fire sirens wailed in the distance. Michele glanced at the blaze, hoping against hope that some could be saved. She shook her head slowly as she realized it was already too late. The smell of burned hair and bodies wafted through the air.

"Michele!" Will screamed through the phone. "Let me talk to him." Michele held the phone out to Zack as the Swiss Guard team arrived.

"Zack," Will said sternly, "it's over for you. I have records of all the funds you stole from Kurtoglu. I'm going down the hallway as soon as I hang up to clue him in."

Zack stared fiercely at the phone, his face frozen in an aspect of contempt. And then the contempt slowly dissolved. His eyes turned red and filled with tears. His shoulders slumped. "D-don't do that, Will," Zack begged. "I'll do whatever you want. Just don't tell Isa."

Will ignored his plea. The sirens were closer. Will spoke louder to be heard. "Did you kill Gloria and the others?" he asked.

"I only killed Gloria," Zack answered. "The police killed the others."

"H-how did she die?" Michele asked.

"I shot her. It was all recorded." Zack grinned. "I sent the recording to your uncle."

The Swiss Guard arrived quickly. They immediately patted down Zack, Chastity, and the driver, relieving Zack of his pistol and his phone. Will spoke to them, "I need two of you to accompany him back to Jerusalem on his plane. I'll have a detachment meet you there to take him into custody. I need two of you to escort my family back to Castello Pietro. The other two, turn the driver and the girl over to the local authorities."

Two of the officials handcuffed the driver and Chastity and led them away, and another two cuffed Zack. One put him into the back of the limo and sat beside him. The other took the wheel of the limo and drove away. The blares of sirens were deafening as the fire trucks and ambulances pulled up to the gate. The Swiss Guard moved the Hummer to allow them speedy access.

Two guards slowly took Jimmy and Michele's weapons. They helped the couple and the baby to the back seat of the Hummer. Manny cringed and wailed in Michele's arms. She held him tighter and cuddled him as Jimmy cradled her. Something had snapped inside her. The pain of the tribulation had been horrible until now, but in the final analysis, the tragedies affecting the world had only had a peripheral impact on her life. Now it was personal, and she knew she would never feel safe again until Jesus returned.

She leaned her head against Jimmy's chest. "The book of Revelation says Isa will be given the power to overcome even the saints for a time." Her voice broke, and they both cried.

Once Michele and Jimmy were safely in the Hummer, Will signed off the phone call. He called Kurtoglu's security team to learn of his whereabouts. As luck would have it, the imperious leader was just arriving at his office from a visit with the pope to plan the upcoming Resurrection Day celebration. He gathered the documentation of Zack's treachery and ran through the front hall of the basilica, his steps chasing swirls of colored lights on the floor as the sun shone through stained glass windows.

As he approached Isa and his security entourage, he slowed to gather himself. It would be a violation of all protocol to interrupt the ruler of the world. Clearing his throat, he called softly to Isa as he approached, "I beg your pardon, Excellency, but a major security breach has come to my attention. I beg a few moments of your time to explain."

Isa looked at him with disdain for a brief second, followed by a sarcastic grin. "Of course, William. We both know how interested you are in my welfare."

Will swallowed hard and followed Isa and his team to his office. The security team stood guard, but their captain, Sharif, followed Will and Isa into the latter's office. Isa pushed a button on the side of his desk, and the office door slammed shut.

"You were saying ..." Isa said drolly to Will.

Will's throat was dry. He had to make this stick so Zack wouldn't have the opportunity to tell Isa about the fake detention centers. "Excellency, if you take the time to look at the summary sheet on top of these pages, you'll see I have documented how Zack has absconded with nearly a billion dollars' worth of credits from your accounts."

"What?" Isa screamed. A chill went through the office. Will was stunned for a moment. He felt sure Satan would have known Zack had no scruples.

Will laid the pages on the desk in front of Isa and then stepped back to stand at attention. Isa looked at the summary and rifled through the backup. He looked at Will through the corner of his eye. "And you decided to bring this to my attention when Zack is on holiday. Why?"

Will thought fast. "Actually, Excellency, Zack's absence was the occasion for the search. A long family history with Zack had aroused my suspicions, but they weren't confirmed until I could get to his data. That was obviously easier to do when he wasn't around."

"Yes," Isa said suspiciously as he looked through the pages again.

Will added, "If I may, Excellency, I think Zack left Jerusalem for good."

"Ran off with the money, eh?" Isa said with a sharp cackle. "To tell the truth, it's a series of actions I admire. But not when they are perpetrated on me!"

"I've located him, sir. At this moment, he is flying back to Jerusalem under the care of the Swiss Guard."

Isa slammed his hand on the desk. "Good for you, Will! Even without the inoculation you are more loyal to me than the assistant who shares my DNA."

Will swallowed some vomit that crept up his throat. "Thank you, Excellency."

"And where have you been?" Isa demanded of his own security chief. "Why didn't you know of this outrage?"

"Um, sir, I, um," Sharif stammered. Will cringed at the look of betrayal in Sharif's eyes.

"Excellency," Will interceded, "I only just found this information today. Normal protocol would have demanded that I tell Sharif. The fact that Zack had already escaped drove a sense of urgency to inform you directly."

"Sticking up for Sharif now, are you?" Isa asked slyly.

Will responded, "I'm just relaying the facts, Excellency. Zack is very crafty. If my family hadn't known him for years, I wouldn't have suspected him. And for what it's worth, sir, I think Sharif runs a tight ship."

"Barring the current leak." Isa grunted. He waved his hand to Sharif. "You're dismissed. You will live to serve me another day. No more screwups, though, do you hear me?" Isa said in a menacing voice.

Sharif blanched and said, "Yes, sir." His voice cracked. He saluted and left the room.

Will felt a sense of terror envelop him as the door closed. He had never been in a room alone with Satan. He silently prayed for strength.

"Will you stop that?" Isa screamed. "I'm not going to hurt you, you imbecile!"

"I beg your pardon?" Will asked, confused.

"You don't need to pray when you're around me. It won't do you any good anyway. And I find it most annoying."

"Yes, Excellency," Will answered. He stopped praying for the moment. He had no idea Isa could hear his silent prayers.

"Not always," Isa answered in an aggravated tone. "But they were coming in loud and clear a few moments ago. Back to the matter at hand, what should be done with Zack?"

"I hadn't actually thought of his punishment, Excellency," Will offered as he fought to stop his mind from thinking about Zack as a matter of expediency in protecting the other fake detention centers. He panicked and in his mind sang "Mary Had a Little Lamb."

"Well, if you won't say it, I will. Zack must die," Isa proclaimed.

"Yes, Excellency," Will said somberly.

"But not because you find him offensive—because of what he did to me."

"I don't follow, Excellency," Will said softly.

"Come now. You said it yourself. Your family has a history with Zack. In fact, that is the main reason I made him my assistant. I wanted to keep your uncle Michael on his toes." Isa folded his hands, and his eyes grew bright with glee. "You see, Benny wanted Zack here as sort of a love interest. Nergal wanted him here as a vehicle to keep Michael off-balance. I listened to both of them, of course, but I had my own reasons. Throughout my existence I have always been fascinated by human grudges. I thought the pitting of Zack against Michael would give me great pleasure. To be sure, I like Michael better, but my odds were on Zack because he has a more devious nature."

"So, you were hoping Zack would take action against Uncle Michael, but instead he stole from you," Will summarized.

Isa shrugged. "An aspect of Zack's character I hadn't counted on, his greed. You see, I was looking for more court intrigue between the two of them—like that old television show *Game of Thrones*."

"So they're pawns on a chessboard to you?" Will asked, stifling his rising anger.

Isa laughed, first a little and then very hard. "Not 'they,' William! All of you!"

Will blanched.

Isa continued. "But you have just given me the most delightful surprise. All along I thought either Michael would take out Zack or, more probably, Zack would take out Michael. I hadn't even considered you a contender, and look at you! You've risen to the top in a most remarkable display of cunning. Clearly I've underestimated you!"

"Thank you, Excellency," Will said with a forced smile. He was breathing in rapid, shallow breaths, wondering if there could be anything more repulsive to him than praise from Satan. He felt a surge of self-recrimination, and then the presence of the Holy Spirit calmed him.

"Well, you've done marvelously, Will. Zack will be killed, all right, but he'll be made an example to anyone who would dare to cross me again. I have just decided to place him on the commemorative pyre at my resurrection celebration." He laughed at the thought of it.

"Oh," Will said briskly as his mind conjured the abysmal image.

"And in honor of your excellent service, you may light the fire!" Isa proclaimed.

"I don't think I can do that, Excellency," Will said softly. "I'm grateful you considered me, but I don't think I can light the fire. Perhaps someone who has received your DNA in the inoculations ..."

"I'll have to think about your reluctance," Isa said dismissively. "Perhaps I'll choose another. What good would it do the celebration if you look uncommitted to our cause while performing your task?"

"Thank you, Excellency," Will said with a slight bow.

"Yes. Yes. Now get out of here." Isa waved him off.

Will made a beeline for the door. As his hand grasped its handle, an unseen force slammed him into the door, backed him up, and threw him into the door a second time. Will felt his nose swelling from the first hit. The second hurt his left arm as he'd extended it to brace against the impact.

"Just a little warning in case you ever decide not to accept an honor from me in the future," Isa said. He laughed fiercely as Will scampered through the door.

Michael sat on the couch in his small apartment. He thought he had cried until there were no more tears, but he was wrong. Why had he allowed himself to think of a happy ending? Just days ago he was excited to raise Manny with Gloria in the millennium. He knew the worst of God's judgments hadn't come yet. He should have known there was a chance one of them wouldn't survive until the end. He pounded the arm of the sofa as he picked up his phone and hit the play button one more time.

"Thought you'd get away from me, did you, Gloria?"

"You sent me away, Zack. I didn't leave you," she said defensively.

"But your lover Michael set you up in this place," Zack said with a snarl. "It wasn't bad enough that he took my ministry; he tried to take my revenge as well."

A cry sounded in the background. Gloria moved to the playpen behind her desk to pick up Manny. She turned to Zack and said, "A woman left him with me. This is all I want, Zack, to be left alone and to be a mama to this baby. I'm no threat to you."

"Give me the baby, Gloria," Zack said sternly.

"Never!" Gloria screeched. The baby wailed. Gloria hugged him and spoke softly to him.

"You have a choice, Gloria. I can kill you and the baby right now, or I can kill only you if you hand him to me."

Gloria's face melted into an expression of grief and horror. "No, Zack!" she cried, her words barely discernible through the tears and the dread in her voice. "He would be better with me in heaven than with you in hell!" Gloria cried.

Zack moved closer, putting the barrel of his pistol against Gloria's head.

"Zack, please," she whined in a half voice.

Michael watched intently. This is the part he needed to see again. There was a flash of light off camera. It was barely discernible, but it was there. Gloria's eyes moved toward the light, and she smiled.

Michael quickly froze the video before the gun blast ruined her beautiful face. She had seen something at the very end. Was it Jesus? Was it her parents? Michael guessed he would never know. But one thing was sure: she was at peace in that final, brief moment of her life.

He looked at her face one more time and then tossed the phone onto the couch beside him. The emptiness he felt was beyond emotional. There was a physical hurt in his chest: the loss of Gloria, the horror Manny had just endured, the ache for a life as a husband and father—a life that would never be. He put his head in his hands and cried violently.

Sobbing and gasping for breath, he wished he could be with his mom or Chris. They would know how to help him through this, but they were gone as well. He felt a puff of air as someone sat next to him and then the tug of an arm that hugged him. He turned to see Will and returned the hug.

The two men cried.

TWENTY-ONE

Will massaged at a migraine beginning in his forehead as he spoke to Michele through his computer. "Jake is doing his best to carry on, but he looks bad. He's not eating, and the circles under his eyes tell me he's not sleeping much either."

"I get it," Michele said. The conversation was early in the morning for Will but in the middle of the night for Michele, who had called after rocking Manny back to sleep. She looked exhausted herself. "I'm numb from the shock of losing not only Gloria but also John and all the others at the camp." Her eyes welled with tears. "I keep thinking we left them there like sitting ducks. Maybe they would have been better fending for themselves ..."

"No!" Will exclaimed. "They wouldn't. Michele, you had a mandate from the Lord to help those people. And you did. You have no guilt in this. All guilt begins and ends with Zack. And to tell you the truth, I'll be happy when he's no longer on earth." That having been said, he was definitely not looking forward to his front row seat for the execution. With his thumb and forefinger, he pressed along the bridge of his nose to try to ease the migraine.

"You look like you're not taking it too well yourself," Michele said softly.

"I feel sad about Gloria's loss, but I'm concerned as hell about whether Zack left an evidence trail that could endanger our other detainee centers. And," he said, hemming, "I'm afraid for Jake's sanity. Did you know he and Gloria were planning to coparent Manny?"

"He told me," Michele said through tears. "Then he said Jimmy and I should adopt Manny now that Gloria is gone. Of course we love

Manny and will do it, but it feels like I'm hurting Uncle Michael in the process." The sight of her tears brought tears to Will's eyes as well.

"Listen, Jake is nothing if not reasonable and rational. Manny needs a mom and dad to raise him. But that doesn't mean Jake hasn't been very hurt by the recent turn of events. We have to find a way to stop him from falling into depression."

"What do you have in mind?"

"Even if you feel bad, like it's rubbing salt in a wound, make sure you involve Jake in Manny's life. Send him updates and photos. He may be more of a grandfather than a father to the boy, but he still needs to be there for Manny."

"I can do that, especially if you think it will help Uncle Michael."

"I know it will," he said. "I have to sign off now. I need to get ready for the 'big burn,'" he muttered with a scowl.

Will quickly changed into a dress uniform and met his men in Abraham's Courtyard. As it had been for all events since the reopening of the Temple Mount, security for this one was intense, including full body searches for all the green people coming to watch the show. Since the inoculations, the recipients of the invasive frisks barely seemed to notice.

Today's crowd would be limited to religious leaders and political dignitaries, all of whom had been burning the midnight oil in Jerusalem the past two days. The inoculations may have turned rank-and-file citizens into obedient little drones, but the higher-ups in the satanic hive just became more indulgent. Alcohol, drugs, and male and female prostitutes had ruled the streets of Jerusalem for a fortnight. And now the spent, hungover elite gathered to recharge their spiritual batteries with Zack's immolation.

Not that Zack was the center of attention. Cities all over the world were enacting the same ritual with live enemies of the state to be incinerated while crowds partied uncontrollably. For today and tomorrow, the worker bees were instructed to exalt in the resurrection and glorification of their imperious leader.

"Satan really is lord of earth now," Will said under his breath as he marched his squad across the courtyard to the front steps of the basilica, where Sharif and his security team were dressed in military attire. Sharif and Will saluted one another. Will admired the smart look of

Sharif's military uniform and shook his head imperceptibly at the thought of the broad-striped balloon pants of his Swiss Guard attire.

Two of Isa's security team opened the huge double doors of the basilica. In the open doorway stood Isa and Benny. Isa wore a simple tailored black suit, white shirt, and thin black tie. Benny wore his standard tailored white tunic with diamond buttons that caught the sun as it flickered through the intermittent clouds above. They descended the stairs gracefully to a fanfare of trumpets from the band to their right. Behind them, in single file, walked a line of lesser luminaries, led by Michael. His face was set like stone.

As the trumpet fanfare ended, Will and Sharif saluted Isa. Sharif and his men fell in behind Will's men. They were followed first by Isa and his entourage and then by the band, which played "Hail to the Chief" as the group paraded across Abraham's Courtyard to the dais and funeral pyre. The audience rose as Isa and Benny mounted the platform. Will's men and Sharif's men surrounded the pyre in alternating positions. Michael and the others stood in front of seats on the courtyard along the front of the dais. Will had ensured his position would be closest to Michael.

Benny came to the microphone first, speaking in Nergal's rich baritone voice. "On this most auspicious anniversary of Lord Kurtoglu's resurrection, we come to express our thanks that he took up his life a second time to lead us to a bright future." The standing crowd cheered.

Benny continued, "I offer a brief invocation today, not to a mythical, unknowable deity, but to the one true god who has chosen to come to us not once but twice. I will never forget the day he rose like the phoenix from the flames of his funeral pyre. Posterity will show through video evidence that we are the only generation blessed with indisputable evidence of God's presence on earth!" Again the crowd cheered.

"So, my dear friends, I make this simple petition to our ever-present god: Bless us, Excellency. Bless us with your presence and with the remarks you have prepared for us today."

Will swallowed bile and prayed to the true God as Benny completed his prayer and bowed submissively in Isa's direction. The crowd bowed as well. The security team remained at attention. Will looked toward Michael, who stood as well, his face like flint.

Isa smiled broadly as he strode to the microphone amid another herald of trumpets. The crowd cheered mightily, as did crowds throughout the world as shown on giant screens surrounding the courtyard. Isa spread his hands in a benevolent blessing.

"Ladies and gentlemen! Citizens of what is soon to be the newest member of the galactic federation of worlds!" The crowd cheered again. Isa smiled and waited for the cheers to diminish. "Ascension to the consciousness of Divinity was not on my list of aspirations a few short years ago." The crowd chuckled. "Rather, it was a destiny unknown to me, and to my alien creators for that matter. As a hybrid being, I sensed the uniqueness of my nature, never realizing that this extraordinary pairing of dissimilar DNA made me a receptacle for the very creator of the universe! I didn't know, couldn't know, until that moment when my spirit combined eternally with His and pulsed back to life on a pyre like this one." Again the crowd erupted.

"Having died, been imbued with the divine spirit, and returned to you from the dead, I can look at you honestly and tell you unabashedly that I am the three-dimensional representation of the very Creator God of the universe. I created you. I reside with you, and I will lead you to your destiny in the stars!" The roars of the crowd grew even louder.

"I have come to lead you, but not to protect you from the Anu." The crowd hushed. "For the spiritual benefit of every man, woman, and child, you must learn to band together and forge a planet of beings united in love and respect for one another. I encourage you not to be fearful of the Anu but to embrace the challenge before you, the challenge to cast off the burden of their existence so you can rise to the heights I had planned for you from the beginning of time." Again the crowd cheered. Will looked at Benny, who seemed to be in some sort of religious ecstasy. Without breaking his attention stance, he scanned the crowd to see that they, too, were very moved.

"I must warn you. There will be hardships between now and the day we throw off the chains of the Anu. Many will die, but I'm here to tell you from my experience that death is not the end. Just as I was able to raise myself from the dead, so will I raise my followers once we enter the galactic federation. Anyone who dies in my good grace, committed to the future, will rise with me to enjoy that future." The crowd again roared in religious ecstasy. Will winced against the increasing pain of his migraine.

Isa continued, "But we have among us those who deny the future, who have placed their own needs beyond those of the collective good." The crowd booed. "Many have denied the gift of my DNA. They mock my divinity, holding to myths and legends of a world that has already passed. They look to the past instead of the future. For these men and women, there is no hope. No hope they will participate in the fight for our freedom. No hope they will participate in the joyous new world. And may I state categorically"—he paused for effect and then continued in a grave voice—"no hope I will resurrect them." The crowd hushed.

"But there are even worse among us," Isa continued. "Some have accepted the life-enhancing benefits of my DNA. They have gloried in their new stamina and immunity to all disease, and yet they have grown traitorous to our cause! They think they can have all the benefits without any of the sacrifice. Well, ladies and gentlemen, these people are a plague among us and must be stamped out. For this reason, our Resurrection Day traditions have been enhanced this year. Starting this year, cities all over the globe will burn in effigy a representative traitor who has abused the gift of my life for personal gain.

"That these individuals exist disgusts me. That such a person was found in my inner sanctum appalls me." A gasp rang out from the crowd. "Yes, ladies and gentlemen, it is true. Just this week I learned my personal secretary, Zack Jolean, a man who had access to my most personal records, used that access to steal hundreds of millions of dollars from our fortification efforts, diverting the funds to his own account." The crowd booed. "He will be executed this day on the Jerusalem pyre. Let the Resurrection Day ceremony begin!"

Two of Isa's military guards marched Zack to the pyre to the lonely cadence of a single drum. Will guessed it was the first time Zack had appeared in public without his hair combed and a smile emblazoned on his face. His greenish pallor accentuated the dark circles under his eyes. Will supposed they were due in equal part to beatings and lack of sleep. His normally clean-shaven face was littered with the beginnings of a gray beard. The military escort led him to a wooden platform. There he was stripped of his clothing and chained to a nine-foot square board. He briefly fought the men who were tying him down, but they pistol-whipped him into submission. Will cringed at the sound of metal on flesh. Once Zack's arms, legs, and torso were bound to the board with thick chains, the entire piece of wood was lifted by a crane and placed upright in a notch at the top of the pyre. Zack hung there, arms splayed in a grotesque mockery of the Crucifixion.

Will took back anything he had ever thought or said about how he would be relieved when Zack met his punishment. What he was witnessing was grotesque and inhumane. He wouldn't wish this treatment on anyone. To make matters worse, Zack's greenish pallor guaranteed only hell awaited him. His existence would never be better than it was at this moment. The weight of those thoughts combined with the migraine to make Will momentarily light-headed. He drew several deep breaths, counting as he exhaled, to ward off his body's urge to faint.

Isa left the dais and stomped down the stairs to Sharif's side to grab a lighted torch with which to set the pyre ablaze. He walked toward Will with the torch extended. If Isa handed him the torch, he would pass out for sure. There was no way he could participate in this barbarism. Isa walked close to him, torch extended before him, and then he chuckled just a bit as he looked Will in the eye and turned to light the pyre himself. The entire strut had been done to tease Will. Will closed his eyes briefly, praying never again to have to face Satan's cruel sense of humor.

As Zack found consciousness after the pistol-whipping, he began to scream at the sight of the growing flames. In those screams, Will heard not only fear but also betrayal. Zack's love of Isa had been for naught.

"Oh God! Oh God!" Zack screamed.

"Finally he knows who he's dealing with," Isa said with a smirk to the crowd. They broke into uproarious laughter.

Will thought Zack's screams would never end. They became more high-pitched and plaintive as the board on which he hung caught fire. He screamed, "Oh, Jesus! Jesus, I'm sorry!"

The crowd gasped at the invocation of an old god. Isa said to them, "So there you have it. He never really gave up the old ways. Tell me, do you think his Jesus will save him?"

"No!" shouted the crowd exuberantly.

Will's disgust moved to physical nausea. He didn't know if he could take this much longer. The plea to Jesus was the last discernible thing Zack said. The rest were screams of abject horror and pain.

Finally, Zack's hair caught fire. He arched his back, screamed one final time, and fell limp on the board. He hadn't burned to death. Will assumed something like a heart attack had mercifully ended this ordeal—only to send him to an eternal torture that was far worse.

The air filled with the acrid smell of burning hair and flesh. The scent motivated Isa to dance with joy. Benny came off the dais to join him, and then the crowd began to dance as well, spinning around like whirling dervishes, psyching themselves into some weird trance state seen in ancient pagan rituals.

Will looked over to Sharif only to find the man staring straight ahead with glassy eyes and a silly grin. The other men around the pyre looked the same—like they were enjoying some form of religious ecstasy. He then turned his gaze to Michael, who stood rigid, unmoving, as he stared at Zack's flaming body.

After a time, the board to which Zack was attached collapsed into the pyre along with anything that remained of him. The whirling slowed and then stopped. With giddy grins on their faces, Isa and Benny blessed the crowd and proclaimed the Resurrection Day celebration to be in full swing. Around the world people would eat and drink food and liquor they had saved for the past year for this special occasion and rare day off work.

Their blessing was punctuated with fireworks launched from the four sides of the Temple Mount. The gathered crowd oohed and ahed at the fireworks spectacular, until one of the pyrotechnic devices careened into the funeral pyre, spraying wood embers and char everywhere. There was a brief quiet pause from the crowd. Another one hit the Jewish temple behind the dais with a loud explosion. Someone in the crowd screamed. Then another.

Benny and Isa looked at each other with shocked expressions, and then they looked to the sky. Will followed their gaze. Above them, the atmosphere was filled not with pyrotechnics but meteors. Isa and Benny called the guards around them and beat a quick retreat to the basilica. The guards at the entrances to the Temple Mount abandoned their posts as the crowd pushed through the security lines to leave.

Will marched with his group to the basilica. He and his men stood guard while everyone entered—everyone but Uncle Michael, that is. Where was he? Will turned around to see him standing in place, with the same rigid gaze he had displayed throughout the ceremony. Will tapped his second-in-command, pointed to Michael, and ran out in the courtyard to get him.

The bombardment continued. A meteor would hit with an awful explosion, the rumble of which would barely subside before the explosion of another strike followed. Alarms sounded throughout the city. Flames shot up as buildings were destroyed.

Will stood next to Michael and gently put his arm around his shoulder. "The trumpet judgments have started, Jake."

"I know," Michael said in a distant tone.

"We have to take cover!" Will said loudly as he cringed from a close explosion.

"I'm not sure I want to do this anymore, Will," Michael said somberly.

Will understood Michael was in pain—most probably he was in some sort of posttraumatic shock—but at the moment it didn't matter. He was as angry with his uncle as he had ever been. He got his nose to within a centimeter of Michael's and screamed, "I don't care if you *want* to do this anymore, Jake! Michele and Jimmy and I need you—you owe it to my dad to be here for us. And Manny needs you—you owe it to Gloria to be here for him."

Something broke in Michael. He wiped at a tear forming in his eye and said, "You're right. There's no time for me to entertain these feelings. Let's go!"

Will sprinted with his uncle across the courtyard as the impact of a large meteor shook the Temple Mount. Before entering the basilica, they stood in the doorway to witness the destruction.

"Nothing will ever be the same," Will said sadly.

Breathlessly, Michael agreed. "You're right. The wrath of God has begun in earnest."

TIMES

TWENTY-TWO

Michael and Will rode out the meteor storm in Will's apartment in the basement of the basilica. Will opened his link to the underground Petra base, and they watched events as they unfolded around the globe.

"So, the meteor storm affects this hemisphere only?" Will asked as they examined images of horrific destruction from Isa's worldwide database of security cameras. What remained of Rome's Vatican City after the Dark Awakening had been turned to rubble, as had the Coliseum.

"For now," Michael answered. "Imagine the world spinning. Our side is heading into the debris field, but as Earth rotates, different areas will face the meteor storm." Will was relieved to see Michael rise above his own pain to deal with the current crisis.

They watched in stunned silence as Africa went up in flames. The burning metal meteors ignited acres of dry savannah. Soon the fires spread to jungle areas. Population centers in Europe not previously destroyed by the recent nuclear exchange were now the target of the Nemesis debris field. Rome, Glasgow, Zurich, Madrid, Munich, and Saint Petersburg were all aflame, as were population centers in the Middle East and Africa. Johannesburg's devastation was incomprehensible.

"What the meteors don't destroy, the fire will," Will said dismally. They heard the distant wail of alarms in Jerusalem above them.

"We have feeds from some skyward weather cameras," the agent said. "They're very telling. Take a look."

The images were startling. The sky looked like patchwork as streaks of white-hot and red-hot metal careened in every direction. Many of the meteors had burned up completely in the atmosphere, but other, heavier meteors plummeted to Earth as smoldering red-hot bombs.

Thinking aloud, Michael said, "The outer debris field isn't as dense or expansive as the inner iron oxide cloud close to Nemesis. If I'm right, we'll just skirt the edge of it on Nemesis's inbound leg. On the outbound leg, it will come really close."

"Let me see if we can find anything from Isa's astronomers," the agent said. "I can't imagine anything more practical than his quantum computer for calculating the space weather from the orbits of millions of projectiles like this."

"Good point. You've been in those records before?" Michael asked.

"The route for our hack has been established. Luigi laid the groundwork once the preacher told of his dream that the trumpet judgments were about to start."

"Good job, A-aalvin!" Michael exclaimed.

"A-aalvin?" Will asked with a raised eyebrow.

"Your uncle's feeble attempt at humor," the agent said with the slightest smirk. "Don't let it enter your vocabulary, young man."

"I won't," Will said with a chuckle. He hadn't seen Michael this animated since Gloria died. "But I have to tell you, I didn't think Jake would ever joke again after recent events."

"My condolences to all of you on that score," the agent offered. "I've seen a lot of tragedies in my career. It is never easy when the good guys lose."

"Thanks," Michael said with a sigh as he patted Will's shoulder. "It hurts a lot, but Will put me on solid ground. There's a lot to be done—no time for despair."

The agent said, "He's right, and to tell you the truth, those poor men and women in your camp got field promotions. They're in a far better position than we are—buried underground while watching God stone the hell out of us."

"Interesting turn of phrase," Michael mused. "In the early days of Christianity, stoning was a prevalent cause of martyrdom. Maybe there is some poetic justice in the type of terror the Lord is using to bring judgment."

"No coincidences in heaven, right?" Will asked. A thunderous crash echoed above them, and an explosion rocked them. "That was close," Will pronounced.

Alert warnings went off in the building, sounding a shrill upward tone, followed by a mechanical announcement. The vaguely female automated voice declared, "An alarm has sounded in the rotunda area. Prepare to evacuate."

"Yeah, right," Michael said. "Like we would fare any better at ground level."

"Sounds like Saint Peter II took a black eye. Couldn't happen to a better place or a better pope," the agent said drolly.

"Amen to that," Will said. The alarm sounded again. This time the automated voice told everyone to shelter in place.

"And for your local space weather," the agent intoned, "cloudy with a chance of bombardment."

"Funny," Michael said. "What does it really say?"

"It looks like you're right. This is a long-duration event, twenty-four to thirty-six hours."

"So that means the entire globe will be hit and this hemisphere will get a double dose. Soon the barrage will stop here as evening falls, but it will continue in the Atlantic, then America, the Pacific, Australia, and Asia," Michael commented.

"It looks that way," the agent said, glancing at his computer screen to confirm.

"Have any of the global communications satellites been hit?" Michael asked.

"Not that we would notice," the agent said, "but I know from some of my former assignments that there is far more redundancy planned into that system than most people know."

"Man-made redundancy or God's protection over the communication grid. Either way, we have the opportunity to warn the rest of the world if Isa doesn't," Michael said.

The agent responded, "Actually, there have been worldwide alerts advising people to take shelter until nightfall tomorrow, whatever their geographic location."

"Well, we can take advantage of the communication grid to tell them who is really behind these catastrophes and that it isn't too late to be saved if you haven't taken the mark."

"The preacher would certainly have everyone's attention if he went out with a message right now," Will said hopefully.

The agent said, "If he sends a recorded message, I could quantum-digitize it and have it ready for broadcast in about an hour."

Michael and Will heard laughter and commotion in the background. The agent corrected himself: "I'm reminded that I can barely get my own email. Rather than using the pronoun *I*, I should have said 'my dedicated team whose English is getting better and better.'"

Will chuckled as Michael moved away from the screen to grab some paper and a pen. "It looks like the preacher is pulling together some thoughts as we speak. In the meantime, are there any new Hubble shots of this thing?"

Giacomo came into view. "The latest was a couple of days ago. It looks like they shut Hubble down after these were taken, maybe to weather the storm."

"Let's see what you've got," Will said. Michael sat beside him with a notepad, jotting down thoughts between careful examinations of each image.

The screen filled with an angry-looking black and red disk surrounded by a cloud of red haze. Giacomo commented, "This is a close-up of Nemesis. As you can see, it looks a lot like embers at the bottom of a fire. The red spots are warmer than the black."

"How far away is it in this shot?" Will asked.

"Actually, it is just beyond Jupiter, but not on the ecliptic," Giacomo answered.

"And the ecliptic is ..."

"The ecliptic is the plane on which most of the planets in the solar system orbit the sun. Our planets move around the sun in a path near its equator like Saturn's rings."

"Okay ..." Will said.

"But the Nemesis orbit is highly inclined," Giacomo continued.

"Highly inclined to what?" Will asked.

"The ecliptic," Giacomo said.

Will turned to Michael with a wide-eyed, questioning look. Michael barely looked up from his notepad as he clarified: "Think if Saturn's rings were tilted ... a lot."

"Exactly," Giacomo said. "So, we will feel the effects of the Nemesis system before we see Nemesis. You know how Nibiru appears in the sky and then disappears as it orbits its star?"

"Yes," Will said. "Although it's been awhile since we've seen it."

"Well, it's on the other side of Nemesis right now in its own highly inclined orbit, and Nemesis is still below the ecliptic. What we're witnessing right now is the outer part of the Nemesis solar system entering the ecliptic near Earth's orbit. Nemesis itself will keep coming closer and at some point pass through the ecliptic," Giacomo said.

"Meaning ...?"

Michael put down his pen and added, "Meaning we won't really see Nemesis until it is right on us. It's moving really fast, but the solar system is a large piece of real estate. By the time it actually crosses the ecliptic, it will be very close. From the perspective of someone on Earth, it will be as if there's nothing, and then a huge object races through the sky."

"That doesn't sound scary at all," Will said, shaking his head.

"Actually, if it weren't so unsafe, the scientist in me would marvel at the opportunity to actually witness such a rare and awe-inspiring cosmological event," Michael said.

"It's of no interest to me except, of course, how to avoid it," the agent said.

"I'm with him," Will said grimly. "No redeeming science qualities for me."

"We've got some more images," the agent said. "These are from Athens." Will whistled slowly at the devastation. There literally wasn't one stone left atop another throughout the city. For as far as the camera could see there was only rubble, fire, and smoke.

At the sound of Will's whistle, Michael looked up at the screen. "A big one must have hit there. If a meteor is big enough, it can have the force of a nuclear detonation. Do you remember a few years back when a meteor exploded over Chelyabinsk, Russia?"

"Yeah, Chelyabinsk," Will said sarcastically. "It was right on the tip of my tongue."

Michael chuckled and asked, "Are there any other pictures from the area? Can we tell how widespread this destruction is?"

Another picture filled the screen. "As you can see, it's not just the modern city," the agent said. "There's nothing left of the Parthenon or the Acropolis. There are no other photos from the area. It seems all the other cameras have been destroyed," the agent said dismally.

"Probably melted," Michael added. "The people who died in the blast zone would have been dead before their nervous systems could even register the pain."

"For the Christian minority, heaven awaits," Will said. "But for the poor green guys, it was a ticket straight to hell."

"I hate to sound callous," the agent began.

"Really?" Will interrupted.

"Point well taken," the agent said. "But what I was trying to say is this: Jesus said, 'Let the dead bury the dead.' I don't think we have the luxury to mourn those who have taken the mark. From a biblical perspective, they're dead already."

"You're right," Michael agreed. "It does indeed sound callous, but we have to be cognizant of the fact that we can't save the world. The truly tragic dead of Athens are those without the mark who had not yet found a relationship with Jesus. Those are the people we could have helped. It just gives me the motivation to send out a message from the preacher right now. I have some basic notes, and I'm ready to go. Will, set up the camera."

———

Michael sat on the couch in Will's small apartment with a bright lamp shining behind him. Will elevated the contrast in the video so that Michael appeared as only a dark shadow. A voice modulator completed his transformation into the preacher. Will pointed to him and counted down, "Three. Two. One."

"Citizens of Earth," the preacher began, "Europe, the Middle East, and Africa are currently under bombardment from an unprecedented meteor storm. As you are aware, the global government has issued a warning to all citizens to take shelter until sunset tomorrow in your respective time zones." There was a rumble as another meteor hit close to the basilica. Will checked his meters to see if it had registered on the recording. Thanks to a very targeted microphone, it had not. He hoped to keep all the bombardment noise from the tape so that Isa could not pinpoint even their hemisphere once the transmission aired.

"The Nemesis system is beginning to enter the inner solar system from a point to our celestial south, surrounded by a massive debris field from its previous incursions. The bombardment we are currently experiencing is Earth passing through the outermost layer of this debris."

A large blast rocked them for a moment. Michael shifted in his chair and took a drink of water before continuing. "I have just told you the science behind these events, but there is a greater hand at work. In the book of Revelation, we are shown God's judgments on the Antichrist and those who follow him. These coming events are classified as seven trumpet judgments and seven bowl judgments.

"The first trumpet judgments are about to unfold. Here is how the apostle John described them two thousand years ago." Then he read from scripture:

> The first angel sounded: And hail and fire followed, mingled with blood, and they were thrown to the earth. And a third of the trees were burned up, and all green grass was burned up. Then the second angel sounded: And something like a great mountain burning with fire was thrown into the sea, and a third of the sea became blood. And a third of the living creatures in the sea died, and a third of the ships were destroyed. And the third angel sounded: And a great star fell from heaven, burning like a torch and it fell on a third of the rivers and springs of water. The name of the star is Wormwood. A third of the waters became wormwood, and many men died from the water, because it was made bitter.

"I believe the next thirty-six hours will see the fulfillment of this prophecy. The first trumpet judgment is the description of the intense worldwide meteor bombardment we are currently experiencing. The second trumpet judgment is a large, mountainous piece of space debris poised to crash into an ocean somewhere on Earth. This presents an imminent danger to all living along the coast. Because we don't know which ocean will be hit, I can't offer any more detailed information.

"I believe the third trumpet is telling us that some of the Nemesis debris contains a ketone known as thujone, a bitter chemical compound found in absinthe, also known as wormwood. This chemical can be harmful to humans and may have psychedelic properties as well. Disintegration of meteors will release the thujone into the atmosphere. Because it is a heavy compound, we can expect it to rain out of the atmosphere quickly.

"As a practical matter, it is prudent for those living along the coast in areas not already facing bombardment to seek higher ground. Anyone in the bombardment must stay sheltered until nightfall. I encourage anyone listening to me to secure as much drinking water as possible before it turns bitter.

"But there are more important matters. Many out there have not accepted the Antichrist's reign for one reason or another. Some simply have a passionate distaste for global government. Some disavow the new religious system because of a devotion to Christianity, Judaism, Islam, or some other faith. To the Christians, I exhort you to hold fast to your faith. Claim the Lord's protection over you and your family, and make sure your heart is right with God.

"To the others, I offer you a challenge. If events unfold as I have described, then you have a decision to make. If the prophecies in the book Revelation are true and are being fulfilled right now, then you have to know what the rest of that book says. I encourage everyone to read it, but let me provide you a brief summary. The book describes the last seven years of human history, during which a world leader will come to power, appear to die, and rise from the dead. Does that sound familiar? This man will establish a new religion as well as global governance. Through deceit, he will lure many to follow him to fight the return of Jesus Christ to Earth. As his evil plans unfold, God will send judgments to warn the people of Earth.

"If the judgments of Revelation are true, so is its message. There is only one Lord, Jesus Christ. He came once and suffered a horrific death to pay for the sins of the world. To anyone who accepts this gift of salvation, He offers eternal life. But the Bible specifically repeals that offer for all who take the mark of the Antichrist—the DNA offered in Kurtoglu's inoculations.

"Jesus the Savior is coming in a very short time to bring peace and justice to the world. Now is the time to claim your salvation and claim your citizenship in His kingdom, which will be established in less than two years.

"May God bless us all and give us strength in these trying times. In Jesus's name. Amen."

Will stared at Michael and counted him out, raising three fingers, then two, and then one. "Amen," Will said after he turned off the camera. "Do you think anyone will listen?"

"Maybe not because of my expository skills, but the fulfillment of prophecy is hard to ignore."

"By the way, good idea pausing after that one big blast. I can edit it out of the version we send to Petra," Will said as he held the flame of a lighter under Michael's notes.

"Hey, Will," Michael said as he turned off the glaring light behind him. "Thanks for hauling me in from the storm. I almost lost myself for a while." He looked embarrassed.

"Who could blame you?" Will asked.

"Maybe anyone I just preached to. I didn't respond very faithfully to Gloria's death," Michael said with a frown.

"That's one way to look at it," Will said, staring into his computer as he erased the recording following its transmission to the Petra base. "I like to think your grief just shows you're human. I was beginning to wonder."

"I don't know what I would do without you, Will, but ..."

Will interrupted. "But you're sure it would be fun. Yeah, yeah, yeah, Jake. Welcome back."

TWENTY-THREE

Isa was in an absolute rage as he stomped past Michael into Benny's office. They had all returned to their posts after sunset. Things didn't look good in Europe and Africa. Fires were burning out of control in cities where burst gas lines fed the flames. Trees and grasslands by and large fell to the meteor impacts and blistering heat. Michael kept his head down, looking at his computer as he strained to hear Isa's conversation with Benny.

"Did you see the transmission from that moronic preacher?" Isa demanded.

"Who didn't?" Benny asked drolly.

"There are millions of people who resist the inoculation! And that idiot just gave them more reason to defy me. Why can't these people see that the real danger to this planet is from this Jesus they claim to worship?"

"The human heart is unfathomable, Excellency. It can be fickle and change loyalties on a dime. And then at other times, it can cling to the most ludicrous of notions despite all evidence to the contrary," Benny said glumly.

Isa screamed, "I don't need pathetic pandering, Nergal! I need insight into these disgusting monkeys we inhabit!"

"Perhaps I can be of more assistance, Excellency," Benny said in the effeminate voice Michael had grown up with.

"Perhaps you can at that, dear friend," Isa said more calmly.

"Fortunately for you, and unfortunately for me, I understand human nature all too well," Benny said conspiratorially.

"And you'll share that wisdom with me for a price. Is that right, Benny?" Isa asked with an edge in his voice.

"Remuneration is such an ugly concept among friends, Excellency. And to be clear, I seek only your friendship."

"And ...?" Isa led.

"And for me to be more of a friend to you, I would need to be less subjugated by Nergal," Benny replied.

"Fair enough," Isa said drolly. "I've given up hope your personalities would merge harmoniously."

"We are less apart than you may think, Excellency. We are in agreement about most things, but I'm afraid we each want to serve you to the exclusion of the other," Benny said with a slight lilt in his voice. Michael believed him. Benny would consent to be Isa's second-in-command, but he wasn't about to be third behind Nergal.

"You may enlighten me now, Benny, and when I need you again, I will summon you. Generally, I love your lack of allegiance to anyone but yourself. However, I like Nergal's commitment to me unto death."

"Fine," Benny said petulantly. "If boring and predictable subservience is your aim, then clearly I'm not your man."

Isa's temper flared again. He raised his voice and spoke in a harsh staccato, "Enough! If you ever want to see the light of day again, Benny, you'll stop this pathetic attempt to outwit me. I invented deceit before your species set its apelike foot on the planet!" Michael heard a huge thud. He winced, guessing Isa had just thrown Benny against a wall.

"I ... I'm sorry, Excellency," Benny stammered. "My ... my first observation is that most of the world has come around to our position. Even though dissidents number in the millions, they are a small minority. Do we really need to fixate on the few, to the exclusion of the many?"

Isa screamed, "Two thousand years ago, I ignored a handful of men: fishermen, a tax collector, a zealot, and a nearsighted Pharisee. While my back was turned, they created a movement that has haunted me ever since. I will not tolerate a fifth column in my new kingdom. When I knock Jesus out of the sky, I don't want anyone around to help Him." Michael cringed.

Benny responded, "Then may I suggest to you that the time of the deceitful lure has ended?"

"Go on ..."

"We have lured most of the world to your cause—by offering them an end to disease, by giving them a common goal, and by giving them a new messiah. The carrot has worked very well. But there are members of humanity who can only be motivated by the stick.

"There is nothing more to lure them. My suggestion is that we disavow the concept of unity through diversity. Crush the minority, Excellency. Tolerate no religion other than the one we espouse."

"You're right, Benny! Maybe it's time for the truth to be known. Maybe it is time I equate the old masters to the Anu. I can prove to those numbskulls that Jesus and Muhammad are our enemies and that only I can save them!"

"Once you take a bold stance, Excellency, you will see a marked result. Those who could be lured have been. Let fear motivate the rest. There will always be time to kill the stragglers who were too dim-witted to be motivated by either greed or fear."

Isa chuckled, then laughed aloud. "And where better to start than Jerusalem. As soon as I return to my office, I'll send my troops to kill the uninoculated."

Benny laughed as well and then added in a grave voice, "Of course, I am concerned for my nephews, given their Christian beliefs."

"Not to worry, Benny. I have special plans to see their faces when Jesus is destroyed."

"Thank you, Excellency," Benny said. "You don't know how much that means …"

Michael sent an urgent text to Will, telling him to quickly requisition a Jeep and meet him at the Wailing Wall. He sent a second text telling Will not to wear his uniform and to bring along an extra sweat suit.

Isa sighed dramatically. "Ah, Benny, I would let you stay if I could trust you behind my back. Nergal, come forth!"

"At your service, Excellency."

"Of course you are."

After Isa left, Michael told Benny he was running an errand to the mail room and then heading home for the day. Benny waved him off dismissively. He ran from the basilica and across Abraham's Courtyard, seeing for the first time the extent of meteor damage. The courtyard was pockmarked with craters, and the basilica rotunda sported a hole the size of a tractor trailer. Descending the stairs at the Wailing Wall, he saw that Jerusalem looked as bad or worse. The sky was filled with smoke radiating the red glow of the fires that were raging unattended around toppled buildings. He reached the Wailing Wall just as he saw the headlights of Will's Jeep.

"What's going on?" Will demanded urgently as the Jeep screeched to a halt.

"Isa's about to have his men kill the unmarked in Jerusalem. We have to get to the remaining religious leaders of Christianity, Judaism, and Islam to warn them," Michael shouted as he jumped into the Jeep. He removed his priest collar and put the running suit on over his clothes.

"Where to first?" Will asked.

"The closest is Holy Trinity. I know the priest there. Father Andrei has connections to the other mainline churches. After that we need to head straight to Jerusalem Baptist." Michael fiddled with his phone as he spoke.

"I'm emailing Isaac to warn the Jewish community. They'll believe him before they'll believe me," Michael said as his phone made a ping sound, announcing the email had been sent.

"Damn!" Will exclaimed as the Jeep came to a sudden stop. The road ahead of them was blocked with debris from a fallen building. With no help in sight, local residents dug with their hands to free wailing people trapped within the rubble.

"Father," Michael prayed, "I know they probably have taken the mark, but I can't stand to see their suffering. Please help them if You can. At least don't let them die like this ..."

"Amen," Will said tersely as he turned the Jeep around. "I know they carry Satan's DNA now, but the human side of them still pulls at my heartstrings."

"That may be one of the hardest things we have to face. Although spiritually dead already, these poor people have to face the most outrageous catastrophes. I don't know what our response should be."

"I get the feeling the Lord isn't too inclined to help them," Will commented.

"I get the same feeling," Michael said sadly, "but I had to ask."

"I understand." They careened down a broader, more passable street. Within moments, they were at the Damascus Gate of the old city and staring up at the white stone cathedral. Holy Trinity was a Russian Orthodox institution built in the late 1800s during the reign of the Ottoman Empire. In the past few years, the façade had been ravaged with graffiti criticizing the old religions, but it still remained a beautiful building.

Michael jumped out of the Jeep. Will followed. Michael heard the unmistakable click as Will disengaged the safety of his revolver. "Put that away," he demanded tersely over his shoulder.

Michael pounded heavily on the rectory door. No answer. He pounded again. He then proceeded to yell into the door in Russian so as to be less likely understood if overheard. "Father Andrei. It's your friend in Christ. I have urgent news."

A hand pulled back the curtain at the window in the door. The curtain fell back into place, and an interior light came on. As the door opened, Father Andrei stood in a long brown robe. He was easily six feet, four inches tall and weighed all of three hundred pounds. His long beard was streaked with gray. Michael felt like a toy doll as the Russian enveloped him in a bear hug.

"Andrei, this is my nephew, Will," Michael said as Andrei released him. "Can we come in?"

"Of course, come in, friend. Nice to meet you, Will."

"Likewise," Will said, extending his hand. Andrei's hand engulfed it.

"Would you like coffee? Maybe some tea?" Andrei asked.

"We have very little time, Andrei. I overheard Isa planning to purge Jerusalem of unmarked citizens. We've managed to send word to the Jews, and I know you have connections with the remaining Catholic and Orthodox clergy. When we leave here, we'll go to Jerusalem Baptist. After that we'll see if we can get one of the imams to believe us."

"There are surprisingly few of us Christians left," Andrei said. "Most Christians don't want to live in the capital city of the Antichrist. A lot of Jews have fled to Petra. But the Muslims … who knows? Besides, what can we do? Where can we go at this late hour?"

"To the Kidron Valley in the City of David," Michael answered. "There are some catacombs and old archeological digs there."

"By the dump?" Andrei asked.

"Yes," Michael confirmed. "Contact everyone you trust. Tell them to get to Hezekiah's Tunnel within the hour. And bring as many flashlights as you can. Will and I will meet you there after we talk to the Baptists and the Muslims."

"The pastor at Jerusalem Baptist is named Noam Chmarkoff, a friend of Russian extraction. I can call him on your behalf," Alexei offered. "I can have him rounding up his people before you could travel there."

"Thank you, Andrei," Michael said somberly. "We have to try to save as many as we can."

Andrei grimaced. "At least for us Christians, there is nothing to lose, only heaven to gain. I don't know if you will be able to convince the Muslims. Even though Kurtoglu has denounced noninclusive faiths, many Muslims still revere him as the Mahdi. How will you distinguish?"

"I hadn't thought of that," Michael said. He wiped at tears forming as he thought of Michele's camp. "A group we had been helping back in the States just suffered terrible loss of life at the hands of a traitor. I want to try to save the resistant Muslim community if I can."

"I think you run a terrible risk going to any of the mosques," Andrei said gravely. "There is a group of Muslims who live as outcasts because they deny that Kurtoglu is the Mahdi. Its leader is a man named Yasin Naaji. He is a very fierce man, and his group is in Silwan."

"Great!" Will groused. "Do you have any idea where in Silwan?"

Michael's mind raced. The area was a maze of tenement buildings. They would never be able to find Naaji quickly. "How can we find him quickly in that mass of people?"

Andrei shook his head. "They are considered traitors by their own countrymen, and they live without the mark. Hiding is what allows them to survive."

Will frowned. "If Naaji's group dies without the opportunity to come to Christ, they are as bad off as the ones who have taken the mark."

Andrei sighed. "And it is only cockeyed American optimism allowing you to believe you can save them."

Michael shuffled his feet. They were wasting time. "Maybe it's just

Christian optimism," he said. "If you have any more information on this guy, tell me."

Alexei asked, "Do you read Arabic?"

"Yes," Michael said. "And speak it."

They followed Andrei to a small office outfitted with an impossibly large desk. Andrei sat at the desk, turned on a desk lamp, and rummaged around in the top drawer. Finally, he smiled and produced the paper for which he had been searching. "His mother, wife, and sisters live at this address. Naaji sacrificed the women of the group to take the mark so they could buy food to share with Naaji and his men."

"Nice guys," Will said.

"You have no idea," Andrei agreed. "They can get a message to Naaji, but if you tell them where to meet us, then you have given the information to people who have Kurtoglu's DNA."

Michael ran his hands through his hair. He had to decide quickly what to do. "Guys, pray silently while I ask God to lead us." The men bowed their heads. Michael said, "Lord, please give me some inspiration. I want to warn Naaji's group, but I don't want to put the Christian and Jewish groups in harm's way. Please give me an idea, Lord."

They stood silently praying for a few moments. Michael's mind suddenly went to their previous conversation when Andrei said, "Hiding is what allows them to survive." He repeated the line aloud.

"What?" Will asked.

Michael smiled. "The Lord already gave us the answer when Andrei said, 'Hiding is what allows them to survive.' We don't need to hide them. They're already hidden. We just have to warn them of Isa's plans. Andrei, I need a pen and paper."

Andrei's gargantuan hand shoved a tablet in front of Michael as he took a seat in front of the desk.

"You wouldn't happen to have an Arabic Bible and a large envelope, would you?" Michael asked sheepishly.

"I've been known to talk to a Muslim or two about Jesus," Andrei said with a broad grin. He left the room to find the Bible.

Michael thought for a second and started to write in Arabic:

> I know you are a man of faith. I, too, am a man of
> faith—a Christian man who, like you, does not believe

Isa Kurtoglu is who he claims to be. I am writing to you as a friend to warn you. Kurtoglu is about to purge Jerusalem of all who have not received his DNA. I warn you to stay hidden until Kurtoglu completes his raid. As a friend, I also send you this gift, a Christian Bible. Please read the prophecies in the last book. They speak to the time of Kurtoglu's reign and the return of Jesus to Earth (not the Anu).

"Okay. This is what I can do with the limited time we have," Michael said once Andrei returned with the Bible and pulled a large envelope from his filing cabinet. Michael took the envelope and wrote "Yasin Naaji" on the front.

Michael and Will bid a hasty farewell, jumped in the Jeep, and headed to the tenements of Silwan.

The way was bumpy as they drove through debris, but the roads were passable. Will drove as fast as he could. When they entered the Silwan area, all signage turned to Arabic script. Michael read signs and gave directions after consulting with the map function on his phone. Finally, they got to a congested area of tenement housing. The buildings were packed tightly together, and the meteor damage was extensive. A blanket of smoke hung over the area. Will stopped the Jeep. There was nowhere to drive. Close quarters and destruction cluttered every road. The area had been a burned-out mess before the meteor storm. Now it was worse with tattered cinder blocks blasted from buildings swallowing any sense of separation between them.

"It's a sea of concrete," Will said in an exasperated tone. "We might have to forget this part of the plan, Jake."

"We're only a block away. We can go by foot," Michael said, jumping out of the Jeep.

"What?" Will shrieked. "The most dangerous section of the city!"

"Look around, Will. Everyone is taking shelter. They're probably more afraid than we are."

"I doubt it, Jake. I really, really doubt it," Will announced as he moved quickly to catch up to Michael.

Michael stepped gingerly over a pile of rubble. "See, it's not going to be so bad," he said when a smell assaulted him: the smell of burned flesh from a smoldering building up ahead. His mind reeled. For a moment he was back on the Temple Mount, smelling the death of Zack and knowing the bodies of Gloria and the others had burned the same way. He stood like a statue, frozen in the flashback, until he felt a slap to his back.

"Come out of it, buddy," Will said sternly. "I recognize the odor, too. Let's either go back to the Jeep or move on up the block, but we can't stay here."

"You're right," Michael said vacantly. They continued to climb through the postapocalyptic landscape until they came to the remnants of a corner. Michael checked his phone and pointed to the remains of the building diagonal to where they were standing. While the top of the building was damaged, the first floor looked habitable.

Michael knocked on the door and called out, "*Ahlon. Ahlon. Assalamu alaikum.*" (Hello. Hello. Peace be upon you.)

No answer. He pounded the door again. "*Ahlon?*"

The door opened slightly. An eye peering from a burka glanced at Michael. Then the door slammed shut.

Michael knocked again. "*Ahlon. 'Abhath ean Yasin Naaji,*" he said, indicating that he was looking for Yasin Naaji.

The door opened again. This time Michael stared into the barrel of a machine gun pointed at his head. He willed himself to appear calm even as his mind raced. "*Laday hizmat li Yasim Naaji,*" he said. (I have a package for Yasim Naaji.)

"*Aftahah!*" shouted the man behind the gun. (Open it!)

Michael heard Will's startled jump as the man screamed. He said calmly to Will, "He just wants me to open it for him. Flaw in our plan—he might think it's a bomb."

Michael could make out only the man's eyes, no other features. The gun obscured his face, and a keffiyeh covered his head. Michael opened the package in slow, steady movements. He removed the contents and passed the note to the man.

The man read the note. Michael watched his reaction and felt sure this man was Naaji.

"Yasim?" he asked softly.

"*Nem fielaan.*" (Yes.) Yasim lowered the gun. He placed one hand on Michael's shoulder and said, "*Ashkurk sadiqiun.*" (Thank you, my friend.)

Michael placed his hand on Yasim's shoulder. *"Aismi Maykil."* (My name is Michael.)

"Thank you, Michael," Yasim said in English.

Michael chuckled. "Is my accent that noticeable?"

Yasim smiled. "I heard you talk to your friend."

"Right," Michael said with a nod. "Read the last part of that book to learn about our common enemy. Now go hide. We're going to do the same."

"Peace be on you," Yasim said as he shut the door.

"Can we get out of here now?" Will asked nervously. "I like to be the one pointing the gun!" They moved much more quickly through the rubble on their return to the Jeep.

Sirens wailed as they left Silwan. "I think Isa's boys are out and about," Will said, pushing the Jeep to go faster.

"Do whatever you have to do, Will, but get us to Hezekiah's Tunnel."

"I'm trying my best, Jake," Will said tersely.

They rode in silence. Michael prayed they would make it there before an encounter with Isa's men.

When they arrived, Andrei was there with about fifty people.

"This is all we have in Jerusalem?" Michael asked.

"People are in hiding from the meteors. These are all we can find," Andrei answered sadly.

"Okay. Stay here for just a couple minutes with Will," Michael said as he rushed off.

"Where are you going?" Will demanded in a taut whisper.

Michael softly called back to him, "Just around the corner. I had Isaac ask the Jews to meet further up. I didn't want the two groups to scare each other off."

"Good thinking," Will called after him.

In short order, Michael returned with around one hundred fifty Jews. Will took the flashlight from the Jeep and stood next to Michael, who led them behind a boulder to a cave. Everyone turned on their lights and followed Michael through a maze descending into the dank ancient tunnels beneath the city. They came to an opening, a large room with a dry floor and more than enough space for the small crowd. The ceiling of the space was high. Only the brightest of their flashlights could penetrate the darkness to see to the top of the cave.

Michael addressed the group in a low voice that nonetheless echoed off the rock walls. "Like dictatorial regimes throughout history, Kurtoglu has chosen the darkness of night to initiate a cleansing action. By tomorrow, his troops will have moved on. Stay here at least until dawn. There will be repeated meteor showers tomorrow, so you might wish to ride out that storm here as well. For the long run, though, Jerusalem is not safe for you."

"What is safe in this time?" Andrei asked somberly. The crowd murmured.

"The Jordanian desert," Michael answered. "Head toward Petra."

When they left the tunnels, Michael and Will found their Jeep undisturbed. Isa's men hadn't been near. They drove to the motor pool with no resistance, but they cringed at the repeated sounds of screams and gunfire coming from the city.

"They're finding people we couldn't," Will said sadly.

"We saved those we could with the time we had," Michael answered, none too hopefully. The gunfire made their effort seem paltry and ineffectual. He wiped at his tired eyes.

"Bunk in my apartment," Will offered. "It's so far below ground that we won't hear any of this, and I have the connection to Petra up and running on a secure line."

"Actually, that's a pretty good idea. I think I'll take you up on that," Michael said.

As they walked to the basilica from the motor pool, Will asked, "Are you ready to catch a few z's?"

"I'm going to try," Michael said with a tired grin. "At least until dawn. Somewhere shortly after that, the next bombardment will begin."

While they ascended the basilica's stairs, an earthquake knocked them to the ground. Will fell flat to the stairs. Michael fell down a few stairs until he was able to steady himself. "Ouch," he yipped, and placed his hand to his head, feeling the moisture of blood.

"What the heck was that? An explosion?" Will asked as he walked down the stairs to help Michael stand.

"If it's what I think it was, Earth was just rattled by a collision with an asteroid. Given the time, it would mean the Pacific Ocean was struck."

TWENTY-FOUR

Michele, Jimmy, and Manny had spent the day in the shelter beneath the estate's chapel. She and Jimmy left Manny to sleep in a portable crib and went into the office. Michele refreshed her email inbox and looked at her secure phone for text messages. Nothing from Will or Uncle Michael. "I wish I knew if Will and Uncle Michael were okay," she said yet again to Jimmy. She caught herself. "Sorry for repeating it. I know wishing doesn't make it so."

"They were okay the last time they contacted us. By then the bombardment should have been nearly over in Jerusalem. That means they made it through just fine," Jimmy said as he rubbed her shoulders.

"Yes, but why the cryptic text? 'Fine for now. Take cover. Talk to you later.' Something else is going on."

"Listen," Jimmy said quietly.

"What?" she asked.

"It's quiet." He looked at his watch and smiled. "Five thirty. It's twilight, babe. The storm is over for the East Coast."

"You're right," she said as she typed into the computer. "The baby should be up in about half an hour. Let's look at the news feed before we tally the damage to our home."

The news wasn't good. The eastern portion of the United States and Canada had taken a pounding. The once-thriving population centers in the Northeast had been decimated by Russian nukes a couple of years before. There the meteors just created new craters on top of old ones.

Rural residential areas in southern Virginia, the Carolinas, Georgia, and Florida fared badly, but not as badly as Michele would have thought. "You know," she said, "America is a pretty vast landmass. There's a lot of space where a meteor can fall without harming anyone."

"Yeah," Jimmy said cautiously. "See if you can get any information on Atlanta, Savannah, Jacksonville, or Miami. We still have pretty dense populations there."

Given their proximity to Atlanta, she pulled up images of that city first, drawing a sigh once she looked at them. The downtown area was ablaze. Local fire departments had their hands full trying to contain the flames. The suburbs fared better, but areas further to the west were taking a beating. It didn't look like the Blue Ridge Mountains would survive. Individual small fires from a multitude of impacts were merging. There were calls for everyone in the area to evacuate.

"There'll be nobody to stop those fires," Jimmy said with concern. "The fires are going to have to burn themselves out."

"Uncle Michael seems to think sediment from meteors will soon drive heavy rains. Maybe that will help with the fires," she said.

"And pollute the water," Jimmy added grimly.

Michele, unable to wait any longer to check the damage, said, "Call up images of Miami. I'm going to pick up Manny and let him awaken in my arms, so we can go check the house."

By the time she reentered the room with the baby, Jimmy had retrieved the images. It was a lot of the same. Global news channels showed shattered buildings going up in flames. The story repeated itself throughout the Midwest, where St. Louis, Oklahoma City, and Dallas had taken beatings. The West had hours to go until sundown, but preliminary reports showed extensive damage to San Francisco and Mexico City.

"Do you notice something different about how these stories are covered?" Jimmy asked.

"I'm not sure what you're getting at," Michele answered. As he responded, she cooed with Manny. "Are you waking up, Mr. Sleepyhead?" His eyes stayed closed, but he stretched and wiggled in her arms.

"We haven't seen one man-on-the-street interview or a single human interest story."

"I hadn't noticed it until you mentioned it," Michele said. "Why do think that is?"

"I think it's evidence of how far from human that people with the mark have become. They only want to know if they have to take a different route to work for the war effort."

"That's scary to think about," she said anxiously. "I can't wait anymore. I'm going upstairs." She changed the baby's position, and he snuggled his head on her shoulder.

As they exited the bunker, Michele and Jimmy both breathed a sigh of relief. The chapel had survived intact. "God's hand," Michele said. "Hopefully, He kept the house safe too."

Leaving the chapel, Michele noticed the air smelled lightly of smoke. She looked at the house. It was intact and not aflame. Then she looked toward the sky to see it filled with haze, the smoke of distant fires caught by the wind. As they proceeded, Michele saw a crater in the flower garden. She stopped short, wrinkled her nose, and asked, "Isn't that where we ..."

Jimmy nodded and grimaced. "Where we buried Billy Watt the day after the rapture. We're going to have to fill that in again."

"I did it the last time," Michele said with a sardonic smile. "Your turn now." She had to laugh at his look of bemused disbelief that she would say such a thing. The backyard evidenced more craters and scorching of the grass, but no burning.

He drew her attention to a hole in the roof nearly four feet wide.

"Given the speed of these things, it must have been a very small meteorite that caused the damage," Michele said.

Jimmy weighed the situation. "Even though it was small, it had to have been hot. We're lucky the entire house isn't aflame."

"We're blessed," Michele said decisively.

"Agreed," Jimmy said with a nod. He put his arm around her as they walked into the house.

Things were pretty much as they had left them. Michele breathed a sigh of relief. Manny yawned and wiggled in her arms, ready for a diaper change and a bottle.

Jimmy went to the refrigerator to grab a bottle and then met her at the stairway. The foyer, with its many-storied leaded glass windows, had survived as well. Stopping off in the nursery, they changed Manny and then continued to the fourth floor to find the damage.

Again, it seemed startlingly minimal. The meteor had burst through the roof and the attic, ending as a small stone in Grandpa

Chris's shower. They looked up through the hole in the bathroom ceiling to the hole in the roof and the hazy twilight sky above.

"Do you think you can patch it?" Michele asked hopefully.

Jimmy bent his head to see through the hole. "I'll have to go up to the attic to know for sure. I think I can patch the roof. It won't be pretty, but we'll keep the rain out. We have some old scrap wood in the barn and some plastic. I'll do what I can."

Jimmy puttered with fixing the hole in the ceiling while Michele checked in on the Swiss Guard members at the gatehouse. They were fine, busily going about their duties like the Isa zombies they had become.

Periodically she checked the news reports for damage. It was the same story over and over again. The United States was on fire, and there was nobody to put out the flames.

She brought the baby's playpen to the fourth floor so she could help Jimmy, or at least be with him, as he tried to repair the roof from the attic. "What's it like up there?" she called though the hole in the shower ceiling. "Chris and I were always too afraid to go up there when we were young, and then we didn't care to when we hit our teens."

"Spooky," he answered with a humorous lilt to his voice. "There's a lot of old stuff up here. I mean, really old."

"The place was quite the hot spot in my great-grandpa Stan's time. Mimi used to tell stories about how he and her mother would hold these big parties that would go on for days," she said as he grunted to hold a board in place over his head and hammer a nail into it. It slipped and fell to the floor. He cussed.

"Are you okay?" she asked.

"Fine," he said in a soft voice. "Just a little embarrassed."

"At talking like that in general, or for speaking like that in front of your wife—or in front of your baby?" she teased.

"All of the above," he said with a grunt as he lifted the board again. This time it stayed in place as he nailed it to the underside of the roof.

She could see through the hole in the bathroom ceiling that the board held. "Congratulations. That's one board down."

"I wonder how Noah did it," he mused.

"With the constant cheering of his wife, I would imagine," she said pertly.

"No doubt," he said as another board went up smoothly. He was getting the hang of it. Michele often marveled at how good he was at fixing things. She had no doubt he would get the hole patched. In fact, it was one of the reasons she was standing below; she loved to watch him do things at which he excelled. First his orphan status and then the rapture had interfered with any chance for him to further his education. She wondered what he would have been in different times. For that matter, she wondered how her life would have been different if she had graduated high school and gone to college.

"Do you ever wonder where we would each be if the rapture hadn't occurred?" she asked him when he finished pounding another nail.

"No," he said briskly. "I know it's only been five and a half years, but it's hard for me to remember when we weren't in the tribulation. I can't relate to the old world now."

"Really?" she asked with dismay.

He put down a board and knelt beside the hole to make eye contact with her. "Before I met you, I didn't have a family. I had lived the bulk of my life with no one who really cared for me. Sure, your parents were wonderful to me, and I'm thankful for everything they did, but in the end I was still an orphan. Since the rapture, I found you and I found Jesus. So, even though these are horrible times, they're kind of warm for me compared to the past. Does that make any sense to you?"

She tried to speak, but her voice caught. Her life before the rapture had been a storybook existence. Her frame of reference going into the tribulation was so different. She wiped at tears in her eyes—tears of sadness for the lonely, scared little boy he had been, and tears of joy that she could be a part of his happiness now.

"I didn't mean to make you cry, crazy girl," he said softly. "I just want you to know that for me, life began when I found you and Jesus." That was all she had to hear. The waterworks were fully on.

As if on cue, the sound of her tears caused Manny to cry as well. She ran to the playpen and lifted him. "That's okay, Manny," she said softly. "Everything's okay."

The sound of feet hitting hard on the attic stairs was followed by a bear hug from Jimmy, and the two of them comforted Manny together. As they embraced, the entire estate shook for several seconds. Michele felt herself sway as Jimmy braced his feet and held her.

Soon Michele's cell phone signaled an incoming text message. Looking at her phone, she said, "Will just texted. He wants us to go to an encrypted computer." She texted back that it would be a few minutes until they would be able to make it from the fourth floor.

Once they reached the bunker office, Michele responded to a communication link sent from Will. The computer screen glowed with an image of Will and Uncle Michael.

"I'm so happy to see your faces," Michele said tersely. "Your response to my earlier text was a little bit cryptic, Will."

Michael spoke, "Isa sent his men to kill the unmarked people of Jerusalem. Will and I were incognito, trying to get some people to safety when you texted us. Sorry our brief response caused you concern, honey, but it was the best we could do at the moment."

"I'm just happy you're okay," Michele said. "How's the damage there?"

Will answered, "Jerusalem was hit pretty hard. The Temple Mount and the basilica took direct hits. How about you guys?"

"We did surprisingly well. A hole in the roof above Grandpa Chris's bathroom. Nothing caught fire."

Michael said, "We've been looking at some feeds from our Petra base. An asteroid hit in the Pacific."

"Does this mean tsunamis?" Jimmy asked.

"There was a study done by NASA back in 2016," Michael said. "They concluded tsunamis were not inevitable if an asteroid strikes in the ocean. There are a lot of variables, of course, such as ..."

Will chimed in, "Short answer, Professor. Tell us before Jesus gets back."

Michele and Jimmy chuckled at the anger briefly crossing Uncle Michael's face.

Michael continued, "I forgot what a tough crew you guys are. Long story short: Tsunamis are not guaranteed after a strike, but a combination of special circumstances can create them. It appears most of those special circumstances have been met. Hawaii was devastated almost immediately because the asteroid strike was so close. There are currently waves traveling toward America's West Coast and Asia. They'll dissipate as they travel, but Japan, Indonesia, Vietnam, Thailand, and the north shore of Australia will be hit pretty hard, and the West Coast will see flooding pretty far inland in low-lying areas like Los Angeles."

"Do they have time to get to higher ground?" Michele asked.

"Technically, yes," Michael answered, "but practically, no. Traffic and torn-up infrastructure will most likely result in life-threatening delays for anyone who tries to get far enough inland. Japan will be decimated. The prospects for the east coast of China are pretty bad too. The waves for them won't be as large or powerful after traveling across Japan and other easterly islands, but so many people live along the coast that China will have difficulty getting them to safety."

Michele could scarcely take it all in. Uncle Michael was telling her billions would be dead in mere hours. She thought back to the Dark Awakening and the nuclear strikes. The number of people lost was horrific indeed, but this one event would dwarf that destruction. "I don't know what to say," she said glumly. "Are you sure?"

Michael continued, "Preliminary reports and scientific measurement of the seismic reaction indicate this was a big rock. John's description of a burning mountain cast into the sea is pretty accurate. The impact most likely went the whole way to the ocean floor and left a crater there. This in turn sent up a column of water and water vapor miles high. Some of it will precipitate back to Earth. Some of it is likely to obscure the sky for a good while."

Michele had been trained from her years of running the family businesses to quickly think of crop impacts. "Uncle Michael, the growing season ..."

"It could be years before there are again bountiful harvests," he said with despair.

Will looked at his phone. "Text from the agent. We have camera footage from the global surveillance system uploaded right before Hawaii was hit." For a second Michele and Jimmy saw only Will's face as he used the laptop's keyboard to call up the footage. As his face filled the screen, Manny made the pretend talking sounds of a baby his age.

"Manny just said hi to you," Michele said with a chuckle.

Will looked up into the screen and said in a high voice, "Hi, Manny! How are you today?" Then he said, "Okay, here goes."

The screen turned to a view of Waikiki Beach. No longer a vacation hot spot for the masses, the area looked pristine, serene, and beautiful. In the Kurtoglu economy, vacations were doled out only to the most loyal of Isa's supporters. The few people on the beach were the crème de la crème of the modern world. They were happily swimming, sunning, and enjoying themselves as a horde of regular "little" people met their every need. Then a bright, white-hot ball flew past them at supersonic speed. People on the beach pointed to the streak of light as it arched across the sky and then held their ears as the sonic boom raged above them.

Still enthralled with the sight and worried by the sound, most stood silently looking in the direction of the object. Suddenly the entire view of the camera turned white with the most brilliant flash of light. Seconds later, earthquake shock waves rocked the island. Debris from the hotel fell around the camera. Its position shifted as the wall to which it was attached crumbled to the ground. Pointing skyward, the camera recorded the sky filling with white steam and a jet of water. Seconds later the camera was flooded and the video feed ended.

"That's horrible," Michele said, choking back a sob.

"There's more," Will said. "Here's data from a weather satellite." A series of still photos showed the Hawaiian Islands and then a monstrous splash of water from the ocean. The third showed waves radiating out from the impact site, one perilously close to Hawaii. The fourth showed more waves expanding from the impact, but Hawaii was gone—submerged.

"Oh, Father God," Michele prayed. "Have mercy on those people."

"I'm afraid the days of mercy are complete, Michele," Michael said sadly. "These are days of judgment."

At that moment, all of their cell phones pinged. Isa was about to address the world.

"Do you guys want me to switch our screens to Isa, or would you rather watch him in replay later?" Will asked.

"We need to be on top of what he's doing," Jimmy said gravely. "Put him on."

They waited for a few moments as music played while the camera was focused on the dark blue curtain backdrop in Isa's briefing room. Soon Isa strode confidently to the podium. He stood behind it for a second, staring into the camera.

"Uh-oh," Michael muttered. "He's mad. This isn't going to be a condolence speech in the wake of tragedy."

Isa began, "Ladies and gentlemen. I'll be brief. As I look at my news updates of the calamity striking the world, I sit in abject horror at the frailty and recalcitrance of humanity."

"Say what?" Will muttered.

"He says we're weak and stubborn," Michael whispered.

Jimmy touched Michele's arm and said softly, "I thought I was the only one who didn't understand."

Michele caught up to what Isa was saying.

"When I first took this role, I was adamant that our survival depended on us forging unprecedented unity. I even provided you with the means by which this unity could be achieved.

"The universe reacts to the consciousness of sentient life. I don't know how to say it more plainly to you. If we were truly united as a planet, the events we are seeing would not have occurred. A unified population would have created a psychic energy shield around Earth to mitigate, if not obviate, the effects of the debris field through which we are passing."

"I don't like where this is going," Michael said cautiously.

"And yet we still have those among us who cling to the old religions, refusing to commit to the future, refusing to work with us, refusing to unite with us in spirit. These people are to blame for the catastrophes blanketing the world.

"Well, I've had enough, and I would think you have too. Today, as a show of my resolve to protect this planet, I have purged Jerusalem of those who have refused inoculation. Furthermore, in order to demonstrate my commitment, I renounce my Muslim heritage with an attack on Mecca. Within minutes, the Kaaba will be no more. There is no reason to worship a meteorite in a box when I, the living god, am in your midst. Worship me, or be damned!" He stomped off the stage.

"Well, that was nice," Will said with a roll of his eyes, as the broadcast camera fell to a long shot of the Kaaba. One minute it was there, surrounded by a few thousand faithful followers. Then there was a bright light. When the light diminished, there was nothing but smoke and a crater.

Michael commented with fascination, "The book of Revelation says the Antichrist will turn against the religious system he rode to power. The book of Daniel says the Antichrist will disavow the gods of his fathers. Isa is right on schedule."

TWENTY-FIVE

The first bombardment had come as a surprise to the Kurtoglu team, but everyone expected the second. Isa was still livid with the belief that those disloyal to him were the cause of the disasters, but his fury was mixed with great glee. He held no esteem for humanity. In fact, it was quite the opposite. He hated them. Created in the image of God indeed! There was only one being with the attributes to warrant such a claim, and it was Lucifer!

Despite their frailty, ineptitude, and faulty intellect, these monkeys, these sons and daughters of Adam, were the beloved of the Creator, clearly an indication He had gone mad and that a more suitable ruler of the universe was needed, even mandated. But to get to the throne, Isa would need to unseat the monkeys. There was no doubt in his mind the bombardment was the Creator's doing, but to what end? To show His favor to the comparatively few people on Earth who had not yet given over to Isa's DNA inoculation?

Clearly, he had to up the ante. Oh, he would always keep around a few just to lure Jesus back, but they would be people of *his* choosing, not the Creator's. Michael and Will would do nicely, but as for the rest of the feeble population who rejected him? He wished them death—no, he wished them excruciating death!

The only good human was a dead human. Every death brought Isa an exquisite feeling of power and grandeur. The moment he rid the universe of these apes, including the half-human Christ, would be the moment the Creator would finally go fully mad.

Isa mulled over all these things in his subterranean office. Peering through the window into the control room, he saw rows of desks and computer screens happily humming away. Things seemed to be running more smoothly now that he had murdered the scientists who neglected to tell him the precise timing of the bombardment. How embarrassing to end the Resurrection Day celebration like that! That's how he knew the Creator was behind it. Somehow He had hidden the event from the scientists.

Into the control room strode the pope, followed by Michael and Will. Isa had requested their presence for today's bombardment. He rose from his desk to enter the control room.

"Ah, Holiness! I see we have some guests with us as we weather today's gift from Nemesis," he said with a cheery smile.

"Indeed we do, Your Worship," Benny said. Isa mused that it was Nergal's baritone but Benny's oversolicitous pandering. Perhaps the two personalities would merge after all.

"Michael, Will, welcome," he said in a brief staccato.

"Thank you, Excellency," Michael said softly. Will repeated him.

"These are grave days, gentlemen," Isa said with a twinge of a smile. "Sad, indeed, but each disaster brings us closer to the glorious day when the Anu will be defeated and our beautiful planet will be free from the celestial mechanics of the Nemesis system."

"Yes, Excellency," Michael said with downcast eyes.

"Oh, come now," Isa taunted. "I'm sure you are interested in the state of the world. Come closer. Let's take a look together, shall we?"

"I don't mind if I do," Benny cooed in a deep voice.

Isa spoke to the new head scientist, "Let's show our visitors the Pacific. Maybe we could start with what used to be Hawaii." The screens turned to drone photos of islands swept clean. There wasn't a single building left.

"Oh no," Michael said softly. Will cringed.

"Oh yes!" Isa exclaimed cheerily. "Really, Father, I understand the underlying tragedy of the situation, but you must try to understand the hidden beauty. Earth was never meant to sustain the number of people we have. As much as the Anu are our enemies, the Nemesis system itself has enabled the continuation of humanity because of periodic cullings of the herd. Let's face it, humanity breeds like rabbits. Present company excluded, of course."

"Of course," Michael said sullenly. Will winced.

Isa tapped the head scientist on the shoulder. He couldn't contain a grin. "Let's show him Hong Kong." The image changed to a flooded city. The buildings of the great city were intact, but the streets had turned into rivers, dead bodies floating along with the current.

"And then there was the beautiful city that used to be called Sydney," Isa said with a chuckle. "I'm afraid it truly is 'down under' now. Japan, Indonesia, and Singapore look a lot like Hawaii, I'm afraid," he said with saccharin sadness. He was taking great joy from the horrified reactions of Will and Father Michael. So weak—and so fun to watch!

"Do you have any images of the sky?" Benny asked with grim fascination.

"I sure do," Isa said as if he'd just been asked to show photos of his kid's graduation.

The screens showed gray, cloudy skies from every location. Smoke from worldwide fires had risen to encircle the globe. There it combined with the monstrous water canopy from the asteroid strike. As they watched, the image moved to Abraham's Courtyard above them, the low clouds reflecting architectural lighting from the three massive buildings there. Streaks of red burst through the cloud canopy as the second bombardment began. Distant booms found their way to the subterranean lair as the meteors blew up in the air.

"It doesn't seem as if they are quite reaching Earth," Benny said with puzzled fascination.

Michael explained in a quiet voice, "The water canopy and smoke provide greater resistance, causing more of them to burn up in the atmosphere this time around."

"Always have the answer, don't you, Father?" Isa asked with a sneer.

"I'm sorry, Excellency, I didn't mean to speak out of turn," Michael said somberly.

"Just joshin' you," Isa said glibly. "You're 100 percent right, of course. Let me show you a few more things." He addressed the head scientist, "Let's show our guests Mecca."

The screen changed to a moonscape. Barren and lifeless gray dust filled the entire screen. Isa chuckled as he closely watched Michael and Will recoil in horror.

"All gone, I'm afraid," Isa said. "Not only Mecca, but also the commercial zone the late prince was so proud to develop. It is hazardous to one's health to worship the old gods.

"Don't let that worry you two, though. Like I told you, I'll need someone to clean Jesus's blood from my boots." He raised his right foot to show off his boot. "Tanned human hide. Pretty nice, don't you think?"

No response.

"Don't you think?" he demanded with aggravation.

"Oh, they're lovely, Excellency," Benny oozed.

"Specially made for me," Isa said with a self-satisfied smile. He leered at Will and Michael just to make them squirm. And they did. What fun!

"Holiness, stay with me through the duration of the bombardment. Gentlemen, before I turn you loose, I should tell you that soon it will be advisable for you to remain indoors. I have it on good authority that people without my DNA will soon face their very own terror from the sky."

"When should we plan to remain indoors, Excellency?" Will asked. "I'll need to change my duty roster."

"Well, let's just say if you have any shopping to do, maybe you should do it in the next twenty-four hours," Isa said with a grin. "You are dismissed."

They turned to leave. Isa felt his mouth salivating. There was something fun about the human body's autonomic responses. His pulse quickened, and his groin pounded with anticipation. Just as they made it to the door, he called out, "Oh, gentlemen, one more thing ..."

As they turned to face him, the screen behind him displayed the destruction of Hezekiah's Tunnel. Their faces were precious as they tried not to cry. This was so much more fun than Isa had anticipated.

"You wouldn't believe what we found hiding in the catacombs by Hezekiah's Tunnel," Isa said with a sinister grin. "I'm afraid none of them made it." His face dropped the grin as his mouth moved to a snarl. "Now you're dismissed, gentlemen!"

Michael wept on the way back to Will's apartment. "I really thought we were able to save them," he said plaintively. "Instead we rounded them up for Isa to kill."

"I guess it was a risk all along," Will said somberly. "But we had to warn them. It would have been wrong not to try."

Michael wiped tears from his eyes. "I thought things were bad before, but they are becoming unbearable now," he said in a tense soft voice as they walked through the underground hallways. He was about to say more, but they ran into some of the Swiss Guard. Will saluted them, holding his hand in the air for a moment after the salute. Michael understood the gesture to mean they needed to be quiet in the public space.

Once in Will's apartment, Michael waited until Will turned on a generator of white noise before he spoke. "Isa is going mad. Satan knows his time is short."

"Yes," Will said gravely. "And for some reason, probably your parentage, he is keeping us close. Too close, Jake. I really don't want to spend the time we have left in Isa's shadow."

"I don't either, but the very unique nature of our situation leads me to believe we are where God wants us to be. The locust swarm is the perfect example. Oops, the locusts! You need to log into the Petra base so we can make sure the programmers are ready to go."

"Got it," Will said as he typed his password into the computer. Within seconds the agent's face appeared on screen.

"We just had an unnerving meeting with Isa," Michael said, dispensing with pleasantries. "Are you guys ready for the locust swarm?"

"Yes. We can change the programming once they are online. We have added a virus to our upload transmission. It will disallow any further orders to the drones. The government won't be able to undo our changes."

"Good idea," Will said.

"But it turns this into a one-shot deal," Michael said somberly. "If your initial programming doesn't work, there will be no second chance to get it right."

"True," the agent conceded, "but there was limited opportunity for a second chance anyway. If our first attempt failed, the government would quickly find and seal the back door we're using. For practical purposes, this has been a one-shot deal all along."

Michael grimaced. "I really wish there was a backup plan. Isa just bested us. We hid Christians and Jews from his purge of Jerusalem.

He found them and killed them. All Will and I succeeded in doing was gathering them together for an easy kill."

"This is different," Will said seriously. "What we're doing now is in the book of Revelation. It has already happened from God's perspective."

Michael smiled. "If I didn't know better, I'd say you've been listening to me all these years."

"Listen to yourself, Jake," Will said with a grin. "This is a good plan, and it's going to succeed. If ever a plan didn't need backup, this is the one."

"Good point," Michael said to Will. Then he looked to the agent. "Have you found out where the locusts will deploy?"

"Isa literally has them staged all over the world. There are billions of them, Father. The technology is advanced, but the construction isn't. Your company has been stamping them out since Isa took over. He can't very well send them while the bombardment continues, so I'm predicting they won't be released until at least tomorrow afternoon our time."

"That timing fits with something Isa said. He told Will and me we should plan not to leave the basilica twenty-four hours from now."

The agent grimaced. "It must be nice to have Satan looking out for you like that."

"It is really unnerving me," Michael said with a nod. "I feel like he's a cat and we're mice. He's keeping us alive for his own amusement."

"At least that's what *he* thinks," Will said contemplatively.

"Your point?" Michael asked.

"Actually, it's your point," Will replied. "He only thinks he's in control. The Lord is in control of our lives. Isa can't kill us until God allows it—whether Isa knows it or not."

Michael's mind filled with memories of conversations he'd had with Will when the latter thought killing Benny and Isa would save the world. Michael had repeatedly told him God was in control of the situation even though circumstances looked bleak. "I talked my face blue telling you this same thing," he said. "I would have bet the family fortune you hadn't listened to a word."

"Well, it looks like today is the day the handsome nephew is right and the withered old priest has been schooled," Will teased.

The agent laughed as Michael shook his head. A rumble in the distance drew his attention. Michael's forehead wrinkled. "I don't like your characterization of it, Will, but you're right. I'm not myself right now. The things you said are things I would normally come up with."

A look of concern crossed Will's face. "Hey, Jake, I was just teasing you."

"But you called attention to something," Michael said. "I'm not reacting well to things."

"It's grief," Will said defensively. "Gloria's death. John's death. The feeling that at both the detention center and Hezekiah's Tunnel we gathered Christians to protect them, only to have them killed en masse. That's a lot to deal with, buddy. Not to mention a daily dose of Benny."

"You've got a point," Michael said cautiously, "but I think there's more." Michael stared into the computer. "And I think you know what it is," he said to the agent.

The agent sighed. He was silent for a second. "The program I put you through was moderated. I didn't think you were really in danger of a disintegration of your personality."

"What?" Will demanded in a shrill tone. "Jake, do you think he damaged you?"

"I'm not sure," Michael said calmly, "but it's worth the question."

"I highly doubt it," the agent said. "But you may be having some posttraumatic stress from the entire episode. Add to that strong feelings of survivor's guilt following all those deaths. There is a chance you are not functioning to full capacity, Father," the agent said sadly.

"So what's that supposed to mean?" Will shrieked. There was another rumble as a meteor exploded in the air above Jerusalem. The lights blinked off and on.

"It means I'm more sad and less able to deal with stressful situations," Michael said offhandedly. "It really doesn't much matter now. The world is in a period of stress unlike any other. I won't be the only one with difficulty coping."

The agent said sadly, "For what it's worth, Father, I never meant to do you harm. From my perspective, it was an elegant way to prove you had really made a commitment to Christ and win the souls of the programmers. As to the resultant psychological effects, well, I apologize."

"Apology accepted," Michael said.

"Not so fast, Jake," Will said sternly. "This guy put us through the mill. We were all traumatized by your abduction!"

"Meant to be," Michael said calmly. "If the agent hadn't done what he did, we wouldn't have the programmers in our corner. We wouldn't be able to reprogram the locust horde."

"I hear you," Will said in a seething tone. "But God could have accomplished those things in a lot of different ways. He probably didn't need the agent's abusive methods."

"Maybe not," the agent conceded, "but that's the way it happened, Will. Frankly, your uncle's way of looking at it is the only way our little group will survive this."

"Actually, we wouldn't be a team if the agent hadn't done what he did," Michael added.

"So, you're okay with this?" Will asked.

"Yes," Michael said decisively. But he wasn't. The knowledge didn't make him angry, just sadder. He was too tired to go on like this, but there was no option other than death—and Will put it pretty succinctly when he said Michael owed it to Gabe and Gloria to be here for their kids. So he swallowed it all, buried it, hopefully deep enough to protect himself for the remainder of the tribulation.

"Then I guess I can be, too," Will said with forced resignation. "But I don't think I'm all that happy to work with you," he snapped at the agent.

"Understood," the agent said crisply.

"Let's get back on track here," Michael said. "To sum up, you are poised to broadcast a signal to reprogram the locusts."

"Yes," the agent said. "It will be sent out via an untraceable quantum signal that will hit all the drones simultaneously to reprogram them and disable any further programming."

"Perfect. That is exactly what we need," Michael said encouragingly.

"So, are we done with today's meeting?" Will asked, a hard edge still in his voice.

"There's one more thing," the agent said. "We're getting reports of rain in Jerusalem. You might want to pop upstairs and look for yourselves."

"Will do." Michael sighed. He had little doubt as to what was occurring. He pushed a button to end the communication and said, "Come on, Will. We might as well get a firsthand look."

They took an elevator to the ground floor and walked through a quiet hallway to the front doors of the basilica. The hallway shone brightly with a blast of lightning, followed almost immediately by a roaring peal of thunder. For a brief second Michael shuddered as he relived the lightning at the rapture. In a flashback, he was standing in a Roman piazza hugging his brother. He drew a deep breath and came back to the present.

Will had kept walking. He called behind to Michael. "Are you okay, Jake?"

"Yeah." He caught up to Will, realizing he had just experienced a PTSD flashback. He shivered and resolved to get it under control. A lot of people depended on him. He wouldn't let them down.

As they approached the doors, they heard the pounding of torrential rain outdoors. Will pushed the enormous wooden door open and yelled above the pounding rain, "Oh God!"

Michael joined him on the portico just outside the doors. Buckets of red rain poured from the sky. The gray granite of the basilica's stairs ran red. The tiles of Abraham's Courtyard were buried in a river of blood that was flowing toward the edge of the Temple Mount.

"What's that bitter smell?" Will asked.

The sky turned brilliant white in another flash of lightning with an immediate roar of thunder. Michael jumped. He raised his hand to wipe at a tear and noticed how his hand shook. He forced it to stop, but not before Will saw it.

He stared back at the younger man, each mirroring the other's concern. "It's thujone," Michael said in answer to Will's original question. "Wormwood."

TWENTY-SIX

Michele was preoccupied on the drive to the office. She hated to leave Manny, and it seemed ludicrous to worry about the family business when they had entered God's wrath. The drive was desolate and dreary. The bombardment had done horrible damage to the infrastructure, and the resultant fires had blighted the landscape. The roads were clear for the most part, although what had once been multilane highways were often reduced to single-lane paths around meteor craters. Ash from the fires blanketed the landscape, except where trails of red were left by crimson rainwater finding its way to streams and rivers. Tim Burton could have designed the landscape.

The surreal nature of the scene was highlighted by the strange glow of the sun. Despite the rain, dust from meteors and resultant fires still filled the atmosphere. Because of this, even at noon the world was bathed in the soft tones of twilight. Saint John had written that the world would lose a third of its light in the trumpet judgments, and to Michele's reckoning, he was dead-on. At night, the effect was also noticeable. The image of the moon was no longer sharp, its craters, mountains, and plains no longer visible. In fact, even its round shape was distorted as its light bent around smoke and water vapor in Earth's atmosphere.

Michele had known this day would come, but it was beyond her ability—beyond most people's ability, she suspected—to actually prepare for such devastation. Knowing it was coming and preparing against it helped, but one could never prepare emotionally to witness planetary destruction. She felt a tear on her cheek. Mourning for the sun. "It will all be fine soon enough," she told herself. "We just have to hang in there a little bit longer."

Her phone rang. She pushed a button on her steering column to patch it through the car's speaker system. "Hello."

"Michele, it's Will."

"Hi, Will. I have you on speakerphone. I'm driving to the office. And before you gripe at me, I really wanted to drive today—no Swiss Guard taxi."

"You should be home," Will said. His voice sounded tired and remote. "The locust swarm will probably be released today."

"You guys will reprogram it, right?"

"Right, but still," Will said. Again she heard the distance and sadness in his voice.

"Will, what's going on?" she asked.

"I'm concerned about Uncle Michael."

"What's the matter?"

"He's super nervous and a little forgetful. He and I talked to the agent. It's likely there are psychological effects as a consequence of that crazy man's abduction and torture protocol."

Michele batted at tears before they could smudge her makeup. "Will, I was so happy to get him back, I didn't really consider what he had been through."

"Neither did I. I had a long talk with the agent last night. He held Jake in an isolation chamber—too short to lie down, not high enough to sit up. All the while he was on mind-altering drugs, derivatives of LSD. Periodically they would heat the box, cool it, and flood it." Will's voice cracked. "I can't stop thinking of the terror he faced."

Michele lost the battle to preserve her makeup and pulled the car to the shoulder of the road. By the time she shifted the gear to park, she couldn't see for tears. "I ... I'm just starting to process it now. Will, I can't stand even to think about it."

"Well, he went through it. And to be honest, he seemed to have handled it okay at first, but then when Gloria was killed he was nearly catatonic. No lie. I don't think he even blinked through the entirety of the Resurrection Day fiasco. Even when the crowd ran to avoid the meteor storm, he just stood there staring at the funeral pyre."

"I knew it was devastating for him, but I figured he was emotionally crushed like we were. I didn't think he also might be sick," she said sadly.

"I appealed to his sense of duty. I told him he owed it to Dad to be there for you and me, and to Gloria to be there for Manny. Then he suddenly snapped out of it and said, 'You're right.' He seemed like the usual Jake, but now I'm not so sure."

"Listen, Will, he's bound to be hurt by the times. We all are. But Uncle Michael is one of the mentally strongest men I've ever known. I can't imagine him losing it," she said, fighting a memory of how hollow his cheeks were when she last saw him and how vacant his eyes were.

"I understand, and I agree. He's tough as nails, but what he underwent was a protocol to disintegrate his personality. It's a miracle, and a tribute to his strength, that he came through it, but the torture combined with grief may be taking a toll."

Michele wanted to argue with him to prove him wrong. She was silent for a moment as she examined her response. Was she angry with Will? No. It wasn't anger at all, but fear. She had come to believe Uncle Michael was unmovable and would always be there to help.

"Michele?" Will asked. "Are you still there?"

"Yeah," she replied, still distracted by her thoughts. "Will, I think I have come to rely on Uncle Michael always to be there for me. It's like he's Mom, Dad, Mimi, and Grandpa Chris all rolled into one. I feel angry because I don't want you to take away my security."

"I'm way ahead of you," Will replied dismally. "I had to sort out my own reaction to this. I feel ashamed that I had to call the agent to find out what Jake had been through. I never asked Jake about it, like maybe it didn't even matter. Then to snap him out of his funk, I pulled a guilt trip on him. Can you imagine how horrible I feel about that?"

She commiserated with him. "I can imagine, because I've been oblivious to his pain as well. But I need to tell you not to take your action or inaction too much to heart. Dad was probably closer to Uncle Michael than anyone, but often he was annoyed that Uncle Michael never confided in anybody. He kept his own counsel, probably because he was smarter than everyone else in the room. He just trusted his own judgment more than advice from others."

"I get that, but he's no longer the smartest guy in the room, and that puts him in a dangerous position," Will answered with grave concern.

"Who do you know who is smarter than Uncle Michael?" Michele asked with disbelief.

Will's voice cracked. "Satan. Michele, Jake is in a horrible position. It's sickening. Isa plays with him like a cat plays with a mouse. Jake turns to stone, trying to ignore the things he says and does, but it's bound to wear him down."

The phone was silent for a few moments except for his sobs. Hearing Will cry brought more tears to Michele. When he was calmer, he continued. "Remember I told you we hid some Christians and Jews at Hezekiah's Tunnel?"

"Yes. That was great news," Michele said.

"No. Isa invited Jake and me to his stupid underground control room. He showed us coverage of the tsunami damage and was totally gleeful about it. Then he lowered the boom. He killed the people we hid away."

"I didn't realize," Michele said softly. Their deaths must have been too reminiscent of the recent detention center deaths for both Michael and Will.

Will continued, "It's hard to explain the glee Isa took in hauling us in there to tell us what he had done. He gets some perverse pleasure out of hurting Jake."

"Uncle Michael is a DNA link for Isa's body. Maybe Satan doesn't like being physically related to anyone," she offered.

"Except that it's sick and twisted. Isa would have no problem killing anyone he didn't like. He's fascinated with his connection to Uncle Michael—and by extension to you and me. Think of it. We have a pass on taking the mark. Do you know why? Isa said he wants to keep Jake around to have him lick Jesus's blood from his boots once he wins the final battle."

"Satan is delusional if he thinks he can win," she said with conviction.

"My point exactly. He's bat-crap crazy, and he's fixated on a man who just underwent horrendous torture and grief."

It all came together for her. Uncle Michael was extremely vulnerable and in the crosshairs of Satan himself. There could be nothing worse on earth. "Will, we have to pray for strength for him. He can't hold it together on his own. The Holy Spirit will have to do it."

"I know," Will said sadly, "but it can be real hard to pray and to feel God's presence when you're depressed. And depression would be light compared to what Jake is dealing with."

"All the more reason for us to stand in the gap. Pray for him, Will. Pray harder than you ever have."

———————————

The conversation with Will had made Michele late for Naomi's meeting. Her dragon of a mother-in-law was bound to be annoyed. "Too bad," Michele said aloud as she turned off the car's engine in the office's parking garage. She had bigger fish to fry, like making sure her family survived until the Second Coming.

Naomi was waiting for her at the elevator bank. Because of their conflicting schedules, it had been a week since Michele had dealt with Naomi in person. Over that time, the transformation had continued. Naomi was even thinner, and the greenish tint to her skin was deeper. What was worse, her hair had thinned considerably.

"Naomi, I'm sorry I'm late. Will called from Jerusalem, and I pulled over to take the call," Michele explained.

"I'm just happy you're okay," Naomi said robotically.

The new DNA has made her more gracious, at least, Michele thought as she smiled and offered her mother-in-law a half hug.

"How's Jimmy?" Naomi asked.

"He's fine. Today's he's happy to have some alone time with the baby."

"That's right!" Naomi exclaimed. "I'd love to see him. Work is keeping me so busy. What's his name again?"

"Manuel. We call him Manny."

"It's a shame about his mother dying," Naomi said. It didn't come across as very sincere.

"You should stop by to see him sometime," Michele offered.

Naomi winced. "Since running afoul of your uncle Benny, I'm leery of being on Vatican property. I didn't like being hauled out of there in cuffs on suspicion of Michael's abduction."

Michele saw her point. Naomi wasn't being manipulative or throwing a dig. There was good reason for her to fear Uncle Benny, although she was delusional if she thought he couldn't take her down as easily in suburban Atlanta as he could in Castello Pietro. "Maybe Jimmy and I could drive him here one day to have lunch with you."

Naomi smiled. "That sounds great! I'll have my secretary set up a date with yours."

They walked to the conference room. Michele took note that one side of the building had taken the brunt of the meteor damage. Broken windows had been hastily covered with plastic, but not before the red rain stained the carpet. "I see we took some damage during the meteor storm, but it doesn't look too bad," Michele commented.

"I wish the businesses had fared as well as our headquarters building," Naomi said dismally as they entered the conference room. A skeleton crew awaited them, just Patricia O'Brien from human resources and Enrique Jones, the CFO. Both wore grim expressions.

"Hi, guys," Michele said. "You don't look like you have good news for me."

Patricia sighed and said, "As if things weren't bad enough today, I was late with my allegiance pledge this morning. One more and I'll be scrubbed for a month!" Michele hadn't really thought much about the day-to-day lives of those with the mark. Each morning, they were required to scan their inoculation chip into a computer and complete an allegiance oath form while they listened to a message from Isa. Miss three in one month, and you were not allowed to buy or sell in the following month. They called that being "scrubbed," because it was as if all of your information had been scrubbed from the beast's computer system. Michele shook her head slightly. For years men of God had wondered how the false prophet would bring an image of the beast to life. They postulated all kinds of things, like robots and demon-inhabited statues. Meanwhile the image John saw was nothing more than a computer screen and a program to verify allegiance.

Naomi sat at the head of the table. In an unprecedented move, Michele sat along the side. She no longer cared who ran the company. Naomi began, "We've had some damage to our factories. We lost our largest cheese plant, a processed meat plant, and several warehouses to fire. That's excluding the West Coast. Basically, we lost everything there to the tsunami. It's total devastation and loss of life. We just have to assume there is nothing salvageable."

"I see," Michele said solemnly.

Enrique added, "Probably the most damaged was our energy business. Meteors hit several oil and gas wells. They burned hot, taking with them the surrounding neighborhoods. Our wells are probably responsible for half the damage done to the Oklahoma City area."

For Michele it was hard to fathom that their business could be the source of so much damage, and harder to fathom what it would matter with the entire world careening to hell anyway. Nonetheless, she dutifully played her role. "Why our wells? Were our practices unsafe?"

"Absolutely not!" Naomi exclaimed. "It was purely luck of the draw. Our wells were hit with some large, hot meteors."

Michele nodded. "Do we bear any legal liability for the damage?"

"The short answer is no, because it's an act of God," Enrique said, "but that sword cuts both ways. We have no insurance coverage for the same reason."

Michele waved her hand dismissively. "Is there some kind of fund set up for the affected area? If so, we need to be the largest donor by far. If not, we need to establish one."

Patricia spoke. "The affected people have been moved off-site to work in munitions factories. With the tsunami destruction on the West Coast, there is a strong need to increase armament production in the center of the country. Simply put, those people won't be returning to their homes anytime soon," she said without passion. Then her face brightened. "We could make a donation to the war effort on their behalf though," she said.

"No. I don't think so," Michele said with a knit brow. "I don't mind helping individuals harmed in part because of our wells, but I'm not going to make blind donations to the government."

Enrique nodded. "Good point. Given all the write-offs we have for destroyed property, we won't turn a profit. Effectively there would be no tax advantage to the donations, because we'll have no income to offset."

"My point exactly." Michele lied.

There was a roar from the hallway. They all looked up, listening to determine the source of the sound. Shortly after, there was a loud scream and a cry of pain, followed by another, then another. Soon the hallway rang with pandemonium.

"What could it be? A shooter?" Naomi asked anxiously.

Enrique strode to the door, raising a solitary finger to ask for silence. He placed the palm of his hand on the door. "Not hot," he said quietly. "I don't think it's a fire."

He opened the door a crack to peer out into the hallway and was blown back into the room by a swarm of locusts. Michele was overwhelmed at the sight of them. They certainly looked like insects, even though she knew they weren't. What shocked her was the sheer number of them. They were everywhere, obscuring her view. A primordial fear rose in her, and she screamed fiercely as she batted them away. The buzzing of their wings gave her involuntary shivers of revulsion.

Her screams were not in isolation. The other three in the conference room screamed in fear too at first, but then their screams turned to shrieks of pain. Naomi was hit first.

"Aaagh! Oh Lord, Isa, what the hell was that?" she screamed. The next screams were without words and dissolved into the opera of pain coming from the hallway.

Michele shut her eyes and prayed. There was nothing else to do and nowhere to hide. Within two minutes, the buzzing of the insects stopped.

When she opened her eyes, the locusts had left the conference room. She slammed shut the door and appraised the situation. Naomi, Enrique, and Patricia lay on the floor moaning and crying out in pain. Large red welts formed where the locusts had bitten them. She knelt next to Naomi. "Naomi, are you all right?" she asked sympathetically.

She winced as she said, "Oh God, Michele. I've never been in this kind of pain. I think this is killing me."

Michele knew the prophecy. Those bitten would wish to die, but they would not be able to—no doubt because of the enhanced immune system from the same DNA that had made them targets of the drones. "Don't say that, Naomi. We'll get you some help," she offered.

Naomi clutched at her. "Before I die, I have to tell you something. In my own way, I do love Jimmy. Please tell him for me."

The raw emotion struck Michele, not only because it came from someone as cold as Naomi, but also because emotion was rarely displayed by those who had been inoculated. "I'll tell him, Naomi, but I can assure you that you'll live through this to tell him yourself."

Michele ran to the phone to dial 9-1-1. The line was busy. "Of course!" she snapped as she hung up. The locust nightmare would be global. No urgent care could attend to it.

Trying to sound calm, she said to them, "I'm going to see if I can get help."

As she opened the door, she was overwhelmed by the noise of thousands of wings as the locusts sped down the hallway. Her first instinct was to close the door and hide. "They won't hurt you, Michele," she said to herself. "The Bible says so." Closing her eyes and gritting her teeth, she slid into the hallway and closed the door behind her.

She was partially right. The locusts neither landed on her nor bit her, but they were large and flying fast. They buffeted her as they flew past her to their next victims. They were surprisingly heavy, and it hurt considerably when they banged into her. She bent at the waist and ran in a crouched position to be under the bulk of the swarm.

The hallway was a mass of human suffering. Michele staggered through, stepping over fallen employees in her crouched position. She went to the bay of windows behind her secretary's desk. They had been damaged by the meteors and were covered over with plastic until the locust swarm broke through. What she saw outside looked like a sci-fi movie—an undulating swarm of greenish-gray insects silhouetted against the dark gray sky and ash-covered landscape. She felt a bump on her head, followed quickly by another and then more. The bumps to her head came from individual locusts leaving the building. Michele shrieked when one was momentarily caught in her hair. The entire horde followed, and the air filled with an endless thunderous drone of their wings as they found their way to the outside.

She ducked under her secretary's desk to find the poor woman already hiding there, barely conscious from the pain of a welt on her face.

She called her name. "Mary. Mary, can you hear me?"

"Agh," Mary moaned. "Just let me die in peace, Michele." She raised her hand to the grapefruit-size welt on her cheek and shivered with pain when she touched it.

Frustrated, Michele knelt closer to her. "I ... I don't know how to help you," she cried.

"You can't," Mary said in a cry of pain before passing out again.

Horrified at her inability to help, Michele left her faithful secretary. The only relief available to the poor woman was the loss of consciousness. Michele had to figure out what to do next. These people were beyond help, and she wanted nothing more than to be safely at home with Jimmy and the baby. Wiping at tears of self-recrimination, she moved into the hallway again, stepping over writhing bodies and ignoring calls for help as she headed toward the elevator. She raised her hand to push the call button and then pulled it back.

"I can't help them," she said to herself as she tried in vain to push the button. No matter how difficult their relationship, Naomi was still her mother-in-law. Michele may not be able to help everyone, but she could help Jimmy's mother.

"Naomi took the mark," she said to herself as she pushed back through the hallway to the conference room. "If Manny doesn't get to know his grandmother now, he never will," she said aloud, partly to convince herself and partly to steal her attention away from the bodies littering the hallway. She wanted to stop and cry. She wanted to pray for them. She wanted to help, but from an eternal perspective they were the walking dead.

"I hate that I just had such a thought," she said to herself as she opened the conference room door. Patricia and Enrique were out cold. She knelt beside Naomi, who had managed to sit up and prop herself against the wall.

"Naomi, the locusts have attacked most of the people in the building. Emergency services will take forever to respond. Do you think you can walk?"

"Yes," Naomi slurred. The left side of her face drooped as if she'd had a stroke. Michele saw the huge lump on Naomi's left arm where she had been bitten.

"Naomi, can you move your left leg?" Michele asked.

"Of course I can!" Naomi snapped out of the right side of her mouth as she moved her left leg spasmodically.

"I'm taking you home with me," Michele said.

"No. No. I don't want to be in a Vatican facility," Naomi slurred as she whimpered.

"Jimmy and I can take care of you there!" Michele screamed.

"Benny's in Jerusalem?" Naomi asked plaintively.

"Yes," Michele reassured. "He hasn't been in the United States for years. You'll be safe."

"Well, maybe for a couple days—until this wears off," Naomi mumbled.

Michele straddled the older woman, placing her hands under Naomi's arms. "Okay, on the count of three, we're going to try to stand you up. One. Two. Three." Michele held onto Naomi and threw her own weight backward. Screaming in pain, Naomi rose for a few moments and then stalled. "Push, Naomi. Push!" Michele screeched.

Her head bobbing to the left, Naomi let out a guttural yell as she slowly completed her stand. On her feet again, she leaned back against the wall. "Hard to keep an old bitch down," she said with a slur and a half smile.

Michele smiled in return and chuckled at the improbability of the situation in which they found themselves. "Naomi, I'm going to have to support you from your left side. Will it hurt you a lot if I get under your left arm so you can lean on me?"

"It'll hurt like hell, but do it. I've always been more John Wayne than Maureen O'Hara anyway," Naomi said toughly.

"All right, here goes," Michele said. She winced as she raised Naomi's swollen, paralyzed arm and slid herself under the older woman's shoulder. Naomi yelped with pain the entire time.

TWENTY-SEVEN

Terrifying screams of pain filled the dark night in Jerusalem. The manufactured locusts were no respecters of daylight like their biological cousins. When they came into an area, day or night, they wreaked havoc. Hours before, Michael had awakened to the screams. Now he lay in his bed with his hands over his ears.

The plan to reprogram the locusts had seemed genius at the time, but he didn't know if his nerves could stand to live with the consequences. His resources were the cause of all the suffering he heard in the streets below.

"I'm not stupid," Michael said to himself. "I didn't invent this technology, and I certainly didn't unleash it on the world. All I did was initiate programming changes."

"Is that all you did?" a voice rang out in his room.

Michael sprang from his bed. "What? Who's there?" he called into the darkness, but the sinking feeling in his spirit told him it was the satanic image from his nightmares.

An evil, menacing laugh preceded a soft glow in the corner of the bedroom. As the light from the corner of the room intensified, the form took shape. Easily seven feet tall with pale blue skin and a face that was at once handsome and twisted, the being flexed large dark wings jutting from his back. From tip to tip, the wings rose over the beast's horned head and extended downward to his midcalf.

Michael was startled by the apparition, which was more vivid and realistic than in his dreams. Diving across the room, he hit the light switch, anxious to disrupt whatever display of light and shadow was catching his eye. To his dismay, the light only clarified the horrendous vision.

"You didn't answer my question," the beast said with Isa's voice and haughty grin.

Michael closed his eyes and prayed. As he did so, he felt hot breath on his face and smelled an intense odor of decomposition, reminiscent of his trek to Georgia in the aftermath of the Dark Awakening. Michael slowly opened his eyes only to see Isa's staring back at him. The beast form remained, but the eyes were definitely the unique gray-blue eyes he shared with Isa. Michael swallowed hard, having fully expected his prayer to force the demon to leave. Then he remembered what the apostle John said in Revelation: the beast would be given the authority to make war with the saints and to overcome them. He stared back at the blue image but said nothing, refusing to answer the question.

"Maybe I should help you," the beast said in a condescending tone. "You sinned the best sin of them all, Michael: the sin of pride. You took great pride in turning those locusts against their creator, didn't you?"

Michael said nothing, but he knew there was a measure of truth to it. He had been happy to plan the locusts' revolt. He prayed, "Oh Father, am I really guilty of the sin of pride in this matter?" His mind raced. Remembering what he had read about spiritual warfare, he commanded the beast, "Be gone, in the name of Jesus!"

The beast laughed. "Admit it, Michael! There's great fun in turning a creation against its creator. The unexpected turn of irony is worth all the work!"

Michael ran from his apartment. As fast as he could, he descended the stairs to street level. Better to be in the pandemonium on the street than in a room with Satan. The locusts buzzed all around him. Their whirring sound around his head was distressing. Even more distressing was the fact that they weren't totally ignoring him. Every so often, one would land on him. When this happened, he would shake it off. His chest pounded with fear as his mind raced. He definitely shared his eyes with Isa, but what else of his genome had passed through to the monster? Could it be that the locusts were confused by the similarity of Michael's DNA signature to Isa's?

Michael didn't know where to run, but he had to seek cover. There was no place for him to find comfort. As he stumbled into a narrow alley, he was nearly run down by a car driving at excessive speed, its stung driver trying in vain to escape the terror. He wedged himself against the stone wall of an ancient building to escape the car and then slid down the building after the vehicle passed, covering his head with his arms. The sounds of the night seemed deafening to him. The roar of the locust wings and the agonized screams of the people were more than he could bear, but he didn't want to go back to his haunted apartment on this night of horror.

Despite the fact that the Temple Mount was now the home of the world's worst evil, it was the only place that felt even remotely safe to him. He ran through the night to the Wailing Wall and then sprinted up the stairs. Security personnel recognized him and immediately authorized his entrance. The locusts hadn't descended on Abraham's Courtyard. He walked briskly toward the basilica. Lights in the courtyard bounced off low-lying clouds. For a few seconds he heard only the sound of his rapid breaths echoing through the empty plaza.

He took a deep breath, maybe his first since the locust attacks began. He slowed his pace, the need for panic abating. For all intents and purposes, this could be any other night in Jerusalem. Looking around, he saw nothing out of the ordinary.

"You've got to get control of yourself, Michael. Nothing is a surprise. It's all laid out in the Bible," he said aloud and mentally began to question himself. Had he really had an encounter with Satan in his room? Was it real? Had Isa somehow moved from world leader to a bogeyman who hid out in the corners of darkened bedrooms?

"It doesn't make sense, Michael," he said to himself as he sat on the basilica stairs to think. What made sense was that he had imagined it, like some kind of flashback. But this time the vision was so much more realistic. If some sort of mental fatigue had brought it on, he was in worse shape than even he had thought.

"Lord," he prayed, "am I losing it? I've always thought too much about things. Please help me, Lord. Don't let my mind run amok in the little time we have left. There are too many people depending on me."

"You'll be fine," a voice called from the shadows behind him. The thought of the horned beast speaking to him again sent him into a new panic. Not knowing what else to do, he took off running across Abraham's Courtyard.

"Where are you going?" the voice called out. Michael heard

footsteps on the cobblestones matching his own. He had to find a safe place. *There is no safe place!*

Michael wiped at his face as he ran. Where indeed? You can't outrun a demented mind. His foot hit a raised cobblestone, and he fell. Not taking the time to stand, he crawled to the nearby obelisk, chanting, "No. No. No. No. No."

A hand grabbed his shoulder. Physically, he reacted with a start and rose quickly to defend himself. Mentally, he felt instant relief. Whatever had touched him was real; it wasn't in his mind. He made a fist and swung as hard as he could.

"Jake!" Will screamed as he dodged the punch. "It's me ... Will!"

Michael nearly fainted from relief. He rested his hands on bent knees and tried to calm the fast panting of his breath. "I'm sorry, Will. I thought you were someone else."

"Who?" Will asked as he rubbed Michael's back. "You're the only one in the entire courtyard."

"Isa, I guess," Michael said. He wanted to tell Will what he had experienced, but it seemed suddenly unreal as the words came to mind. "I couldn't sleep with the locust attack. It all got to me. I know we did the right thing to protect the saints," he said with a sob, "but at the same time, we're responsible for all those shrieks of pain."

"Oh ... okay," Will said suspiciously. Michael knew Will thought he was hiding something. Well, Will would have to think what he wanted to think. Michael wasn't about to mention a blue Satan in his bedroom.

Michael's breathing regulated, and he stood upright. Gathering his composure, he tried to sound matter-of-fact. "Can you stand a guest sleeping on your couch? It's pretty loud in town. By the way, why aren't you asleep?"

"Well," Will said, grimacing, "I was until I got a call from the security staff that you were wandering around the courtyard in your jammies talking to yourself. I figured I needed to come out and get you before everyone on staff started to believe you were running around at night drunk, crazy, or both."

Michael was embarrassed. He had forgotten he was in his pajamas. Clapping his nephew on the back, he said, "Thanks. Let's get inside. I have a feeling it will be a long night once Isa and his minions find out they've become the targets of their own demonic technology."

"I think that's about to happen," Will said, pointing to a cloud moving across the courtyard. Soon they heard screams of pain from the guards at the stairs leading to Old Jerusalem below.

"Let's get inside!" Michael yelled with an embarrassing amount of panic in his voice. In the time it took him to say it, the locusts swooped overhead. A cloud of darkness surrounded the two men as the horde blocked the soft glow of the streetlights along the courtyard's perimeter.

"I'm with you, Jake," Will said with a panicked tone matching Michael's. He placed one arm around Michael's shoulder as they ducked and ran toward the basilica.

Their steps echoed through the courtyard as the cloud of animatronic locusts descended. Ignoring Will, one after another landed on Michael. Will shooed them away as he and Michael ran headlong to the basilica.

It seemed like time was standing still. Everything moved in extreme slow motion for Michael. He felt each thundering clop of his feet against the cobblestones. No matter how they pushed, the basilica was still a few steps away. After what seemed like forever, they found the stairs and jaunted upward. Will opened one of the large doors to the basilica when it happened: a locust landed on Michael's neck—and stung him.

The rush of pain sent a bright flash of light to Michael's brain. He screamed, and as the flash subsided, he focused on the expression of horror on Will's face.

Will furiously grabbed at the locust attached to Michael's neck and flung it to the ground. In anger he stomped it.

The pain was overwhelming. It was as if every nerve in Michael's body was on fire. The pain began at the spot on his neck where he'd been bitten and radiated outward. His field of vision reeled as his head lolled from side to side.

Will grabbed him to steady him, but his nephew's touch grated harshly on nerves already set aflame by the toxin. Michael shrieked in pain when Will touched him.

Will jerked away, and Michael began to fall to the pavement. Will caught him again, setting off a fresh round of agony. Michael screamed.

Will didn't let go. "I know it hurts, Jake, but I have to get us inside."

Michael swallowed hard against the pain. "D-do it," he muttered through clenched teeth.

Will opened the door with one hand, holding it open first with his foot and then his back, as he half guided, half carried Michael through the door. As he did so, the locusts took full advantage of the chance to enter. They swarmed past Will and Michael with such velocity that Will had trouble keeping the two of them upright. Michael moaned in pain but pushed in fear against the horde. He wrestled free of Will's grip and threw himself onto the floor inside the door. Will followed suit, and the heavy door slammed shut behind them.

"Good move, diving in here like that," Will said as he landed on the floor next to Michael.

"Tell that to my aching body," Michael said, trying to get to his hands and knees. Will helped him stand as the first shrieks echoed throughout the immense stone architecture.

"So, the programming worked?" Will asked. He was clearly confused.

"Yes," Michael said with a grimace.

"But ... but they bit you!" Will asked gravely, "Jake, you're saved, aren't you?"

"Of course I am!" Michael screamed through a fresh burst of pain. His voice echoed throughout the hallway, mingling with the screams that were coming more regularly now. He lowered his voice. "The drones focus on Isa's DNA signature delivered in the mark. Guess who happens to share DNA with Isa?"

"His physical father ..." Will said with dawning awareness.

"Just another thing to thank the Lady for," Michael said through grunts of pain. His flesh felt like it was burning. He could barely stand the pressure of clothing against the searing pain encompassing him. He moved slowly, deliberately, down the hallway toward the elevator to Will's apartment. Will followed.

"Jake, you're a child of God! This punishment isn't for you!"

"Tell me about it," Michael snapped as he struck violently at the elevator call button, only to wince at the pain it brought to his hand.

Will paced and wiped at his forehead in exasperation. "But, but, there's got to be something we can do. Your face, Jake, it's swollen ... everywhere."

"It hurts, Will." Michael grunted as the elevator doors opened. "Everywhere. My clothing is driving me crazy."

"There's got to be something we can do!" Will half screamed over the echoing shrieks of pain from the hallway as the elevator doors closed.

"I've got to get out of these clothes," Michael said, ripping his pajama top down the front, sending a cascade of buttons to the floor. Will gasped at the flaming-red flesh underneath. The elevator dinged, and the doors opened at the subterranean level housing Will's apartment. He reached out to help Michael off the elevator. Michael stopped him. "Please don't, Will. Every touch brings incredible pain." He hobbled out of the elevator into the hallway, which was littered with bitten Vatican workers rolling in pain. Michael looked around at the debilitated figures. They showed no signs of recognition that he and Will walked past.

"Will," he called out as he stared at a catatonic victim of the venom.

Will stopped ahead of him.

"Look how much worse they are," Michael said in a faraway voice, his mind racing with thoughts.

"Because they've taken the mark," Will said. "You're a mistake, only partially susceptible."

"The Bible says the effects will last for months. It says that people will long to die to alleviate the pain, but they won't be able to die."

Will continued the thought, "Because Isa's DNA resists illness and death."

"I don't have that enhancement," Michael said cautiously.

"So, you're thinking this could kill you?" Will asked.

"I'm not sure. Part of me thinks it should, but then I look at how much worse they are."

"Maybe it will only be temporary for you," Will offered.

"It will be," Michael assured him, "because when we get to your apartment, you're going to pray for my healing."

Will stammered, "B-but … but, Jake, I've never done anything like that."

"It's either that or be my nursemaid while I hang out naked in your apartment for months," Michael growled.

"Well, when you put it that way …" Will said with a forlorn shrug of his shoulders.

Will paced and prayed. Michael lay on the couch in his underwear. His body was disfigured, bloated, and swollen, like a beet-red Pillsbury Doughboy. Still, Will had never prayed for a healing. He had read about them in the Bible, but he had never been witness to one. He prayed for guidance and thought about the situation. Scripturally the locust stings were reserved for those who had taken the mark. Michael obviously had not. Therefore, according to scripture itself, it couldn't possibly be in God's will for Michael to fall prey to the locusts' venom.

But then again, he reasoned, the venom was already affecting Michael. How could that possibly have happened if it weren't within the will of God? Will rubbed his eyes. The bottom line was that he was afraid nothing would happen if he prayed for Michael's healing.

But what if God had allowed Michael to be stung so he could be healed in a demonstration of Jesus's love and power? Michael moaned in pain on the couch.

"This is ridiculous," Will said aloud to himself. "It's time to get off the fence. The Bible clearly says this suffering is not for the children of God. Only my unbelief is keeping him in pain."

He squared his shoulders, strode resolutely to his uncle, and said, "Uncle Michael, in the name of Jesus, Lord and Ruler of the Universe, I command you to be healed of the effects of the demon locust."

Michael's body arched on the couch as if it had undergone an electric shock, and then it lay still. Will peered over him. There was no sudden change. It wasn't like in the Bible where blind people saw or lame people walked. But the lack of tension in Michael's body looked like he was experiencing some sort of relief.

"Uncle Michael?" Will asked quietly.

No response.

"Jake, can you hear me?" he asked a bit more loudly.

"Uh-hum," Michael affirmed.

"Do you feel any different?"

"A lot of relief. Going to sleep now. I think it worked."

That was it for Michael. He lay deathly still on the couch. Will checked on him periodically. At first he thought he could see a decrease in the swelling, and the bright red skin seemed to have softened to a lighter pink. Was he really improving, or was Will seeing what he so desperately wanted to see?

The phone rang, startling Will. The caller ID showed it was Benny.

As Will answered, Benny shrieked, "Oh God, William, you have to help me! I've never been in so much pain!"

Will looked at Michael, who was resting peacefully. By comparison to the panic he heard on the phone, it was clear the Lord was at work in Michael. "I don't know what I can do, Benny," Will said nervously.

"Just get over here!" Benny screamed. "I'm frightened, Will," he moaned.

Will left Michael a note and rushed to Benny's quarters. He navigated an obstacle course of bodies either writhing in agony or unconscious throughout the hallways and past the Swiss Guardsmen at the entrance to Benny's apartment, lying incapacitated on either side of the door. Rushing in, he caught sight of Benny. He wiped at his eyes. It wasn't the Benny he had come to know, but the original Lucky he had met years before, except Benny's flesh was red and swollen as he lay naked on his bed.

"Benny, I'm here," Will said in a soft moan as he looked away. He knew Benny deserved this. Everyone who had taken the mark deserved it, but Will's heart was struck with compassion when confronted with the tremendous human suffering before him.

"Can you help me, Will?" he whined.

"Listen to me, Benny. There's a spiritual component to this. It's affecting people who have taken the inoculations you and Isa forced on the world. If anyone can offer you some relief, I think it would be Nergal."

"Huh!" Benny shrieked and then cussed a blue streak. "He believes he wasn't created to endure human suffering, so he's decided to hide out somewhere deep in my subconscious. I hate him," Benny barked.

Will felt helpless and trapped. Faced with the sheer torture before him, he wished he could pray for everyone to be healed. He wished for the world to be a happy place once more. He wished ... for all this to end. He wished Jesus would come quickly and set things right.

Since the administration of the mark, people hadn't gotten sick. Hospitals had closed, and doctors had stopped practicing. Not knowing what else to do, Will looked through the contacts on Benny's phone. There he found the number of Benny's former doctor. He called and was surprised the man answered.

"Um, hello, Doctor. This is Will Marron. I'm Pope Peter's nephew." Will winced as he said it. "The pope has been stung by the locusts."

"I remember you," the doctor said in a strong voice. It didn't sound to Will like the man had been stung. "Can I be honest with you, young man?"

"I hope you will be," Will said resolutely.

"There is no relief for anyone who took the inoculation. There's only hope in Jesus."

"Amen," Will said. "I serve Him too."

"Must be hell with that thing as your uncle."

"I won't lie, it isn't easy. But the suffering is too much for me to witness. Is there anything you can do?"

The doctor sighed. "I have tons of unused morphine. Everyone will want it soon. I can be there in ten minutes if your guards will allow me entrance."

"I'm most likely the only guard who isn't rolling on the floor in pain."

"Well, then I'll be there in ten minutes. Just so you know, I'm doing this for you because you are a Christian brother in the enemy's camp. As far as your uncle is concerned ..."

"I understand. And I am thankful," Will said.

The doctor indicated that he had no intention of lingering in the Antichrist's home. Will didn't blame him. The doctor didn't even flinch at the excruciating pain his needle caused Benny. Neither did he show any compassion when leaving more vials of medicine and needles.

"Don't ask me to do this again," the doctor said sternly as Benny nodded off into drugged bliss. "I won't help him anymore. If you or any Christian needs medical service, give me a call."

Will began, "Well, my uncle Michael was—"

"Sick for a while this evening," Michael interrupted him from the doorway. The change in him was truly miraculous. He was dressed in one of Will's sweat suits, and his face looked normal. "But I'm feeling better now. Just a little tired." Will could tell Michael wasn't fully recovered by the way he leaned in the doorway trying to look casual. He had to. There was no quick, easy way to explain why the locust had bit him.

The doctor shook Michael's hand. "I've seen you look better," he said cautiously.

"To tell the truth, I was pretty sick earlier, but Will over there prayed for a healing, and the Lord was kind enough to deliver."

"Good to hear," the doctor said quickly, obviously still anxious to be out of this place.

"Before you go, Doctor," Michael said softly, "if life gets too tough for you and your family, call me. I have connections to the group in Petra. And they would love to have a doctor on staff."

"I'll discuss it with my wife. Expect a call from me tomorrow," the doctor said as he left.

Once the doctor was gone, Michael's demeanor flagged. Will hugged him. "You had me really worried for a while, Jake."

"You and me both," Michael said as they headed through the groaning masses back to Will's apartment.

TWENTY-EIGHT

For four months the world lay dormant as if it were dead. The cataclysms of the meteors and the asteroid-induced tsunamis had crippled infrastructure. On top of those devastations, the locust venom had produced a global population without the will or the ability to improve its condition. Relief efforts, construction, and even social media slowed to a near stop.

"The Bible says that soon spirits will go out to mobilize the world for war," Michael said in an encrypted video conversation with Isaac at Petra.

"Still, it has felt like a respite. The only people not too sick to grow crops are the Christians, and God graciously allowed their gardens to thrive despite the nuclear and natural disasters. It enables us to stock up for the final phase of judgment," Isaac said with a grin.

"I hear you," Michael said. "But people are beginning to heal. The pope is back to his old demonic self, and Isa has been pretty active the whole time. He was covered in red welts and puffy flesh, but the suffering of others brought him glee."

"That must have been a pleasure to be around," Isaac said sarcastically.

"It has been its own kind of hell. Will and I are the only ones not affected by the locusts. Isa goes from being entitled and demanding to being secretive and threatening. It galls him that he has to depend on Will and me. It's a constant reminder the locust program backfired."

"In a big way!" Isaac chuckled.

"I have to tell you, I feel bad about some of it. The people responsible for the project worked at a company my family owns. They were

259

all summarily executed when Isa saw what happened. I feel responsible for their deaths." Michael pushed a hand through his hair. Although the effects of the locust poison had left him months before, the entire experience weakened him somehow. He was constantly tired. His daily exposure to Isa had fueled more appearances of the blue beast in the middle of the night. His kidnapping and torture hadn't fragmented his personality, but his grip on reality had certainly weakened.

"You have to choose to feel proud about saving the Christians," Isaac said. "This is a battle to the death, Michael. You are on the right side. Casualties are inevitable. The people who died were doomed in any event once they had taken the mark."

"I know. I know," Michael said somberly. Maybe it wasn't so much guilt as fatigue. He was tired of the pain and suffering.

Isaac encouraged him, saying, "We're down to the wire, Michael. Before we know it, the battle will be over. You have to align yourself with God's will. That means you have to become more callous to the suffering of His enemies."

"I second that motion," Will said as he entered Michael's apartment.

"Hi, Will," Isaac called out. "You might have to toughen up your old uncle Mike."

"He's tougher than he looks," Will said with a grin as he moved into camera view. He took a playful swat at Michael's head.

"Of course I am," Michael said. "I may not be as young as the two of you, but I'll give you a run for your money."

"We might have to save the remainder of this conversation for another day," Will said into the camera. "Uncle Michael and I have a meeting with Scarface Kurtoglu."

The walk from Michael's apartment to the Temple Mount was quick. There were still no cars on the roads or people in the streets. Shops remained untouched since the locust attack. In a different world, before the mark of the beast, people would have looted, if for no other reason than to get food. But food and drink were the last things the afflicted wanted. More than anything, they wanted to die to gain relief from the constant pain. As the Bible predicted, their one wish would not be granted.

"I could go for a Starbucks," Will mused as he kicked a spent locust carcass down the street, "but other than that, I've grown accustomed to the empty streets."

Michael muttered his agreement. The newfound silence of the times led him to speak in hushed tones on the street, as if a loud voice would interrupt some sort of sanctified stillness.

"It's especially beautiful today," Will said. "The red haze from the Nibiru encounter has finally left the atmosphere."

"Well, it won't be long now until we're in the debris field again," Michael said softly as they ascended the stairs to the Temple Mount. A skeletal man waved them through security. His greenish pallor was accentuated by red blotch remnants of the locust attack.

Once in Abraham's Courtyard, Michael stopped for a moment to orient himself. Then he turned due west. He pointed to an orange ball on the horizon. "See that?"

"It's the sun," Will said with a shrug.

"Really? Then what is that?" Michael said, pointing to the yellow ball to the east, just peeking out between the new Solomon's Temple and the new Dome of the Rock.

"Wow!" Will yelled. His voice echoed through the courtyard.

"The orange ball is Nemesis," Michael said. "The red dust in the atmosphere has hidden it, but on a clear day like today, it's visible."

"It must be close," Will said with concern.

"Judging by its size in the sky, I'd guess it's less than one AU away," Michael said absently as he studied the orange-red globe.

"An AU?"

"Astronomical unit, roughly ninety-three million miles, the distance between Earth and the sun."

"Oh," Will muttered.

"Notice how it looks more orange than red?" Michael asked.

"I guess," Will said.

"I don't know if it is reflecting the sun's light or if its proximity to the sun is warming it and changing it," Michael said as he stared.

"Does it matter?" Will asked.

"In the long run, I guess it doesn't," Michael said as he continued to the basilica with Will in tow. He wasn't really sure if it made any difference, but he wondered if the orange hue was an indication Nemesis was warming, pushing its atmosphere further into space, enlarging the debris field Earth would soon pass through.

Michael braced himself against an involuntary chill running down his spine. He looked one more time before entering the basilica. There was no doubt about it: they were definitely heading into the most dramatic judgments of the tribulation.

They were in Isa's conference room at the scheduled time. Neither of them knew what the meeting was about. It could be anything from Isa not liking his coffee to a rant that nobody was well enough to work in his munitions factories.

Before long, Isa entered with Benny. As the pain from the locust attack had subsided, Nergal again came to the foreground.

"Gentlemen!" Isa called out merrily.

"Excellency," Michael said, followed by Will. They both stood as he entered the room.

"Good afternoon," Benny said.

"Holiness," Michael said, again followed by Will.

They all took their seats.

"Michael," Isa began, "I need you to get a memo out to the employees at all our munitions factories. Explain to them I have exhibited patience beyond that of any god before me. Now, however, the effects of the locust attack are beginning to subside. It is time to get back to work. We are perilously close to the appearance of the Anu, and there is much work to do."

"Yes, Excellency," Michael said, staring into Isa's eyes—the same eyes that plagued him in nightmares.

Isa returned the stare and then smiled an arrogant smile. Isa was toying with him!

"William," Isa said briskly.

"Yes, Excellency," Will replied crisply.

"I want you to visit each of the scientists from our facility downstairs. Explain to them that their failure to report to work tomorrow will result in immediate termination of life."

Will stuttered a bit in his reply. "Y-yes, um, Excellency."

Michael's mind raced to stories he had heard about Adolf Hitler's growing madness when he was holed up in a bunker, awaiting the German defeat. If it was a valid comparison, they were seeing Isa's descent into insanity. Michael and Will were on the front line in the push to depravity. The key was not to follow Isa in the descent. Michael unconsciously reached to his wallet and the photograph it contained, his link to sanity, the relationships of the past and the hope of the future.

Isa continued, "Nibiru's orbit soon will bring it out of its hiding place behind Nemesis. From the moment we are in sight, the Anu will launch their attack. I want every telescope on Earth and in orbit tracking their ships as they approach."

"Yes, Excellency," the guys said.

"William," Benny said with Nergal's imperial stare, "I'll help motivate the scientists. Excellency and I have functioned with the locust poison while the scientists lay around and moaned. It is time for them to step up."

Will cast a sidelong glance at Michael to show his annoyance and disbelief at what Benny had just said. Benny's dependence on them had been extreme, even for someone as spoiled as he. Only as he began to feel better did Nergal reemerge and show a bit of self-sufficiency. Michael couldn't stifle a grin.

As his grin faded, he said, "The sky is clearing. Will and I saw the Nemesis system on our way here today."

"I saw it as well," Isa said with a grimace. "As our orbit around the sun progresses, we are moving toward it. It is also moving toward us."

"So it won't look static in the sky," Michael said with a furrowed brow.

"Hardly," Isa said. "Imagine two high-speed trains bearing down on each other. The Nemesis system will grow dramatically in the sky as each day passes. It is time for us to mobilize the world."

The meeting ended without fanfare, but things had definitely changed. The world would be back on line by the next day. The reprieve for the church was over. Final events would mushroom and overtake the world as surely as Nibiru would overtake Earth.

That night, the infamous preacher pirated state television channels. His message to the world was short and to the point.

"We are nearing the end of the effects of the locust plague. The world is racing to finalize its preparation for the Nibiru cataclysm. On a clear day, the northern edge of the Nemesis debris field can be seen plainly in the sky. Nibiru, the largest planet, is currently on the far side of Nemesis, obscured from view. As we continue our orbit around the sun, and as Nibiru continues its orbit around Nemesis, we will come perilously close in the coming months.

"Saint John in his book of Revelation has predicted all this. To the Christians among us who follow the Word of God, let me explain where we are in the scheme of things. The trumpet judgments are completed. The plague of the locusts has given us the opportunity to prepare for the end. In the next month, as the government regains its focus, it will be time for you to harvest anything you have planted. The final judgments will come in rapid succession. Make no mistake: these judgments are from the throne of God, but He has orchestrated them through the passing of the Nemesis system. As our orbits draw Earth closer to the interloper system, the effects will be similar to those we just experienced, but with greater intensity.

"These are the coming bowl judgments:

"First, there will be horrible malignant sores for those who have taken the inoculations.

"The second bowl judgment shows the seas becoming like blood. From this I interpret that the iron deposits from our next passage through the debris cloud will again penetrate the atmosphere and rain out quickly, polluting the remainder of the seas.

"The third bowl is concurrent with the second bowl as it describes freshwater sources also turning blood red.

"The fourth bowl describes scorching heat as the sun ramps up its output due to the extreme magnetic pull from Nemesis.

"The fifth bowl judgment is darkness. As we pass through the Nemesis debris field, our atmosphere will dim again. More than that, however, there will be a period of days when the Nemesis system will be between Earth and the sun. The Bible describes this as palpable darkness that is fearsome in its oppressiveness.

"The sixth bowl judgment describes the drying of the Euphrates River, long acknowledged as the symbolic border between East and

West. The Bible says this is in preparation for the arrival of armies from the East to Israel, ostensibly to defend Earth from the Anu.

"The seventh bowl is widespread destruction from a global earthquake. I believe this quake will be global because the entire crust of the earth will slide over its mantle as Nibiru's south pole attracts Earth's North Pole. In a matter of minutes, Earth will change its position in space. Earth's crust will struggle to keep up. Global earthquake. Global tsunami. The mind struggles to form an image of such widespread destruction.

"But the good news is that Jesus's return immediately follows. He will make things right again. So, despite the horror of the coming storm, there is a wonderful rainbow on the horizon. Between now and then, though, persecution against Christians will resume with a vengeance.

"I pray for you, my friends. Stay well and look up, for our redemption draws nigh."

TWENTY-NINE

The preacher's comments were sobering. Of course, none of the information was new to Michele or Jimmy. Yet hearing it made Michele anxious. She was tired.

"Well, the end is near," she said with a raised eyebrow to Jimmy.

"If you believe that drivel," Naomi said with a brash tone as she entered the family room. She had run Michele and Jimmy ragged while she recovered in their home.

"Yeah. I'm not having this conversation with you, Naomi," Michele said briskly.

"Nice way to speak to your mother-in-law. What do you think of that, Jimmy?"

"Do you really think I would take your side over Michele's?" Jimmy asked incredulously. "She has bent over backwards to be kind to you, and you've done nothing but complain, argue, and demoralize."

"Well, I can tell when I'm not wanted!" Naomi shrieked.

Her yelling woke Manny from his nap. To put an end to the confrontation, Michele asked Jimmy to go get him.

Once Jimmy left the room, Michele said in a quiet but stern tone, "Naomi, you're getting feisty again. I think that means you're feeling better."

"Actually, I am," Naomi said in a more quiet voice.

"I have to tell you, it has been tough keeping on top of our businesses while being a wife and mother. Manny is walking now and gets into everything. He needs constant attention."

"And?" Naomi asked as she took a seat in one of the family room recliners.

Michele sat in the recliner next to her. "And, I constantly feel like I'm cheating Manny, Jimmy, or the company. I don't have time for all of them."

"I see," Naomi said with a smug grin. Michele grinned as well at the ridiculousness of the upcoming conversation. Naomi was about to get everything she'd ever wanted.

"Here's what I propose. Since you are well enough to take care of yourself, it's time to start your life again. Maybe go back to your own place—not because of harsh words with Jimmy, but because it's time."

Naomi nestled into the chair and sighed in comfort. Clearly she was in the mood to negotiate her departure. This was no surprise to Michele, but she knew she would have to make Naomi feel like the winner.

"There's more," Michele added. "I don't think I have time to be the company's CEO. I propose that I take the chairman of the board title from Uncle Michael. He won't mind. And I'll make you the CEO."

"And you'll let me run things my way?"

"Well, the day-to-day," Michele said. "Some things don't change. It is still a family-owned business. Uncle Michael, Will, and I are the board of directors. We still have final say."

"Maybe I should have a seat on the board," Naomi said with a grin.

"Maybe I should have the Swiss Guard remove you," Michele said with a grin designed to match Naomi's. She picked up the phone to dial the Swiss Guard barracks at the gate.

Naomi laughed. "Put the phone down, Michele. You can't blame an old gal for trying."

Michele laughed as well. "For what it's worth, Naomi, I think we do okay with each other."

"That's because you're one tough broad, like your grandmother. And despite what Jimmy just said, I really am thankful for the care you guys have given me. All my life, I've been the only one who really gave a damn about me. As appreciative as I am, I find it hard to accept the concern and help of others."

Michele looked at Naomi with a fresh perspective. It was one of the rare moments the older woman had opened up to her as a friend. She wasn't ready to go to town shopping with Naomi, but the candor did a lot to cement a feeling of friendship. As soon as Michele had that thought, another formed. This poor woman who had just offered an olive branch of sorts had taken the mark. Her only future was torment and despair. Michele knew Naomi had chosen it—maybe more than anyone she had known. Selfishness, lack of regard for others, and a browbeating personality had been the hallmarks of her life. But, the overwhelming consequences for her decisions struck Michele. What a futile existence!

"I guess because we have worked together, I get you, Naomi, probably a little better than Jimmy does. Even though I think I understand you, I am grateful for admissions like the one you just made. They make me feel closer to you."

"And that's good for business," Naomi said. Michele recognized the response as Naomi's cover for what she perceived to have been an admission of weakness.

"And for mother-in-law–daughter-in-law relations," Michele said with a smile.

"Well, Manny and I don't hear any screaming," Jimmy said as he entered the room, cuddling the still-tired little boy. He kissed Manny's dark, curly hair.

"Far from it," Michele said with a smile. "Naomi and I just had a nice family moment."

"Yes, we did," Naomi said as she slid to the edge of the recliner. "And if you'll excuse me, Jimmy, I'm going to my room to pack. You and Michele have been wonderful to me, and I'll always be grateful. But it's time for me to get back to work."

"Oh," Jimmy said with a start.

Naomi stood from the chair and motioned for him to bend toward her. She kissed him lightly on the cheek. "Thank you, Jimmy, for being more of a son to me than I was a mother to you," she said as she wiped furiously at a tear forming in her right eye.

"You're welcome, Naomi," Jimmy said. He paused for a moment, winced a bit, and then ventured, "Mom."

"That means more than you'll ever know."

She left the room while Jimmy sat in her chair. Manny laid his head against his dad's chest. It looked like he may fall back to sleep. Jimmy spoke softly so as not to disturb him. "What happened just now?"

Michele chuckled and then answered in a soft voice, "I think she meant everything she just said, but I primed the pump by offering her the CEO title at our business."

"I'm sure she jumped at it," he said as he patted Manny's back rhythmically.

Michele stifled a laugh. "Well, that coupled with my threat to have the Swiss Guard remove her from the house when she tried to demand a seat on the board."

"That's my mom!" Jimmy chirped. "What prompted you to make her CEO?"

"The message from the preacher. Uncle Michael's right. We are down to the wire. As the population gets better, there will be a huge push to get ready for the Anu. Given Isa's contention that we all must be of one mind to defeat them, there will be a new push to execute Christians and Jews."

"What does that have to do with Naomi?"

"We'll need to take shelter in the bunker, but if Naomi knows about it, it would blow our cover. I need her not to be here."

He chuckled. "Have I told you lately how much I love you?"

"No," she said. "You don't have to say it all the time. I know by your demeanor and the tender care you take of Manny and me. Still, it's good to hear it every once in a while. You're my heart, Jimmy. I love you more than I can put into words."

He took her hand in his, and the two of them sat quietly. Before long, Michele heard Manny's soft snore, followed by his father's. It was the last thing she heard before joining them in a nap.

"Hello, Michele," Will's voice rang from the computer in the bunker's office.

"Hi, Will. I'm here with Jimmy and Manny," Michele said as Jimmy came into camera view with the baby.

"Well, hello, my little guy!" Will beamed.

Jimmy laughed and replied, "Hello back, my big guy!"

"Funny," Will said with a shake of his head.

Jimmy pointed Manny's attention to the screen. "Look, it's Uncle Will. Say hi."

"Hi," Manny said in a whiney voice.

"Manny, can you say 'Uncle Will'?" Will asked in a singsong voice.

Manny uttered similar sounds, much to Will's satisfaction. After a brief chuckle, Will spoke to Michele. "It looks like you guys are in the bunker."

"A little spring-cleaning. We'll take up permanent residence here once the persecutions turn furious."

"Good move," Will said. "I don't want to be indelicate, but where's your mother-in-law?"

"She moved out," Jimmy said.

"With a little bit of a deal," Michele added. "I made her CEO of the business. I'll take the chairman of the board position to keep tabs on her, if Uncle Michael agrees. By the way, is it me, or does he seem really aloof these days?"

"It's not you. I'm telling you, he's been unsure of himself and distant since the agent put him through that stupid program. It left him unprepared to deal with Benny and Isa during the past few months when the regular staff was down and out."

"Not to mention the fact that he was bitten by the locusts," Jimmy said, wrestling with Manny, who had lost interest in the conversation.

"I was super scared when that happened," Will confessed. "So many things ran through my mind: Did the reprogramming of the locusts not work? Was Jake not saved? It sounds unthinkable now, but in the heat of the moment it was one of the things that crossed my mind."

"Totally understandable," Jimmy said as Manny fussed. "It's been nice talking to you, Will, but I'm going to take your nephew out of the office and to his toys."

"Bye-bye, Manny," Will sang, waving in an exaggerated motion.

"Bye-bye," Manny replied, clearly happy to be leaving the room.

Once they left, Michele continued, "You know, it wasn't just the torture. It was also losing his love that hurt Uncle Michael. I wish we could do more to help him."

"Reach out to him. He's in his own head. I engage him as much as I can just to try to get a laugh out of him. Constant exposure to Benny and Isa is daunting enough for me. And I'm not doing it on the back of the kind of torture and grief he's been subjected to."

"I'll do just that, Will," Michele said softly. Her heart broke for her uncle, and she wished there was more they could do for him.

Will encouraged her, saying, "And whatever you do, remember that it's almost over, Michele. It will seem darkest before the dawn, but things will get better."

"I hear you," Michele answered vacantly. She knew he was right, but she dreaded the things to come.

THIRTY

Michael and Will took the scenic route to the desert test site. Yet again, they would be present while Isa tested a new weapon. This was supposed to be the pièce de résistance, the ultimate integration of CERN and weapons technologies.

"You'd think after all this time around you, I'd understand these things better," Will said as he wheeled their Jeep down a dirt road mountain switchback.

Michael braced himself against the bouncing ride with his right hand on the Jeep's roll bar. It felt good to be out in the desert—liberating after the time on the Temple Mount. And Will's driving was a bit of a roller-coaster ride as well. He grinned as he said, "So you took the lonely mountain road for the excitement, not the scenery?"

"Both!" Will answered.

"Well, I'm happy you did. I'm just now beginning to see how hemmed in I felt over these past few months with Benny and Isa," Michael admitted, although he knew there was more to his mental frailty than the influence of those two. The visions of Satan and his fear of coming events were crowding into his day-to-day existence, fast becoming the sum total of his reality.

"I've noticed. So has Michele," Will said.

Michael sensed the caution in his voice. "I guess I haven't kept it hidden too well," he said.

"There's more to it than Isa and Benny," Will said. "There's probably a lot of grief over Gloria. You know, she also told Michele the two of you were planning to raise Manny in the millennium."

Michael took a deep breath and shrugged, feigning nonchalance.

It was like a punch in the gut to have that memory foisted on him. "It was a lovely thought a long time ago, Will."

"It must hurt, though. Michele feels some guilt in parenting Manny. She loves him as her own but doesn't want to hurt you in the process."

"That's ridiculous!" Michael exclaimed. "I'm thrilled he has a stable home with a mom and a dad. And I've been in love with Michele since before she was Manny's age. I would never let these circumstances come between us!" He meant every word. Of course the situation hurt, but it didn't for a moment put him at odds with Michele.

"Maybe you could give her a call just to reassure her," Will prodded.

"I'll definitely do that," Michael said. "Listen, Will, I'm going through some stuff right now, but none of it has to do with even the remotest displeasure with you or your sister. I love you guys more than life itself."

Will ruffled his uncle's hair. "I'm happy to hear that!"

"Good." Michael beamed in return. "But until we get off this mountain trail, I'd appreciate both hands on the wheel, please."

"You got it. So what is this problem you're having that has nothing to do with Michele or Gloria or Manny or me?"

Through a pained expression, Michael said, "I can't even explain it. All my life I relied on my intellect, but now I feel like my mind is failing me."

Will downplayed Michael's admission. "I don't want to hurt your feelings, Jake, but you're not exactly young anymore. A little forgetfulness is to be expected, isn't it?"

"It's not forgetfulness," Michael said glumly. He wanted to tell Will what he was feeling and seeing, but the words wouldn't come. He hesitated and then tried to explain. "Do you remember when we were with Benny at the hajj?"

Will offered a sardonic grin. "Not going to forget that anytime soon."

"Do you remember how I saw the demons Nergal called forth, but you saw nothing?"

"Yeah, until you prayed that I could see them too."

"Well, I'm seeing things again, Will. Not necessarily spiritual things. I feel like maybe my sanity is slipping away."

They were about to exit Will's shortcut and join a paved highway.

He pulled the Jeep over and put it in park. Looking deeply into Michael's eyes, he said, "Look, Jake, that stuff the agent did was designed to bend people's minds. He didn't break you, but he must have stressed you out more than we realize. If you had been a prisoner of war, the government in the old world would have gotten you treatment for PTSD. We just put clean clothes on you and put you back to work for Benny and Isa, a task nobody would like to have."

Michael wiped at unexpected tears. "I don't like the pain I'm carrying, but the agent did the right thing. His actions allowed me to right a wrong that had haunted me for years. I *did* break the personalities of the programmers, Will, much to my chagrin."

"That was some pretty nasty stuff you did," Will said somberly. "But the programmers are whole now. You've paid in spades for any damage you did."

Michael sighed. "I know. I know the Lord forgives me, and so do the programmers. It all worked out to God's glory."

"So, we've learned you're human today, Jake. You've done some not so good things, but you've repented. You've also done some wonderful things, like bringing me into the family. ... And someday I may even forgive you for this ridiculous Swiss Guard outfit."

They both laughed.

Will continued, "My point is, you're human. It's okay if exceedingly stressful situations have led to PTSD. Considering what you've been though, I'd say you're incredibly strong."

Michael hadn't even considered that he had shown any strength in the battle for his mind. He had focused exclusively on his loss of control. "You really think so?"

"Dude! You're a badass, like Rambo!"

"Okay, now I know you're pulling my chain." Michael grinned.

"Just a slight exaggeration, Jake. You're my hero, and you always will be."

"I'll remind you of that after you've spent some time with your father. He's the real Rambo of the family."

"Michele knows you both, and she also puts you in the hero camp," Will offered.

"Idiots!" Michael exclaimed with a grin. "My niece and nephew are idiots!"

Will laughed heartily as he pulled the Jeep onto the highway. "So, Rambo, would you mind explaining to your idiot nephew again what Isa's super-duper weapon is going to do today?"

Michael furrowed his brow. "If I'm right about it, this should dwarf the last tests."

"Those were scary enough!" Will exclaimed.

"These weapons set me ill at ease," Michael said as he crossed his arms over his chest. "Remember that I learned my physics from the Lady's disc, so for all I know it's all lies. Also remember that this is my English interpretation of a very complex code of information ..."

"Caveats aside," Will said as he made a rolling motion with his right hand, inducing Michael to speed to the conclusion.

Michael shook his head and rolled his eyes. "Isa and the CERN scientists believe they have captured and weaponized dark matter."

"Dark matter for the Dark Prince," Will said. "Kind of makes sense."

"The problem is that most scientists don't have a handle on the nature of dark matter. The information on the disc ties it to the un-collapsed waveforms surrounding matter."

"Yeah, now you're losing me."

"Quantum mechanics posits the thought that our perception of matter is a collapse into discrete particles of an endless waveform of probabilities."

"That whole idea that subatomic things don't actually exist until they are perceived," Will said, a shocked expression on his face that such a thought came from him.

"Very good!" Michael said, patting his shoulder. "I think you only pretend not to be paying attention."

"Oh, I'm not pretending ..."

"Some scientists believe the wave never collapses. They think observation only chooses the one possibility we see. The others still exist, but interdimensionally. Sometimes this thought is called the 'many worlds' theory because its corollary states that every decision point in the universe creates a separate time line for each outcome."

"Yeah. I don't even think Captain Kirk would buy that one," Will said. "That's a lot of universes."

"I agree. But the information on the disc hinted at another solution.

Perception chooses one of the possible solutions from the wave field, but the field doesn't collapse. Neither does it branch off into separate universes. Rather, it forms hypothetical superpositioned particles that are partially in our universe as dark matter and partially outside our universe."

"So, the science on the disc hints at other worlds, a multiverse?" Will asked with a shake of his head.

"Not so much other worlds as other world," Michael said glumly. "The opposite side of the dark matter is the light outside the universe—the true heavenly realm."

"Wait!" Will screamed. "So they think they have a weapon to crack open the universe and enter heaven?"

"There are no Anu, Will. Isa isn't looking to defeat some space enemy. Satan inside him thinks he has the technology to destroy Jesus and His followers when they return to Earth."

"But that's crazy!" Will said with exasperation. "It's doomed to fail."

"And that is where my intellect is failing me, Will. It kind of makes sense to me based on the information on the Lady's disc, especially when you consider that Jesus and our resurrected family have roots in this reality."

"You *actually* think Isa can stop Jesus or hurt Him in some way?" Will asked.

"My faith and my spirit say no, but I spent so many years believing in the science of that disc that it makes me wonder. Also, Satan must at least think there is a chance it will work. That's why he's taking a stand."

"But he's delusional," Will said.

"And very intelligent. The fallen angel technology I saw on that disc was far beyond anything our science currently understands," Michael said glumly. He felt an irrational fear rising from within. Of course Jesus would win, and decisively. But why did he feel so unsure?

They were back at the test site again. The retinue of politicians and military brass certainly looked worse for wear. The locust illness had done a number on their already gaunt, greenish forms. To a person, they looked like something from a movie about the walking dead.

Will rolled his eyes at the sight. Michael just stared in disbelief. His mind flashed back to an old film called *They Live*, a cult classic from the 1980s in which a popular wrestler of the day played a character who found a special pair of glasses allowing him to see the true skeletal form of aliens pretending to be human. These people were just about as gruesome, but in some sort of satanic joke, they couldn't see how they looked.

These sycophants had been down and out for months. Benny and Isa clearly gloried in the opportunity to see them again, freeing Will and Michael to take up seats at the very back of the recently erected viewing stand, easily three rows behind the closest of them.

"I can't get over how bad they look," Will whispered. "I should have known. It's not like they look much worse than the Vatican staff."

Michael winced. "It's not the shock of their appearance that gets me. It's the realization that they are no longer human. We can imagine they're people, but they've been genetically modified into something else entirely."

"Almost too scary to think about," Will said dismally. "I can't wait for it to be all over. Speaking of which, isn't that our old friend Nemesis on the horizon?"

"Yes," Michael said. "Notice how much larger it looks today. It's grown a lot in a week."

"Low on the horizon," Will stated. "If I hadn't come by way of the mountain road, we might have seen it on our way here."

They could clearly see its orange disk, smudged by the cloud of debris surrounding it. Small points of light, little round balls, floated nearby.

"None of the planets out there is Nibiru, right?" Will asked.

"No. Nibiru is a lot larger and further away from Nemesis. Soon enough it will come roaring into view."

The beginning of the program interrupted their conversation. All rose and placed their hands over their hearts to join the loudspeaker in a pledge of allegiance to Kurtoglu. Michael and Will did not participate.

Following the pledge, Isa welcomed the audience and called for the weapon's unveiling. Onto the field, a massive missile carrier delivered a black tube. Just a black tube! Michael was overwhelmed by the simplicity. It didn't look like it had any moving parts. Yet there was something ominous and deceptive in its appearance.

The missile carrier slowly positioned the beastly cannon. From this perspective, Michael guessed it to be about a hundred feet long and thirty feet wide.

"Aim!" Isa screamed into a megaphone.

The bed of the missile carrier raised the front end of the tube to place it in line with the image of Nemesis on the horizon. It moved slowly, with incredible precision. For at least five minutes, the mechanism shifted position in tiny increments to find its target.

"Not a particularly fast weapon," Will said under his breath.

"If they're actually targeting Nemesis, precision would have to be measured to the nanometer. A small error here would translate to miles and miles of error at the other end of the beam's trajectory."

"How long would it take a beam to get there?" Will asked.

"At the speed of light, a little over eight minutes," Michael answered.

"Do you think they'll do it?"

"We'll know soon enough."

There was a pregnant pause. The crowd held its breath once the machine quit moving. Isa held his hand to his ear, obviously hearing from his technicians that the weapon had been successfully aimed.

"Fire!" Isa screamed through the megaphone.

The arena was silent. Then a soft purring sound came from the cannon. Soon the purring escalated to a roar, and within a few minutes the roar was deafening. The end of the cannon pointing toward Nemesis glowed white with heat, distorting the atmosphere in front of it.

Michael sat transfixed, awed by the technology but fearful of its power. Looking intently at the space in front of the cannon, he saw a flicker. It was very fast, but something happened. As he stared, it happened again. "Did you see that?" he asked Will above the cannon's roar.

"What?" Will asked.

"Look at the area in front of the cannon. Something in the air is flickering there."

"Okay, but look at the horizon as well," Will said in response.

Michael stared at a wisp of smoke and a darkening spot on the horizon where Nemesis stood. That made very little sense to him. There was no way a wave from this cannon could affect Nemesis so soon, not to mention the time it would take for the image of a scarred Nemesis to return to Earth. The effect must be in the atmosphere. The dark spot grew larger and resembled a singe. That's it! The cannon was burning a hole in the atmosphere.

"That dark spot is a singe mark where the cannon's rays are affecting the atmosphere. Think HAARP on steroids," Michael said.

"Really?" Will asked. "Look at the crowd. They think they're seeing damage to Nemesis."

Michael looked at the generals in the crowd. They were now cheering and patting each other on the back.

"Then Isa is deceiving them," Michael said sternly. "It's impossible that the mark is actually on Nemesis. Einstein still has something to say even in this day and age ..." Michael stopped midsentence. He saw it again, but this time the flicker was slower. A spot of bright white light opened in front of the cannon.

"There! Will, do you see it?"

"The light? Yeah."

The atmosphere in front of the cannon no longer flickered. It was now a bright white spot about twenty feet in diameter.

"I'm guessing it's something like superheated air, right?" Will asked.

Michael thought about it. He supposed the cannon could create plasma at its mouth, but it was in an open field. The atmosphere should cool it before a plasma could form.

The white spot grew brighter as the dark spot on the horizon grew darker. Michael couldn't shake the feeling that the event on the horizon was the distraction. The main event was in front of the cannon. "You're a magician, Will. The horizon is the misdirection."

"Well, the crowd certainly is falling for it," Will answered.

"Not us, though," Michael said. "Concentrate on the white light." They both stared into the light, but its brilliance began to hurt Michael's eyes. Then he saw it. Inside the white orb a scene unfolded. A large muscular man of light moved in front of the cannon. He held out his hand as if to stop the cannon's beam.

"What the heck!" Will exclaimed. "Jake, there's a person in there!"

"If it's what I fear, Will, that's not a person. It's an angel."

"An angel?"

"The dark matter cannon was successful in boring a hole through the universe. What we see in the orb is heaven, a place outside of time and space, somewhere beyond the universe." Michael cringed at the thought of it. Satan had manipulated humanity to build a weapon that could bore a hole through reality to the dimension of heaven. It was unthinkable, and yet he was looking at it!

"So, you're telling me he opened up a window to heaven?" Will asked.

"More like punched a hole through heaven's front door. This is Satan's last stand, Will. All the deception is about this stupid weapon."

"Could we destroy it?" Will asked.

"I'm sure this isn't the only one."

As they watched, the angel's brow furrowed and his face became a visage of agony. He remained like that for a second before he turned to flame. The orb turned solid white and then disappeared as the cannon throttled back.

"Did we just watch an angel die?" Will asked.

"I'm afraid we did," Michael said dismally.

"But, Dad and Tina. All of them will be flying right into a beam like that."

"I know," Michael said in despair.

Will shrugged off the implications. "The book of Revelation would have mentioned it if Satan could actually do real damage to the resurrected saints."

"You would think so," Michael said deliberately. He wished he weren't so well versed in ancient literature. An ancient epic was likely not to mention the casualties. History is written by the victor, even if it is written in advance.

He shuddered. His worst nightmare was coming true.

THIRTY-ONE

Events began to cascade. Earth had entered the Nemesis debris field. The sky was again as red as at sunset all day long. For those who had taken the inoculation, the atmospheric dust was corrosive. Large lesions of pus broke out all over their skin. The lesions looked painful, and Will had no doubt they were, but they didn't elicit even a glimmer of compassion from Kurtoglu. He pushed his oozing subjects at a frenzied pace to prepare for the coming invasion.

Will was patrolling Abraham's Courtyard. It had been closed to the public for the installation of dark matter cannons at each corner of the Temple Mount. They were positioned on carriage assemblies to allow maximum exposure to the sky. He watched the engineers fine-tune the aiming mechanism. The cannons could be pointed independently or used in unison to concentrate against a specific object. The cannons themselves were currently not functional, as the critical dark matter was held in a specially constructed containment safe below the basilica.

Will bristled at the horrendous sound of air force jets bearing down on them at top speed. Even at those tremendous speeds, the artificial intelligence was able to lock on them and shoot them with harmless lasers as they went past.

For a brief second, Will's mind retreated to better times. Could it have been only less than seven years ago that he was happily performing a crossbow act with his girlfriend? It seemed like another lifetime—another person.

He reached to the face mask dangling from his neck. The jets had pulled down with them more of the red dust. Time to breathe through a filter. Nonetheless it was good to be outside. The walls of the basilica closed in on him. In the past there had been some camaraderie among the staff, but that was all gone. Isa's DNA had taken the sense of humor out of most. People barely acknowledged one another. They stayed on task. And Isa was quite the taskmaster.

"Oh crap!" Will said to himself as he looked across the courtyard. "Speak of the devil!" The underlying truth of the expression caused him to chuckle. Benny and his pus-oozing face made fawning eyes of adoration at Isa as the two walked toward Will.

That was definitely Benny. Apparently, Nergal wasn't too much into the most recent pain. The sores had taken a toll on Isa as well. His gait had slowed and his temper flared these days. *Hah, too bad for you, Satan. Maybe your flesh will be your undoing!*

Michael ran up behind them to show Isa an iPad, no doubt a progress update for construction of larger dark matter cannons along the Jezreel Valley—the site of Armageddon in the book of Revelation. Will wished there were more he could do to help Michael. After the destruction of the angel, Michael had retreated again to a place of measured emotion and secret thoughts.

As the three came near, Will saluted. Isa returned the salute with a boil-scarred hand. Will thought Isa's boils were demonstrably worse than others'.

"William," Benny said with a bit of familiarity uncharacteristic of Nergal.

"Lucky," Will said with a grin, testing the waters.

Benny clucked at the name but didn't protest. Michael looked up from the iPad with a glint of devilish mirth. *Ah, nice to see the old Michael is still in there. The old Benny, not so much!* Will chuckled at his own joke as he removed his air filter from his face.

"Yes. Yes. How nice to be surrounded by your family," Isa said with dripping sarcasm. "Nonetheless, William, I insist on far more decorum going forward."

"Yes, Excellency," Will said as he stood to attention.

"Did I just hear the roar of fighter jets?" Isa asked sternly.

"Sir. Yes, sir!" Will snapped.

"And the result?"

"The engineers have details, Excellency, but the AI tracking systems found their targets."

"Excellent!" Isa exclaimed. Will hadn't heard him be this exuberant since the sores broke out. He strode toward the engineers with Benny in tow. Michael attempted to follow, but Benny waved him off, so he stayed behind.

"At least the führer cracked a smile today," Will said with a grimace. "I'm guessing a smile hurts with all those lesions on his face."

"The lesions are giving him a lot to complain about," Michael said. "He is laying the blame at the feet of Christians."

"So, he's acknowledging the sores are a punishment from God?" Will asked, incredulous.

"I'm sure somewhere in the combined schizophrenic brain Isa and Satan share, there's the Satan part that knows it. But he is ranting about a plot from the Anu. He says the lesions will cease when the world becomes one mind with him. He's even devoted some of the armed services' precious time to hunt down and kill Christians."

"That's frightening. I told you that Michele, Jimmy, and Manny have moved into the bunker, right?" Will asked.

Michael nodded. "Yes. I've been toying with the idea of trying to get them to Petra, but Michele wants to stay at home. She feels safe there."

"It's a nice setup, Jake, and it's not at the center of the action like Petra. Speaking of which, will we ever cut and run to Petra?"

"You mean to avoid persecution from Isa?"

"Duh. Yeah," Will said as Michael scowled at him.

"I've been praying about it, but I don't think God is leading me in that direction. Have you heard anything from Him telling you we should leave? Or that you, at least, should leave?"

Will offered an embarrassed grin. "Most of my prayers have been more like 'Get me out of here, Lord!' than asking for His direction."

"It's easy to feel that way, trust me," Michael said with a nod.

"Well, He hasn't removed me from my post, so I'm taking it to mean I'm not relieved of this duty," Will said somberly.

Michael clapped him on the back. "As the Klingons used to say, it's a good day to die."

"Yeah, not a Trekkie," Will said with a half smile.

"Just a small flaw in an otherwise sterling character," Michael said with a grin.

Out of nowhere, a flash of light filled the sky with the brilliance of an atomic bomb. Michael pushed Will to the cobblestones and lay next to him. Seemingly endless sonic booms followed. "What the heck was that?" Will cried.

"I don't know," Michael said. He lay prone to the ground with his face close to Will's. "Nuclear?" he asked. Will noticed involuntary shudders of fear from his uncle.

"I don't know, but I don't think so. I think I saw a bolt of lightning," Will answered.

"Another discharge ... like the day of the rapture?" Michael asked, his voice quaking.

The echoing booms were immediately followed by the rapid-fire bullet sound of thick raindrops. Michael appeared to calm himself by analyzing the situation. He explained, "The discharge has set off a chain reaction in the atmosphere. The iron particles are going to rain out in spectacular fashion."

"Spectacular?" Will aped as he stood. Michael followed. Already their clothes were soaked with the deep crimson liquid.

Michael stretched his palm to the sky to catch a few drops. The red was so deep as to appear brown. "Imagine what this will look like when it gets into all the rivers and seas."

"Blood," Will said.

"Blood," Michael agreed.

Above the showering sound of the rain, they heard Benny screaming. Looking in the direction of the scream, they saw Benny and Isa under the tarp used by security to keep out the heat of the sun. Benny was pantomiming for Michael and Will to get umbrellas and escort Holiness and Excellency back to the basilica.

Will crossed his arms and shook his head. "The leader of the world and the spiritual advisor to us all, pantomiming for an umbrella. You couldn't even put this in a movie."

"No one would believe it," Michael said as they walked to the basilica.

The lightning burst had caused the power on the Temple Mount to short out, but it didn't take Michael and Will long to find a couple of umbrellas. As they did, the backup generators came roaring to life. Already soaked to the bone, they didn't bother to raise the umbrellas on their trek back to the stranded god and his helper.

Will snorted. "It actually smells like blood," he complained.

"It's the iron content," Michael said. "I can see why John thought it was blood when he experienced it in his vision."

Will grinned. "I hate that we're living through the tribulation, but I get a charge when I see the Word of God coming to life."

"I know how you feel," Michael said, matching his grin.

"What the hell are you two Cheshire cats grinning about?" Benny barked.

"Well, you have to admit that Will looks like a drowned rat," Michael answered off the cuff.

Will played along. "Tell me Jake looks any better!"

"Well, I've seen both of you look worse," Benny said with a quick smile. *Nope. No Nergal here,* Will thought.

"I want to see those smiles wiped off your faces!" Isa demanded.

"Yes, sir," Will said with a quick stand to attention.

Michael said nothing, but his smile faded. He opened his umbrella and held it over Isa's head. "Allow me, Excellency," he said.

"That's better. You know I have the likes of you to thank for this mess," he groused.

"I'm not sure I follow," Michael said. Will knew better; Michael understood all too well what Isa meant.

Isa screamed, "These sores are an Anu plot. This latest electric discharge could easily set off another Dark Awakening. If Christians and Jews had heeded my plea to come into agreement with me, none of this would be happening right now!"

Michael offered no response. Will kept his head down.

Only Benny tried to appease him. "You are right as always, Excellency. But if I may, the number of Christians and Jews is a very small percentage of the population. We have routed all fake reeducation camps, and now that our own people are well enough to serve in our munitions factories, we have sent the Christian detainees to their imagined eternal reward."

"There are enough of them, Benny!" Isa screamed. "Benny! Why the hell am I talking to Benny? Nergal, get out here!"

Benny faltered for a second. Will almost walked on ahead but caught himself in time to keep the umbrella over the pontiff's head. His countenance grew fierce and his gaze red hot. "Apologies, Excellency,"

Nergal said with a shiver. "I never have grown accustomed to these flesh suits. I find them irritating on a normal day and excruciating with these lesions."

The remark sent Isa into another bout of rage. A thick vein came to the surface on his lesion-riddled forehead as he yelled, "Do you think for a moment I care about your comfort? If you aren't up to the task, I can send you to hell now!"

"If my only alternative is dismissal," Nergal said briskly, "then I prefer to serve." Will stifled a grin at the decidedly Benny-like response. He stared at Michael, noting he had caught it too.

"You *prefer* to serve! *You prefer?!*" Isa screamed.

Benny fell to his knees in a puddle of red water. He begged Isa's forgiveness.

"Forgiveness isn't my thing, Nergal," Isa said softly, a bitter smile on his face. He kicked at Benny, leaving a gash on his forehead. Benny fell backward to the soaked cobblestones with a howl. Will winced at the callous brutality and looked to Michael as his mouth formed a silent O of awe.

"Now get up and serve me," Isa barked.

"Yes, Excellency," Nergal said in a panicked whine as he accepted Will's extended hand to stand. "I'm at your service, Excellency, through eternity," he added, groveling.

Isa glowered and shook his head. "Just concentrate on today," he said with disgust. "The moment we get to the basilica, I want you to issue an edict. Rather than wait for another Dark Awakening, I call on all citizens of the world to turn in known Christians. I want them all dead ... ah, present company excluded."

Pointing at Michael, Isa said, "This one and his pet still amuse me."

"Yes, Excellency," Nergal said compliantly.

Will caught Michael's eye and mouthed, "Pet?"

Michael made a wide-eyed expression at Will, telling him to knock it off.

"Excellency," Michael said delicately, "you have amassed the most advanced and most powerful weapons known to humankind. Surely you feel confident of the coming victory. Is it really necessary to eliminate the Christians? After all, there are so few left."

Isa pointed his index finger at Michael and said slowly, his voice full of displeasure, "When I want your opinion, Father, I'll ask for it. But to answer your question, I have offered this world nothing short of eternal health and prosperity. By and large, my offer has been gratefully accepted. Even the Muslim population has fallen in line, but the band of morally bankrupt Jews in Petra and the scattered Christian enclaves of this world mock me. They *mock* my gift to them!"

Michael said nothing as Isa paused and stared at him.

Isa began again with very deliberate words. "And *you* mock me, Father. You and the young pup over there. I hate the look of disdain in your eyes, and I loathe your lack of respect. But I long for the day when I bring you and your miserable Messiah to your knees."

Isa looked furious. Michael's knees began to bend. At the same moment, Will felt his knees weaken. Isa was trying to force them to kneel before him. Will saw Michael close his eyes in prayer, and he followed suit. "Jesus, please don't let us fall to Isa." Immediately, his knees strengthened. He opened his eyes to see Michael standing strong as well.

Isa screamed in anger, and then his cell phone rang. Snatching it up to his ear, he barked, "What is it?"

Isa listened and then said, "We'll be right there." He put the phone back in his pocket and spoke to the group as if he hadn't just lost it a few seconds before. "We've been summoned to the command center. The scientists have something we need to see right away."

———

Looking grim, the current head scientist greeted them as they exited the elevators to the large underground command center. On the wall of screens ahead of them were close-up images of the sun, blazing orange to yellow light. They stood behind the desk of the head scientist. Puddles of bloodred rain dripped from Michael, Will, and Benny.

"Start the film," the scientist barked at his subordinate. The screens, ten in all, went black for a second and then displayed the sun's churning surface. Will saw flames shooting out from the circumference.

"These images from our IRIS satellite are half an hour old. What you're about to see is a burst of white from an electrical discharge."

True to his words, the screens all glowed an eye-piercing white as

287

the scientist continued his narrative. "This is the electrical discharge that recently rocked the entire planet. Our hardened electrical grid is by and large able to handle its effects, but minor local outages have hampered our ability to assess the extent of any damage. As local power grids come on line, we are learning that damage has been minimal."

"Excellent, Dr. Rudolf," Isa said with a self-aggrandizing grin. "It is always good to see the benefits of my planning come to fruition." Will wanted to gag at the comment, but he stared straight ahead. The earlier confrontation with the madman had been too aggressive for his taste. Isa was losing it; Will was sure of it.

"Absolutely, Excellency!" the formerly chastised Benny cheered exuberantly.

On the screens, the brilliant white faded to a new image of the sun. It looked different than it had. It looked to Will like a blob had formed along its side, right in the middle.

Pointing to the blob Will had just noticed, Dr. Rudolf continued, "You'll notice an extrusion along the side of the sun in this view."

"Uh-oh," Michael said softly. The blob broke free of the sun, revealing itself to be a floating orb of plasma.

Dr. Rudolf said, "You see the implications, Father Martin. This is a coronal mass ejection of massive proportions. It will take us a long time to analyze the data, but I'm convinced the ejection of such a mass will have a destabilizing effect on the sun for thousands of years."

"Thousands?" Isa asked incredulously. "With all due respect, Dr. Rudolf, you rushed us here because you said this was an urgent matter."

Michael interjected, "Is the ejected plasma on the orbital plane?"

"Yes," the scientist answered grimly. "Excellency, there *is* a sense of urgency. The ball of plasma you see on the screen is headed toward Earth."

"That ball of fire is on a collision course with Earth?" Isa asked.

The scientist nodded his head. "In four or five days' time."

"Which hemisphere will be affected?" Isa asked.

Dr. Rudolf winced. "Excellency, it is many times the size of Earth."

"That doesn't answer my question," Isa said tersely.

"There are variables we have yet to quantify," the scientist said, hedging, "but it looks like the Western Hemisphere will take the brunt of the initial encounter."

"Initial encounter?" Michael asked.

"Father, this is a huge plasma field. It will sweep past Earth, envelop it for a time, and pass on. So, the side facing it will take the initial hit, but all of the planet will see its effects."

Will stared at the screen, trying to get his head around it. Clearly, it was the fourth bowl judgment when the planet was destined to be scorched by the sun. He knew it was coming, and it was ahead of him on the screen, but he still couldn't imagine it.

THIRTY-TWO

Michael sat at his computer watching coverage of the massive rainstorms brought on by the electrical discharge. All over the world, torrential rain pulled red dust from the atmosphere. He marveled at the timing.

"I never really saw the genius in the timing of Your judgments, Lord, but living through them sure has changed that." The damage from the coming solar mass ejection would have been less if the dust particles had stayed trapped in the atmosphere. But the discharge changed all of that. Across the world, thick red floods raced toward rivers, and rivers toward the sea. By the time the coronal mass ejection hit Earth, the atmosphere would be clear and the air would be dry.

The coverage was interrupted by yet another global transmission from Isa. Again he urged the citizens of the world to take cover. That was easier said than done. The rains had flooded many basements and underground facilities. Isa again ranted about what he considered the root of the problem: lack of unity, specifically, the failure of those who refused the inoculation to become part of the global community.

"How can we expect to take our rightful place in a galactic federation when we cannot achieve global unity?" he asked, incredulous. "At what point must I stop asking for cooperation and begin to demand it?"

That question led to his rant. He called upon all citizens of the world to turn into authorities anyone who didn't bear the mark. "In fact, why not spare the authorities the bother and kill them yourselves? Rise up, citizens of the world! Fight for your place among the civilizations of the galaxy! Eliminate those who stand in the way of our glorious future!"

Michael turned down the volume. In the past two days, as the world flooded and superhot solar plasma barreled toward Earth, Isa's major concern was killing Christians. Any sane person would know he was crazy, but the only remaining sane people were his targets.

Michael clicked into an encrypted telecommunication program and called Isaac at Petra. He answered immediately. "What's up, Michael?"

"Just checking in. What do things look like there?"

"The desert is flooded with bloodred rain," Isaac said with a grin, "but the sun is shining over Petra. God has protected His chosen."

"That's good to hear," Michael said as he looked out his window at the streets of Jerusalem flooded and stained with red. "Jerusalem is floating in blood."

"No doubt," Isaac answered. "How is the führer these days?"

Michael grimaced. "Your analogy is closer than you think. Isa is increasingly temperamental and not in touch with his subordinates. He's reminding me more and more of stories about Hitler's mental state in the bunker beneath Berlin."

"Huh," Isaac muttered. "As it turns out, antichrists are somewhat alike. It proves my theory that Satan is and always has been an uncreative being. With the Lord, all things are new because He *is* a creator. With Satan, it is the same rehashed insanity over and over."

Michael concurred. "Agreed. The only thing that changes is the audience. Each generation gets the same show, it's just fresh for them."

"Satan's eternal nature contrasted with the finite nature of humanity. It's really the only edge he has. At any rate, we're on the cusp of his demise," Isaac said with the hint of a smile.

"His time is short, and he knows it," Michael affirmed. "He'll ramp up his war on believers."

"I've seen the images," Isaac said with a grim expression. "TV coverage is showing mobs all over the world beating and killing Christians and Jews in the streets. I was hoping the bulk of it was propaganda forged in Kurtoglu's studios."

"I'm sure there's some spin on it," Michael said, "but a lot of it is real. I spoke to the agent earlier. He's lost contact with nearly every community he's helped over the years. There was a particular kid in

Kazakhstan of whom he had grown fond. The agent is pretty sure the boy has been martyred."

"I'm sorry to hear it," Isaac said. "It seems there's more than enough heartbreaking news to go around these days. How is the remnant in Jerusalem?"

Michael answered with a sigh. "Between the killings and the exodus to Petra, Jerusalem is pretty much devoid of faith. The town is mostly comprised of Kurtoglu loyalists and sycophants. What used to be a city that at least paid homage to three religions is filled with mindless worker bees who spend their off-hours in bars and whorehouses."

"That sounds pretty grim."

Michael wiped at his forehead. "As nice as it is to talk with you, Isaac, I have a reason for my call. The preacher is about to come out with a message. As a courtesy, I wanted to tell you it's coming. I'm going to advocate Isaiah 26:20." Michael gave the reference with assurance, having witnessed for himself Isaac's legendary Bible memorization.

"You're telling them to dig in, go into hiding," Isaac said with dismay.

"I know, it's a bit different than the message you preach from Petra, but there is a major difference. Your group is the prophesized 144,000 Jewish believers. You are being shown special protection. Even the blood rains aren't affecting Petra."

Isaac sighed. "But, Michael, I keep thinking about scriptures saying we should be about the Lord's business when He returns. To my mind that means resisting the Antichrist."

"And yet, Isaiah wrote that prophecy for a reason," Michael said. "You won't refute me publicly, will you? I don't want any disagreement in the church at this late hour."

"No. No public denouncement from me. You may be right, Michael. We are called to follow the same Messiah, but He has different plans for my group. We weren't left behind at the rapture; we were born of the rapture. And there's a difference."

"Thank you for your consideration, Isaac. I don't think my message will come as a surprise to anyone. Between the ramp-up in persecution, the blood rains, and the coming fire, I imagine most Christians have gone to shelter already. More than anything, I want to teach on Isaiah's prophecy so they don't feel like they are doing the wrong thing.

The rapture seems like a long time ago, but a lot of us have very vivid memories of thinking we were doing the right thing, only to learn we were on the outside of God's will. I don't want analysis paralysis to stop Christians from taking shelter for the final events."

"Analysis paralysis!" Isaac chortled. "That is the best description of the phenomenon we have been witnessing. It is a fairly constant conversation in Petra that the left-behind church seems reluctant to act, while we seem reluctant to think things through. Your side has analysis paralysis, forever mulling over contemplated actions. My side has ... I'm going to call it 'cognition remission.' We are reluctant to think about any of our actions. The thought process throws us back to pharisaical interpretations of scripture that led us away from Messiah, so we tend to act first and think about it later."

Michael smiled. "Well, soon enough we'll be one community. Maybe we can learn from each other to come out somewhere in the middle."

"All of the differences will fade to nothing in the brilliance of Jesus's reign," Isaac said.

Michael sat at his computer, the camera covered with black tape, as the preacher began his message.

"My brothers and sisters, this may be my last message to you. We are coming down to the wire, and our Lord will be with us soon, but these last few weeks will be fraught with danger. As Nibiru's orbit brings it from the opposite side of Nemesis, it will cross very close to Earth, concluding the bowl judgments and ushering in the Lord's return.

"I know there is some confusion regarding the next steps for Christians. We are all aware of the biblical command to occupy until He comes. We are reminded of the parable of the ten virgins. Only five had enough oil for their lamps. When the unprepared five went to buy more oil, the master came, and they were left out in the cold.

"None of us wants to share the fate of the unwise virgins. None of us wants to be found lacking when the Lord returns. Now the current regime has declared war on us, enlisting even average citizens to hunt us down and destroy us. If you feel the Lord has called you to martyrdom, then by all means fulfill your destiny, but I don't think it's a requirement.

"We must rightly divide scripture to determine the Lord's will for us in these final hours. I submit to you that the parable of the virgins and the command to occupy until He comes were fulfilled at the rapture. Our loved ones who were raptured fulfilled these commands to be faithful until His coming. Sadly, we already fulfilled the role of the unwise virgins.

"I believe at the current time, we fall under the following verse from Isaiah 26:20, where the Lord says through the prophet: 'Come, my people, enter your chambers, and shut your doors behind you; Hide yourself, as it were, for a little moment until the indignation is past. For behold, the Lord has come out of His place to punish the inhabitants of Earth for their iniquity.'"

Michael paused for a moment to allow the weight of God's pronouncement to hit home. "Surely the approaching Nemesis incursion is the wrath spoken of by Isaiah. We are in the very end of the tribulation. Now is the time for the fulfillment of that verse. So, my brothers and sisters, I urge you not to misunderstand prerapture verses as a condemnation for seeking cover in this final hour. The very opposite is true. You are encouraged by the Lord to take cover until His wrath has passed.

"Hide. Stay well. Devote yourselves to the Bible and prayer, praying that the judgments will pass quickly and that you will be safely delivered to the time of His glorious appearing."

For a second, Michael was grateful for the anonymity because his viewers wouldn't be able to see the tears cascading down his face. Many would hide, but many would be found by Isa and his cronies. His voice caught in his throat as he concluded. "I ask the Lord God to deliver you and bring you peace in Jesus's name. Stay well, my friends. I hope to meet you soon in person on the other side of the Lord's judgment."

The dream came again that night, more vivid than it had ever been. Michael tossed and turned on his bed.

He was in the Jezreel Valley. The sky was dark with foreboding clouds that roiled above. The ground was barren, deep red, and cracked, stained with the bloodred rain and dried to ash by the coronal mass ejection.

The swirling vortex of clouds parted slowly, revealing not a blue sky, but the dark blue orb of Nibiru, many times the size of the moon. A hand touched Michael's shoulder. He turned away from the monstrous sight in the sky to see Will.

They were standing with Benny and Isa. As Michael looked on, double vision formed, in which the shadowy blue-skinned image of Satan surrounded Isa. Michael shivered involuntarily.

Earth had turned into a scene from hell. Death and destruction were everywhere. Not so much as a blade of grass had survived the ravages of the solar twin's passage.

Hot wind raced as Michael turned to look behind them. The entire valley was filled with every type of military vehicle and thousands of soldiers. He identified flags from each of the ten regions of the world. The sum total of earth's military might stood behind Isa. In the distance, Michael saw squadrons of jets approaching. They quickly closed the gap and began their flyover. There must have been thousands of them, flying in tight formations rows and rows deep.

Then the sky cracked. A blistering flash tore it asunder. As the light faded, Michael saw the host of heaven, led by Jesus on a white horse, coming from the horizon.

"Jake, they're here! We made it! We made it through the tribulation!" Will screamed.

Isa screamed as well, commanding the dark matter cannons to aim. Michael fell into a panic. He knew he should be happy to see the Lord, but fear raged in him.

As the armies of heaven approached, a pair of horsemen split from the group. They were distant in one second and close at hand in the next, their speed too quick for the eye to see or the mind to comprehend. In an instant, Michael saw the riders clearly. They were Gabe and Chris, coming to extract him and Will from the battlefront.

"It's Dad!" Will screamed.

At the same time, Isa yelled, "Fire!"

The culmination of Michael's worst nightmares unfolded before his eyes. The dark energy rays found Chris and Gabe. Both shrieked in agony for a second before disintegrating.

Michael screamed himself awake. He was shaking. He wiped sweat from his head as he untangled himself from his sheets and jumped from the bed.

It was still dark outside. He said, "Time," to his computer.

"5:30 a.m. Kurtoglu time" came the response.

"No way I'll get back to sleep after that," he said. He turned on a light, dressed, and opened his wallet. As with the other times he had this vision, he found comfort in the old photo left by his mother. One day he would ask her its secrets. He prayed that the vision was only a nightmare. He didn't think he could bear to lose Gabe and Chris again.

Rapid pounding at his door startled him. For a second, he thought it must be a Gestapo raid to haul him away in the middle of the night. Well, whatever that would entail, it was bound to be better than being in the Jezreel Valley, the Valley of Decision.

The mere thought of the dream brought a shudder. He heard a voice with the pounding. "Uncle Michael! Jake, are you asleep?" It was Will.

He unlocked the door, trying to chase the sleep from his eyes. "What's up, Will?" he asked.

"You didn't answer my texts. I assumed you were either asleep or in trouble," Will said breathlessly. "Pack some clothes and come with me."

"Why?" Michael asked, his mind still in a fog from the dream.

"The scientists got it wrong. The coronal mass ejection thing traveled faster than they thought. It's about to hit."

"How did they misjudge it?" Michael asked vacantly.

Will shrugged and quickly shook his head. "I'm not an egghead, Jake, just someone here to move your butt. But I heard them say they overestimated the effect of the solar wind, although I'm not sure what they meant."

"The solar wind speed seems to be the speed toward which solar ejections gravitate. If one is blown off the sun with little energy, it's slower than the solar wind, which pushes it along to speed it up. If the mass is blown off the sun with greater energy, that is, greater speed, the solar wind tends to slow it down. Apparently, this explosion was so violent that the solar wind had minimal effect." It felt good to look at things scientifically for the moment, taking his mind off the horror of his dream.

"Yeah," Will said tersely as he threw several outfits, some underwear, and socks into a bag. "Look in the bag, Einstein. Is there anything else you need?" Will spoke hastily.

"My iPad," Michael said as he removed it from his desk and chucked it in the bag. "I have a lot of Bibles on it."

"Good," Will said, zippering the bag. "Let's get out of here."

"I just need to make a quick pit stop," Michael said as he moved to the bathroom.

He finished, washed his hands, and threw some cold water on his face in an attempt to interrupt the lingering stupor of his dream. Coming out of the bathroom, Michael saw his apartment bathed in gold and red light.

"Jake! It's here!" Will threw open the curtains to reveal a blinding sight. The sky churned with fire. "We should be underground now! How will we get back to the Vatican?"

Motivated by adrenalin, Michael finally felt fully awake. He now understood Will's urgency, and more to the point, he rose to the occasion to calm Will's fears. "We can do this, Will," Michael said as he moved quickly to rummage through a hall closet. He pulled out a tent he had used years before in archeological digs. It was designed to provide shelter from heat in the day as well as warmth at night. The exterior was made of thermal Mylar.

"We'll cover ourselves with this. It's highly reflective thermal material. It should keep us safe until we get to the basilica," Michael said with a command-and-control tone.

"Good job, Jake!" Will said with hope. As they left the apartment, Michael took a last look around, not sure if it would be safe for him to stay there again.

They unfurled the tent and held it above them as they left the building. Already the temperature in the street was stifling. In the time it took to get to Will's Jeep, they were drenched in sweat. They moved deliberately, careful to cover themselves all the way. The heat of the Jeep's seats burned through their pants.

"Ouch!" Will screamed shaking his hands after touching the steering wheel. He reached for a bottle of water in the cup holder, pouring it first on the steering wheel and then on the gearshift, each hissing when hit with the water. With a grimace, he started the engine.

"The engine is already in the hot zone," he said, staring at the dashboard.

"We're only about a mile away from the Vatican garage," Michael said, feeling the hot air take his breath.

"We'll give it a try," Will said, carefully putting the Jeep into reverse. It lurched backward, leaving marks on the pavement. "Look at those marks. Could the tires be melting?" Will asked as he put the Jeep in gear and raced down the empty street.

Michael shook his head. "Modern tires aren't made only of rubber. They're made from a recipe of components, each of which has a different melting point. Some of those materials, like the rubber component, may start to melt, but others will stay intact. The net result is a softening of the tire that can lead to ..."

An explosion rocked the Jeep as Will struggled to keep it on the road.

"... blowouts," Michael said, completing his thought.

Will slowed the Jeep to a crawl. The front left tire had blown and now made a flopping sound with each revolution. He said, "We're still three-quarters of a mile from the garage entrance, but we're only blocks from the Wailing Wall. We might have to take the stairs. Are you up to it in this heat?"

"Let's do it," Michael said, noting that breathing was becoming more uncomfortable.

The rear passenger tire blew with a bang as Will turned onto the square in front of the Wailing Wall. He drove the crippled Jeep right to the foot of the stairs. They climbed out carefully, being sure to keep the Mylar around them.

Michael could barely see for the sweat pouring into his eyes. After the first few steps, his legs felt like lead. Each breath assaulted his nose and throat with blistering heat. "It won't be safe for us to be out in this much longer," he said, panting.

Will didn't look good either. "Hang in there, Jake. Follow me," he said with a raspy voice.

They climbed the stairs to the Temple Mount in silence, not having the energy to talk further. At the top of the stairs, Will pulled Michael to the right, away from the basilica.

"We're closest to the Dome of the Rock, and I have security clearance to enter," Will explained. "We can get some shade there for a couple of moments, then cross to the Temple. It's a zigzag approach, but we'll have respites of shade."

"As long as we don't take too much time. Things are heating up fast," Michael warned, looking at the undulating red sky.

At the door to the Dome of the Rock, Will placed his hand in a palm reader. The computer granted him access to the vestibule, and they ducked inside.

The air in the building was easily fifty degrees cooler than the air outside. Michael and Will fell to the cool floor, taking deep breaths.

"How hot do you think it is out there?" Will asked.

Michael chuckled. "Hot as hell."

"Literally," Will said with a roll of his eyes.

They sat back for a few minutes, allowing their breaths to regulate. Finally Will said, "So let's give it a few more minutes, then we'll move under the Mylar cover to the Temple. I can get in there as well with my security clearance."

"Sounds good," Michael said. "From there it's not a long way to the basilica."

Will wiped at his forehead. "I can't wait for this to be over, Jake. I seriously don't know how much more of this I can take."

"I want it to be over too, buddy," Michael comforted. Nearly immediately after saying it, he had a flashback to the dream, to the destruction of Gabe and Chris. He shuddered and reached to his wallet just to touch the photo, his tether to sanity.

THIRTY-THREE

The massive stone structure of the basilica kept air temperatures a livable ninety-eight degrees. Will carried his uncle's bag to his quarters. "You take the bed. I'll sleep on the couch until this passes."

"I haven't been such a sound sleeper these days anyway," Michael said with a grimace. "I'll be happy to take the couch."

"Can't do it, Jake. I would never let my old—did I say old?—uncle sleep on the couch while I took a bed."

Michael chuckled. "Fine."

Will checked his computer. Michele had tried to reach him. He initiated a return video call. Within a few seconds she was looking at him from her computer screen.

"You rang?" Will asked glibly.

"I was worried. Are you guys okay? The news coverage is saying the solar mass ejection came earlier than expected and that your hemisphere is getting it right now."

"That's the truth. I just ran out to get your uncle Michael. He wasn't answering my texts, so I had to ruin a Jeep to extricate his butt from his apartment."

"So now he's *my* uncle?" Michele asked.

"Stop fighting over me; I'll get a swollen head," Michael said as he came into view.

Michele and Will chuckled. Will continued. "The truth is, we're a little giddy right now to be out of the heat. For the first time in a long time, I was actually happy to enter this ugly basilica."

"He's right," Michael said. "I guess we are a little goofy with relief. We just got in. What have you been hearing?"

Michele turned the view to her computer screen, showing the spontaneous combustion of trees and steam boiling off lakes and rivers. "How long is this supposed to last?" she asked.

Michael's brow furrowed. "Make no mistake about it. This is a large cloud of hot plasma. The good news is that it's moving faster than we anticipated. That will shorten our exposure to somewhere between a day and two days."

"That's a lot of time at this heat. News reports are saying Jerusalem has passed one hundred fifty degrees," Michele said.

"And it is still the wee hours of the morning here," Will added.

"What is going on in Georgia?" Michael asked.

"It's heating up. Already ninety degrees, and it's midnight. The sky looks like sunrise, but it's not the sun. It's literally fire. Right now it's only on the horizon, though."

"You are staying underground, right?" Michael asked.

"I might have stepped outside the chapel to get a look at the sky," Michele said defensively.

"But you stayed away from security cameras, right?" Will asked.

"I stayed away from all Swiss Guard security cameras, if that's what you mean."

"You know that's what I mean. I told the Swiss Guard you've come to the Vatican. They're under strict orders not to enter the house or grounds, but to defend them from the perimeter," Will said with an edge in his voice.

"I kind of wish you hadn't done that," Michele answered. "They're nice guys. I could help them through the coming disaster."

Will chided, "They're marked by the Antichrist, who has deputized every citizen to kill Christians on sight. I know they're nice guys, but we're down to the wire, and I don't trust anyone. Let them think you're not at home."

"Fine," Michele said glumly. "We're all getting a bit of cabin fever, but I know you're right. By the way, the preacher's message last night was wonderful, Uncle Michael."

Michael smiled. "If I see him, I'll pass along your compliment."

"You do that," Michele said with a grin.

Will's cell phone sounded, followed immediately by Michael's. Both checked their phones with a grimace.

"Looks like we're being called to Adolf's bunker," Will said with a scowl. "I was just telling Uncle Michael I can't wait for this to be over."

"I hear you," Michele said softly, "and I'm sorry if it sounded like I was complaining when I said we have cabin fever. We're blessed, and I know it. We pray all the time for you two, knowing you're in the belly of the beast."

"You don't know how much we appreciate it," Michael said.

"Got to go now, Sis. A hug to Jimmy, and a kiss to the baby," Will said with his finger poised above the key to disconnect the call.

"Will do. Be safe."

———————

Will sighed as the elevator stopped on the bottom floor. He wondered how Michael actually survived in his underground laboratory at the Vatican all those years. To him, the fluorescent lights and the recycled air were a turnoff. Nonetheless, on this particular day, Will guessed the bunker was at least ten degrees cooler than his apartment.

They strode to Benny's side. Will saluted.

Michael said, "You called for us, Benny?"

"Address me as Holiness," Nergal said sternly. *No Benny here.*

"Yes, sir," Michael said, clearly avoiding using the term. Will was tempted to crack a smile. Michael could be bent, but never broken.

Isa pointed their attention to the wall of screens. "Father, as you are by now aware, this group of self-proclaimed geniuses missed the arrival time of the coronal mass ejection. I was hoping to get your appraisal of the situation."

For a second, Will felt sad for the greenish eggheads who had spontaneously erupted in massive boils with the rest of the unsaved world. To be under such physical stress and at odds with your savior must be hell.

"Show him Antarctica," Isa demanded. The screens moved to satellite photos of the deserted continent, its once pristine white ice shelf sheathed in a coat of blood red. Along the edge of the continent, the red gave way to deep crevices of white.

Michael studied the image for a few long, quiet moments. "The fragmentation at the edges of the ice sheet is troubling," he said. "They could indicate massive calving, huge icebergs set free into the ocean. The most likely result will be coastal flooding as they melt."

"Well, score one for my geniuses," Isa said with disdain. "They've been telling me the same thing."

"Frankly, I'm amazed our satellites are still functional," Michael said.

"You shouldn't be. Information you derived from the Lady's disc enabled the world to equip a fleet of satellites with magnetic field generators specifically for this likelihood."

"I remember the promise of such a system. I didn't know it had been implemented," Michael said softly, still staring at the image. "Do we have any indication of the atmospheric temperature right now where the ice sheet is calving?"

The scientist at the desk directly ahead of him turned to say, "Around ninety-five degrees."

"Hotter than I would have imagined," Michael said deliberately. To Isa he said, "Anyone still alive along the coasts of the continents should be alerted to move inland." Will thought about the billions who had already been killed in the plagues thus far.

"I've ordered all military to evacuate," Isa said gravely. *So much for your citizenry.*

Isa snarled as he barked out, "We have to save our most precious resources, William, and at this juncture, that means our armed forces."

"Yes, Excellency," Will said in military fashion, wilting under the madman's stare. All the while he warned himself to control his own thoughts.

Michael provided cover. "I assume we are seeing the same activity on Greenland's ice sheet, Excellency," he said briskly.

"Yes, Father, we are." To the scientists, he said, "Show him the Amazon."

Several images filled the screen, all showing South America shrouded in smoke.

"The canopy has dried out and caught fire," Michael said glumly.

"Yes," Benny said with a hint of a smile. "There's no way to extinguish it. It will have to burn itself out."

"It will get worse before it gets better," Michael said. "We still have at least another day of this extreme heat, and then the smoke from these fires will be like a nuclear winter cooling the world for several growing seasons."

Will watched in horror as Benny picked open one of the huge lesions on his face. It made a popping noise as pus and water escaped. He looked at Michael for a reaction and found none. *How does he do it?* Will wondered of Michael.

Isa answered Michael, "Fortunately, we no longer have a large population to feed, a goal your uncle espoused for years."

"Benny always wanted all the food for himself, trust me," Michael said, which inspired uproarious laughter from Nergal and Isa. *He's actually charming them!*

"Nonsense, William, but it is good to laugh once in a while," Isa said. Will blushed. Michael stared hard at him as a warning to bring his thoughts into line.

Isa said condescendingly, "Don't be too hard on yourself, William. This is why I keep you around. Your uncle is inscrutable. You, however, are not, and you know him well enough to sense his motives and broadcast them to me with that loud, but less impressive, brain of yours."

Will was immediately hurt that he was being used against Michael. The thought drove a smirk from Isa. Will forced the current conversation from his mind, imagining in detail the performance of a crossbow trick.

Isa turned toward Michael and asked, "So you think the extreme heat will last another day?"

"It's a guess, Excellency," Michael said, hedging. "Clearly the plasma cloud is moving more quickly than we thought. It is huge. I doubt Earth will put much of a dent in its speed."

"So, twenty-four more hours then?" Isa asked.

"Please don't hold me to a precise time, Excellency, but somewhere around that."

"Is there a way to clear the atmosphere of the Amazon smoke?" Isa asked.

"I guess you could seed the clouds to get rid of the low-lying stuff. The atmosphere was very dry after it rained out the red dust, but this extreme heat should be evaporating significant amounts of water," Michael responded.

"Show him the Ataturk Dam," Isa demanded of the scientists.

The screens changed to satellite images of the Turkish dam, as well as local shots from the shoreline. Already, boats along the shore sat in fast-drying mud where earlier a harbor had been. Will's mind flashed to the prophecy in Revelation saying the Euphrates River would dry up. The Ataturk Dam was on the Euphrates River. Will glanced quickly over to Isa to see if the man had read his thoughts. No indication if he had. Again he moved his mind to a crossbow trick, counting clicks as a woman spun on a wheel.

"That seems extreme," Michael said as he scrutinized the photos.

The scientist in front of him said, "There have been strange reports of fire actually touching the lake. We think this was a point of plasma contact."

"Unsettling," Michael commented. "It means the atmosphere is yielding to the plasma."

"Perhaps not," the scientist said. "The Turks resisted our demands to harden assets at the Ataturk hydroelectric facility. It was unshielded and producing at near capacity when the plasma storm arrived."

"More to the point," Isa said sternly, "the Kurtoglu family, my so-called brothers, kept the money and sent falsified reports of its completion."

The scientist winced at the description. Ignoring the Kurtoglu family dysfunction, Michael asked, "So it actually attracted the plasma cloud?"

"Yes, sir," the scientist responded. "There are only a handful of other electric plants that haven't been shielded. We've shut them down until the plasma storm passes."

"Wise decision," Michael offered.

"So, to sum it up," Isa said officiously, "the storm is showing us more damage than we had previously envisioned and will likely lead to coastal flooding, the destruction of the Amazon rain forest, and a possible nuclear winter. But at least the storm won't last as long as we had originally thought."

"Yes, sir," the scientist said.

Michael added, "If I may point out, Excellency, the storm is more intense than first predicted, but the outcomes may not be so different. Longer exposure at slightly less intensity could well cause all the disastrous effects we're witnessing."

"So, faster, but not much of an increase in damage," Isa summed. "Pulling the Band-Aid off quickly rather than slowly."

"There's no way to know for sure what would have happened, but that is a very reasonable conclusion," Michael offered.

"Well, then, given that our scientists' miscalculations didn't really result in any additional damage, I guess I will allow them to live. Too late for Dr. Rudolf though," Isa said with a mock frown.

The statement pulled Will back to the conversation. He watched as a silent tear rolled down the lesion-riddled cheek of the scientist who had been conversing with Michael.

"Get back to work!" Isa demanded of the scientist. "Try not to disappoint me again!"

To Benny, Michael, and Will, he commanded, "You three, in my ready room." Then he strode off to his office—the same one in which Will had witnessed Isa's declaration of nuclear war. Will couldn't wait for this day to end.

Nergal followed immediately. Michael held back. As Will caught up to him, he asked softly, "Drying up of the Euphrates?" referencing the prophecy.

"Uh-huh," Michael said, keeping his eyes forward.

They entered Isa's office overlooking the command center. Isa went to his desk and flipped a switch, making the windows opaque. Benny sat at one of the two chairs in front of Isa's desk. Michael and Will gravitated to a couple chairs at a small conference table in the corner.

"It is time for the world to come together around me, Holiness. The Anu are close at hand."

"Yes, Excellency," Benny said gravely.

"Their flesh is willing, but theirs spirit are weak," Isa said. Will blanched at the inverse quote of Jesus. His eyes darted to Michael's. They made brief contact, and then Michael shook his head slightly.

"There's only one way the world can be saved. We must impart to the world leaders our sense of urgency," Isa declared.

"With all due respect, Excellency, we are in daily contact with them, and our media coverage blasts a message of preparedness twenty-four hours a day," Benny said with dismay.

"What I have planned will instill the armies of the world with our very nature. It, ah, may be painful, but it is necessary," Isa said as he stared into Benny's eyes. Will wondered what they could be talking about. He glanced at Michael, who had gone pale. Whatever Isa had planned, Michael knew what was coming.

The lights in the room grew dim as Isa stared intently at Benny. While Will watched, a strange doubling of reality obscured his vision. In shadow all around Benny a reptilian form took shape—first as a thin greenish vapor. Soon it coalesced into a huge, scaled green monster. If it weren't so terrifyingly real, Will would have thought it to be bad sci-fi. He guessed he was looking at Nergal's true form. While the form was decidedly more solid than at first, Will could still see through Nergal to Benny underneath. He was old and fat as he had been when Will met him. He looked pathetic and scared.

Michael touched Will's arm and spoke in a whisper. "You may want to close your eyes."

Will patted his uncle's hand as he whispered, "I'm okay."

Next, the doubling occurred around Isa's body, but the spectral form rapidly took shape and moved beside Isa. Will gasped at his first view of Satan. His blue-tinted skin shone with a soft light as he stretched himself to his full height. Unfurled wings nearly touched the ceiling. Despite the feeling of rampant evil in the room, Will was taken with the exquisite beauty and awesome power of the being before him. Surely he must have been the treasure of creation before his fall. Now the beauty was marred, and the smile that had once undoubtedly caused heaven itself to smile with him had degenerated into the Joker's mad grin.

And it was the grin that finally moved Will to a near panic. He wanted to run from the room, but he knew better than to rile Satan. He looked toward Michael to see an expression of unbridled fear. Michael panted, his breath taken by the palpable evil in the room.

As Benny fell backward in his chair, the other three joined hands to form a small circle. In unison they began to chant. Will felt himself shrink back into his chair. He wanted to hide. He wanted to run. He wanted to die—anything that would take him away from this room.

At once, Satan howled a vicious scream filled with pain and resolve. Next Isa followed, and then Nergal. As their screams ended, small reptilian beings crawled from their mouths. Will swallowed his own vomit and shut his eyes. He couldn't watch anymore.

Eyes shut, he felt Michael clutch at his arm and scream in panic.

Will wanted to help him, but some primal sense of self-protection prevented him from moving. Eyes still closed, he felt the brush of evil come past him and stop in front of Michael. Michael's hand clutched again at Will's arm and then went limp.

Finally, Will forced his eyes to open, but he saw nothing. The room had turned to total blackness. He was in some ludicrous hellish funhouse, and he was afraid to move. The oppressive darkness weighed heavy on his chest. As he struggled against it to breathe, he noticed Michael's arm was no longer on his.

Just as he thought he could take no more, the lights in the room came back on. In front of him sat Isa and Benny, chatting as if the horrible events had not transpired. He looked toward Michael to confirm the reality of what he had just experienced. It was then he saw Michael lying on the floor.

He jumped to Michael's side and held his wrist. There was definitely a pulse, and Michael was breathing. He patted Michael's face, saying, "Jake. Wake up."

Michael stirred groggily. Isa and Benny turned at the sound of Will's voice.

"It looks like your uncle needs some rest," Benny said coldly.

"*Your nephew* has passed out," Will said with an edge.

"Family fun aside," Isa said coldly, "get him out of here, Will. Make sure he stays hydrated."

"Yes, sir," Will said as he helped Michael into a seated position.

"I'm ... I'm okay now," Michael said groggily.

Will put his arms under Michael's to pull him into a standing position. Nearly dead weight. Michael was certainly not okay.

"Put your arm around my shoulder, Jake. We're going to get you some sleep."

"Good," Michael said with half-lidded eyes.

As they left the room, Isa said, "Oh, Will ..."

"Yes, Excellency?"

"Call all Swiss Guard back to Jerusalem from their posts. I want every serviceman on the field with us when the Anu attack."

"Yes, Excellency," Will said sharply as he led Michael out of the room.

The room was in total darkness, but Michael could still see the pale blue of Satan's face, just inches from his own. Satan laughed, his acrid breath hot on Michael's face. "You know I'm going to win this battle, don't you?" he taunted in a coarse whisper.

"No!" Michael screamed as he awoke on Will's bed. He sat up, rubbing at a massive headache. The bedclothes were wet, the air-conditioning unable to keep up with the oven-like temperatures outside.

Will appeared in the doorway with a glass of juice. "How are you feeling, Jake? You've been out for close to four hours."

Michael pushed sweaty hair from his brow. "Tired. And I have a headache, but I'm fine."

Will sat on the edge of the bed, handing the glass to Michael. As his uncle drank, Will asked, "What did we just see in there, Jake?"

"Revelation 16:3," Michael said after a long drink. "They just sent out powerful demonic entities to gather the world's armies to the Jezreel Valley. We're headed to Armageddon, Will."

THIRTY-FOUR

The extreme heat took its toll on the estate's plant life. The orchards were ruined. Barring the miracle of restoration at Jesus's return, there wasn't a chance that any of the trees would produce again. The grass and flowers of the yard were burned to the root. Walking over them produced little puffs of dust. The house and the chapel hadn't fared well either. Michele was convinced that the old timbers were creakier and looser now than they had ever been. Several sections of roof had turned ashen.

"I wonder how close we were to the whole thing catching fire," Michele said to Jimmy as they walked around the property with the baby. Manny, excited to be outside, laughed each time a puff of dust accented his step.

"I'm thinking pretty close, babe," Jimmy answered. "It only feels cool now because it was so hot before, but it's still ninety-five degrees."

"I guess we could turn the air-conditioning back on in the house," she suggested, and then regretted it almost immediately. Something had changed in her. As much as she loved the old house, the terror of the times had gotten to her. She preferred the bunker. She shook her head involuntarily, hardly believing she felt that way.

"We could," Jimmy said with a furrowed brow, "but I don't want to stay in the house. I really think I'll sleep better in the bunker."

She smiled. "I was just thinking the same thing. As much as I didn't care for our Vatican status, I guess I had grown used to the protection of armed guards. Now that they're gone, the place feels less safe."

"And too big for just the two of us to keep watch over. I don't want

310

to try to sleep wondering if every creak is someone on the stairway," he added.

She chuckled for a minute. "Do you remember right after the rapture when you thought Uncle Benny was an intruder?"

He laughed at the memory. Then he sighed. "Those times seem blissfully innocent compared to where the world is now."

She agreed. Even though it felt like they had lost everything in those first days, the ensuing years had shown them there was much more to lose, much more to fear, and much more to loathe. "For a while, when we were fighting Kurtoglu with the forged FEMA camps, it felt like we could at least stand against the rising evil. There was an earthly reason to get up in the morning. Now I just want Jesus to return and put a stop to things."

He scooped up the baby and then took Michele's hand. "I know it feels like the walls are closing in on us, but some of it has been for the refining of our character. When we were working resistance, we were still tied to the world. Now those ties have been beaten out of us. Our only hope is Jesus. Everything else has been stripped away."

"At least we still have each other," she said reflectively.

"Of course. It's like Paul said in Corinthians; in the end there are three things that last: faith, hope, and love." He squeezed her hand when he said the word *love*.

"Think how blessed we are, not only to have found each other, but also to have made it this far in the tribulation. And we have Junior here to boot," she said as she moved the baby's hair from his face.

Jimmy said somberly, "I could be truly happy if it weren't for the green oozing faces out there. As much as I want this to end for us, I know they're headed to something even worse."

Michele thought of the changes in her employees. They thought the mark would bring them long and healthy lives, but their health was dismal and their prospects worse. "I know they all made the choice, but my heart goes out to them. Isa sold them a bill of goods."

"He did, and they won't realize it until they see it's Jesus in the sky, not the Anu," he said.

"And maybe not even then," Michele noted. "Their minds are so twisted. I don't know if they'll fully comprehend until Isa is defeated and his spell over them is broken."

She heard a sound like a footstep coming from the house. In the old days, she would have wanted to investigate it, but not now. Isa had turned all of his people into vigilantes against Christians. It was doubtful they could have a good encounter with a green person at this point. Michele looked at Jimmy. Having heard it too, he cocked his head to hear further sounds. Nothing.

"Do you think someone's in the house?" Michele whispered.

"Could be," he whispered in reply as he pulled her down the path toward the chapel.

"Maybe a squatter," she said. "The Swiss Guard thought we were in Jerusalem. They might have told people ..."

He pulled harder on her arm. "Doesn't matter anymore."

At that moment, a gust of hot wind blew past, to Manny's delight. He squealed happily, causing the adults to break into a run for the chapel.

Michele silently thanked her grandmother for having built the bunker. She said to the baby, "Let's go home, honey. Do you want to go home?"

The noise startled Naomi. She stood at attention, waiting to hear it again. Footsteps. It was definitely the sound footsteps that were moving quickly.

She moved quickly too, not away from the sound but toward it, through the family room and the kitchen, then into the mudroom. From the window there, she saw them running into the chapel.

"Jerusalem, my butt!" she exclaimed as she scratched at a boil on her arm.

The air in the bunker felt cool and refreshing. Fresh vegetables from the hydroponic garden awaited them, along with freeze-dried pasta. Michele and Jimmy both breathed a sigh of relief as the bunker entrance closed above them.

After they had eaten a late dinner and relaxed awhile, Michele said,

"Will should be awake soon. Would you mind rocking Junior to sleep while I call him? Unless you want to call Will ..."

"I love your brother, but I'll take time with my Manny-Man any day of the week," Jimmy said with a grin.

"I hear you," she said with a smile. She quickly set up the video call. Will answered with a very bad case of bedhead. His long locks frizzed to frame his face like a rock star from the 1980s. She looked at her watch. She was about half an hour early.

"You're early," Will said with snark.

"And either you have the worst case of bedhead or you've joined Van Halen," she teased.

"The heat has made the air really dry," he said, wiping the sleep from his eyes, "and my couch is pretty small, so I move around a lot trying to get comfortable."

"Uncle Michael is still staying with you?"

"Yeah. He may go home tonight. The heat is starting to abate."

"How is he doing?" Michele asked.

"He wakes up screaming several times a night, usually only when I finally get comfortable on the couch," he said with a sardonic grin.

"Is he asleep now?"

"In the shower, for what it's worth. Our filters get most of the red out of the water, but it still has that irony blood smell. Also not good for my hair."

Michele giggled. "If you had known the tribulation would be so hard on your hair, you might have accepted Christ earlier."

"Ha-ha," he answered with a grin.

Michael appeared behind Will on the screen, looking tired but well-groomed. Michele remembered how he had always looked so clean and smelled so good when she was growing up. "Well, hello there, handsome."

Michael smiled. "You're in a good mood."

Michele sighed. "I wasn't just a bit ago. We went out to check the damage. Every living thing has been burned in the heat. I only started to feel better once we were sealed back in the bunker."

"Good," Michael said. "I'll tell you, if I had a bunker, I would be in it."

"I've been getting frantic emails from our business. Between the heat and the tsunamis, not a single crop has survived. There will literally be no food in the world in a few weeks. The devastation is unthinkable," she said.

"Jesus said He would cut the days short or else nobody would survive," Will said somberly.

"It won't be long now," Michael pronounced with a sigh. The sigh seemed strange to Michele. They were talking about Jesus coming to put an end to their sorrow. What about that scenario did Uncle Michael fear?

"You say it almost as if you dread this coming to an end," Michele said cautiously.

Michael shrugged. "I just dread all that has to transpire between now and then. Speaking of which, now that the heat wave is ending, prepare for extreme darkness."

"The next judgment," Michele said somberly.

"They're coming rapid-fire now," Will added. "No time to recover from one before the next one occurs."

Michael continued. "The reports of our scientists show Nibiru soon will swing very close to Earth—so close that it will fill the sky. It will be like a three-day eclipse."

"Total darkness," Michele said.

"And worse," Michael added. "Three days without sunlight will really upset weather patterns. As if that weren't enough, Nibiru's movement is counter to Earth's spin."

"Meaning?" Will asked, wincing against the pain as he dragged a comb through his hair.

"Meaning our rotation could slow. I said there would be three days of darkness, but I meant seventy-two hours, give or take. Only one day may pass in terms of Earth's rotation."

"So, one long day ..." Will said.

"The slowing won't be abrupt, so it shouldn't cause tsunamis, but it will cause a sloshing effect. The coasts will flood again," Michael explained.

"I honestly don't even know if anyone is left alive along the coasts," Michele said sadly.

"Before all this started, about 40 percent of the world's population lived within a hundred kilometers of a coastline," Michael said with a shake of his head. "If they all died along with the people who were killed in the nuclear exchange and the fires, then Earth's population must be far less than half of what it was at the rapture."

"And most of them are headed here," Will said. "The armies of the world have been relentless in their trek to Israel. Even through the ridiculous heat they have kept coming."

"They'll come through the darkness as well," Michael said. "They'll hate it. They'll suffer, but they'll come nonetheless because they believe the Anu will launch their ships during the darkness."

"Everyone will be gathered to protect Earth," Michele said. "How long does Isa think it will take the Anu ships to reach Earth?"

"Given that the Anu are a figment of Isa's imagination, does it really matter?" Michael asked.

"I guess not," Michele answered.

"I heard him say something about three days," Will said, "but he lies just to lie."

"The truth is, he doesn't know," Michael answered decisively. "Satan knows his time is short, but that's all. Jesus controls the details, and it's driving him insane."

"All the more reason for you two to cut and run to Petra," Michele said sternly. She knew they wouldn't. Uncle Michael believed the Lord wanted him there as a witness for history.

"I can't," Michael said decisively, "but I would have been happy if your brother had gone to Petra."

"If I were going to leave you alone, Jake, I would have done it long before you contributed to the demise of what was once a lovely head of hair," Will said with a goofy grin. He looked at his watch. "We have a meeting with His Holy Butt in forty-five minutes. I have to take a shower."

"Is there anything I could say to convince you to leave there right now?" Michele asked Michael as Will left the room.

"The short answer is no," Michael said decisively. "And the long answer, the one Will and I don't really talk about in front of you, is that Jerusalem is locked down tight. Isa is demented and paranoid. If we tried to leave, we would be shot instantly as traitors. The time for us to escape to Petra is long gone."

Michele drew a sharp breath. She knew the answer didn't change their circumstances in any way, but there was something heartbreaking about the knowledge that they couldn't leave even if they wanted to. She wiped at a tear in her eye. With that bit of knowledge, she understood her uncle's reticence about coming events.

"Don't cry, honey. We'll be okay," he said, offering hollow assurance.

"I know," she said somberly.

There was an awkward silence for a second. Then it was broken by an ear-piercing blast. Michele cringed at the sound even several feet below ground. In the background, Manny screamed. Jimmy came into the office holding the baby.

On her computer screen, Michele saw Michael holding his hands over his ears as the blast diminished to a loud hum.

"You hear it there, too?" Michele yelled above the sound.

"Yes," Michael said, shaking his head.

"The trumpet blast of the Lord?" Michele asked hopefully.

Michael shook his head no as Will ran into view with a wet head wrapped in a towel. "Nibiru's gravitational pull. Earth has started to slow down its rotation, but the atmosphere hasn't. We're hearing the result—windstorms with greater speeds than we've ever experienced."

"We have to go, sweetheart," Michael said to Michele above the drone of the wind. "It's all going down. Stay in the bunker. Don't come out until Jesus comes!"

THIRTY-FIVE

ergal gave way to Benny's tears as he lamented the destruction of the dome of Saint Peter II basilica. The wind had ripped the dome from its base, blowing its shards to Jerusalem below. The Dome of the Rock fared no better, but its golden dome blew onto the Temple Mount, littering Abraham's Courtyard with debris and obliterating the obelisk, pillars, and sacrificial pools in front of the Jewish temple.

"My life's work, crashed around me," Benny moaned to Michael and Will as they assessed the damage.

"Don't take it so hard," Michael said. "This isn't really your life's work. Your life's work is written on the hearts and minds of Earth's population."

Benny grinned sorrowfully. "What a kind thing for you to say, Michael. I appreciate it."

Michael opened his mouth to explain that it was no compliment, but Will cut him off. "Look up in the sky," he said, pointing to the east. A large dark sphere commanded the eastern sky.

"Nibiru," Michael said. "It will fill the sky soon." The sight of it brought him deep dread.

The mention of the interloper planet drew Nergal to the surface. "Gentlemen," he barked, "we don't have time to mourn this rubble. We have to prepare for battle with the Anu."

Michael did a double take. Nergal's presence came on so suddenly that the incongruity took him aback. Benny marched off toward the door of the now dome-less basilica. Michael offered Will a quixotic shrug as they followed along.

Shadows lengthened as they walked through the rubble that had once been Abraham's Courtyard. On the steps of the basilica, Michael turned to get a better glimpse of Nibiru. It would no doubt become terrifyingly huge in the sky.

"It will be dark soon," Michael said glumly to Will.

Benny answered, "The enemy is filling the sky, gentlemen, just as predicted by our glorious leader. Bear in mind that he also predicted our victory." He entered the basilica and led them yet another time to the elevator, which they rode to Isa's underground control room.

This time the screens were filled with glowing dots on a world map. As Michael studied it, the significance of the dots became apparent. They were position markers for the armies of the world, who were making short order of their trek to the Middle East.

Isa greeted them with joy uncharacteristic of the past few months. "Ah, gentlemen! Welcome. What you see here is the formation of the largest army ever assembled on this planet. In a matter of days, every man and woman with a weapon will be on the Plains of Megiddo. Every armed ship will be either in the Mediterranean or the Persian Gulf. Air bases around the area will be filled with the most advanced aircraft ever seen by humanity."

"A beautiful sight, Excellency!" Nergal fawned with a remnant of Benny's personality. "There is little doubt the Anu will fail miserably in this coming attempt to enslave mankind!"

Michael winced. Nergal and Satan were clearly aware that the intended target was Christ and the host of heaven. Yet Benny and Isa also believed in the Anu myth. The personalities spoke of both opposing ideas with complete conviction.

"You are hampered by your ability to see things in only three dimensions," Isa said in response. "From a multidimensional perspective, my actions make tremendous sense. We *will* win against the Anu, Father, despite what you choose to call them."

"Clearly, I can't see things as you do, Excellency," Michael said cautiously. For a brief second, he thought about the lunacy of gathering all the world's forces to a particular spot in advance of a planetary attack. From orbit, a space enemy could simply choose to attack at the 99.9 percent of Earth Isa had left unprotected. Isa's plan only made sense if he believed the prophecies of Jesus's return. Catching himself,

Michael chased the thoughts from his mind. He looked toward Will, who stared straight ahead in an obvious attempt to control his own thoughts.

Isa commanded the screens be changed to a sky view. Immediately they showed a panorama from a satellite feed. The image was truly disturbing. Nibiru was a huge dark blue sphere bearing down on Earth.

Michael leaned forward to stare at its image. "Do we have a map of its trajectory?" he asked softly.

The head scientist, whose face was nearly obscured by leaking lesions, mechanically put up on the screen a view showing a series of paths described by dotted lines. "Like with predicting a hurricane, we have a cone of probable tracks," the scientist said. "We have literally no previous experiences on which to base our models, and Nibiru has largely been hidden from us by the Nemesis cloud. Only now are we able to get clean data about its density and magnetic strength."

"And?" Michael asked.

"And preliminarily, both are much higher than we had originally assumed," the scientist said without emotion.

"I'm concerned about the Roche limit," Michael said cautiously.

"As are we," the scientist said gravely.

"So, if I'm reading this correctly, in about a fifth of these possible paths ..."

The scientist finished the sentence without emotion: "Earth passes the Roche limit."

"Is that bad?" Will asked.

Michael answered, "At the Roche limit, Nibiru's gravity will overwhelm the gravity holding Earth together."

"So Earth would break up?" Will asked.

"Yes. Its remains would form a ring around Nibiru," Michael answered.

"Utter rubbish!" Isa screamed. "Enough with the science-fiction voodoo, Father. Just as I have prophesied where the Anu will land, I have prophesied their defeat. Therefore, there can be no destruction of Earth."

"His Excellency is right, Michael." Benny snorted.

"I don't believe we will enter the Roche limit either," Michael said calmly, basing his opinion on his knowledge of Bible prophecy. "Yet, as a scientific curiosity, I'm astounded by how close we will come."

"Well, if your intellectual curiosity is satisfied, Father, can we move on?" Isa asked with dripping sarcasm. He demanded the screen view be changed to the Jezreel Valley. The screen displayed the plain of Armageddon, lined with dark energy cannons. Markings showed where the armies of the world's ten regions would con-gregate. Isa had placed the North American and European forces closest to the front.

Michael drew a hard breath. He knew from scripture it would happen, but the idea of the totality of earth's firepower pointed at one object was overwhelming. He swallowed hard and found himself reaching to his wallet and the photo it contained.

"Prepare, gentlemen," Isa said with pride. "In two days' time, we will join the converging armies, and I will lead Earth to a victorious future."

At that moment, darkness overwhelmed the room. "Lights!" Isa screamed to the men manning the consoles. Emergency lighting cast a dim red glow. Isa yelled, "Report!"

"Nibiru has moved into occlusion," said the scientist. "Earth will be totally darkened for three days." Michael pondered the remark. Occlusion was no reason for the power outage. He suspected it was supernatural—God's way of announcing to Isa the arrival of darkness.

"All the more reason to have electric lighting!" Isa barked.

"Yes, Excellency," the scientist said. "I'm sure the power will be back shortly. This is merely ..."

Isa turned his back on the explanation and stomped to the ele-vator. Michael, Will, and Benny followed. Isa stabbed angrily at the elevator call button to take him to the surface.

"I think we'll have to take the stairs, Excellency," Will said.

The great Lord of Darkness couldn't get a lift to the surface! The thought brought a brief smile to Michael before he was body-slammed by an invisible force. As he fell to the floor, Isa's voice rang in his head, saying, "Careful with your thoughts, Father. You want to stay alive to see your Lord's destruction, don't you?"

The power kicked on and the elevator dinged while Michael was still on the floor. A shocked Will bent to help him up as Isa and Benny boarded the elevator. Pushing the button to close the door, Isa intoned, "You two can take the stairs."

"What just happened?" Will asked.

"My fault. I wasn't guarding my thoughts," Michael said with self-recrimination. "I was dwelling on the irony that a recalcitrant elevator stymied the Lord of Darkness."

"Uh-hum." They were startled by a cough from behind them. The head scientist with all the lesions.

"Can I help you?" Michael asked.

"I don't think anyone can," the scientist said with deep foreboding. In an almost silent whisper he said, "I don't think the Anu are real."

"Who do you think is coming?" Will asked.

The man was silent for a second as tears overwhelmed him. He fought for his voice, which cracked as he moaned with fear and longing. "Jesus."

"I think you are right," Michael answered.

"Then I am pitiable, am I not, Father? Wouldn't the Roche limit destruction be preferable to the events soon to transpire?"

Michael felt overwhelmed with compassion for the man. Most people who had taken Isa's DNA bought fully into the lie. This man had spent a lifetime thinking through problems. His musings had led him to a truth that most of the world wouldn't share until Jesus arrived. Michael answered the man. "With all my heart, I wish it could be different for you," he said somberly.

The man winced as salt from his tears stung the sores on his face. "The promises of a bright galactic future brought such hope," the scientist said sadly. "When I was young, I went to summer Bible school. I believed in Jesus, but soon science took over my imagination, and then subsequent revelations like the Antakya Codex called the veracity of the Bible into question. I guess I just bought into the lie."

Michael swallowed a sob at the mention of the Antakya Codex, his work on a forged Gospel of John to disprove Jesus's message. He had repented of it and released documents to prove the forgery, but people had been hurt by it nonetheless. The most horrible act of his life had a face—the swollen, disfigured face of the man crying in front of him. He hugged the strange half-human being for a brief second. Then the scientist quickly gathered his composure, broke the embrace, and abruptly left.

Michael followed the man's lead as he wiped the tears from his eyes. The die was cast. Everyone on Earth had made a choice, and within a few days the consequences of those choices would be made manifest. He poked at the elevator call button.

"No stairs?" Will asked with a smirk.

"To hell with Isa," Michael growled.

———

Isa and Benny looked jubilant as they sat in front of the camera, broadcasting to the world. Isa spoke as the screen behind him changed to his image at the podium of the now defunct United Nations building. "Seven years ago, I stood before you at the UN with a plan for the world, not just a plan to survive, but a plan to thrive.

"I told you much destruction would come and all would have to sacrifice. I also told you the end result would be our liberation from the tyranny of the Anu, a species that has plagued ours for eons. I told you our actions would win our accession to a galactic federation. I told you humanity would enter a golden age where we would live as gods.

"Well, those days are now at hand. You have worked tirelessly and sacrificed more than any generation before you. You have put an end to war, division, and hatred. Where once we were a quarreling group of nation-states, you have worked with me to forge a global identity.

"We are poised to succeed, my friends. In the next few days, the Anu will surely attack." The screen behind him changed to a map with several arrows pointing toward the Jezreel Valley. "I am amassing the greatest armed response ever seen by this planet and, more importantly, ever seen by the Anu. They are expecting the docile reception of our ancestors and will be unprepared for our military might. The battle will be brief, and it will be decisive."

Benny took up the narrative. "The Anu cannot defeat us. But, my children, we are creatures of habit, and old habits die hard. At my UN address, I explained that only *we* can bring about our own defeat. A great man once said, 'We have nothing to fear but fear itself.' To translate his thoughts to the current day would be to say that we have nothing to fear but disunity. Our victory is contingent upon unity of purpose, unity of consciousness, unity of belief, and undivided loyalty to our future. Despite our best efforts, there remain those among us who have refused to join our quest. You know who these dissidents are. They are few, but they are disruptive—the Jews and the Christians who try to undermine our efforts with a misbegotten belief that their Messiah will soon part the clouds.

"These men and women promote a false narrative that the Anu are not enemies, but the reincarnated souls of loved ones lost in the murders of the Dark Awakening. Unable to come to terms with the tragedies of these past seven years, they have spiritualized the Nemesis crossing."

Isa picked up the conversation. "To bring home the point, I want to state that we cannot tolerate an Anu fifth column among our ranks. We have done every kind thing we could think of over the past seven years to educate these people, to show them with hard science that their beliefs are fraudulent and dangerous to the rest of us. There aren't many of them left. There is an enclave of Jews in Petra to which I am sending a full legion of our world army.

"The Christians pose a different problem because they have gone underground. Our armed forces cannot root out this remnant because they are needed here with me to repel the Anu. Therefore, I call on all citizens to join the cause by hunting down and killing everyone who has not accepted our DNA. They have neither worked for nor deserve the benefits coming to us once the Anu have been defeated.

"Even more importantly, their existence constitutes a continuing threat. There must be nobody here to support the Anu in their efforts. Such people are traitors. They go against their very nature as human beings to support a vile race bent on our servitude."

Isa ended the address. "Loyal citizens of the world, I adjure you to perform your duty in this dark hour by killing Christians wherever they may be found. Do not give the Anu a foothold.

"And now to you and your loved ones, my fellow citizens, I bid you warmest wishes and peace, for I will not address you again until after the Anu have been repulsed. Good night and good fortune. Look to the bright day when next we will speak."

Michele turned off the broadcast. She couldn't listen to any more. She sat in the darkened office of the bunker. Jimmy and Manny were asleep in the other room. Before joining them, she decided to look at the camera feeds from the house and grounds. Nothing. The darkness of the Nibiru occultation was stifling. There was simply no light anywhere—at least not enough to trigger the cameras.

And then she heard a sound. Either her mind was playing tricks on her, or she had just heard someone walking in the chapel above.

THIRTY-SIX

T he darkness was palpable on their drive north to the battle formation. Michael winced as he watched Will strain to see.

"I've never seen anything like this, Jake," Will complained. "The high beams just die in the darkness about three feet ahead of the Jeep!"

Michael fidgeted with the heater. After two days of no sunlight, Earth was cold. Even the most temperate zones were below zero. Ice formed around smoke in the upper atmosphere from the burning of the Amazon forest, causing it to precipitate as snow. Israel might well have been situated on the Great Lakes for the snow piling up there.

Generally the four-wheel drive did its job, but on occasion they found themselves sliding on patches of ice. "Not really good driving weather for two boys from Georgia," Michael quipped.

Will grunted a chuckle as he stared ahead for signs that he was still on the road. The combination of utter darkness, howling winds, and snow dancing in the narrow field of the headlights was very disorienting. Normally the drive would be about two hours due north on the Yitzhak Rabin Highway. Today, two hours had gotten them less than a quarter of the way.

"It could be worse," Will offered. "We could have flown there with Isa and Benny."

"Thank God there was no room for us in their chopper!" Michael exclaimed. "That had to be a horrible ride."

"For the company alone," Will mused. "But the air had to have been rough as well."

"I don't know how Nergal took it, but I can guarantee Benny was pooping his pants," Michael said with a tired smile.

"The roads are really terrible," Will said.

Michael sensed he was leading to something. "Yeah?" he asked.

"Nobody would miss us if we got lost. What if we just don't show up? Do we really want to be on the front line anyway?" Will questioned.

Michael thought about it. He would love not to be standing with the Antichrist when Jesus split the sky, but he felt he should be there. What if Isa's stupid ray could actually harm Gabe? Didn't Michael owe it to his brother to be there for him?

"Will," Michael began carefully, "you saw what happened to that angel. What if Isa's weapons can actually harm the army of God?"

"You don't really believe that, do you?" Will asked incredulously.

"You saw the angel disintegrate in the ray," Michael said.

"I saw what Isa wanted me to see," Will said judiciously. "We don't know that we witnessed reality."

"Fair point," Michael said. Frankly, the demonstration fit so neatly with his nightmares, he hadn't even considered that the angel's destruction could have been a deception. "But what if we can help?"

"Help how?" Will asked. "I already killed Isa once. That didn't go so well, if you'll remember."

"Honestly, I don't know, but I want to be there to offer aid and comfort to any of the saints who are hurt and, if need be, maybe run Benny and Isa down with the Jeep."

"Great plan," Will said sarcastically.

"I have no plan, Will. That having been said, God has placed us at Isa's right hand all this time. I want to be there, ready to assist the invasion if the Lord calls on me."

"Fair point," Will said. "And it will be great to have a front row seat when Isa realizes his plans mean nothing to Jesus."

"Agreed," Michael said softly, reaching to his wallet in the familiar gesture to chase away the image of Gabe's death at Isa's hands.

They continued in silence for about half an hour. Then the Jeep swerved violently. Will barely managed to steer it to the side of the road. He slammed the gearshift into park, but the vehicle continued to rock. They were buffeted by an ear-piercing sound that started as a low rumble and kept increasing in pitch and volume until they held their hands against their ears, praying for it to cease.

After what felt like an eternity, the sound diminished and the shaking stopped, leaving them in eerie silence. On the horizon, a ray of light shone as the sun crept around Nibiru.

"Look over there in the sky," Michael said, pointing to the sun.

"Yeah?" Will asked.

"That was no simple earthquake. That was a crustal displacement. Earth's crust just shifted in response to Nibiru's magnetic field. The reason we see the sun is that we have shifted miles, maybe hundreds of miles, to the south in a few minutes."

"That's impossible, isn't it?" Will asked.

"The surface of the earth floats over its core. It's possible for it to move suddenly in response to stress on a celestial scale. But the atmosphere ..." Michael didn't get the chance to finish his statement before hurricane force winds whipped the Jeep back and forth. Screaming above the wind, Michael continued, "The atmosphere will have to catch up. Winds could be hundreds of miles an hour!"

The Jeep flipped as Will screamed, "Hold on!" Michael felt his head bouncing against the vehicle's roof when it rolled again, landing unsteadily on its tires, shoved tightly against a wall of rock along the road.

The Jeep rocked back and forth for a minute as the winds died down. Michael looked ahead along the road in the growing light. "Do you see the overpass up there?"

"Yeah," Will said with a questioning look.

"Get under there quickly. The destabilization of the atmosphere is about to produce ridiculously large hailstones."

Michael didn't have to tell Will twice. He put the Jeep in gear. It whined against some unknown damage from its roll, but soon Will had them parked safely. Then hailstones the size of the Jeep's hood fell with resounding thuds along the roadway. It was only a few at first, followed by a barrage that echoed all around them.

"I hope the overpass holds!" Will screamed, pointing to stress cracks in the corner. "I think the earthquake already did a number on it."

"I hope so too," Michael yelled in reply. Within several minutes, the hail slowed and then stopped.

"Is it safe to continue?" Will asked softly, as if savoring the silence.

"Maybe we should give it about half an hour," Michael said, looking out to the sky. "I think we'll have full-fledged daylight by then."

Michael's cell phone rang. Bemused, he said to Will, "Must be local. There's no way the satellites could have adjusted so quickly to the crustal displacement." Looking at the phone, he identified the caller as the scientist from Isa's bunker. He quickly showed the display to Will before answering on speakerphone.

"Father Michael?" the scientist intoned.

"Yes. What just happened?"

"That's why I'm calling. We haven't yet established contact with His Excellency. I was hoping you were near enough to give him a report."

Michael winced. "I'd say we're still hours from his location. We were sidetracked by the earthquake and hailstorm. How big was the crustal displacement?"

"Well, at least I don't have to explain a crustal displacement to you," the scientist said smugly. "About twenty-five degrees."

"To the south," Michael said, checking the sun's position in the sky.

"Mostly," the scientist answered, "but there definitely has been a shift in longitude as well."

"I can't imagine the destruction."

"That's my report, Father. We've managed contact with some of our satellites, and the images are frightening. The damage was catastrophic. There is not a viable city left. The Temple Mount has collapsed on top of us. I suspect this barracks will become our tomb." The scientist spoke clinically, no emotion.

"I ... um ... I'm sorry to hear that," Michael said, trying to sound as unmoved as the scientist.

"The best I can hope for at this point is to rest in peace," the scientist said, "but I doubt Jesus will allow us that mercy. I'm beginning to understand why His Excellency hates Him so."

"I have no answer," Michael said, stumbling for a reply.

"No reply needed. When you see His Excellency, tell him everything is gone. For all practical purposes, Earth is destroyed." He hung up without saying goodbye.

"Sobering," Michael said grimly.

The drive to the front was more comfortable in the daylight. Although the sky was filled with clouds, the gray of the sun's ambient light seemed wonderful compared to the darkness of the past three days.

Travel was slow as Will pushed the Jeep through the snow and navigated around melting chunks of ice and debris from the crustal displacement. Driving was made more difficult by the spiderweb of cracks littering the windshield.

Michael fiddled with his phone for hours, trying to get a connection to the United States. "Crap!" he exclaimed at the latest busy signal.

"Still no service to the States?" Will asked nervously.

"No. I have to trust them to the Lord, but I'd love to go into this day knowing Michele, Jimmy, and Manny are okay."

"I hear you," Will said as they pulled up to a military checkpoint near the Valley of Decision. "Well, here goes nothing," he said as he rolled down the cracked window and handed his orders to the greenish soldier on duty.

Upon inspecting the orders, the soldier saluted. Will casually returned the salute. "Sir, I didn't realize you were with His Excellency's team."

"Relax," Will said as he looked to the man's uniform for an indication of rank, "Sergeant. Just tell us where to report."

"Sir, you will proceed two kilometers down this road to another checkpoint. There you will be given an escort to His Excellency's location."

"Thanks, Sergeant," Will said kindly.

"No problem, sir," the young man offered.

It looked like the young man had more to say. "Is there anything else?" Will asked.

"Well, sir, you know His Excellency personally. Do you think we'll survive the Anu, sir?"

"I can tell you there is life after this battle, soldier," Will said with a catch in his voice. "Take care." He wiped at a tear as he raised the window.

"I know they've changed their DNA," he said as his hand pounded the steering wheel, "but they're human enough to pull at my heartstrings."

"I know," Michael said, patting his nephew's shoulder. "I know."

They drove another two kilometers as the sergeant had directed. The closer they got to their checkpoint, the more activity they saw along the road. At the checkpoint, they were directed to follow a military truck for another three kilometers. As they rode, they ascended slightly in elevation, offering a view of the full valley. Michael drew a deep breath. The valley was about twenty-five miles long, yet it was crammed full of army vehicles, weapons, and people—rows and rows of soldiers awaiting the battle to save the planet. The only breaks in their ranks were occasional pockets of destruction caused by the wind and hail.

"Will, look," Michael said in awe as he pointed out the passenger window.

The Jeep swerved a bit as Will took his eyes off the road to grab a quick look below.

"I've never seen such a crowd," Will said somberly.

"It is the sum total firepower of Earth poised to shoot the Lord out of the sky," Michael said in awe. "I knew it would happen, and yet somehow I could never fully imagine it." His heart sank at the thought of all those lost souls. "It just makes me wish we could have done more to stop them from taking the mark," he said with a wince.

The vehicle in front of them stopped. Will pulled in behind. The soldier exited his truck and appeared at Will's window. As Will lowered the window, the soldier said, "If you will follow me, sir, I'll take you to His Excellency."

Will and Michael followed the soldier downhill to an open tent, inside of which Isa and Benny sat on folding chairs looking over final battle plans.

"You made it!" Isa said as if they had shown up for a party. "I thought maybe we had lost you in the earthquake."

"About that," Michael said deliberately. "The guys at your Jerusalem command center have been trying to reach you. The earthquake was a full crustal displacement, Excellency, a worldwide quake. Every urban area was decimated." Michael paused, waiting for a manic fit of anger. Instead, Isa grinned, softly at first, but then the grin caught hold and grew broad.

Isa said, "Well, between you and me, Father, we probably would have had to knock down much of that stuff anyway. My plans for a new earth include architecture much more glorious than the blighted urban landscapes of the past."

"I see," Michael said quietly.

"No. You don't," Isa said deliberately. "But you will. Once you see your so-called Messiah for who He really is, you will be anxious to follow me into a future filled with scientific advances and intergalactic trade. I know you, Father. You have dreamed of such a society."

Michael shook his head somberly. "In times past, I did."

"And you will again!" Isa said, slapping his back. Michael cringed. "My forces are undefeatable!" he crowed. "You cannot bring me down today. This is the day I throw off the shackles that have bound me for millennia. Today I will raise my throne above the stars of God, and I will sit on the mount of the assembly!" Isa howled with maniacal joy. Then he leaned close to Michael and said softly, "A little secret, Father. The prophecies you studied aren't etched in stone. They are more like the musings and dreams of an old God who has failed His creation." He pulled away from Michael and screamed, "Well, there's a new god in town, and this one ain't hanging on no cross, I can tell you that!"

Getting in Will's face, Isa grinned insanely. "What do you think about that, William?" he yelled.

"I think you might be in error, Excellency," Will said derisively. Michael winced.

Benny gasped. "I think young William may have outlived his usefulness, Excellency," he said disdainfully.

"Nonsense!" Isa exclaimed. "What fun will it be to win if I don't have the faces of these two morons to watch when I crush their God?"

Michael began to bristle at being called a moron, but then he brought his thoughts in check. He forced his mind to be blank and then stared at Will, who was obviously doing the same.

An alarm sounded in the valley below. They all moved to the front of the tent to see what was going on.

"Excellency," a voice rang from outside the tent.

"Yes, General?" Isa called.

"Our sources tell us they have pings on space radar. The Anu fleet will arrive within the hour," the voice announced.

"Excellent!" Isa cried out. "Prepare for battle!"

THIRTY-SEVEN

The dim light of the sun broke through the gray clouds above. For the first time in days, Michele could discern images from the estate's camera feeds. What she saw was not hopeful. It showed massive damage.

The camera from the front entrance showed the collapsed stairway that had once graced the four-story entrance to the home. Fallen plaster and broken glass filled the foyer. There were no signals from cameras in the upstairs hallways. Michele guessed the upper floors of the estate had either crumbled or blown away, or both.

A tear came to her eye as she showed the images to Jimmy. "I know I shouldn't care," she said quietly. "In the scheme of things, it's just plaster and wood, but all I can see is the beautiful memories that used to reside there."

"Jesus says in scripture, 'Behold. I make all things new,'" Jimmy said softly. "I guess that's because all things get destroyed."

"I guess you're right," she said, turning to news feeds showing destruction from all points of the globe. "They're saying there's almost nothing left. Crowds of green people are in the streets cheering on Isa's army. They want revenge for the destruction of the world."

"They just want it to end," Jimmy said resolutely. "In that way, we are all alike. We envision different outcomes, but ultimately, we all just want this to end."

"You're right," she said, taking his hand. The news feed halted for a breaking alert. The green face of a young woman filled the screen. Makeup barely hid her facial lesions. A sprayed-stiff cotton candy tuft of yellow hair surrounded her spindly, malnourished face.

"They think they still look the same," Michele said, shaking her head.

The woman held one hand to her ear as she listened to an update. Finally she nodded and began her report. "Ladies and gentlemen, we are getting word that global forces have detected long-range radar signatures of Anu ships. They are expected to be in Earth's atmosphere within the hour."

News coverage shifted to fuzzy satellite coverage from the Jezreel Valley and images of Isa conferring with his generals. Michele's heart skipped when she saw Uncle Michael and Will in the background. "At least they survived the earthquake," she said quietly as the report continued. "His Excellency President Kurtoglu has issued a statement advising all citizens to be courageous and to take heart. He tells us that victory will be ours before the day is through."

"Talk about fake news," Jimmy said anxiously.

The report continued. "With respect to His Excellency's comments, we would like to point out that scientists are unsure at present as to the length of the day since the recent crustal displacement. For certain there was a longitudinal shift that should shorten the day by at least two hours. However, there is some indication Earth's rotation slowed as well. As we get more details, we will let you know. We continue now with our regular programming." The screen filled with more drone shots of rubbish that used to be cities.

Michele gasped at the damage. It was a wonder anyone was left. "It's hard to believe anybody survived this," she said aloud.

"I know," Jimmy concurred. "It's weird. We're sitting here all peaceful and quiet, while on the other side of the planet the bulk of the population is poised for war. I wouldn't want to be there for the world, but the calmness here is unnerving."

"I agree," Michele said. "I wonder what will occur in the skies here when Jesus appears above the Jezreel Valley. Surely we'll see something too. We won't have to watch it on a screen from a hole in the ground, will we?"

"We could maybe take a look around the yard, get a sense of the damage, and keep our eye on the sky for the Lord's return," he said with a grin of anticipation. His grin faded as he said, "But Manny's asleep."

"He'll sleep another hour at least," Michele said. She grabbed the baby monitor and attached it to her belt. "And, we have the monitor."

"Maybe we could take a quick look outside," Jimmy said. "I'm too anxious to sit around the bunker."

She grinned. "Let's do it."

They opened the stairway to the chapel. When they got to the top, they decided not to close it so they could more quickly get to Manny. The chapel had several broken panes of glass but was by and large undamaged by the quake and hailstorm.

"Looks like a miracle," Michele said, taking in the smell of beeswax and polished wood. She had always loved this place.

Jimmy opened the door and said in a foreboding voice, "Prepare yourself. The house didn't fare nearly as well."

She joined him at the door to see the house in tatters. The entire third and fourth floors were gone. Brick, wood, and plaster dust filled the yard. "Oh," she said with a start when she saw it. "From the camera images, I expected it to be bad, but I wasn't prepared for this." She zipped her jacket and braced against the cold.

They walked hand in hand through the snow to the house, constantly checking the monitor to ensure they were in range. Michele placed a hand over her mouth as drapes from the family room blew through broken windows. Looking inside the back door, she saw a jumbled mess of plaster and smashed cabinetry in what used to be the kitchen.

Her mind flashed quickly through a cascade of memories in the house. She had loved it there. She assumed it would survive the tribulation and belong to Manny one day.

"It's so strange," she said. She was in shock. "I didn't imagine the house would be gone. Somehow I guessed it would continue into the millennium. How stupid was that?"

"Not really all that stupid," Jimmy said. "When you think of it, this house has been the only world you have known. After the rapture, it was a form of security. I think that's why Uncle Michael fought so hard to keep it away from the Vatican. He wasn't protecting the wood and plaster, just preserving the memories."

"I know," Michele said, stunned by the tears landing on her cheek.

He held her close. "The memories aren't gone, Michele, and the people who made them with you are on their way back to us. It's a win-win."

"I know," she said. "But I'm shell-shocked from the tribulation. I wish the Bible said more about Jesus's reign. I feel like my nerves won't take any more change … even good change." She buried her head in his chest for a second, thankful for his warmth and relaxing in his scent.

They walked along the side of the house, just far enough to get a glimpse of the front, while staying in range of Manny's monitor. The front porch and its pillars were gone, having collapsed in the same winds that ripped away the top floors. The once beautiful wooden front doors were battered and swinging in the wind, making vacant screeching sounds with each movement. The peach and apple orchards along the front driveway were burned and withered stubs encrusted with ice. Michele shook her head in disbelief. It certainly didn't look or feel like home anymore.

"I loved growing up here," she said dismally, "but now the bunker feels more like home."

"It certainly feels safer," Jimmy agreed. Then he sniffed at the air. "Do you smell smoke?"

The smell hit her as he spoke. "Yeah, I do. Maybe it's from the Atlanta fires."

"No," he said. "It smells like something's on fire now. We should get back to the chapel."

At that moment, they heard a soft half cry from the monitor on Michele's belt. "I'd say we better," she agreed. "Manny's waking up."

He took her hand and led her to the backyard. She felt his hand stiffen as they turned the corner. The chapel was ablaze.

"Jimmy!" she shrieked. "We have to get the baby!"

Jimmy let go of her hand and broke into a dead run toward the flaming chapel. Michele felt her heart in her throat as she followed him. Her mind raged with possibilities. Could they make it through the flames to get Manny and get back out again? Would the mechanism work to seal the bunker off from the chapel? If they sealed themselves in, would they be able to get back out if the chapel collapsed over the bunker's entrance? None of the scenarios felt good except to get the baby and get back out.

Jimmy was easily twenty feet ahead of her when she heard the shots. One. Two. Three. On the third shot, Jimmy fell to the ground. Ahead of him stood Naomi, green and covered with lesions, an insane grin on her face.

"No!" Michele screamed. "Naomi! What have you done?"

Naomi lowered the gun. "Oh, hi, Michele," she said nonchalantly. The woman was stark raving mad.

"Hi, Naomi," Michele said, forcing a chatty, conversational tone. "How are things at work?" She tried to focus on Naomi, to find a point of weakness so she could take the gun, but her fears for Manny kept pulling her gaze toward the fire.

"Things are a little slow," Naomi said casually.

Michele took a step toward her. Slowly, steadily, she attempted to close the distance. Jimmy moaned on the sidewalk. "Naomi, I think Jimmy's hurt. He needs our help," Michele said cautiously.

"No," Naomi said, shaking her head. "His Excellency needs our help. He is about to save us from the Anu, but Christians are the weakness. We can't allow a fifth column."

"Oh, Naomi, Jimmy and I aren't a fifth column! You know that," Michele said with feigned kindness. "If we were, we wouldn't have asked you to live with us, would we?"

"I don't know," Naomi said indecisively. "Maybe that was some sort of plot to convert me."

"But we didn't, Naomi. We never tried." One step closer. The monitor broadcast the baby's cry. Michele bit her lip.

"No, I guess you didn't," Naomi muttered.

"Naomi, did you forget Uncle Benny is the pope?"

Naomi looked confused. "You know, I ... I did forget that."

"Did you forget Uncle Michael is his advisor and Will is his protector?"

Naomi crinkled her mouth. "I guess I did. I forgot that too."

Michele advanced another step. She wiped at huge tears. "Naomi, the baby needs me. I have to get Manny."

"The baby," Naomi said with a nod and a look of confusion. "I guess I forgot about the baby," she mumbled.

"He's your grandson, Naomi, and he's in trouble because he is in the chapel's basement, under the fire. We have to help him." Michele lost the ability to sound calm. She cried at the thought of Manny alone and in danger.

"Help him?" Naomi asked vacantly.

"Yes, Naomi, we have to help Manny. Come on. Help me get him to safety." Michele quickly closed the distance, but her action was too abrupt. The fog lifted, and Naomi brought up the gun to Michele's eye level.

"You nearly confused me, Michele, but I won't let the Anu win! That's why I set that damned chapel on fire!" Her voice rose to a scream as she pointed the gun at Michele's head. "No fifth column! Do you hear me?"

Michele stood stone-still. Her eyes locked on Naomi's. "Yes. I hear you," she said bitterly. At that moment she heard a scream from behind her as Jimmy pulled himself up and rushed his mother.

It was over in a second. Naomi calmly moved the gun from Michele's head to Jimmy's, taking him down with one loud boom. Michele looked on in horror as Jimmy's face disintegrated into a mass of flesh and blood. He fell with a thud as blood spattered the snow. Michele fell immediately on top of him, shrieking with grief.

As she felt Jimmy's wrist for a pulse, she felt the barrel of Naomi's gun on her forehead. Everything moved to slow motion, and a strange feeling of peace came over her as death approached. The flames in the chapel danced red and gold as puffs of smoke gave flight. The only sounds she heard were the cries of her baby and the roar of Naomi's gun.

THIRTY-EIGHT

The wind blew fiercely as Michael and Will took their places next to Isa and Benny at the head of Earth's combined military might. They were to the right of the firepower on a gargantuan mobile platform like those used by NASA to position a rocket for launch. Around them, below the platform, were a host of generals and admirals locked on computer screens to coordinate the movements of the disparate forces.

The clouds, blown by the harsh wind, began to part, revealing a horrifying truth. Nibiru had passed to display its parent star. Nemesis filled the center of the sky—an enormous red-orange orb surrounded by red iron oxide dust blown into wings by the solar wind.

Michael braced himself and squinted his eyes against the wind to discern the details of the interloper. It was much larger in the sky than several full moons. He estimated it was less than twenty million miles away, spitting distance in celestial terms.

"That's absolutely terrifying," Will muttered.

"Take heart, William," Isa said confidently. "This is the moment we have been waiting for. Now we can prove ourselves worthy of congress with the other intelligent life-forms in the galaxy. It is perhaps the most important date in history!"

"Second only to the date of your resurrection," Benny added with pride. The man clearly believed victory was at hand. Michael's mind rushed as an inner voice wondered if there was a possibility of the prophetic narrative being wrong—or at least unsettled. Could there actually be a satanic victory? He wiped at his brow, forcing the thought to go away.

His eyes were drawn to Isa, who stared at him with a grin. "As I have told you before, I am particularly interested in your reaction to the day's events, Father. Nothing will cap off the day's victory like the look of desolation on your face when you realize how wrong you have been. Imagine that! Your enhanced intellect may well have made you the smartest man ever to have lived, but you're not smarter than me, my friend."

Michael pondered a hundred responses but decided instead to simply ignore Isa. He stole a glance at Will, who stood looking into the distance.

"There!" Will said with excitement, pointing toward Nemesis.

"What?" Michael asked as Isa raised a hand to his earpiece to hear a notification.

"Look carefully," Will said. "There's a small white dot in front of Nemesis."

"The Anu vanguard," Isa said resolutely. "We have radar confirmation." The atmosphere around them buzzed with electricity and monstrous roars as the dark matter cannons came on line.

"How exciting!" Benny exclaimed, licking his lips. Michael was sure the expression was full-on Benny. No Nergal there.

As they watched, the small white dot doubled in size within a few seconds. Then it doubled again. And again. Soon they could discern a multitude of small white craft headed their direction.

"There must be millions of them!" Will yelled excitedly.

"Aim the dark matter cannons!" Isa ordered. A hundred cannons growled at once as their aiming mechanisms filled the valley with a relentless whine.

Soon the response came from below. "Cannons aimed. Automatic tracking engaged."

"Wait for my order, gentlemen!" Isa commanded as he yelled over the edge of the platform to the generals below, his voice crisp with excitement. "Wait until we see the whites of their eyes!"

But the advancing host was too fast for human reflexes. Within milliseconds of Isa's last command, the forms were close enough for the onlookers to discern individuals riding on white horses. Two broke from their ranks, descending at dizzying speed toward the command platform. In that moment, everything fell into slow motion for Michael as his tortured brain contrasted reality with his nightmares.

"Dad!" Will screamed.

Looking up, Michael saw the smiling face of his brother, Gabe, riding an incredibly muscled white stallion. Next to him was Chris, also atop a white horse. They both glowed brilliantly, the white of their tunics nearly too bright for Michael's eyes.

"Fire!" Isa screamed in a terrified voice, his former confidence waning.

The cannons erupted in dazzling displays of white-hot light. It was Michael's recurring dream superimposed on reality. As in his dream, Gabe toppled from the horse when the dark matter beam overtook him. Chris fell as well. Michael fell to his knees in anguish as Will cried, "No!"

In the next second, Michael felt strong hands seize him by the shoulders, lifting him from his knees. He looked into Chris's blue eyes.

"Your ride is here," Chris said with a broad smile.

"But ... but the dark matter beam," Michael stammered.

"Was never really a threat. Only a deception to fool the chief deceiver," Chris said as he pulled Michael onto his stallion.

"I tried to tell him that!" Will protested from Gabe's horse. "Have you ever tried to tell him something?"

"All my life!" Gabe laughed.

"Most of mine!" Chris added with a chuckle.

"Some things never change," Michael said with a grin. He took his thankful gaze from Gabe to look around. Nergal had left Benny and was standing to the side. Likewise, Satan had left Isa to stand braced against the oncoming horde.

Repeatedly Satan screamed maniacally, "Fire!" as the heavenly host flew past.

"Are you guys ready to go?" Gabe asked as he placed a stabilizing arm around Will.

Chris held Michael in the same manner and said, "Yes." The horse felt immensely powerful beneath them. Michael breathed deep the aroma of Chris's cologne, a scent he had associated with strength and protection from the time he was a child.

They took off, flying in the blink of an eye to the top of Mount Tabor, looking down on the valley.

"Where's Jesus?" Michael asked as Chris helped him from the horse.

"Defending Petra from the Antichrist's troops," Chris responded with a smile.

"That's right!" Michael said. "The prophets said He would go to Bozrah first!"

"And Bozrah is Petra?" Will asked.

"You bet!" Gabe said. "But He should be here any minute now. Chris and I have to rejoin the army. You guys will be safe here."

"Go kick some butt!" Will encouraged.

"Actually, we're only here to protect the Christians. The angels will gather the bad guys, but the battle belongs only to Jesus," Gabe said with a smile that brought Michael greater peace of mind than he had known in the past seven years. They flew away faster than the eye could follow.

Michael could no longer stand. His nerves crashed with relief, and he fell to the ground.

Will sat beside him, crying. As he wiped at his joyful tears with one hand, he hugged his uncle with the other arm. "It's over, Jake! It's finally over!"

Michael wiped at his tears as he hugged his nephew. It was then he noticed a solitary figure in ancient garb standing at the edge of the cliff overlooking the valley. Michael stared in awe as he realized it was the apostle John, carried forward in time from his exile in Patmos to record these very events in the book of Revelation. As the thought crossed his mind, the man turned to offer him the slightest grin. Michael returned the gesture.

They were rocked backward by a sudden crack of lightning that split the sky. Picking themselves up as thunder filled the valley, they saw piercing bright light cascading from a hole in the sky. Telescopic vision flooded Michael's mind as he saw through the brilliance to the loving face of his Savior, Jesus. He went to his knees in adoration, in frightful awe of the power He commanded.

Will got to his knees beside Michael and hugged him fiercely. As they watched, Jesus spoke with the power of the thunder that had just rocked the valley. "It is finished!" He cried in all languages simultaneously.

From His utterance, the atmosphere in front of Him roiled with heat in a wave that descended to the Jezreel Valley. As it moved through the armies, they burst like so many grapes in a winepress. Blood cascaded through the valley below. First one then another jet crashed, screeching into the mountain on the other side of the valley. Huge plumes of smoke blew high into the atmosphere as the rest of the world's air force followed the same pattern. Each crash rocked Michael's tired nerves, each intensifying his longing for war to be gone from Earth.

Finally, the rapid-fire crashes and resultant explosions ended. There was nothing but silence in all the area. Michael cried with relief. He also cried with sadness for the deceived who had just perished. And most of all, he cried with gratitude that Jesus had called him to life after he had spent so many years in darkness.

Jesus descended gracefully from the clouds until His steed rested on Isa's command platform. In that instant, Isa, Benny, Nergal, and Satan fell as if dead in the presence of His power.

Lightning cracked the sky, followed by a peal of thunder that rocked the earth. In the millisecond before the bullet struck, Tina pulled Michele to the ground.

"Mom!" Michele screamed with surprise.

"It's all over now, sweetheart. Everything is fine."

Michele hugged her mother fiercely and wailed with relief. Looking over her mother's shoulder, she saw her grandmother.

"It's over, Naomi," Kim said sternly as she took the gun.

Naomi fell to the ground with a shriek. "Kim!" she cried with sudden mental clarity. "It's true! The rapture, all of it! It's true! And I've been a fool!" She wailed uncontrollably.

"Yes, Naomi," Kim said softly. In the next millisecond, Kim knelt over Jimmy. As she touched his forehead and prayed, his wounds healed and his face was restored.

Michele yelped with joy. "Mimi! Thank you!" She left her mother's embrace to hug Kim.

"Yes. Thank you, Miss Kim," Jimmy said as he sat up.

"I think you can call me Mimi now," Kim said with a smile.

"I want to go by the name Grandma," Tina said with a grin.

Michele's heart sank as she thought of Manny in the fire, but as quickly as she had the thought, she saw a form moving through the blaze. She felt Jimmy's arm embrace her as they watched Gloria come out of the flames, holding Manny in her arms.

"You have grown so much!" she said to the boy as he cooed.

Michele ran to get her son, but she stopped short with the knowledge he had been Gloria's son first. This could be awkward.

"There's your mama," Gloria said as she handed Manny to Michele.

Michele cried and hugged Gloria as she took the baby. "I'm so sorry, Gloria," she managed to say through sobs.

"Nonsense!" Gloria exclaimed. "Manny needs a mortal mommy and daddy. He's *your* baby. But he has a resurrected aunt who loves him with all her heart," she said, pulling Michele close. Jimmy joined the hug, followed by Tina and Kim.

Some unheard signal pulled Tina, Kim, and Gloria from the hug.

"We have to go," Kim said deliberately as three large white stallions clicked their hoofs down the sidewalk. Kim took Jimmy; Tina took Michele; and Gloria took Manny.

"I can't believe it's finally over," Michele exclaimed through tears as she joined her mother on the horse. Tina held her close as she shook with relief. "Almost over, at any rate. We're on our way now to the Valley of Decision."

There was a dramatic pause as Isa, Satan, Benny, and Nergal lay prostrate before Jesus, who had left His horse and stood staring down at them. In that brief moment, resurrected saints brought millions of believers to the mountain with Will and Michael. The group from Petra arrived, along with the agent and the programmers. Michael and Will hugged each in turn. Michael smiled broadly at Yasim Naaji, who waved to him from fifty feet away.

Michael's heart thrilled when he saw Gloria, his mother, and Tina bringing Michele, Jimmy, and Manny. Hugs and tears abounded for the few seconds the glorified family members remained. Then they took to the sky on their horses, joining the heavenly host, where they floated at attention above Jesus.

Jesus turned to the crowd on the mountain to say, "Well done, My faithful servants." In a hard-to-fathom expansion of reality, each person there heard his or her own name in the single utterance of the statement.

As Michael heard Jesus, He stood before him. When Michael looked into Jesus's eyes, he saw a happiness, peace, and contentment he had never known. The most powerful being in the universe, who had just slain with His breath the total military might of humanity, stood before him, radiating unconditional forgiveness and love. Jesus caught him as he fell to his knees with the knowledge of how unworthy he was to stand in his Lord's presence. Then Jesus hugged him and held him close for a second. And then reality contracted and Jesus was on the platform again.

"Dude, you won't believe what just happened!" Will screamed to Michael.

"Somehow, He changed time and space and hugged all of us at the same time, Will," Michael said, cutting him off.

"The most amazing thing I've ever experienced!" Michele exclaimed in awe.

As Jesus raised His hand for silence from the crowd, the raptured saints descended to join their family members who had just experienced His embrace. Chris and Kim flanked Michael. Arm draped around Will, Gabe stood with Tina and their kids. Manny watched everything in silence with eyes wide as saucers as Jimmy held him. Gloria was with her parents. They all looked on as millions of angels descended in a dazzling white cloud to the battlefield, depositing there those who had taken Isa's inoculation.

Michael was in awe of the might and spiritual power of the angels. For too long society had passed them off as little Valentine's Day babies. In reality, they were fearsome creatures of radiant light. Into the field behind Isa's platform, onto the bloody mud and fallen army, angels dropped millions of greenish people. Still deceived, none of them realized their actual situation, believing instead they had been captured by the Anu. Michele gasped when they deposited Naomi there.

Michael watched as realization struck them en masse. They moaned in heart-wrenching agony at the choices they'd made to exclude Jesus from their lives. They all fell to their knees in the bloody dirt, weeping with intense sorrow before Jesus, whose bright white robe was spattered with the blood of the decimated armies. Michael had a sense Jesus was bending time and space again and was sure that each who knelt did so from an unseen private encounter with Him—but their encounter with the Judge of the Universe wasn't beautiful, comforting, and kind as his had been.

"There but for the grace of God go I," Michael said, quoting Englishman John Bradford from the sixteenth century.

"All of us," Chris concurred.

"Maybe me a little more than most," Michael said with a wry smile.

"But you have suffered greatly as a result of your decisions," Kim said as she rubbed his shoulder.

"And the time spent with Benny and Isa is a fate none of us would have been able to endure," Chris said decisively. "Benny alone nearly drove me crazy."

Sudden silence filled the valley as if all had been told to pay renewed attention to unfolding events. They all watched, riveted to the scene below. With one great cry, Jesus yelled, "Esh!" Michael recognized it as the Hebrew word for fire. At His mere utterance, the ground shook all around them. Michael could not stand in the shaking. He turned to see that Will, Michele, and Jimmy were similarly affected. Not so for those in resurrected bodies.

In front of Isa's command platform, a whirlpool opened. Michael strained to see as his mind reeled with scientific discoveries of his past. Not a whirlpool, it was a wormhole! A passage to a horrible dimension opened. From inside radiated an orange-yellow flickering glow and an occasional lick of flames. A blast of astounding heat rushed past them. For all Michael knew, this portal led to the surface of a star, maybe the sun. His mind fell to the passage from Revelation describing this scene. John called it the lake of fire.

"Po!" Jesus commanded. (Here!) Isa's body lifted from his prostrate position and floated in front of the Lord of the Universe. Jesus looked at him with disgust. Michael was sure a lot of communication was going on between the two as Isa hung there. Not knowing the precise words, he was allowed to sense the emotion of the encounter. Jesus was forlorn at the loss of eternal life brought about by Isa. For the destruction of earth and, more importantly, for the destruction of souls, he was banished to the lake of fire.

Isa struggled to open his mouth. Finally, the Lord allowed him to speak, but only a scream of terror came forth. Jesus glanced to the portal, and Isa was sucked, screaming, into the lake of fire.

Next up was Benny. Like Isa, Benny was held aloft as he had his exit interview with Jesus. Like Isa, he was given the opportunity to speak. Unlike Isa, he did more than scream incoherently. He called on the only people for whom he had ever felt true affection. "Kim, talk to Him, please! Michael, help me!"

Despite his knowledge of the evil inherent in Benny, Michael had a sudden moment of compassion for his uncle. He wiped at a tear forming in his eye and heard a soft cry come from his mother. He reached to take her hand. She squeezed his in return.

In the milliseconds that followed, Jesus stood in front of them, even though He hadn't left his position on the platform below. He was beautiful to Michael as His eyes filled him with peace. With one nail-scarred hand He touched Michael's face, and with the other He touched Kim's, wiping away their tears.

"Be at peace," He said softly. Then with a hint of a grin, He said, "No tears in heaven." Michael grinned in return.

"Thank You, Lord," Kim said in response.

"Yes, Lord, thank You," Michael said, and then Jesus was gone as quickly as He had come. In the intervening moment, they had been spared Benny's descent into the lake of fire. As Michael watched, Nergal was flung into the portal just before it closed with a resounding roar.

Jesus raised his right hand to the sky as an introduction for the archangel Michael. A burst of light appeared in the air above the platform. The light coalesced around the form of an incredible being. Surrounded by a multicolored aura, the archangel Michael was a hugely muscled man of incredible beauty. To Michael, he looked like Michelangelo's *David* in ancient military attire. He drifted slowly to the platform and knelt before Jesus, bowing his head to the ground.

With a flick of Jesus's hand, another earthquake rocked the area.

As it subsided, the valley floor split to reveal a cavernous depth spewing sulfurous gases that irritated Michael's nose and eyes.

Jesus looked lovingly at the archangel Michael and nodded. The archangel stood to attention. Then the blue beast that had haunted Michael's nightmares was held aloft in front of Jesus. Without thinking of it, Michael touched the wallet in his back pocket. Again, the watching crowd didn't know the exact words, but they could sense Jesus's sentiment, His rage at a being He had created—a being wanting nothing more than to destroy every good thing in existence.

Unlike Isa and Benny, Satan was given no opportunity to speak. Michael drew a sigh of relief. He never wanted to hear that insane, rabid voice again. With a subtle move of His hand, Jesus commanded the archangel to take action. With inhuman speed, the warrior of old bound Satan in thick chains, grabbed him by his blue hair, flew with him over the pit, and dropped him into it. Instantaneously the earth was healed of the breach, and Satan was no more.

With the dismissal of Satan, Jesus stared longingly at the crowd of Isa's followers who had been deposited on the battlefield. With sadness, He said, "Be gone." They instantly dissolved into the field of blood on which they knelt.

Then Jesus shone brightly as the crowd on the mountain cheered. He simultaneously hugged all present. Only then did Michael's nerves finally relax. He felt more joy than he had ever known. Something else changed in him that moment. With a bit of thought, he understood. With Satan and his minions gone, sin had been removed from the planet. And not just sin, but also the propensity to sin, along with the weight of sadness and despair that follows in its wake.

This change felt to Michael like the lifting of an incredible burden. Until that moment, he hadn't realized how constant the pull toward sinful anarchy had been on his life. And now, for the first time in his existence, he knew true peace.

EPILOGUE

It had been two weeks since the Lord's return, and Earth was flourishing like it had in the days of Adam. Already the trees of the family orchard were bearing fruit. The re-creation of Earth was moving along rapidly as the resurrected saints worked with tireless abandon to restore the planet.

At home in Georgia, Kim, Chris, Gabe, Tina, and young Chris had nearly completed the restoration of the family estate—creaking stairs and all. The place had never felt so warm and inviting. After morning devotion in the chapel, Michael settled onto the patio behind the family room, allowing the sun to warm his face as he deeply inhaled the fresh air.

Morning devotion! Michael thought the phrase couldn't possibly explain prayer in the new dispensation. Each morning as he prayed, Jesus stood before him, as He did for every believer in the world. Instantaneous, face-to-face communication with the Creator! It was unheard of until this time. Michael shook his head in disbelief.

Kim came out to the patio with a glass of water. One of the first things restored after Jesus's return was the water, now crystal clear and refreshing beyond belief. Michael gratefully accepted the glass.

"Mom, when am I going to get to help out around here?" he asked.

"You guys were put through the mill during the tribulation. Relaxation is what the doctor ordered." Her brow furrowed as she added, "Besides, in terms of the reconstruction, you would only get in the way, honey. We're much faster and have more abilities."

"I guess I'm going to have to hear that for about a thousand years," he said with a chuckle.

"Soon enough, we'll each be given kingdom assignments. Life will look very different, but it will be full, interesting, and joyous," she said as she patted his arm.

For the first time since Satan's dismissal, Michael thought of the wallet in his pocket. There was no need of money, credit cards, or identification now, but out of habit he still carried the wallet. He pulled it from his pocket, opened it, and retrieved the worn photo he'd taken from Kim's safe.

Laying the photo on the table in front of him, he turned to his mother and asked, "Can you tell me the story behind this photo? How did you guys all manage to be together for a photo years before you met?"

She picked up the picture and looked at it as if it were an old friend. "It's a long story," she offered with a sigh.

"Time, we've got," he said with a grin. And there, under the bluest sky he had ever seen, Kim led Michael through the haunting details of the family's past.

Stay tuned, folks. We're about to see how it all began!
Here's an exciting excerpt from my next novel:

PRECEDENT

THIS GENERATION SERIES: BOOK 5
THE PHOTO SERIES: BOOK 1

ONE

Jürgen Orsic stared out his bedroom window in the Palace Hotel at Mondorf-les-Bains, Luxembourg. At one time the town had made a name for itself because of the peacefulness of is parks, lake, and healing mineral spas. The Palace was the quintessential luxury spa hotel in its heyday. But that was before the war. As one of the few buildings unfazed by the years of battle, the Palace now served a different function. The fine furnishings, paintings, and statues had yielded to metal desks, army cots, and utilitarian military equipment. The fountain in front and the sculptured lawn had fallen to a fifteen-foot-high fence with two rows of barbed wire. Jürgen wasn't a guest of the hotel but a detainee in Central Continental Prisoner of War Enclosure Number 32, also known as Camp Ashcan.

Ashcan was reserved for the interrogation of high-ranking Nazis. Jürgen spent his days in the company of the likes of Hermann Göring, the great mobilizer who galvanized the German economy into a war machine. Other residents included Walther Funk, minister of the economy, and Wilhelm Frick, minister of the interior. Old farts. Jürgen was lucky to be half their age. His presence in the facility had far less to do with a distinguished career and much more to do with a distinguished parentage.

Jürgen's mother was the famed Maria Orsic, the woman who headed the Vril Society. As an accomplished medium, she had for years psychically placed the Third Reich's leaders in the presence of an advanced species from Aldebaran, a solar system sixty-eight light-years from Earth in the constellation of Taurus. The ascended masters of Aldebaran claimed to have long ago lived for a while on Earth. They were adamant about their connection to Earth's Aryan bloodline and advocated the sanitation of society from the infestation of other root races.

Maria held trance sessions with the most significant members of the Nazi high command. Der Führer himself sought the advice of the Aldebaran masters on numerous occasions. Maria charmed them all with her legendary beauty. Her perfectly symmetrical face sported soft porcelain skin, full red lips, and haunting blue-gray eyes. In contravention to the style of the time, she allowed her thick, luxurious honey-blond hair to adorn her shoulders or else pulled it back in a simple ponytail. The entirety of the high command succumbed to her charms, but only one fell to her bed.

In November of 1924, Maria had been called to the apartment of Rudolf Hess in Munich. There she put Hess and Rudolf von Sebottendorf, founder of an enlightenment think tank known as the Thule Society, in touch with their dead friend. Sebottendorf felt better after the séance. Hess felt better after the ensuing sex. Nine months later, Jürgen came into the world, the son of the deputy führer who would one day humiliate the nation when he took it upon himself to fly to Scotland in a vain attempt to broker peace with England.

Jürgen was strikingly handsome. He had his mother's eyes, nose, and full lips. His father contributed a thick head of dark hair, high cheekbones, a cleft chin, and a tall, muscular body. But Hess had never cared enough to contribute his name, so Jürgen used the surname Orsic. And in truth, it served him well. His parentage was no secret to the Nazi high command. Having the deputy führer in his corner held untold benefits in Hitler's society for most of Jürgen's life. Add to that the information channeled by his mother, and Jürgen was something of a favorite grandchild to Hitler.

Beyond that, he had become a secret advisor to their Austrian king when the leader of the Aldebaran home world had chosen him to be the vehicle through which the aliens would communicate detailed plans and information crucial to the development of the Nazis' famed V2 rocket program. Of course, that was just the beginning. Jürgen's head swam with ideas for supersonic flight, spacecraft, and an anti-gravity technology tested in the Reich's supersecret project known as *Die Glocke* (the Bell).

Things had been perfect for Jürgen until his father's defection. For a brief period, he too fell under Hitler's suspicion, but as more and more of the Aldebaran technologies transmitted to him came to life, all doubts of his loyalty and usefulness were swept away. And more information kept coming. The head of the Aldebarans was a lovely woman who bore a striking resemblance to his mother. When Jürgen met her in visions, he knew immediately why she had chosen his mother as Earth's first point of contact. There was no doubt that there was some genetic connection between the two. But as time passed, the Aldebaran leader, who went only by the title Lady, realized that she needed more than Maria Orsic's beauty. She needed a brain capable of receiving, remembering, and reproducing the incredible technological advances she wished to communicate.

Jürgen was thrilled with the transmissions from the Lady, and he gloried in the attention the information elicited from the führer. Unfortunately, his newfound attention was a trial for Maria. While still beautiful, her body had started to succumb to gravity and age. She no longer commanded the attention of every man in the room. To complicate things even further, her connection to Rudolf Hess did not bode well for her once he was branded a traitor. The final straw for her was the Lady's transition to Jürgen. There was little left for her. In order to gain attention and retain relevance, she set about a series of "revelations" that came not from Aldebaran but from the pain of her loss of utility for the powerful men at the pinnacle of German society.

In time, her fraudulent prophecies annoyed the Lady nearly as much as her constant haranguing and self-pity frustrated Jürgen. The Reich was failing, and her continued existence threatened plans he and the Lady had developed to take the advanced technology to the Americans, the country with the greatest resources to secure a future filled with untold scientific advances and travel to the cosmos.

Her murder was surprisingly easy for Jürgen. Disposal of the body involved more physical labor than he desired, but the entire event was largely painless. Considering his mother's false transmissions about leaving Earth to visit Aldebaran, he sent a final communication to members of the Vril Society in her hand, ending it with the cryptic message, "*Niemand bleibt hier*" (No one lives here). The note did much to foster the contention that she indeed had left Earth on a journey to Aldebaran. In reality she found her way only onto the street, looking like any other victim of the Allies' relentless march to Berlin.

After leaving her, he was supposed to give the Lady's final transmission to the führer. It wasn't good news. She said that Hitler had squandered the Aldebaran technology, and for that reason his reign would end. Jürgen had heard rumors of Hitler's fading sanity. He doubted he would gain admittance to the führer's bunker and entertained serious doubts that he would live through the experience if he were to deliver the message as dictated by the Lady. He decided instead to travel to Bavaria to discuss the message first with Hermann Göring. Uncle Hermann would know best how to proceed. That's when he was taken. The Allies scooped him up along with Uncle Hermann and delivered them both to Camp Ashcan.

While no longer a site of luxurious pampering, Camp Ashcan was not nearly as bad as Jürgen had supposed a detention facility would be. The baroque hotel was a marvelous structure retrofitted with utilitarian furnishings. Because of the wall surrounding the former resort—and because there was nowhere to run in decimated Luxembourg—the prisoners were free to meander about the facility. The older detainees, pretty much everyone but Jürgen, spent long hours sunning on the hotel's large veranda, chatting endlessly about the proper way to parlay information into freedom or reduced sentences when the Nuremberg trials moved ahead.

Jürgen didn't join them. Instead, he spent time with his captors to ingratiate himself to them. The endgame was not to find their favor, however. His purpose was more devious. He spent hours in mournful conversations with camp interrogator John Dolibois. He told of Nazi horrors, some real, some fabricated. He bewailed his situation as a nice young man who'd been thrust into the heart of the Reich's warped mentality as a consequence of his parentage. Dolibois seemed sympathetic, but Jürgen couldn't be sure.

Then again, it didn't really matter. All he had to do was project the image of a young man who was heartbroken by life. He consciously looked forlorn and retrospective in every moment outside his room.

He was sadly courteous and kind toward his captors. In no event did he betray his facility with languages. Nobody at Camp Ashcan, not even Uncle Hermann, had the slightest idea that he spoke English fluently, without accent.

And at night, Jürgen sat by his window to listen. The night guard at the gate was a glib, happy young man. Each night he joked with the guards at the four corners of the wall about how many more days until he could go home. It was just a few days left at the camp and a couple of days of leave before he set sail on a ship from France to the United States. When questioned by the other guards about what he would do when he got home, the young man was vague. He said he was an orphan. He had grown up a loner and would probably live his life that way. Maybe he would head back to his home state of Georgia. Maybe he would go out west.

Jürgen liked to listen to the stories. He also liked the way the guard said the word *Georgia*. "Gee-oor-jah" Jürgen would say softly to himself. But it was far more than the man's accent that Jürgen found intriguing. It was his face and body. The man was nearly Jürgen's double. Of course, Jürgen hadn't seen him close up, but from afar, the two looked strikingly similar. The Lady told Jürgen that she had arranged the young man's post specifically for their ensuing plan. Too bad she was only an ephemeral being. Jürgen thought she was someone with whom he could fall deliciously in love. He fell asleep hoping that one day he would meet a real woman who carried the Lady's regal beauty.

Jürgen awoke to great activity at Camp Ashcan. Dolibois was rounding up detainees for transfer. Within days the camp would be closed. From the looks of it, within the hour, over half the camp would be relocated to Germany for the beginning of war crimes trials.

Jürgen knew that tonight would be the only opportunity for him to pursue his daring plan. Uncle Hermann came to say goodbye. That one hurt, but the rest meant nothing to him. Nonetheless, he played the part of an innocent youth caught up in something far beyond his ability to comprehend. He stood with tearstained eyes, manufacturing the look of trying to be brave.

Dolibois patted his shoulder as the last of the detainees on his list joined the formation headed to Germany.

"*Und ich?*" Jürgen asked in a soft moan. (And me?)

Dolibois explained that he would return the next day to discuss Jürgen's next destination.

The transferees were broken into smaller groups and loaded into ambulances as protective cover from the many people who would prefer swifter justice than that promised at Nuremberg. When they left, they took with them the sense of heaviness that had pervaded the camp. Jürgen went to the back terrace to think—and to listen.

As he had suspected, the guards were jovial in their conversation. Their extreme vigilance gave way to joyous chatter once they no longer held responsibility for the most reprehensible of the Third Reich. Of course, they had no idea Jürgen could understand every word. They spoke with joy that the camp would be fully emptied by tomorrow evening. They rejoiced that this assignment was coming to an end. And they talked anxiously about returning home to the United States. All the while, Jürgen retained the look of a traumatized youth.

"I wonder what they're going to do with the young pup over there," one of the guards said. Jürgen looked out to the horizon, careful to give no hint that he understood.

"I can't believe they'll go hard on a kid like that. What could he have done to land him here with the most bloodthirsty?" the other asked.

"I hear he was one of Hitler's favorites." They laughed. Jürgen had no doubt the man implied a sexual relationship.

"Then that should be punishment enough," the other responded.

Dinner was a quiet affair. Jürgen sat alone at a table in the large dining hall. He ate quietly, being careful to pick at his food as if he hadn't the will to eat. When dinner finally ended, he walked disparagingly to his room.

Once the door was shut, his attitude changed completely. Quickly he removed the sheets from his cot. Tying them together, he looped one end over a pipe running across the room near the ceiling. He smiled at the thought that the unsightly external plumbing of the old hotel would be his salvation. He quickly fashioned a noose from the hanging sheets and tested it repeatedly to ensure it would hold his weight.

Next he removed his shoelaces and tied them together to form the beginning of a garrote. Sneaking quietly from his room, he entered the recently vacated room next to his. Moving quickly and silently, he turned upside down the small wooden chair tucked neatly into the room's desk. He rocked the chair's leg back and forth to loosen the glue holding it together. It was slow going at first. He had to fight the temptation to bang the chair on the floor to break the leg. He worried that he was wasting time in his fight against the stubborn glue.

He looked at his watch, and his mind raced. He soon would have to act, with or without the chair leg. He pondered how to revise his plan if the damnable thing wouldn't come loose. It would be harder to meet his objective, but he thought he could do it.

"What choice do I have?" he asked himself in a voiceless whisper.

Frustrated, he placed the chair on the floor. Standing on one of its legs, he grabbed the one on which he had been working and threw his body weight backward. Catching himself against a fall, he got into position to repeat the move. Finally the leg loosened. Frantically, he jerked the leg back and forth until it came free of the chair.

He sat quietly for a moment with the chair leg in his hand as he regulated his breathing. He wanted to scream for joy. He wanted to run. He wanted to do anything to express the rush of energy he felt in anticipation of his freedom.

"Not now, Jürgen," he told himself. "There's still a lot to do."

Silently he crept back to his own room to tie the ends of the shoelaces to the chair leg. He opened his window, checked his watch, looked at the guard at the hotel's gate, and listened. If they followed their normal pattern, in ten minutes the guards at the front corners of the wall would skip out for a cigarette break together. They would notify the guard at the gate to be extra vigilant while they took their break. But who would be vigilant tonight, their last night at Camp Ashcan?

They followed their normal pattern, but with a little less military precision and a lot more joy to their steps. As the two guards stepped down from their posts at the corners of the wall, Jürgen slipped softly down the back stairs of the hotel. At ground level, he pushed carefully on the door to the outside patio. Because there was a wall surrounding the facility, the Allies had not taken the step to barricade all entrances to the building. In fact, this staircase was used frequently to access the patio by day. The door was prone to a loud screech when opened. Jürgen pushed softly, opening it a centimeter at a time to avoid alerting the guards. When the door was only slightly ajar, he squeezed through, leaving one of his shoes to prop it open.

Staying close to the building, hiding in its shadows, he crept up behind the guard who looked so much like him. Gripping one end of the chair leg, he raised it high and swung down with all his might at the guard's head. The guard fell immediately unconscious, but Jürgen was momentarily frozen, stunned with fear at the noise the hit had made. He closed his eyes and took a deep breath. Holding his breath, he listened carefully. Nothing. If the other guards had heard the crack of contact, they dismissed it.

Now he moved with lightning speed. Slipping the shoelace garrote over the man's head, he twisted the chair leg, tightening the laces around the man's neck. He twisted the leg until he physically could not move it another centimeter, and then he held it there to a slow count of two hundred to ensure the man's death.

Now came the hard part. Grabbing the body by the belt, he bent forward and folded it over his shoulder in a fireman's carry and bolted as quickly as he could to the comfort of the hotel's shadows. Breathing heavily and straining against the weight, he marveled that he was able to carry the man so far without a break. The incredible power of adrenalin astounded him. He made it to the open stairway door before needing to rest.

He threw the body to the floor, sat down beside it, and rested to a twenty count. Grabbing the body under the arms, he pulled it up the stairs to the first floor. For a second he thought he would need to rest again midway in the climb, but he forwent the opportunity, motivated by the image of the body crashing to the bottom of the stairwell while he rested. It felt like forever, but he finally made it up the stairs and into the hallway.

He checked his watch. Time was running out. He had to hurry. Again he threw the body into a fireman's carry and darted the short distance from the stairwell to his room, where he dropped the body on his bed. Stopping to catch his breath, he wiped at the sweat streaming from his forehead and wondered if he could complete his task in time.

Manhandling the body to remove its clothes and the garrote was much more difficult than Jürgen had imagined. Redressing it in his own clothes was even harder. To complicate matters, he had to do it with great stealth. One loud thump could awaken neighboring detainees. He didn't need Germans finding him any more than he needed the Allied guards finding him.

Standing in his underwear, he admired his work. The guard certainly resembled him with the clothing change. The bloating of his face from the strangulation would obliterate subtle differences in their appearance.

He threw on the US military uniform haphazardly. There would be time to make sure every button was buttoned when he reached his post. In a final, exhausting move, he cinched the body's neck into the makeshift noose. Grabbing the garrote, he ran down the stairs and took up the guard's post just seconds before his compatriots returned from their break. He tossed the garrote over the wall, wincing at the muted crack it made when it hit the street. The returning guards signaled, and he waved to them.

The night passed without incident. At daybreak, Jürgen was relieved by the next shift. He hustled out of the facility and walked down the street as a free man, a new man. He chuckled. In all the tension of his escape, he hadn't taken the time to learn his new identity. He retrieved the wallet from his back pocket and opened it with a grin. It wasn't a lovely name, but he would make it work. Jürgen Orsic was dead. From now on, he was Stanford Martin from Alpharetta, Georgia.

"Stan Martin," he said to himself with a grin. He could get used to it.